The
Apex
Theory

Written by N. M. Camacho

To my mom, Esmeralda, for never telling me to stop doing what I love.

And to my father, for letting me watch Jurassic park as many times as I wanted.

Instinct guides the animal better than the man. In the animal it is pure, in man it is led astray by his reason and intelligence.

- Denis Diderot

PROLOGUE

The branches of the tall acacia trees brush up against each other. They scrape and pluck the leaves off as they strike one another, the leaves fluttering down to the cold floor below. Each tree sways side to side, this particular night windier than others. The tops of the trees block the bright moonlight, the tree canopy like a thick blanket of impenetrable green leaves. And because of this, it's pitch black, making the dense foliage down below seem like dark walls meant to keep you trapped.

A single human being tumbles in the dark, his shoulder bumping into a tree with full force. The human staggers to the side, and he falls to his knees after losing his balance. The rigid tree roots burrowed in the dirt scratch his knees as he lands on them. But he pays no mind to the pain; he quickly stands up, his knees creaking from old age as he scrambles to his feet again.

He continues darting forward, never looking over his shoulder, never slowing down. His breathing is shallow, desperate, his loss of stamina wanting to make his feet give way to the ground. But he won't stop. He cannot stop, the blood trickling from his left bicep reminding him what could come next if he does. He holds his hand up as he runs past the thick ferns in his way, the thorns of sprawled out bushes making tiny breaks in his skin along his wrinkled face.

In his terrified pace through the forest, he trips on a rock and flies forward into an open area. The moonlight, finally free and present from the tree canopy, illuminates the human's whereabouts.

He has finally reached an opening in the woods, which reveals a clearing, with a single trailer home in the center. The trailer home is old and weary from constant exposure to the elements, with piles of random trash and appliances surrounding it. He stops about twenty feet from the trailer home and turns around, facing the forest.

He can hear bird chirps and sounds of the tree branches moving in the wind, but he can see nothing. Everything is pitch black in the forest he emerged from.

He kneels down and reaches into his pants pocket and pulls out a matchbox. He pulls out a single match, then frantically tries to light it, striking it multiple times against the matchbox. When all of a sudden, the chirps and cicada trills of the forest stop, followed by complete silence.

They're here.

The man finally strikes the match one more time and it ignites. He stands up and flicks it on the grass in front of him. Fire erupts, the man holds up his hand to his face, cowering from the heat. The blazing fire furiously gushes around him; it starts to form a giant fiery circle around the trailer home. Fuel was dumped to surround the trailer home, a premeditated action by the man to keep something out as a last resort. The man squints at the burning fire. He puts his hand back on his wound and winces. His face is a little clearer, and he looks like he's in his 50s, with long white hair, a beard, and a look of terror accompanied by disbelief.

Whatever he's running from, he does not seem to believe it himself.

The man turns around and runs to the trailer home. He reaches a set of appliances and starts to climb them. He then climbs to the top of the trailer home, struggling to get up due to his injured arm. He makes it up and sits on top for a couple of seconds, trying to catch his breath as his heart pumps more blood out of his wound, the dark black blood trickling in between his fingers.

Something breaks the silence.

The sound is not dissimilar to a hawk screech. It's loud and guttural as it bellows through the night air. The man looks around the circle of fire surrounding his home, trying to catch a glimpse of the terrifying sound. Then more screeches are heard, a series of them, one after the other, almost making a chorus from every direction surrounding the circle of fire. Each sound makes the man more frantic, his heart pumping faster as the weight of fear in his chest begs for a miracle.

He's surrounded.

He pulls a revolver from the waistband of his pants; he opens it and dumps out empty shell casings. He pulls out more bullets from his pocket, but his panicked breath lets some of them slip through his fingers, rolling away and off the edge of the trailer home. He starts to load the revolver with whatever he has left. The screeches still resonate as he loads three bullets in the cylinder, his visitors still waiting. The man finally stands upright, overlooking the circle of fire from his high ground.

He looks around again, but still doesn't see any sign of life. The chorus of determined attackers seems to get louder by the second; the man's ears are pulsing. The man searches. He slowly turns, scanning the ring of fire, looking for anything, anything at all that gives him the opportunity to-

Eyes.

He finally sees them. Two eyes staring right at him, glowing orange in the fiery light. The man is stricken. He hesitates at the sight but then raises the revolver to his eyes, to aim it. And just as the revolver's iron sights reach his line of sight, a single drop of water plops on the barrel of the gun. Then another on his hand, and another on his arm.

It's starting to rain.

The rain starts to get heavier after a few seconds, and the fire slowly starts to extinguish. The man looks around helplessly, as the only hope of survival starts to fade. He locks his gaze again with the pair of eyes, they have not moved or blinked. The glowing eyes slowly start to disappear as the fire smothers, but just before the eyes completely disappear, the glowing eyes *squint*. The eyes then disappear as the fire finally dies.

He has nowhere to go, and now there is nothing keeping them away.

The screeching stops, the forest is silent again, and only the man's shaky breath can be heard. The darkness of the night blankets his peripheral vision, the moonlight now dim as his eyes need to re-adjust. He stares at the revolver in his hand, a brand-new ultimatum coming to fruition in his head. Either let his attackers subject him to their appetite or...

Take a quicker way out.

apex predator.

(\ã-, peks 'prə-də -tor\)

n. Predator with no predators of their own, residing at the top of their food chain. Apex species occupy the highest trophic level(s) and have a crucial role in maintaining the health of their ecosystems.

PHASE ONE

"An invasive species of seemingly apex stature arrives and begins to create turmoil within the balance of the current ecosystem. Without fault, shortly after, evidence of a broader, more instinctual and intelligent species of apex stature comes to fruition. Why it occurs has an answer closer to Gall's law and is rather more simple than it seems."

— Excerpts from *"The Apex Theory: An In-Depth Analysis of Apex Predators in Arbitrary Environments."* Published in the *Journal of Wildlife Biology*, submitted by Dr. Anika Irving, PhD.

DISCOVERY

A secretary types away on her computer, never looking away, busy. The waiting room is large with a number of chairs, big enough to hold almost thirty people. However, it's mostly empty, except for the secretary, and one lone woman sitting in the lobby. The woman in the lobby sits in a slouched position. She looks tired and annoyed, like her patience is wearing thin. Bags under her eyes, disheveled hair in a ponytail, she yawns. She's been looking around this particular waiting room for an hour, wondering why there are so many chairs. Or why this company makes it seem like they receive many visitors, the parking lot was practically empty. She's listened to the secretary type away furiously, and wondered what on earth she could be so busy with. She shifts in her chair for the tenth time, uncomfortable to be sitting for so long.

The woman in the lobby is Anika Irving. She has an athletic build, but she looks worn out, a few gray hairs already showing in her dark brown hair. Even at twenty-seven, her physique would make anyone think she has had manual labor for too long. Her arms and hands are strong and chiseled, with small indentations and scars that can only be seen at a closer angle. Her t-shirt is a bland gray with a Metallica logo, faded by countless washer cycles. Torn cargo pants cover her worn and mud-crusted hiking boots. Anika takes an impatient deep breath and reminds herself why she is glad she never took an office job.

Still weary from the jet lag, Anika raises her hands and rubs her temples. After nearly eight hours of flight time, Anika has nothing but disdain for this waiting room. She flew in from Iceland, after spending almost four months in the wilds of the isolated country. Anika would have preferred to stay longer in the peaceful plateaus of Iceland; actually she would love to never leave at all. But the Department of Biology at the University of Washington could only justify so much within its research and travel budget. Anika was forced to fly back to Seattle and report her findings to the university board. Eventually, she would appear with her trusty journals and laptops, but she was first intercepted by her godfather, William Burns.

After finally deciding to charge her phone once, she made it to a populated city in Iceland. She noticed she had a few missed calls from Burns. She called back and was greeted with Burns's scruffy voice, inviting her to meet with one of his colleagues as soon as she makes it back. Anika was tired to say the least, and she was still upset at having to go back to the realm of civilization. After being on her own, chasing wolves for nearly four months, Anika didn't really feel like talking to people just yet.

Yet, against her wishes, she agreed to meet with Burns as soon as she landed at Sea-Tac International Airport. Once at the airport, she picks up her luggage, finds her parked Suzuki Samurai in the airport's garage, and speeds off to the address Burns gave her. Now here she sits; after checking with the secretary, who told her to wait a few minutes, which dreadfully turned into an hour.

I miss my bed, is the only thought right now on her mind.

The phone on the secretary's desk finally rings, and she answers it immediately. She speaks softly; Anika is unable to hear. The secretary hangs up the phone.

"Mr. Valente will see you now," the secretary says to Anika.

Anika stands up, her joints softly cracking, and she walks towards the door. She tugs on the handle, but it won't budge.

Anika tilts her head slightly towards the secretary, annoyed. The secretary hits a button on her desk, and a small ring is heard behind the door. A lock is disengaged, triggered by the secretary. Wouldn't want your twenty appointments barging in at the same time, would you? Anika wonders what's so damn special about the room she's stepping into.

Anika opens the heavy door and steps in. A large office, with walls full of certificates, framed pictures of yachts, wilderness, and animals, all of them with the same man at the center. She continues past the wall of adventure and sees the man in the pictures sitting behind a desk. He stands up when Anika walks in. She recognizes him immediately, now that he is clean-shaven. Forrest Valente, a strong-looking man in his mid-thirties. As he walks toward Anika, she notices his very expensive suit. It appears Valente can alternate between his adventurous side and his corporate side with the help of a razor. He wears a smile, but it's hard to tell if it's real or not. Next to Valente's desk sits another man, William Burns, who doesn't stand up and instead watches as Valente casually strolls over to Anika. Valente extends his arm for a handshake when Anika reaches the desk. Anika shakes his hand.

"Dr. Irving, nice to finally meet you in person, glad you could make it. Please have a seat," Valente says, offering her a seat next to Burns. Valente walks back to his mahogany desk and sits behind it; Anika takes the empty chair next to Burns. Burns gives her a short wave of his hand as soon as she makes eye contact with him.

"Hey Ani," he says in a direct, no bullshit voice.

"Bill," she responds politely.

"I'm really glad you could come in for this meeting. I have been hoping to speak with you for a very long time, Dr. Irving," Valente says.

"At Bill's request, otherwise I wouldn't have. My waiting room is much bigger than yours," Anika says. Valente gives a short chuckle, amused at her joke. Anika can't help but notice that Valente laughs like a supervisor who is trying to relate to his employees. Like a corporate foreman who knows nothing about the job, and then proceeds to tell everyone how to do it. His first impression already creates a dislike in Anika Irving. It isn't surprising, however, Burns explained it all the night before. Burns asked her to come meet Valente and listen to a proposition from him. He didn't say what the proposition was, at least he couldn't over the phone. The only reason Anika agreed was because Burns never asks her for anything.

Valente clears his throat and gives Anika an admiring smile.

"I'm sorry, I know you must get this a lot, but I was a massive fan of the show, especially when you were still in it. Such a profound and insightful one." Valente shifts in his chair, "I'm really glad you stayed loyal to animal conservation after you went on to do your own thing. Your focus is on wolves now, right?"

Anika nods.

"Magnificent. And of course, your father is still going strong with the show, never gets old. Never miss an episode. Although it does miss your presence, I must say," Valente says.

Valente speaks with such admiration, like a little boy who is finally meeting his childhood hero. But Anika remains silent; she simply keeps her stern and blank stare at the fanboy before her, *get to the point.*

"Told you not to mention her father," Burns says. Burns told Valente to stick to the topic and to refrain from attempting to socialize with Anika; Valente immediately realizes Burns was right after all.

"Right, I apologize. Just a big fan is all," Valente says, defeated.

"You requested to see me?" Anika reminds him.

Valente shrugs off the awkward moment and says, "Yes,

there is something we want to discuss with you. Before we do that, unfortunately, I must ask you to sign a non-disclosure agreement."

Anika gives him a reluctant look.

"Why?" she asks sternly.

Valente is at a loss for words, "The topic is... delicate," he says.

"And what's the topic?"

"Not until you sign."

"You want me to sign without knowing what we're talking about?"

"That is how an NDA works."

Burns sighs. "Once you sign, you'll know why. Just sign it, Ani."

Anika thinks for a moment, *fine*. She trusts Burns, and that's the only reason she agrees. Valente hands her the document and the pen, and she starts to sign.

"I don't do hits, you know," Anika says.

Valente doesn't get the joke; he simply stares straight-faced, and then Burns chuckles.

"Told you she has a strange sense of humor," Burns says.

Yes she does. Anika's jokes often don't land, her cynical attitude the cause of that. Valente just continues to stare and chooses not to laugh at this particular joke. Anika finishes signing the NDA and hands the paper back to Valente, who gives it a brief skim to make sure all the needed lines are signed.

"Dr. Irving, I want to be clear. After signing, if for whatever reason you decide to talk about what we're about to show you, I have every bit of power to discredit you and I will seek swift legal action. Do you understand?" Valente explained.

Valente's admiring tone is completely gone. In a second, he has switched gears to something a little more serious. Burns mentioned Valente's law background in the phone call the night before, and Anika can finally see the lawyer in Valente's eyes, indeed a very powerful individual. Anika has been threatened with legal action before, but Valente's threat has actual weight. That, coupled with the fact that his chest seems bigger sitting down, he looks like a *very* intimidating lawyer. Even then, Anika keeps her face neutral at the football quarterback with the law degree.

"I know how a non-disclosure agreement works," Anika says.

"She signed it, Forrest. Just show her," Burns says to him.

Valente agrees; he takes a pair of glasses from his suit pocket and puts them on. He turns his attention to his MacBook computer and starts to type. Valente begins to talk as he clicks around on his laptop.

"As you are aware, Bill has been working with me for the past four years. I've been funding his show on animal conservation, seeing that I myself am an avid supporter of the cause. We often focus on putting a stop to poaching in several countries, but occasionally we research rare or supposedly extinct animals." Valente stops typing on his computer and looks at one of the walls with a projector screen already pulled down. "Two months ago, I sent Bill on an expedition to Tasmania. We were making an episode on Tasmanian wildlife and on the Tasmanian Tigers, mostly about the doubt surrounding its extinction. They went deep into the forest, setting up bait and motion-sensor cameras around the supposed sightings. I'm sure you're familiar with the process. The whole trip was only meant to last a couple weeks."

Valente turns on the projector, Burns reaches behind him and dims the lights in the office.

"A week or so in... they encountered something

magnificent," Valente says.

Valente is mesmerized at the thought as he pulls something up on his computer. Anika quickly makes her own assumption and haphazardly interjects. "Please tell me you didn't bring me in here just to tell me you found a Thylacine. I mean, *congratulations*, but not really *my interest*," Anika says in an exasperated tone.

Burns scoffs, "Will you just settle for a second and watch?"

Valente opens up a video file and clicks play. Anika decides to watch the video on the projector.

At the top left corner of the video, it says the date: 07/25/24. The camera seems to emerge from the dark, like it was in a pouch. It shakes as someone starts to point it. The camera shows the pickup bed of a truck a few feet away, thick trees and bushes surrounding it, the rain pattering softly. It's dark out but not completely; the sun hasn't quite set yet. The tail-lights of the truck are shining red onto the floor below. A voice offscreen in the video is heard, whispering, "Just point it, right there... yep, there," the voice says.

The camera adjusts and then zooms in a bit. A man slowly walks into the frame. It's Burns; he turns to look directly at the camera, guiding the man holding it. The cameraman offscreen speaks while adjusting the camera. "Bill? I think you're seeing things," the cameraman says.

"Just... quiet. Keep it straight," Burns whispers.

In a quick moment, the bushes rustle, and a faint chirping can be heard, then growling and purring. Burns puts his hands to his ears and points at the bushes that slightly moved. "Do you hear it?" he whispers.

There's complete silence from the cameraman. Burns takes a couple more steps forward, but the chirping stops. Burns freezes. A few seconds go by where nothing happens. No more movement, just pure silence. Burns can't hold his breath any longer; he exhales a cloud of mist.

"Fuck. We scared it off, whatever it was," Burns says.

"Bill, I've never heard sounds like that befo-" the cameraman is cut off.

A dark shadow jumps into the frame, just a few feet away from Burns. Neither Burns nor the cameraman speak a word or even breathe. The shadow walks slowly toward Burns, the red tail-lights of the pickup revealing the shadow's true form. It stands about two feet tall; it has legs like a bird, and it balances itself upright with a lizard-like tail. It has small, slender forearms with claws, and a few feathers on its head. It chirps. The creature bobs its head, examining Burns curiously as it steps toward him, its dark eyes staring directly at Burns. The cameraman finally begins to breathe, his breath getting heavier in awe of what he is witnessing.

Anika watches the footage intently without taking a breath herself; she leans forward.

Burns stands still in the footage. The creature takes a couple more steps. It almost seems docile and chirps again. Burns slowly reaches out with his hand, almost touching its head. The creature seems brave—it feels no fear. Burns's hand is only a couple inches away from the creature, when a short but deep growl is heard in the bushes behind the creature. The creature's behavior changes instantaneously. It hisses and then snaps its small jaws onto Burns's fingers. Burns gasps in pain and retracts his hand. The creature then darts offscreen into the bushes. Burns holds his injured fingers and turns to look directly at the camera, in shock.

"What the fuck?" Burns says, shocked.

The footage comes to a halt. Valente and Burns sit in silence, waiting for a reaction from Anika, but Anika is absolutely astonished. Anika waits for someone to say something, but it's very obvious. Even now, it seems Burns and

Valente are still in amazement; the footage hits just as hard every time. A few soundless seconds go by, then Anika finally breaks the silence.

"Is this real?" Anika asks, reluctantly.

Burns turns the lights in the office back on. He slowly raises his left hand to her face, showing the visible scars on his fingers. Jagged indentations on his index, middle, and ring fingers, imprints of small but sharp teeth. Burns puts his hand down.

"Felt pretty real to me," Burns says.

There is another brief moment of silence while Anika is unable to grasp the concept. She cannot even begin to accept the reality of the animal that she saw. The bird-like features mixed with those of a lizard. It seemed far-fetched, but it was unmistakable; she just saw an animal no one has seen for millions of years. And this animal's first instinct was to draw blood from Burns.

"Now do you understand?" Burns says.

Anika blinks, unsure of what should be said next. This can't be real, how could it? Anika moves past accepting it, instead, she occupies her mind with the intentions of those who changed paleontology from a theoretical science into *practical*. "Why show me this? What do you want from me?" she asks.

"We want an expedition," Valente says.

Anika scoffs and rubs her eyes, then says, "You can't be serious."

"As serious as we can be, we're moving forward with this. We would like you to be a part of it," Valente adds.

Anika's eyes give her away: the disbelief, the fight-or-flight kicking in. Burns knows the look, he knows she needs convincing. "We took saliva samples from my fingers. Most of it was contaminated by my blood, but only one sample wasn't.

Valente's molecular biologists here have been having a hard time with it," Burns says.

"Yes, the DNA is incredibly complex," Valente adds.

"Plus, it was raining and the floor was very muddy that night. There were footprints on our camp and the forest surrounding us, one set of tracks, for a mile or so. We would have followed them if we wanted to, we have photos of those if you want to see them. There's other evidence too that you can look at, but only if you agree to come with us," Burns tells her.

"Agree?" Anika scoffs.

Burns rolls his eyes, "Just say it, Ani."

"I don't know if I believe it," she says.

"Have I ever lied to you?"

"No. Never. And I know damn well you're not an Oscar nominee."

"You're not sure if you want to believe it, I understand, Ani, I'm not sure either."

Anika takes a deep breath, "An expedition? To do what?" Anika says, probing for more intentions.

"To find more proof, footage. More DNA samples, blood preferably," Valente explains.

"And a live subject?" Anika asks Valente, testing his intentions.

"No," Valente snaps. He picks up on her test, to Anika's surprise, "I fully believe in the preservation of these species."

"Really? No theme park ideas floating around in your head?" Anika says sarcastically.

Burns rolls his eyes.

"An expedition," Anika repeats, "Let's say I believe you for a moment and think about this logically. *We know nothing about an extinct ecosystem*, nothing. How could you expect to be prepared to meet this animal in the wild?"

"We have a paleontologist coming along," Valente adds.

"Do you know what paleontology is? The study of prehistoric *fossils*, every piece of information your paleontologist gives you will be nothing but theory, pure conjecture. We'd be going in blind," Anika explains.

"Ani, it's not that different from what we do. Remember the episode on Amur leopards? We knew nothing about those, but we learned. How is this any different than that?" Burns says.

"Oh it's very different, there are other species of leopards that we piggybacked from. What's the closest thing to this? *Parrots*?" Anika argued. "And why do you need me? I mainly focus on wolves, I'm not an expert on prehistoric life forms."

Burns turns his head to Valente, "Are you gonna tell her?"

Valente's face says it, *nope*. Burns has to tell her himself then. He smiles to himself and doesn't bother to look Anika in the eyes when he says, "Your father is coming along."

Anika's face turns bright red. "Why the hell did you bring me here in the first place?"

"Because I know your father. He's good at what he does, but he's disconnected from reality."

"You think? You should have come to me instead," Anika says. She seems a bit betrayed that Burns would go to her father before ever asking her.

"I know," Burns says, "But your father has the most credibility. And I hate to admit it, but he has the number one show in the world, and the audience believes him. Anyone else reveals this and they'll claim it's a deepfake or AI of some sort. I mean, how many contacts and friends does he have in how many countries? *Countless*. Matt has the ability to do this right, but he's a showman, he could just as easily fuck this up. I devoted my life to preservation, and I know you do too. Come with us, even if it's to prove us wrong."

Anika contemplates; she doesn't like the idea of her father going, or working with him, but she clearly has a lot of respect for Burns. She considers everything again in her mind. If she accepts, how prepared do they think they are?

"What's the plan?" she finally asks.

"A full month. Film crew, a paleontologist, me, your dad, you, and a couple ex-military personnel for security."

"Just a couple?" Anika mumbles.

"The point is, if we can bring good, tangible proof to the right authorities, we can work fast to make sure *no one* tries to take advantage of these species," Valente says.

"I know. Especially an intelligent one like this."

"That's quite the assumption," Valente says, intrigued.

Anika considers her thoughts for a second. She's replaying what she saw in the footage in her head. "It was curious," she says, "I mean sure, I've met animals that have never met humans before, so naturally they're not afraid. But it showed genuine curiosity, with caution. It wasn't just looking at Bill, it was probing him. Trying to read his body language as much as possible, trying to figure out if and when he would become a threat."

"It had confidence," Burns says.

"And insurance. The sounds from the bushes before it bit you? I would assume it was a warning. I've seen similar communication in wolves. They must move in packs."

"It came from one," Burns added.

"What?"

"The audio doesn't do it justice. That growl, it only came from one, I'm sure of it. And it sounded much deeper than the ones preceding it."

"Possibly an adult."

The thought of a much bigger version of the creature startles both Valente and Burns. Anika picks up on it. "Have you actually considered the gravity of this? You've seen *Jurassic Park,* did that look like a herbivore to you?"

"You don't need to tell me twice," Burns adds. "I felt its teeth, like tiny razor blades. And most, if not all herbivores had molars like today's species, at least that's what Lucy said."

"Lucy?"

"Our paleontologist," Valente says.

"But I didn't need a paleontologist to tell me it was a predator," Burns continues, "I could tell. Again, the audio sucks. The animal was completely quiet in its approach, there was no sound from its footsteps. The surrounding floor was muddy and had lots of gravel, yet there was utter silence, it was very light-footed."

"Do you think it communicated?" Anika asks.

"Hell yes. Like you said, its whole demeanor changed when it heard the growl and it snapped forward to bite me. It's not just that, there was also a smell."

"Smell?"

"Right before the growl in the bushes, the scent hit me like a wall, like an unnatural... almost chemical smell."

"It's a different world," Anika says, "we'd be going in blind."

"That's why we're bringing ex-military personnel," Valente adds.

"I would've brought more than two if you ask me, do you think that'll be safe enough?"

"I don't know. I mean, we've done this before," Burns says. "Lions, tigers, elephants. You're doing wolves now, which are pack hunters. We've been in apex predator territory before, and we've both had close calls, but this…"

"It'd be incredibly different," Anika remarks.

"That's putting it lightly. I looked into its eyes, it felt like, I don't know…" Burns shrugs off that last thought. Burns is an experienced man, probably has seen it all, but this seems to have shaken him to his core.

"I'm assuming you're funding this?" Anika says to Valente.

Valente snaps out of it. He had been mesmerized by the conversation between Anika and Burns. "Yes," he says, "and I'm making sure you have the utmost protection. Dangerous or not, we have to make sure that this species remains undisturbed."

Anika looks at Burns, a twinkle of fear in his eyes, rare for a man of his experience in wildlife.

"When do we leave?" Anika asks.

"Bill will fill you in on the travel details. Does this mean you're in agreement?" Valente says with a smile.

Anika is much less enthusiastic; she feels as if the world will swallow her whole for uttering her next words. "I guess so," she mutters.

"Good," Valente says, "Well, thank you for dropping by. We have much to do and prepare for, we've got a bit of a get-together tomorrow, I'll see you there. Bill, if you could show her out?"

Anika stands up to leave. Burns follows. Valente also stands up and extends his arm for a handshake.

"I'm glad you agreed to join the team," Valente says. "We are going to make *history*."

"Yes," Anika says, shaking his hand. "I'm sure no one in their right mind would say no."

Anika turns and walks out of the office alongside Burns.

They walk past the heavy door, Anika finally getting her answer as to what's so important about this room. Now she knows; the room changes the course of history. It changes your perspective on your place in the food chain. No one ever walks out of here the same again. They continue walking in silence, past the secretary and out of the waiting room until they exit Valtech Industries. Anika glances at Burns.

"Had anyone else showed me that, I would've told him to go fuck himself," she says to him.

"I know," Burns's face is somewhat pale, and it startles Anika.

"You… don't seem ready for this."

Burns takes a moment to answer; he takes a deep breath. "I don't think anyone will be. I'm going home in the meantime, can I drop by later tonight?"

Anika nods her head, and watches Burns slowly lumber to his car in the parking lot.

Anika drives herself home after her meeting with Burns and Valente, letting her instincts drive while her mind wanders into the unknown. She doesn't know what to think or what to believe. Nothing makes her feel better while the weight in her stomach seems to be getting heavier. She wants to believe that she would be doing the right thing by joining this expedition, she has to. Otherwise her body would run away as fast as possible.

For a few moments, she thinks deeply about the whole idea of this expedition. An aim to re-discover an animal thought to be dead from the last extinction event. And now, it falls into the lap of Forrest Valente. A tall, brooding, and broad-chested handsome man who wants to protect this species like any other conservationist would. Yet, he's not originally a conservationist, is he? Why does Burns trust him with this discovery? She knows Burns is of good character and sound judgment when it comes to other people, but Valente's history is questionable.

When he called her the night before, Burns explained who Forrest Valente was in an attempt to convince her to attend the meeting. Forrest Valente's parents own the second-largest pharmaceutical company in the United States, Valente Pharmaceuticals, and are widely regarded as the most reliable across the nation. Valente Pharmaceuticals is a multinational pharmaceutical, biotechnology, and medical technologies corporation. It started as a medical delivery company in the early 1990s, offering all kinds of medical supplies as requested, within the hour, and without the standard delivery costs. It soon bloomed in 1998, earning contracts and expanding its focus on developing and producing pharmaceutical prescription drugs and medical device technologies. It is expected to soon surpass its number one competitor, Horizon, in the near future.

Valente's parents did their best to make sure he had everything he could ever want, which was the exact opposite of what he'd wanted in his adolescence. At seventeen, Forrest finished high school a year early, and went on to attend Harvard Law School. Valente never asked his parents to bribe or persuade anyone, and instead chose to do it on his own volition. He was accepted almost immediately, as his transcripts and intellect seemed to pave the way for grander things. However, about a year into his schooling at Harvard, he had a swift change of heart.

Valente started working as a laborer for an engineering firm in a neighboring city, as he asked his parents not to give him money for lodging. Valente wanted to work for himself and not use his status to gain the upper hand. During his time, at this engineering firm working for rent money, he was cordially invited to help at an event being held in Montana. Valente helped build and reinforce a new kind of fire tower overlooking the peninsulas at Yellowstone National Park. Valente had never been so close to nature before; he had never spent enough time outdoors to appreciate the beauty of the natural world.

When he finally went home, all those photos made him discover a new passion in his heart. Valente chose to finish law school but his focus was elsewhere in the remaining years. When he wasn't studying, he was reading books on wildlife and biology. When he wasn't in school on the weekends, he was at the nearest park, or forest, taking pictures and sketching animals in his journals. After finishing law school, he pursued another major, biology. His time achieving his degree went by faster than he thought, as his love for the subject was intoxicating.

To his parents' surprise, he asked them for money, which he called "a small loan that I fully intend to return". Valente used his father's loan to purchase the engineering firm he worked for during his time at Harvard. He reoriented the company's focus, specializing in wildlife and environmental engineering, offering services related to ecological assessments, mitigation plans, and habitat restoration. He also broadened the contract parameters by accepting projects internationally. Valente's company became increasingly successful in just a few years, so much so that he did indeed pay back his father's loan, and added more departments, like biology, to his company, *Valtech Industries*. Ever since then, Valtech has been the premiere choice for grants and donations for anything dealing with biology and wildlife conservation.

Of course, all of this meant jack shit to Anika, and she didn't understand why she needed a history lesson on someone she'd only seen in a glance on the cover of TIME magazine. Burns sighed over the phone, and explained to her that he had been working with Valente for four years now. Valente had constantly been funding Burns's expeditions, and his show on Animal Planet. Burns asked her to trust him, and to just hear him out, to which Anika reluctantly agreed.

While driving home, Anika hopes Burns knows what he's doing, she hopes he made the right decision. She also hopes that this extraordinary discovery has fallen in the lap of the right person, and not the complete opposite.

As she drives past the plazas near her home, she notices a discount bookstore between a gym and a diner. She pulls into the plaza's parking lot and parks in front of the bookstore. She strolls inside; there is a smell of used paper lingering in the air. Anika wanders around, headed toward the non-fiction part of the bookstore, passing the history, sociology, and criminal studies sections. She reaches the section she's looking for, *biology*. She scans the subsections while looking at the book spines, wildlife studies, ornithology, and herpetology, until finally one stands out to her, and she pulls the large book out.

The Dinosaur Encyclopedia.

Anika flips to a random page, only to come upon an illustration.

A single predator lunging with its claws at the reader.

Its eyes locked onto hers.

MISSING BIRDS

Naomi Gagnon wipes the rain off her smooth forehead as she steps into her Land Rover. She closes the door firmly as she adjusts herself in the driver's seat of her SUV. Pulling down the sun visor, she flips up the mirror protector. She gazes into her own soft brown eyes for a couple of seconds before she moves on to her hair. Her brunette hair is in a ponytail, the tail ends of it light blue as the dye is almost completely grown out. She runs her fingers through her scalp and feels the heavy moisture on her fingertips. Some of the moisture has accumulated just above her forehand and is running down in streaks as her hands caress her head.

Naomi wipes the streaks of moisture before they reach her brows. She then turns her head to the left and then to the right, examining her head as a whole.

Well, the chilly Tasmanian rain hasn't completely ruined her hair. Plus, she never wears any makeup in the field, so there is nothing for the cold rain to ruin. She flips down the mirror protector and then flips up the sun visor. She reaches for her keys in her jacket pocket, and after finding them, she ignites the Land Rover to life. She puts the rover in drive and begins to move down the dirt road before her.

Naomi Gagnon spent most of her workday in the field. Today, she hiked for almost forty minutes through the Franklin-Gordon Wild Rivers National Park forest, doing her due diligence in keeping up with her cassowary research.

After arriving at her destination in the forest, Naomi meticulously searched for her moody yet erratic gold-necked friends. *Casuarius Unappendiculatus*, or better known as the Northern Cassowary, are an unusual case at the moment. The endangered species of flightless bird is most common to Papua New Guinea, living in the coastal swamps or rainforests of the New Guinea Islands.

The Northern Cassowaries are believed to have less than 20,000 in population left in the world. And although it is on the threatened species list, it is not a priority for anyone at the moment.

Anyone except Naomi Gagnon and her team, her team being Naomi and a colleague named Jason Marks. The reason for Naomi's sudden interest in the Northern Cassowary is their recent appearance in Tasmania. Not native to the island, nor suited to its typical habitat, the bird's presence immediately caught the attention of the seasoned ornithologist.

Reports of locals witnessing or encountering the four-foot "death chicken" were, at first, not taken seriously. A flightless bird found 2000 miles from its natural habitat? Unlikely.

But unbeknownst to Melbourne University, Naomi loves local tales of marvelous and/or mysterious encounters with wildlife. Initially, she was met with ridicule from tenured professors. Not only for the absurdity of the claims, but for believing the word of hermits living in the bush.

Naomi is known for her tenacity as a scholar; she takes every detail seriously. At 43 years of age, her mind is as sharp as it needs to be. So, to the surprise of her ridiculing colleagues, not three days after embarking on her journey through Tasmania, she encountered her prize. Four gold-necked Northern Cassowaries, two males and two females. All of them sharing territories in the northwestern side of the national park. Which was unheard of, but not as much as their presence in Tasmania. For nearly a year and a half now, she has been studying them. Keeping track of their movements and their behavior as well as their health in their new habitat.

Monitoring their health was Naomi's first priority, it's believed that Northern Cassowaries don't adjust well to new environments. Northern Cassowaries only live in humid rainforests or swamps. For them to suddenly emigrate to the dry summers and cold winter rain of west Tasmania is concerning.

Which brought up Naomi's second priority after initially discovering them. Not a question of why they emigrated, but a question of *how*. The only logical possibility Naomi ever came up with is human intervention. Either intentional or unintentional, it's common for animals to stowaway on ships. Whatever the reason may be, Naomi quickly let that avenue of research go and focused on the birds' wellbeing.

Naomi spent countless days in the forest, studying them cautiously from a distance. It didn't take long for the world's most dangerous birds to surprise Naomi again. They were extremely social with one another. Again, a trait extraordinarily unheard of. Cassowaries are shy creatures, often keeping to themselves, and only interact during breeding seasons. Yet, for unexplainable reasons, they were always within sight distance of each other.

And they haven't bred at all.

Naomi made these birds her entire focus, oftentimes wondering if she has discovered a new subspecies of Northern Cassowaries. They ate together, moved together, and slept near each other. These four birds were inseparable. Every night

Naomi went home to her condo, she was left astonished at their social behavior. Naomi knew she struck gold with her new found discovery. She would be remembered for her research into these extraordinary creatures.

These animals became Naomi's life.

After a few months of observing them, she named all four animals. One female was named Grumpy, because she was, as the name implied, always grumpy about something. Naomi always heard Grumpy's low growl resonating through the forest, wherever she was. The other female was named Angie. Angie was an intern assistant Naomi met years ago. Angie was always eager to please, doing whatever she could to win the favor of Dr. Naomi Gagnon. Same was with Angie's cassowary counterpart, always seeming eager to please Grumpy for whatever reason.

Then there was Thumper, the taller male of the two. Whenever he ate a satisfying meal, he thumped his right leg up and down on the ground. His taloned feet thumping the ground was a noise that always brought a smile to Naomi's face.

And the last male, she eventually named Stoic. It was difficult for Naomi to name the last male. For a while, she didn't see any defining traits in Stoic. At first, Naomi speculated that Stoic was the only bird in the group to act like their species are supposed to. Stoic would rarely directly interact with his 'pack'. He stuck around, sure, but almost never socialized like the other birds. Naomi came up with the name Stoic after she ran into him face to face.

Or rather, *he ran into her*.

Cassowaries are very distinct birds; they move in almost

like a wander from place to place. Their interactions with humans is almost always due to humans crossing their paths. They don't seek out human beings or other creatures, they're solitary animals. But whenever a human being has the unfortunate luck of running into the four-foot bird of death, their behavior is usually *on sight violence* if instigated. Cassowaries use their strong thighs and razor-sharp talons to kick you until they are satisfied. The best course of action is not making eye contact to avoid instigating the animal. Back away slowly and let the bird continue on its merry way.

So when Stoic popped out of the bushes next to Naomi, she thought her luck finally ran out. She had been so busy changing the SD card in her camera that she didn't see Stoic step away from the other birds.

Naomi looked away, and very slowly stepped back from the animal, while putting her backpack between her and the bird. In her peripheral vision, she noticed the animal continued to step forward toward her. Naomi braced for the inevitable attack, but it never came. Naomi then did the unthinkable; she looked up at the world's most dangerous bird and made eye contact.

The bird just stared at her.

Naomi felt a chill run down her back; these birds were a sight to see up close and personal. She wanted to look away, and continue to step back from the animal, but she couldn't. She saw something different in this animal's eyes. To this day, she can't quite explain what it was. Naomi eventually came to her senses, and stepped backward again. She expected the bird's signature head movement to follow her location as it looked for a reason to fight. Naomi expected the bird to move its head in a twitch, but it didn't.

Instead the animal slowly moved its eyes and then its head to follow Naomi's location. Its movements were more deliberate than instinctual. Then the bird did something more alarming than the attack Naomi expected; the bird stepped back slowly, and disappeared into the bush. The bird's calmer behavior stumped Naomi for weeks. That's when she came up with the name Stoic. He was calm, nothing bothered him, and there was nothing in his behavior that made him look frantic or unpredictable. That, coupled with the fact that Stoic always seemed to easily spot Naomi wherever she was at whatever distance, made Naomi's stomach turn.

Yes, these animals had all of Naomi Gagnon's attention.

But as Naomi drives down the dirt road, her windshield wipers at full speed, she feels worried. She hasn't seen any of her birds in a month. They seem to have fallen off the face of the earth. At first, Naomi thought they moved, perhaps emigrated to another part of the island. But why now? They never decided to move before, and their habitat didn't at all. So what caused them to disappear? Her colleague, Jason Marks, suggested human intervention was possible. One reason Cassowaries are on the threatened species list, is the hunting of these birds by human beings. Jason suggested the possibility that human beings killed the animals.

No, Naomi didn't want to think like that.

She will find them. They're out there, she knows it in her gut. Even after a month of searching, she won't quit. And it doesn't matter how many times Jason suggests she's wasting her time. It doesn't matter how often Jason suggests Naomi can get seriously lost in the forest looking for dangerous birds.

Which is exactly her point. With an island as dense

as Tasmania, it's completely possible that they're hidden somewhere in the forest. And with that thought process and motivation, Naomi Gagnon drives home to sleep it off, and try again tomorrow.

OLD FRIENDS

Anika eventually makes it home. She lays on her couch, slowly reading through the pages of the book she purchased. She feels as if she has a test to catch up to in the morning, reading furiously through the book like a college student whose procrastination has caught up to them. She takes glances at the illustrations as she reads, trying to put new words into her vocabulary. The different periods in time, different families, different genera and species. Anika finds it surprising that she only recognizes two dinosaurs by name, Triceratops and Tyrannosaurus. Of course she does, they are the most common if not the first dinosaurs people get acquainted with. She reads through the sentences, all of them written in a speculative tone.

This is not the first time she's done this; when she used to make expeditions on other animals, she would often purchase a few books pertaining to the species she was studying. Her small house is mostly bare except for a few bookshelves and hiking gear. The bookshelves are full of books, encyclopedias, and some biographies, all in the subject of wildlife biology. Whenever she studied up a species she was not familiar with, she would feel a sense of confidence. Confidence that the species has been studied over decades and these facts were based on years of observations in the field.

She feels no such confidence reading through this encyclopedia, all these 'facts' make her feel uneasy. Theory can only take you so far. You can analyze as many fossils as you want, like an ancient crime scene, and still learn nothing about actual behavior. The only thing she knows for sure, is that the species Burns encountered was carnivorous. Valente's paleontologist was right, all the herbivores described in the encyclopedia had short, stubby teeth. Like the molars you would see in cows, or sheep. Anika remembers the footage. The creature stood on its hind legs, like an ostrich, its tiny, clawed hands hanging as it watched Burns extend his hand.

She remembers the scars on Burns's fingers, the deep jagged cuts. A creature so small and already able to swiftly tear open Burns's calloused fingers. The more she thinks about it, the more it unsettles her. The illustrations of predators don't help. These books cater to young audiences, so naturally the pictures are meant to look appealing. But in the context of Anika's situation, it makes her feel sick. Most of these carnivores are as tall, if not taller than the average human, and usually ten or more feet in length. Words to speculate their behavior; strong but agile, possibly territorial, cunning, *could disembowel with a swift kick*. Anika feels like she is having a nightmare she can't wake up from. She sits up on her couch, and puts the book to rest next to her. She rubs her face, breathes in, and reminds herself that being a field biologist is always dangerous work.

This the main reason she left it all behind, and instead stuck with wolves. At least wolves are honorable, in a sense, and as long as you don't invade their territory, they respect your presence. Wolves are majestic animals, taking good care of their packs with their designated roles. Anika admires it, the fact that a species can focus on the wellbeing of their pack, without being selfish.

Anika studied other animals before, from the parks in the pacific northwest, to the wilds of Africa and the untamed forests of India. She's been around them all, lions, tigers, bears, hyenas, snakes, and rhinos. Name a species and Anika has been in close contact with it at some point. Her father, Matt Irving, hosts one of the most popular wildlife shows in the world.

His charisma and seemingly brave demeanor has earned him the respect of many institutions. Matt Irving has been hosting this show for twenty years, raising Anika in the world of wildlife conservation. She was a part of the show, along with her mother, Cassandra. Anika learned to be around all kinds of ecosystems while she traveled with her parents, that is until the incident that caused her to leave on her own.

The sudden reminder of the kind of tragedy that can occur in the world of wildlife studies brings up an interesting question to Anika. She grabs her Samsung Galaxy A21 and unlocks it using her fingerprint. The background on her phone is that of a wolf pup, bright blue eyes and dark gray coat. Anika clicks on an icon and opens up Google Chrome. She taps on the search bar. Before she types anything, she hesitates, the voice in the back of her head warning her of this avenue. She gives in; Anika has to know. She begins to type: *Tasmania animal attacks*. There is an article on dogs wiping out Tasmanian penguin populations, another on a deadly taipan snake bite, and one on a close call with a cassowary. Anika keeps scrolling, no other articles stand out to her.

Has no one ever encountered these animals? If the assumption that they have been hidden in the forest all this time is true, no human being has ever seen one? Anika clears her search bar and types in: *Dinosaurs Tasmania*. All she gets are ads suggesting field museums in Tasmania. No record, no reports, not even a single "a dinosaur ate my cat" article written in a conspiratorial tone. Can someone like Valente have the power to keep this quiet? Anika quickly shrugs that away. Valente would never have known if it wasn't for Burns. He only learned about this discovery recently. Anika puts her phone down, and arches her head back, staring at her ceiling.

The world will never be the same.

There's a knock on her door. Anika stands up and walks toward her front door. She opens it to see Burns standing on her porch, wiping the rain off of his jacket. She greets him and lets him step inside. She offers him a beer to which he replies, *whiskey, if you have it.* Burns takes a seat in her living room as Anika looks around her cabinet for the whiskey. Burns pats his wet hair, attempting to dry it, his hair beginning to thin. As Anika approaches him with a bottle of whiskey and two glasses in her hands, she can see the instantly recognizable weight in Burns's eyes.

Burns is a steady-handed, 46-year-old man, whose life is part anguish and part adventure. Burns left his abusive home when he was eighteen. He moved to a different city in his home state, West Virginia, where he joined an EMT academy. He quickly became a methodical first responder, earning his Paramedic certificate sooner than most. He did this until his late twenties, when he decided to continue his education. He attended a university, and it was there that he met his wife, Addison Kimbley. Addie was a wildlife biologist, and she was earning her PhD in Molecular Biology. She was a known supporter of conservation, often pushing back on lumber companies in the amazon. Burns loved her tenacity, and Addie loved his direct attitude; they were married almost immediately.

Together, they traveled the world, fighting injustices and keeping the animal kingdom out of harm's way. They earned an almost legendary reputation, which caught the attention of another wildlife icon, Matthew Irving. The Irvings and the Burnses became great friends, spending most of their time in the field on expeditions. Burns and his wife would often guest-star on the Irvings' show, spiking the viewership drastically. So much so that Animal Planet offered the Burnses their own show, with the Irvings' blessing. They gladly accepted. Addie always felt she needed to reach a wider audience to achieve her goal, and their show granted the need.

Their show, *Saving Our Planet*, consisted of Bill and Addie traveling to various countries to fight for animal rights, deforestation, and poaching. The show ran for five seasons, until it was put in hold due to Addie's declining health. Addie had been diagnosed with lung cancer, stage three. Burns struggled to keep it together while his wife slowly faded away. Addie Burns passed away after battling cancer for two years, leaving Burns devastated.

Burns didn't know what to do with his lonely life. He took a sabbatical of a couple years before returning to his job. The one who convinced him to go back to what he and his wife did, was Anika. Burns and Addie never got around to having kids, but they considered Anika their goddaughter. Anika was smart, dexterous, prudent in a manner that impressed the Burnses. After Anika left her father's show, he and Anika spent a great deal of time together. Burns would always respect Anika's work and often joined her on her trips to Iceland. He liked those trips; they were peaceful, and Anika was always good company to him. Burns became like a second father to her. However, recently, he has been spending more time on his own. This last year, he had minimal interaction with Anika. Anika used to wonder why he suddenly alienated her, but now she knows why.

Anika hands Burns two fingers of whiskey in a glass. She sits down next to Burns with her own glass. Burns takes a long sip from his glass before turning his attention to her.

"How was the flight?" he asks her.

"Quiet. Not a lot of people leave Iceland."

"Have you eaten?"

"Had a granola bar on the plane."

"Gotta eat up, kiddo. You look skinnier than last time."

"Oh yeah? When was 'last time'?" she presses.

Burns nods. "Yeah, I know. I've been AWOL, but now you know why. I'd have told you sooner if I could."

Anika sips her own whiskey. "All this seems legit to you?" she asks.

"I saw it with my own eyes, why wouldn't it be?"

"No, I mean this Valente guy. He seemed pretty uptight for a guy that wants to protect a species."

"That's just the Harvard in him. I've been around him a bit, he's strict but he's legit, I promise you," Bill says. He finishes his whiskey, and at this point, Anika notices that he hasn't been making eye contact.

"Bill, talk to me," she says softly.

He finally looks at her, but then looks away again. "About?"

"Well, there's watching footage, and then there's how you describe things. Tell me, in your own words," she says.

Burns takes a deep breath. "Like nothing I'd ever seen. Like nothing I've ever experienced. It didn't feel real while it was happening. Me reaching out to a wild animal seems like such a stupid thing to do now that I look back on it, but I needed to touch it because I thought I was going nuts. Curious, sprightly little guy, but that's all I could notice. I didn't really study him, not like I usually do," Burns explained.

Anika knows Burns to be exceptionally observant; no detail ever leaves his mind, and nothing ever gets past him that he doesn't notice. Anika always suspected that it was the paramedic in him, the ability to pick up everything in one quick glance. She finds it strange that Burns is being vague.

"Bill. You can't tell me that's all you remember. I know you, you didn't notice anything else?"

Burns's breath is shaky. He has something to say, but it's upsetting him just to even think about it. Anika hands him her unfinished whiskey; she's never seen Burns this upset, not since Addie passed away. Burns takes another swig from Anika's whiskey glass. He sighs, then turns his head and locks eyes with her.

"I did notice something. I wanted to study it like I usually do, to avoid looking it in the eyes... but I couldn't. Its left eye was black, like a shark, or a lizard or a bird, dead doll eyes, not unnatural. But it's right eye... colored, pupil and cornea, iris... it was almost like..." Burns wanders off mid-sentence, not sure how to describe what he's feeling.

"Maybe you saw it during a developmental stage, all the more reason to believe it was a juvenile," Anika adds, attempting to sway Burns back to reason and away from his doubts.

Burns quickly shrugs off her attempt to steer the conversation. "Ani. I brought you along to make sure someone is thinking straight, cause if I can't handle it for whatever reason, we *cannot* trust your father to do the right thing."

"And what is the right thing?"

"I'm not sure at this point, but whatever it may be, it isn't what your father has in mind."

Anika shakes her head; she knows he's right. Matt Irving is going to have other plans for this discovery. "And why does he know?" she says. "If you don't trust him, why is he involved in the first place?"

Burns finishes the second glass of whiskey in one last swig. He clears his burning throat and puts the glass down on the table in front of him. "It was all Valente. It's how I met him in the first place, Matthew met Valente at some event and they've been together ever since. When I showed Valente everything, the first thing he did was involve your father."

"*Why?*"

"Forrest admires him. Obsessed with Matt's show, I think it's a bit of envy. Valente wishes he had a family devoted to this."

Anika scoffs, "If only he knew the truth…"

Burns nods in agreement. He takes a quick glance in Anika's direction. "Light reading?" he asks, pointing at the books on her couch, *The Dinosaur Encyclopedia* by Michael Benton, *The Dinosaur Heresies* by Robert T. Bakker, and *The Rise and Fall of the Dinosaurs* by Stephen L. Brusatte.

"They read like horror novels at the moment."

"I'm sure they do, picked up a couple myself, but I'd rather listen to Lucy. She's got a good attitude, very enthusiastic."

"Speaking of which, how many people in total are a part of this? What's the plan?"

"Well, in total, I'm not sure. Maybe a little over ten people. Mostly the film crew from your dad's show. There's two planes, cargo and passenger, leaving in a couple days out of SeaTac. Eventually landing in Hobart, we should make our way there in a day or so."

"How far into Tasmania?"

"Far, miles away from any town or city."

"Miles. Into that *thing's* territory?"

"Valente had a house built out there, something like a makeshift HQ. Big house, ensured me it was reinforced and sturdy."

"He had a house built?" Anika says, raising an eyebrow.

"He has the money for it, plus his company was originally an engineering firm. Valente's lead engineer is highly recommended, you'll meet him tomorrow."

"What's tomorrow again?' Anika asks.

Burns leans back in his chair. "Debriefing. Everyone involved will be there, get our plan together, look over cargo and supplies. We leave in a few days."

"Shit."

"You didn't expect to leave so soon?"

"I thought I might have some time to decompress."

"Valente is eager, your father is impatient, and impetuous. They're both afraid someone will beat us to it."

Anika sighs in disbelief. The thought of working with her father again after so long reminds her why she left him in the first place. Always so impatient, so careless and selfish when it comes to his so-called work. Anika stands up and yawns. Burns just stares at the floor.

"I'm going to bed, you should too," she says.

"Alright, I'll head out."

"No no, crash on the couch. You're a lightweight when it comes to hard liquor. Besides, you can drive me tomorrow morning."

Burns nods his head and stands up, stepping toward the couch. He sits down as Anika walks toward her room and closes the door. Burns puts his legs up and leans back, then he closes his eyes and goes to sleep.

OCCUPATIONAL HAZARD

"I find this to be pure lunacy at this point, Dr. Gagnon," Jason Marks says with a firm tone.

"Love how you call me 'Dr. Gagnon' when you're trying to be serious," Naomi replies to him. She tumbles back and forth as the Land Rover careens through the bumpy dirt road. She has one hand on the steering wheel, and the other is holding up the BlueCosmo Global Satellite phone to her head.

"Naomi," Jason continues, "This is as serious as can be. Listen to yourself, for God's sake."

"Listen to myself?" Naomi simply repeated.

"You're talking about taking a two-hour hike into the forest by yourself. That's no joke, Naomi."

"I've done it before, dummy."

"Naomi."

"I'm sorry, who's got eight years of experience in the field?"

"Folks with more experience have died for less. This isn't necessary, you've got plenty of data."

"It's not about the data," Naomi says, "it's about the animals, Jason."

"They're just *animals*."

"That's just low, even for you."

"Naomi, you have to- for-it now-"

"Losing you, Jason. Gotta go anyways."

"Godd--n it---"

Naomi hangs up the satellite phone and throws it onto the passenger seat. The idea that they are just animals bothers her the more she thinks about it. These animals became something more than that. Not friends or family, Naomi is not delusional. But it is something akin to those kinds of relationships. It's the responsibility of caring for such relationships. She feels it in her heart, she has to find them and ensure they are safe. After being in their company for more than a year, she can't just give up on them. That's something Jason Marks can never understand.

Naomi stops her Land Rover on the side of the dirt road, the pin on her GPS indicating where she left off the last time she went out. She turns off her vehicle and steps out. Her boots crunching in the gravel and mud, she makes her way to the back of her truck. She opens the back door and pulls out her backpack. It contains all of her camping supplies, emergency food and flares. See? Not as reckless as Jason made it seem. She puts her arms through the straps and stows her backpack on her back. She closes the back door of her truck and turns her attention to the forest before her.

With the GPS in hand, she takes a deep breath and begins her journey into the dense wilderness.

Call it an occupational hazard, the danger inherent in her field, she knows it; she's not naive. It bothers her to a maximum that she constantly has to remind Jason that she's not an idiot. To do this kind of job, to be successful in this career, there are risks that have to be accepted.

Working with wild animals is, and always will be a risk. If you keep that phrase in mind for the entirety of your field career, the easier the job is. To forget your place in the wild, to believe these animals are your friends or family, is the quickest way to become another animal death statistic. You'd think this belief system would be common sense, but unfortunately it happens more often than you'd think.

Naomi knew of two of her colleagues who seriously got hurt when they first went into the field. Another ornithologist by the name of Gino Martinez, a twenty-something-year-old with an ego bigger than his stature. He almost got his head kicked in by an ostrich in Africa. Gino spent three weeks in the hospital, but even that experience unfortunately didn't fix his ego. It did make him appreciate his desk more though. Then there was Judith Gonzalez, a fast-talking and risk-taking marine biologist, who lost her right hand to a bull shark off the coast of the gulf of Mexico. Both stories have the same thing in common; they began to trust the animals they were studying.

There is no trust; most wild animals don't have that capability. Humans are creatures of habits and routines. Seeing the same individual every day for an extended period of time creates familiarity, and then subconsciously creates a feeling of trust. While some animals can learn patterns and routines, they will not treat you as a 'familiar face', much less with a feeling of trust. Wild animals have their instincts and their triggers that change their behavior spontaneously. Especially in predatory animals; give the impression of a fleeing prey and they will chase you, no matter how long you think you've known them.

Naomi never approached the birds, never got close enough to trigger the animals or make them uncomfortable. Except, of course, Stoic was the exception, but he was a special case. She briefly thinks about Stoic. To Naomi, sometimes it seemed eerily plausible that Stoic enjoyed sneaking up on her. Whether or not that's the truth, Naomi may never know. Although, as she walks through the forest, alone, she secretly hopes Stoic would pop out of the bushes and surprise her. Only then would Naomi finally know that all is well and she can go home to a good night's sleep.

As she walks, she scans every inch as far as she can see. She's looking for any sign of their presence. Feathers, tracks, killed prey, or even bird droppings. But just as the preceding months before, she cannot find a single trace. What was the need for their movement? Was it human intervention? Or did they move because of desperation or fear? They couldn't have just migrated, not like that, and to where? They seemed perfectly happy in their previous habitat. Plenty of food and plenty of space, and none of that has changed. So what changed with the birds?

Unfortunately, the only plausible answer Naomi keeps coming back to, is indeed human interference. Only humans have the ability to destroy and make disappear beautiful sources of nature. If that is the case, then Naomi hopes at least one of the birds got a good kick in.

Naomi steps over a bush and feels something crunch under her boot. The crunch is crisp and sturdy. Naomi stops in her tracks and looks down. She sees something under her foot, something ivory white, or is it dark yellow? Naomi kneels down and moves her foot off the crushed object. She reaches with her right hand and pokes at the shattered pieces with her fingers. She picks one up, it's light, but it's also a thick piece of material similar to fragile drywall. She holds it up to her face, and to her extraordinary surprise, her mind recognizes it immediately.

It's an eggshell.

She looks down again at the other pieces on the ground. It's a very large eggshell, bigger than any other bird on this island. For a moment, Naomi feels her heart race, her breath becomes giddy. Did her birds finally breed? Is that why they moved? But something doesn't add up' it's the color of the eggshells. Northern Cassowaries lay light black spotted eggs, while these eggshells are some shade of ivory yellow or white.

Then again, Naomi's earlier assumption of the birds was

that they may be a different subspecies. Either she was right in her assumption, or there are bigger birds out here. Bigger than her Northern Cassowaries she grew so fond of.

No, that's ludicrous. She would have seen them by now. Plus, what species of bird can possibly be bigger than Cassowaries in Tasmania? See? There's no logical answer when you pose the question like that. This eggshell has to belong to her birds. So the question is, is this their nesting grounds?

Naomi begins to look around at the ground. She doesn't see any other broken eggshells. She doesn't see any other traces of-

Her mental alarm goes off. She doesn't know why until she takes a closer look. It's skeletal remains, but they're not of an animal. She knows instantly, no animal or bird in Tasmania has skeletal remains of this size. And against her better judgment, she reaches forward and picks them up in her hand. It's only inches from her face when she realizes she's holding a human femur. The bone's diaphysis still looks oily, the epiphysis still has small tendons attached as well as dark red chunks of flesh.

Naomi drops it, feeling her stomach curl. She takes deep breaths in an attempt to keep herself from puking. She has to report this, she has to let someone know. Someone out there is missing and she has just found their remains. She stands up and struggles to fish the GPS out of her pocket. She checks her jacket and then her pants, but she can't find it. She looks around on the dirt floor until she sees it. The GPS is sitting next to the eggshells she was examining. She bends at the waist to pick up the GPS, and at that very moment, she feels a hot breath against the side of her head.

The last thing she hears is a deafening screech.

DEBRIEFING

Anika steps out of Burns's jeep. They have parked in front of a massive hangar behind Valtech's main building. A large, airport-like hangar, housing multiple kinds of machinery and dozens of projects in various stages of construction. Engineering materials lying in neat stacks against the walls, giant shelves holding pallets of materials. A forklift drives by Anika and Burns as they make their way inside the hangar. The forklift drives up toward the giant shelves and proceeds to start moving a pallet of materials.

"Bill! Over here!" a voice calls out.

A man in welding equipment stands next to a white Ford F-350. He seems to have been adding metal caging bars to the passenger side windows. Anika and Burns stop a few feet away from the welder. He lifts up his mask and reveals a 49-year-old man with a gray beard and black-framed glasses. He's short and barrel-chested.

"Looks like you're the first one here," the man says.

"Looks like it. Anika, this is Lee Ward, lead engineer at Valtech," Burns says.

Ward takes off his glove and extends his hand for a handshake. Anika shakes his hand.

"Another biologist, I take it?" Ward says.

"Yes," Anika says, as she scans the Ford in front of her. "You know, white is not an ideal color for field biology."

"Of course not, I plan on wrapping it later today. A matte

green is what Forrest requested," Ward replies.

"Hmm, green," Anika tugs on one of the metal bars covering the passenger windows, "Kind of thin, don't you think?"

Ward takes off his welder mask completely, his bald head shiny with sweat. He smiles, "It's what those safaris in Kenya have been using. They're field-tested, not even lions can get through it," he says confidently.

"Oh, they might be bigger than *lions*," Anika mumbles.

"What did she say-" but Ward is cut off.

"Bill, Dr. Irving. You're here," Valente calls out behind them. Anika and Burns turn to see Valente walking toward them. He slowly slips off some work gloves. Valente is wearing a dirty, greasy t-shirt and jeans, evidently working in the hangar for a while.

"An hour early, I see. Everyone else will be here soon," Valente says.

"Are these going with us?" Anika asks, referring to the trucks.

"Yes, three of them actually. Packed with enough supplies to last a month, if more is needed you could always make a pick up at Hobart."

Anika is not asking about the supplies, she could care less. She keeps thinking of the pictures in the dinosaur encyclopedia she read the night before. All those potential candidates looked stronger and more versatile than these 'bars' can withstand. Anika expected to see an army, a tank, something state-of-the-art, and all she sees now is upgraded pick-up trucks.

"Is everyone coming?" Burns asks Valente.

"Yes, Dr. Benitez, our paleontologist, is here already, waiting in the main office over there," Valente says as he points to an office in the southeast corner of the hangar.

"Can I see her? I have some questions," Anika says.

"Well, yes, but all questions will be answered in the briefing, if you could just-"

"I have my own questions, if you don't mind," Anika says abruptly.

"Of course," Valente replies softly.

Anika walks past him, ignoring his presence. "We'll catch up later, okay?" Burns says to Valente, trying to distract him from Anika's rude demeanor.

"Sure," Valente responds.

Burns follows Anika, while Valente stares at Ward for a few moments.

"Is that the chick from *Out with the Irvings*?" Ward queries.

"Indeed so."

Ward chuckles and puts on his welder mask again, "Looks like she's not the ray of sunshine she used to be."

As Burns walks alongside Anika toward the main office in the hangar, he takes a peek at Anika's determined stride. Anika has been a little more intense lately, becoming consumed by her work and closed off to everyone around her. Everyone except Burns, of course; she is always honest and open with Burns. She may not say nice things in the nicest tone, but she always tells Burns what needs to be said.

But she hasn't said a word to him all morning.

She's had a gloomy demeanor ever since they left her home earlier today. Burns could feel her brooding energy in the car ride here and now on their walk to the main office. Anika is among the most trusted biologists and friends Burns has, but the only flaw Anika has is her attitude toward other people. Burns can only apologize so many times for her; he knows she doesn't mean it oftentimes.

But then again, Burns can admit their current situation may require a bit more *bruteness*. Burns will have to let these next moments play out, and get a feel for where Anika's head is at.

Anika and Burns reach the main office. A couple of men in baseball caps stand outside the entrance to the office. One of them lighting a cigarette for the other, they both see Anika and Burns approaching. One of them walks over, meeting them halfway—a tall, bearded man in his mid-thirties, he's wide-chested. The man's shirt, 5.11 cargo pants, and his stride definitely scream former military.

"Anika Irving," he says, extending his hand, "Big fan of the show."

Anika shakes his hand as he introduces himself, "Kenneth Kitsap. Everyone calls me Kit."

"Kenneth Kitsap? So your initials are a passive aggressive way of ending a text message conversation?" Anika says mid chuckle.

"According to my ex-girlfriend, *yes*," Kit says, chuckling himself.

Anika has always liked the former military. They always have a good sense of humor. The other man walks to them, blowing a cloud of cigarette smoke. He's also mid-thirties, as tall as Kit, athletic build, and of Asian heritage. He has a bit of scruff on his face, and he hides his eyes under his cap.

"This is Jonas Jeller," Kit says, referring to the other man.

"JJ," he corrects.

Anika shakes his hand too, "I'm assuming you're our chaperones?"

"Yes ma'am. We'll be providing security on this field trip, not to make you feel stupid. We know you do this for a living,"

Kit says. Burns just stands to the side, texting on his phone.

"So, JJ and KK it seems," Anika jokes; she notices they both have jackets with the same logo, Valtech. "Do you work for Valente?"

"Yes, we usually work in the hangar, and sometimes security for his building," Kit responds, while JJ seems to be the quiet one.

"Ready for some actual field work?" Anika asks.

"Yes, we've been waiting for an opportunity like this, we love the field."

"It seems like there'll be a lot of people to chaperone," Anika says.

"Yes, a bunch of newbie film crew, and that over there is our pal-eon-tologist. The pretty one," Kit says, pointing to the office behind him.

"Well, it was nice to meet you both," Anika says as she walks past them. "From my experience, keep an eye on the film crew, they're the ones most likely to get hurt."

"That's why I called them 'newbies'," Kit replies.

Anika opens the door to the office and steps in, an empty room with plastic chairs, definitely not an 'office'. An old banner with purple lettering hangs on a wall, which reads 'Valtech Engineering'. That seems to be the old company name before Valente expanded it to something other than engineering. It appears that he loves putting his logo everywhere he can. In the corner of the room, sitting next to the projector on a table, is the paleontologist. Anika walks over to her; she is leaning forward, looking at her laptop, typing away furiously.

"They tell me you're our paleontologist," Anika says.

She seems startled for a few moments then looks up at Anika through her framed glasses. She is quite pretty, with high cheekbones and green eyes, and looks to be in her early twenties.

"Sorry, didn't see you walk up," she says in a Latino accent, "I'm Dr. Lucy Benitez."

"Anika Irving, Benitez, you say? Where are you from?"

"Texas, my family is from across the border."

"Where in Mexico?"

"Juarez."

"Oh cool, my mom was from Monterey."

"Oh right, Mr. Valente said you and your parents had the wildlife show?

"I used to, have you ever seen it?"

"Not really," Lucy says in a nervous tone.

Anika smiles. "Good, then we might actually get along."

She sits down on a couple plastic crates across from her. "I wanted to talk to you about this whole thing. You saw the video, right?"

Lucy nods. "Yes, I did."

"What'd you think?"

"What do you mean?"

"It seems... real to you?

Lucy understands the skepticism coming from Anika. "Well, if it was just the video I would've been more skeptical, but ultimately it was the rest of the evidence that convinced me."

"The saliva samples."

"Mhm, that and the bite marks on Mr. Burns's hand, the pictures of the prints, the sketches, and the feather."

"Feather," Anika repeats, curiously.

"You didn't know? They found one in the bushes a few yards away from where Mr. Burns encountered the animal."

"Hmm, and... what was it? Sketches?"

Lucy nods. Anika takes a moment to consider; she hasn't yet seen the other evidence. Valente promised to show her the rest of the evidence once she agrees to join the team. She will ask him the first chance she gets.

"Did you get a chance to look at all this?" Anika asks.

"Mhm."

"Thoroughly?"

She nods again; she can tell Anika's testing her. It seems to be upsetting her but she's used to it. Everyone sees a young woman like her and assumes she hasn't earned her PhD; she usually has to prove it.

"And?" Anika presses.

She pushes up her glasses, ready to show her intellect and prove she has a place in this expedition. "The feather doesn't match any bird in our current animal kingdom," Lucy explains. "Neither does the DNA, all I can say is that it's closer to reptilian DNA strands. The footprints also don't match anything in our current animal kingdom."

"And the video?"

"Its legs are like a bird, but its skin, its snout, its tiny arms, the tail. No reptile in our current animal kingdom is bipedal. The only bipedal reptiles or 'therapods' we've ever had are ancient, and extinct."

"It doesn't look like all of them are extinct."

Lucy smiles. "Seems that way."

"Can you tell what species it is? Specifically, I mean?"

"My guess would be mostly conjecture, but its prints-" Lucy holds her hand up and stretches three of her fingers, like a print. "-as far as we could see, like this, but they were apparently very light-footed. There weren't any solid imprints in the mud, could be three identical clawed toes, or two normal toes with the inner one upwards, like a claw."

"Like a *velociraptor*."

"Maybe, of that family at least, could be a dromaeosaurid. But nothing's definite, not until we get better evidence to analyze. In the footage it looked fairly small, Mr. Valente suggested today that it might be a younger specimen, so there's no telling what the genus or species it is. Velociraptor is a good guess, you're familiar with them?"

"No. I've just seen too many movies," Anika says.

"Movies?" Lucy asks, confused. Anika finds it amusing that Lucy has no idea what she's talking about; she must not watch much TV.

"At least you won't be as scared," Anika mutters.

"Just nervous, actually. I've been in the field before."

"Field? Doing what?"

"Eighteen dig sites."

"Interesting. Well this isn't quite *that*."

"I'm aware, I know what I'm getting into. I know there's a possibility it could be carnivorous. Mr. Valente assured me we'd be fine," Lucy says in an irritated tone.

"Just stick close and listen to us, you'll be fine."

The door behind them opens, and a group of people walk in, talking and snickering to one another. Anika recognizes a cameraman, the producer, the boom mic operator, and the editor from her father's show. Burns also steps into the office, behind him follows JJ and Kit, laughing and joking with someone. A man pats Kit on the back as he seems to be giving a punchline to a joke. Kit and JJ howl in laughter. The man, late 40s, tall and lanky, tanned skin, curly brown hair, is none other than Matthew Irving. He wears a tan button-up safari shirt, sleeves rolled up, matching cargo pants, and old work boots. His wrinkly but handsome face wears a charismatic smile with perfect teeth, clearly the face of a prestigious TV show. Matthew Irving walks with JJ and Kit until Burns waves at him to follow him.

"There's our showman," Anika mutters.

"Who?" Lucy asks.

"Matt Irving, my dad."

"Oh right, you were on the show with him."

"Yes, do me a favor," Matt and Burns start walking over to Anika. "If there's anyone you shouldn't listen to, *it's him*."

Lucy has no time to respond to Anika's advice, as Matt and Burns reach them both. "Anika, I didn't know you were coming," Matt says. He has a charming, southern voice.

"She agreed to it last night," Burns remarks.

"Huh," Matt seems a bit surprised to be in the same room as Anika. He turns his attention to Lucy. "Hi there, I'm Matt Irving, who might you be?"

"Dr. Lucy Benitez," she says, trying not to blush, as he seems to smell good too. "I'm Mr. Valente's paleontologist."

"The expert? Aren't you a little young to be an expert?" Matt says.

The blushing stops; this happens every damn time.

"She's pretty smart, I vouch for her," Burns interjects.

"*Cool*. Nice to have you aboard, Ms. Benitez." He turns to Anika, "How have you been, huh?"

"Fine," Anika answers, short and direct, her face telling him to spare her the small talk. She doesn't feel like talking with her father, and Burns notices.

"Hey, uh Ani? I need you for a sec," Burns says to steal her away, and Anika stands up.

"Nice talking to you, Lucy," Anika mumbles as she walks away with Burns.

"Need to show you some stuff I ordered," Burns says to Anika. "Interrogating our scientist already?"

"I was trying to figure out what she was thinking before Matt turned it into a red carpet."

"I know, I know."

They walk over to Kit and JJ, standing next to some packaged equipment. "Did you guys get what I asked you?" Burns asks them both.

"Mr. Valente finally came through with your orders. Took him long enough," Kit says. Kit starts to open three long black plastic gun cases. Anika and Burns peer inside the gun cases. Inside held in place by malleable foam are three brand new rifles for the expedition.

"I should've gone out and bought them myself, I don't know why Forrest took his sweet time getting these. We'll only have a few days to test fire and zero the scopes. Did they come mounted or did you do it yourself?" Burns asks.

"Me and JJ mounted them as soon as they came in an hour ago," Kit says. He notices Anika is examining the details of the rifles. "Are you familiar with rifles?" he asks her.

"I know how they work," Anika replies, "I'm not that familiar with brands or calibers, not anymore at least."

JJ picks up one of them from the case. The stock is laminated with a green mountain finish. It has a 20-inch cold-hammer-forged barrel with an added muzzle brake. The rifle's bolt, receiver, along with the barrel are a matte stainless steel. Mounted on top is a Leupold VX-6HD rifle scope with 3-18x magnification. JJ pulls the bolt back, and it sounds heavy and threatening in his hands.

".375 Ruger Guide," JJ says. "It's a new one in the market. I've test-fired .375 before, powerful fuckin' rounds."

"Fires .375 Ruger bore," Kit says. "270 grain rounds, big enough and fast enough to stop an elephant. Hence the name *elephant rifle*."

"Looks like it'll tear off your shoulder," Anika says. "Is that about right, JJ?"

"The kick doesn't hurt too bad," JJ mumbles, cigarette in his lips "but it won't tickle either."

"We ordered two of these for the ride, and there's this last one. Boss, I'm surprised you even know about this," Kit says as he reaches for the last weapon. It holds up a 12-gauge shotgun; it's nickel plated with black pistol grips and tactical stock. Anika has never seen a shotgun like this; it has no pump, and it simply looks powerful and menacing.

"Benelli M4, semi-automatic shotgun," Kit says, holding it up. "Pinnacle of Italian engineering, used to carry these sometimes in the marine corps. Perfect for turning someone's body into mush."

"How many rounds did you bring?" Burns asks.

"15 for each," Kit responds as he puts the shotgun back in its container.

"Just 15? For each one?" Burns asks, exasperated.

"We're studying extinct lizards, not fighting a war, sir. Besides, we do have the other rifles, the non-lethal tranq guns Mr. Irving ordered," Kit says.

Burns gives Anika an annoyed look.

"What'd you expect from the animal whisperer?" Anika says.

Burns sighs. "Alright Kit, I'll meet with you later today at my place. We'll get these scopes dialed in and make sure everything's working."

"I'll bring the watermelons," Kit says jokingly.

Burns shakes his head, then thanks Kit and JJ for the demonstration. He turns to walk away. Anika admits she does feel a little better now, knowing Burns took the time to think ahead. She knows Burns used to be an avid hunter in his younger years, but not so much anymore. Now Burns can't bring himself to shoot another animal after spending so much time with his wife protecting them. He mainly sticks to the target practice and the survival aspect of being in the wild. Anika remembers the many days and nights she spent with Burns camping as *uncomfortably* as possible. Burns argued to get used to being uncomfortable to build resiliency. He also taught Anika how to handle numerous firearms. Due to Burns's extensive knowledge of firearms, Anika knows these rifles Burns ordered will be enough for the expedition, or at least she hopes they will be.

Anika taps him on the shoulder. He looks at her as Anika wears a subtle look of disappointment.

"I don't want to hear it, Ani."

"Expecting the worst in this expedition?"

"You want to be out there defenseless? Are they not a good idea?"

"The fact that you've already considered the worst proves that we are out of our depth with this," Anika says.

"Your point being?" Burns asks sternly.

"Neither of us need this, not really. You know, we could just *go home.*"

Burns leans in close to Anika. "You trust *him* with this?" he says to her, referring to Matt.

"No."

"Precisely."

Anika and Burns decide to drop the conversation. They find

two empty seats in the room and sit down. Over the next ten minutes or so, a few more film crew trickle into the office, taking their seats in the plastic chairs, all facing a projector screen. Burns and Anika took the seats closer to the front and the projector itself. Matt is busy chatting with Lucy, spending his time pointing and looking at her computer screen. Lucy then grabs a small remote and switches on the projector. Matt watches as it slowly comes to life, previewing a blank screen on the projector. The projector then shows Lucy's computer screen, cluttered with word documents, excel sheets, and files that have no organization to them. She pulls up a PowerPoint slide show and then Matt gives her a thumbs up.

Valente and Ward finally step into the room. Matt sees them both from across the room and waves at them. Valente waves back, and then gestures to start the meeting. Valente and Ward remain standing. Matt then waves at everyone, then tells Lucy to start the slideshow. The first slide is the cliff notes of a set of rules.

"Alright, everyone. Let's get this show on the road, but first of all, I want to take a moment to appreciate you guys for agreeing to this. We are making history folks, and you're a part of it. All these moments are prologue to an accomplishment so amazing, it'll be talked about for decades," Matt says, almost in love with his own voice. Anika can't help but roll her eyes. Matt continues, "Basic rules for y'all, any trash or food wrappers are to be disposed of properly. We are not to leave any food outside the HQ, so as to not attract any attention. Also, no cigarettes, no cologne, no deodorant, and no old spice cinnamon shit shampoo. I'm looking at you, Zeke." The room chuckles; a film crew member gives him a thumbs up after being singled out.

"Ladies and gentlemen, we are going there to observe and document. Not interfere. We are trying to gain as much evidence of these animals' existence as we can, so we can protect them. Film crew, just pay attention to me or Bill... I guess Anika too. We've done this many-a-times before, we'll make sure it all goes smoothly," Matt says, then signals Lucy to change the slide.

Next one is a map of Tasmania. "We will be landing in Hobart, then we will drive from there closer to Tarraleah, and then head east into Franklin-Gordon Wild Rivers National Park. It is a mighty long drive folks, so bring something to do even if it is just a neck pillow. There is a house that Mr. Valente and Mr. Ward have kindly built for us that will be our HQ. Enough rooms and couches for all of us, however it's about an hour and a half drive back to anything civilized."

"We will be moving," Matt points at a few dots on the map, "along here where the tracks stopped, it's as far as Bill followed. We will be placing bait and trail cameras, here and here. If we have no luck, we'll move 'em farther. We don't know how deep in the bush they live. I don't imagine it's far from where Bill encountered it. Now, each time we go out, we will be taking one of these fine gentlemen," Matt points at Kit and JJ.

"They are battle-hardened marines," Matt winks at them. "And ready to kick ass if it comes to it. The reason we have 'em, is because we suspect that these creatures are carnivores, and of a dangerous dinosaur family, thanks to our lovely paleontologist here, who has been working diligently to identify this fine creature. Ms. Benitez, mind taking over for a bit?"

Matt sits down, leaving Lucy unprepared for the spontaneous spotlight of attention. However, this isn't her first time giving a lecture, so she decides to stay in her chair and switches the slides. The first picture is a diagram of dinosaur families.

"Hi everybody, I am *Dr.* Benitez, and from what I could tell, the creature is definitely of the saurischian order, which just means 'lizard-hipped'. In the video, it walked on its hind legs, so a theropod, now as to what specific species, it could be any number of them. Different genera like dromaeosaurs, deinonychosaurs, and other medium-sized carnosaurs are all possibilities. Now, we speculate the creature in the video is not at full size, probably a youngling." Benitez switches the slide to a screenshot of the creature in the video.

"Genera like megalosaurus, spinosaurus, and tyrannosaurs," Benitez says, the word 'tyrannosaurs' sending chills down the crowd's spines, "All have been discounted, typically younglings of those genera are bulky, wider, with identifying features. The creature in the video has a slender body, thin legs and arms, and the neck is longer. All the other genera that I mentioned before, can range from three to eight feet tall, depending on the species. Now, no fossils of any kind have ever been found in Tasmania, so I can't deduct as to what specific species it is."

She changes the slide, the title labeled "Dromaeosaurids", which shows pictures of Deinonychuses, Velociraptors, and Utahraptors, all standing tall, looking almost demonic with their sharp teeth and lifeless eyes.

"Most species of the dromaeosaurid family were known to hunt in packs, never loners as far as we know. Fossils have been found with four to eight members, approximately," she changes the slide again. A raptor pouncing on a stegosaurus, while other raptors are ripping it apart. "It has always been speculated that they were intelligent. Their skulls showed that their brains were larger than other dinosaurs. Probably closer to dolphins or wolves."

She changes the slide; it looks like a comic book panel. Each illustration with a different species of carnosauria. Allosaurus, Monolophosaurus, and Dromaeosaurs, all of them towering over an outline of an average-sized human, all carrying a menacing stare.

"Can they open doors?" Matt interrupts, an attempt at humor. Some in the room laugh, only a couple don't. Lucy doesn't understand the question, or the laughter that follows.

"I swear, if this whole fuckin' trip is just movie references..." Anika mutters, loud enough for everyone to hear.

"Enough," Burns says to the room. "Continue, Dr. Benitez."

"Umm, yeah. Multiple species have their own genera and don't really fit into the other families. Nevonator, Megaraptora, Herrerasauridae, all have their own families and individual attributes. All are under consideration. It will take a lot of evidence, both photographic and material, to determine the exact species."

She changes the slide again to a diagram of a dinosaur, but the slide doesn't have a title, or a label. It stands next to a human, with measurements around it, approximately twenty feet long, ten feet tall. Long and slim arms, claws on its hands like steak knives, powerful-looking legs, and taloned feet like an ostrich. Its snout is broad, lengthy, and its mouth is wide open, rows of blades for teeth. Its eyes look forward at the crowd, a penetrating and frightening gaze meant to shock its prey. These illustrations always seem to have the predators looking at the reader in a starved, lustful manner, while herbivores are composed and passive.

Burns looks away from the illustration, distressed. Anika notices her friend is distraught. A friend she has watched stare down a leopard and scare off a grizzly, a man who now seems like he has met his own predator. Benitez keeps talking, flipping through slides showing other species in detail. The room is completely silent, some mesmerized, some neutral, but all of them with a new, hidden fear.

EVIDENCE

"Quite an interesting briefing. I feel like shitting myself, thank you for that, Forrest," Ward says as he walks out of the office after the briefing ends. Valente strolls with him toward the inner part of the hangar. Valente knows Ward was skeptical about the whole expedition ever since he showed him the video. It took Ward a few days to finally accept the whole situation is real, although he's not entirely sure Ward has completely accepted it.

Ward has always been the kind of man who prefers to see and feel the texture, smell the environment of whatever he's doing to understand it better. He likes to be direct and honest about his concerns toward any project, and rarely ever stands down when he feels safety is being ignored. Valente always liked that about Ward, especially when he worked under his supervision during law school. Ward was the owner of his own company, Ward Engineering, when Valente met him. Ward took him in as a part-time laborer, but after seeing Valente's willingness to work and learn about the business, he promoted him to a full-time employee.

Valente never minded staying after-hours to make sure a project wasn't delayed, to which Ward took notice. Ward was aware he was attending Harvard, and he always found it odd that Valente was in no hurry to get home and study. One time, he asked him if he was getting enough time for school, to which Valente replied, "It's just law, not that hard to understand." Ward decided not to pry anymore, and let the young man work. To his surprise, Valente passed law school with honors, but then decided not to leave Ward Engineering.

Ward had done his research; he knew who Valente was and who his parents were, but he never asked him why he chose to have a job at all. Despite coming from immense wealth, Valente was a good kid, who loved getting his hands dirty and lived for manual labor. Ward found it admirable that Valente liked working with his hands, and picked up things fairly quickly. Ward never married, never had kids of his own, and he considered Valente a good friend, who always stuck by him when he needed it most.

Ward's company usually took in common civil construction jobs, often supplying blueprints and materials for seemingly intricate architectural homes and businesses. Ward helped a lot of businesses on the southeast coast of the US, providing structural advice for hurricane seasons. At one point, Ward received a contract offer for new watchtowers in a national park in Montana.

This wasn't Ward's usual job, and he didn't like going to remote places, but Valente insisted to at least "see what the deal was". Ward trusted Valente, and agreed to take the contract. He made good money in this job, although Valente, for whatever reason, decided to stay a couple more days in Montana. Something caught Valente's eye and Ward didn't know exactly what it was. Valente seemed mesmerized by the local wildlife, even as far as constantly being distracted during the project.

A few days later, Valente came back to work, with one of the last things Ward expected to hear. Valente offered to buy Ward Engineering, with a check big enough to let Ward retire and never work a day in his life again. This made Ward curious; he wondered what Valente had in mind for his engineering firm. Valente explained what he had in mind, mainly international contracts focusing on maintaining wildlife preserves. Ward was intrigued, and he agreed to sell his business on one condition: that he be allowed to stay on as an employee. Ward explained that he wasn't much for sitting at home doing nothing, and he wasn't an 'I'll go fishing' kind of retiree. Valente gave him a big smile, as if he'd been hoping Ward would stay. Instead of leaving him as just an employee, he made Ward co-owner of the business. They've been working together ever since, which is about seven years, even if Ward had to learn a little biology to understand their contracts.

Valente tries to calm Ward down. "You had already seen the video, Lee, there's nothing new you didn't already know."

"Easy for you to say, shit, maybe that chick was right, those bars on the trucks *are* too fucking thin," Ward says.

Valente takes a couple quick steps and stops Ward in his tracks. "Lee, *relax*," Valente says, "We've been over all of these blueprints for months now. The house, and the trucks, will be fine."

"I don't know, Forrest, did you see the estimated dimensions of those fucking things? And they anticipate there are more than one? Are you sure you want to do this?"

"Lee."

"Hold on a sec, kid. Look, I know how you feel about protecting wildlife, but this feels way too dangerous. Christ kid, more so than lions. Lions!"

"Lee, relax for god's sake. You want to look things over? Fine. But stop hitting the panic button when we're this close."

Ward sighs in disbelief. He shakes his head and then becomes more stern with Valente.

"Alright, Forrest, I'll play along. But know this, even if I reinforce everything to withstand a fucking bombing raid, I still won't be able to sit still," Ward walks past Valente. "Christ kid, you got to learn to *let some shit go*."

Ward continues to walk away from Valente, toward the

Fords being worked on by other laborers.

"Marty!" Ward yells to one of the laborers, "Hold on, don't put those on yet, we're starting over!"

The laborer holds his hands up, confused about Ward's new orders. Ward reaches him and begins to explain things in his authoritative manner. Valente watches as Ward angrily tells the laborer that they're changing the designs on the trucks. He's never seen Ward this worried before; he always knew Ward to be a confident individual. Valente remembers seeing Ward in a tank top one day, a tattoo on his left bicep reading *Army Ranger*. It made sense to Valente that Ward was former military. His body still showed great strength despite his age. There was also the fact that most of Ward's employees were former, if not current military. It seems Ward trusted them more and probably missed the camaraderie. However, Ward never talked about it, let alone mentioned his military service. Valente never knew specifically what conflict Ward is involved in, and he never thought to ask such a personal question. Ward is a kind person, and Valente considers him a respectable companion, but he always seems to have a sense of an obscure wrath sometimes.

"Mr. Valente," a voice says behind him.

Valente turns his head to see Anika, her face tired but controlled. "Please, call me Forrest."

"*Mr. Valente*, I'd like to see this other evidence, in person."

"In person?"

"Yes. I need to see it all, whatever you have."

Valente blinks a couple times. He can tell Anika is incredibly determined, and there's no use in denying her access. She would just argue. Everything Burns told him about Anika seems to be true. She's a grim and persistent wildlife biologist, and she has a way of rubbing wrong with people. Valente was assured by Burns that she is an ideal asset to have on the team, 'realistic' is the term he used to describe Anika Irving. Either way, Valente doesn't feel like being alone with Anika and her combative attitude. He sees Burns walking out of the office with Matt.

"Of course, all of our evidence is in the main building over there," Valente points to Valtech' s main building. "In the biology wing. I could take you there myself, can you give me a minute?"

Anika nods, and stays where she is, waiting for Valente. Valente sees Burns talking with Matt, both standing in the middle of the hangar. He strolls to them, and catches the end of their conversation.

"…it'll all be fine?" Matt says to Burns.

"She might keep her distance, that's all I can say," Burns replies. Burns and Matt see Valente approaching them.

"Bill, need you with me. Anika wants to join us in the biology wing," Valente says. Burns doesn't bother to ask; he knows exactly what is going on as he sees Anika in the distance with her arms crossed, waiting.

"Alright, I'll be with you."

"Matt, see you in a couple days," Valente says. Matt salutes Valente and then pats Burns on the arm. He walks away, moving like he's the tallest one in the room. Anika just watches her father with pure disdain in her eyes.

Valente leads the way through Valtech's main building. Burns and Anika follow closely behind. The building's layout looks extensive, a lot of space, a lot of offices and conference rooms. However, it all appears vacant, no employees except for the secretary and security guard at the main entrance. And it's only Tuesday. Anika's been to many office buildings before, like the Animal Planet headquarters in New York and various embassies, and they all seem pretty busy. If Valente owns this successful field engineering firm, Anika expects to see a lot of top tier employees, and seeing practically no one does not boost her confidence in the expedition. The only busy part of Valente's company is the engineering hangar, but even there, there are only about ten employees.

"Where is everybody?" Anika finally asks.

"A lot of personnel doesn't usually mean increased productivity," Valente says without skipping a beat. "We have never been delayed on a project so far, even with the minimal staff we have."

"How many contracts do you usually accept?"

"About fifteen a month."

"With minimal staff?"

"Never been delayed," he reiterates.

Valente reaches the door for the biology wing. Anika notices that it looks like a regular office door, might as well be a closet. Valente slides his keycard and the keypad blinks green. Valente opens the door, revealing the so-called 'biology wing'. A large lab, counters with cabinets, whiteboards, and shelves with laboratory equipment. Four massive industrial refrigerators sit in the corner, and the counter in front of them has laboratory technology sitting on top, microscopes and beakers. Anika feels a sudden rush of nostalgia. This particular room reminds her of all the science labs in high school. Valente is a rich man, then why does every aspect of his company seem to have an improvised appeal?

Valente lets Anika and Burns walk into the room. He closes the door behind him and waits for it to lock. "What did you want to see?" he asks Anika.

"Everything."

"Okay then, let's start with physical evidence before we

get to anything speculative," Valente says. He moves to the industrial refrigerators, and opens one of them. A faint hiss is heard as he swings the door ajar. White cold fumes escape as he reaches in and pulls out a glass case on the top shelf. He sets the glass case on the counter in front of the refrigerators. Burns and Anika have already moved in for a closer look.

Anika peeks into the glass case, the glass partially fogged and murky. But she can see its contents. A feather, about three or four inches in length, the hollow shaft about one inch before the feather sprawls out into its vane with a natural design. The vane seems light brown with black splotches, the barbules not at all neat and soft like a normal bird feather. Instead, the barbules are seemingly pointing in opposite directions, individually, giving it a spiky appearance.

"Different, no?" Valente says.

Anika looks up at him. "Doesn't look like any bird I've ever seen," she says.

Valente nods, then makes his way toward a filing cabinet in another corner of the room. He reaches into his pocket for a set of keys. "I would show you the saliva samples but I'm afraid those have been depleted. We already had a small amount, and we used it all for the tests we ran," Valente says. He picks out a key from his set and uses it to open the top filing cabinet.

"We? Who's we?" Anika asks.

"Molecular biologist out of Berkeley, he's currently out of town, otherwise he'd be here," Burns answers.

"Yes, yes, his name is Sacksteder, Bill recommended him," Valente says as he pulls out a file from the cabinet drawer.

Anika guessed that Burns might have suggested someone in the first place, since his wife knew practically everyone in that field. Valente walks back toward Burns and Anika with a file in his hands. He sets it on the counter and lets Anika take a look for herself. She opens the file and sees a set of photographs. Four photos show a small footprint in the mud, illuminated by the camera's flash, a single ruler sitting next to the print to indicate dimensions. Two toes, left and middle, about six and a half inches in length, one and a half inches wide. Slim toes, the imprinted dots above them denoting that they are clawed. The third toe is harder to see. It doesn't have a good imprint like the other two, actually at this point, Anika notices that they have better imprints in the mud toward the top of the creature's toes. As if the animal stood or balanced on its tiptoes and talons.

Anika flips through the other photos of the muddy prints. "Do you have pictures of the other one's tracks?" she asks.

"Other?" Valente says.

"The one that called it away in the video, it can't have been far," Anika says.

"No tracks," Burns replies.

Anika looks at him, bewildered. "None?"

"Nope, none at all, we looked."

"How… odd. It's clear from these pictures that the creature seems to have padded feet, making it light-footed, but I don't imagine a larger version of it wouldn't leave any tracks."

"We don't have the first clue. It was raining heavily that night, they could have been washed away, somehow," Burns says.

"Maybe it was far away? Made a loud enough cry that you could hear it?" Anika suggests.

"No. It was close, very close. I could feel its presence after I heard it."

Anika trusts Burns's judgement, so she decides to look at the other photos in the file. The others are pictures of Burns's fingers, the jagged cuts from the bite fresh and blood-smeared. The teeth seem to be about two or three centimeters in length.

"Any side effects? From the bite?" she asks.

"None. Valente had a physician take a look at me, blood tests, the works, nada," Burns responds.

Valente is curious about Anika's question, so he asks for elaboration. "You suspect it could have venom of some kind?"

"I was more concerned about diseases," Anika says.

"Diseases? You mean because they're carnivores?" Valente asks, referring to sometimes carnivorous predators carrying bacteria in their teeth and gums.

"No, I mean diseases in general, do you know anything about prehistoric diseases?"

The thought never occurred to Valente. Anika notices his moment of realization. "The world was completely different millions of years ago," she says. "Who knows what illnesses those animals were prone to."

Valente is concerned. "And what is your suggestion then?"

Anika stands upright from bending over the counter and looking at the files. She's now looking Valente in the eye. "My suggestion starts with a question," she says. "What kind of non-lethals are we taking with us?"

"Matthew asked for tranquilizers, air rifles used in zoos. Plenty of sedatives as well."

"Sedatives," Anika says, "That would imply he plans on capturing one."

"For a blood sample, we would release it into the wild as soon as we have it."

"I thought we were just observing," Anika presses. "I'd call that interfering."

"Matthew assured it would all be fine."

"*Matthew* is a very careless and foolhardy person. He would likely expose us to this creature for his own benefit. And who knows what kind of behavior these creatures have? They could be very territorial, and defensive, especially toward anyone trying to capture one of their own."

Valente frowns. He looks to Burns for help, but Burns looks away, unwilling to say a word. "Are these actual concerns? Or are they just ways of being conflictive with your father?" Valente says.

Anika leans forward with her shoulders tense. "Do they sound like bullshit concerns?" she says firmly.

Valente says nothing.

"Let me tell you something. My father has a very distinct and ridiculous belief about wildlife, and he will use that belief to not only get people hurt, but to make himself look better on TV."

Valente still says nothing. He clearly has a good friendship with Matthew Irving, and he doesn't like what he's hearing.

"If you are as smart as everyone tells me, you'll make sure the 'master outdoorsman' doesn't fuck up your mission, or your life," Anika says.

She finally releases the tension in her shoulders. She leans back down and refocuses her attention onto the rest of the file. Valente is shocked, Burns told him that Anika's relationship with her father is dicey, but it's very clear she doesn't trust him and clearly despises his work. Anika holds up a photo to Valente's face, breaking his line of thought. "What's this?" she asks.

Valente recognizes the document, although it's not a picture, it's a sketch. "Drawings, sketches from everyone who saw the animal that night. They all agreed that this is what it looked like," Valente explains.

Anika flips the sketch in her hand and looks it over. It is a very rough drawing of a dinosaur with feathers on its head. The sketch is not very detailed except for a basic outline of the animals features and limbs. It looks like the most generic outline of a random dinosaur. She then puts the sketch back on the table. "What kind of sedatives?" Anika asks, breaking the brief few seconds of silence.

Valente clears his throat. "Xylazine, and Acepromazine, with Naltrexone to counteract any side effects."

"I've used those sedatives before, but the only reason we used them is because we knew the entire physiology of the animals. We know nothing about prehistoric animals, we don't know how their body works or reacts to certain elements. In the end, if we're not careful, we might end up doing more harm than good."

Valente sighs. "I see no fault in your argument… but… well…"

Anika knows; she recognizes the look almost immediately. "But my father has taken over your project."

Valente slowly nods his head in exasperation.

"Yeah, well, he does that," Anika says.

"Way too goddamn often…" Burns mumbles.

Anika flips through the other sketches. "Just be glad me and Burns are coming along, odds would be three against one." Eventually, Anika gathers all the photos and sketches, and puts them back in a neat pile. She hands the file back to Valente. She seems to be satisfied for now.

"Alright then," Valente says, "I think it's best to get back to work. Did Bill fill you in on the travel details?"

Anika gives him a nod, and Valente proceeds to put the file back in the locked filing cabinet, while Burns puts the encased feather back in the fridge. Valente leads them both out of the biology wing, and down the empty halls of his company building. Valente finds his feelings for Anika very conflicting; on one hand, she can be pugnacious, on the other, she is thorough with the information given to her. When Valente showed Matthew Irving the footage, of course he was blown away, but he never asked to see the physical evidence in depth. Matt never brought up any safety concerns or cared too much about the details pertaining to the creature. His main priorities were focused on getting a sizable film crew together, and flying out there as soon as possible. Valente and Burns actually had to convince Matt to wait before doing anything without a plan, to which Matt agreed in an impetuous manner.

Christ, perhaps Anika is right to have her concerns about her father. Valente finally starts having some doubts about a man he has known for years.

"Mr. Valente," his secretary says.

He's holding the door of the main entrance open for Burns and Anika, and they have walked past the secretary's desk. She's holding a large yellow envelope in her hands. "Yes, Susan?" Valente says.

"This came in by messenger today, marked urgent," she says, holding the envelope out for him.

"If you need anything else, talk to Lee in the hangar," Valente says to Burns and Anika as they walk out. Valente lets the door close and then walks toward his secretary, taking the envelope from her hand.

"Messenger? How long ago?" Valente asks.

"An hour or so. I tried calling you but it went to voicemail," Susan says. Valente usually keeps his phone on silent, as he hates to be disturbed during his time in the engineering hangar. He opens the envelope, which is light in weight, but it is the size of a normal piece of paper. He pulls out two sheets of paper and skims the heading and the body paragraphs.

And to his secretary's surprise, he then closes his eyes, and cusses up a storm.

"*A court summons*?" Ward says, exasperated. "What the fuck for? For who?"

Valente has rushed to talk to Ward in the hangar after reading the contents of the envelope, while Ward is in the process of replacing the metal bars on the truck windows. "For Valtech Industries," Valente says, "For withholding evidence, reckless endangerment, and property damage."

The words make Ward baffled and irritated at the same time. "When the fuck did we do all that?"

"I don't know, but this is serious, Lee. The court date is in two days."

Ward shakes his head. "Shit, kid, what about all this? Are you gonna postpone?"

"Absolutely not."

"Then what?"

Valente shakes his head, upset, furious, clouded. He takes an enraged deep breath before responding. "No delays..." Valente simply says.

"Uh-huh. Which means?"

"They leave, without me. No delays."

Ward can see Valente's disappointment. He's been planning this expedition for months.

"You sure?" Ward asks.

Valente turns his head, and sees Matt Irving, laughing and joking with Kit and JJ. Now it would be two against one, he thinks. He will have to put his trust in Burns and Anika. "No delays, Lee," he says. "*No delays.*"

DEPARTURE

Valente stands next to his Mercedes sedan, which is parked in front of his private plane hangar at SeaTac airport. He watches as Ward and his other Valtech employees load the supplies into the cargo plane. He sees his three modified Ford F-350s being pulled into the 747 Dreamlifter, all of them matte green like he requested, with a purple Valtech logo on the driver and passenger door. Thick metal protective bars bolted and welded on the outside of the passenger windows, bulletproof windshield, all terrain tires, and upgraded suspension. The pickups have a canopy installed, the pickup beds filled to the brim with food, cases of water bottles, and camping equipment. Things like camera equipment, GPS, lab equipment, and weapons will be loaded onto the private plane the crew will be flying in.

Things the last couple days went smoothly. Valente and Ward finished work on the trucks a day early. Everyone got their passports and travel details in order and in time for the flight. Of course, Anika called Valente a day ago, and had some suggestions for camera equipment, as well as FLIR cameras. His conversations with Anika over the phone are short but direct. Valente is starting to warm up to her. Anika is proving to be pretty knowledgeable in her field. She's tenacious, but also very attentive to the plan and proper procedures of wildlife biology. Valente appreciates her diligence, as it's his top focus in his own company. It's the reason he's keeping so little personnel, because as long as you know what you're doing and what the deadlines are, things go smoothly.

Valente never believes in having a lot of employees. He believes in looking his candidates in the eyes and deciding if they're steady workers. Plus, if something doesn't go his way, he knows him and Ward would just do it themselves. That's the main thing Ward and Valente have in common. They don't mind working sixteen hours a day, six days a week. Although now, as Valente watches his project load into the plane without him, he feels like a useless laborer skipping out on work. The thought makes the weight in his stomach heavier. He feels sick and frustrated. Who on earth could be suing his company? Who could be keeping him from his beloved project? Valente knows he and Ward have always gone the extra mile for their clients, and their work is always rated top-notch.

Still, no matter what happens, Valente may be able to join the expedition later on. They're planning on being there a month, so the notion makes it a little easier on his stomach. Valente sees Ward signing the pilot's clipboard and then shake his hand. Ward turns and begins walking toward Valente, who's leaning against his car. Ward is wearing a flannel and a black jean jacket, with tan slacks, and trucker hat with a Valtech logo.

"Should be all," Ward says, "When's the other plane leaving?"

"Couple hours, they'll be here soon."

Ward leans against Valente's car next to him, and pats him on the back.

"How are you feeling?"

"Worthless."

"Ah, don't worry too much about it. I'm sure it's all some misunderstanding. Plus, you get to keep me company."

Valente smirks. "Actually, Lee, you can keep *me* company."

"What do you mean?"

"I mean, you are the co-owner of Valtech, you have to be in court too."

The thought never occurred to Ward. He pulls a pack of cigarettes from his jacket, takes one out and lights it while he holds it in his lips. Ward inhales the nicotine and then blows out a thick cloud of smoke. "Who's our lawyer? Do you know anyone good?"

"I do, *me*."

Ward frowns, and gives him a side eye. "You? Kid, it's been like ten years since you went to law school."

"It's just law, and I didn't forget a single thing."

Ward chuckles. "Christ kid, are you ever going to admit something is beyond your control?"

"I don't think anything is in my control. I just know that whatever happens, I can handle it."

"And you'll be able to 'handle' this?"

"Well, Lee, we almost certainly didn't destroy any property, or recklessly endanger anyone, and we most certainly didn't withhold any evidence."

"Hmm... Well, I'm not so sure about withholding evidence."

Valente scoffs, like he's half expecting Ward to tell him about some random double life he's been leading. Ward catches the implication and laughs. "I'm talking about *this*. The expedition," Ward says.

Valente doesn't understand. "This? How?"

"I mean maybe keeping this whole thing out of the public eye might be considered withholding evidence."

"No one knows about this. No one. And it doesn't fit into the other two charges."

Ward feels that this expedition does indeed seem like reckless endangerment, but he won't say it to Valente, as he already looks uneasy. "If you say so, kid."

Eventually, a large transit van makes its way onto the private runway. It's parked a few feet away from Valente's car. Matthew Irving, Kit, JJ, Dr. Benitez, and the film crew slowly disembark the transit van. Each carrying their own backpack or duffel bag, and some have neck pillows around their necks. Matt catches a glimpse of Ward and Valente, and makes his way toward them.

"Where is she?" Matt asks.

"Who?" Ward says.

"My jet."

Matt Irving insisted on bringing his personal jet he uses to fly the crew around, a Bombardier Global Express he's had for years. Matt wanted to fly it, to which Valente suggested otherwise.

Valente points to the hangar. "Being fueled, you'll leave soon."

"Not coming with us?" Matt says, noticing Valente's sharp-looking three-piece suit.

"Got some things to take care of. I'll join you later this week."

"Alright then, the cargo plane has already left?"

"Took off twenty minutes ago, it'll be waiting when you land in Hobart."

Matt gives him a thumbs up, and then walks away, apparently to help his crew move the luggage and equipment off the van. Out of the corner of his eye, Valente sees a Jeep Wrangler rolling in. It moves and parks next to Valente's car. Ward can see Burns and Anika inside. The Jeep settles down as the ignition is switched off. Burns and Anika step out and proceed to grab their backpacks out of the back. Burns locks his

Jeep, and then he and Anika walk toward Valente. "Studying dinosaurs or going on a date with them?" Anika jokes, pointing at Valente's suit. She seems to be in a lighter mood today, surprisingly.

"Got some things to do, I'll catch up later this week," Valente says.

Anika's 'lighter mood' fades quickly. She steps closer to Valente. "What kind of things?" she asks in a challenging tone. Anika isn't much for being tossed into dangerous situations by people who assume to know better. Anika is assuming that Valente isn't going for personal reasons, either because he's scared or he simply doesn't care. Valente matches Anika's confrontational demeanor.

"My company is being sued, Dr. Irving. I have to stay, otherwise, I would've been on the cargo plane that left twenty minutes ago," Valente says. This is the first time he's pushed back at Anika. Anika eases off her stance and takes a deep breath.

"You figure it won't take long to sort out?" Burns interjects.

"Not at all, considering we haven't done anything wrong, it shouldn't take long," Valente says.

Burns nods his head. Anika looks away at the crew putting luggage on the jet. "He brought his fuckin' jet," Anika turns her head toward Valente. "He's not flying it, is he?"

"Of course not, no need to worry."

"Last thing I need is more fuckin' stress," Anika says as she walks toward the jet. Valente just watches her stomp away; his feelings for her fluctuate by the hour.

"Bill, you good?" Ward asks him.

Burns nods his head. "I'll be fine, we all will, hopefully."

"Well, you know the drill, you need anything, don't hesitate to call me or Forrest," Ward says.

Burns gives them a short smile, then shakes both of their hands and thanks them for their help. Burns then walks away, ready to board the plane. As soon as Burns and Anika are far enough away, Ward lets out a scoffing laugh.

"What?" Valente snaps.

"That chick is so goddamn intense all the time," Ward replies.

"Bill says that's her baseline," Valente says, "Would hate to see her genuinely upset."

"Still though, I like her," Ward says. "With that kind of energy, she'll keep the *right people on their toes.*"

Anika takes a seat in the jet, with Burns across from her in the leather seats. It's been so long since she was in this thing last. Spacious, luxurious, with a minibar next to the cockpit, but Anika hates every inch of it. She sees her father take a seat close to the cockpit, sitting next to the two marines, joking with them again. It looks like he's found his audience. Kit is smiling and laughing with Matt's electrifying charisma. Even the quiet one, JJ, who's the hardest to read, is smiling. While watching them, Anika hopes the marines will eventually let their instincts kick in, and see through the bullshit.

Matt taps the secret compartment on the wall next to his seat, popping open a secret cabinet. He pulls out an ice-cold bottle of champagne, and shows it to the marines. Anika can barely hear what he's talking about, but it doesn't matter. She has heard it all before. He's more than likely bragging about his jet. Matt Irving loves his jet. He would often fly Anika and his wife across the globe, filming his show in the late 1990s and early 2000s. Matt came a long way in his life, long enough that he was able to afford a $20 million jet.

Matt started his job as an intern at a zoo in Texas in the early

90s, shadowing zoologists and field veterinarians. Eventually he was hired as a full-time zookeeper, where he began to love animals and the outdoors. The zoo, however, had to let him go, as they considered him a rash zookeeper, usually walking into the animal enclosures on his own with no protection. Matt argued that he had built a sense of trust and mutual respect with the animals, and that there was no cause for concern. Even then, the zoo decided not to keep him around, as he was a potential liability. Matt traveled the country, working in different zoos, most notably Woodland Park in Seattle and Central Park in New York.

He did this for four years, until a man visiting New York from Africa offered Matt a job as a game warden in Kenya, which Matt gladly accepted. In his time in Kenya, Matt worked as a game warden and safari guide, teaching tourists about African wildlife. It wasn't long until tourists began to notice that Matt's safaris were wildly different from the others. He would at times leave the truck full of tourists and walk right up to the animals on the route. Lions, elephants, rhinoceros, and even hyenas, Matt appeared to be quite fearless. He eventually earned some notoriety from tourists, always requesting Matt to be their guide. It was around his second year in Kenya that he caught the eye of an Animal Planet executive, who came across a video played on various news channels. The clip highlighted Matt's audacity by walking up to a pride of lions, and proceeding to hug them.

The lions hugged and held Matt in their giant but soft paws. They were apparently extremely comfortable around him. The executive flew out to Kenya the first chance she got, and offered Matt Irving a once in a lifetime deal: his own educational wildlife show. Matt was both confused and thrilled. He had never thought of that, but it was everything he could have ever wanted. His premiere episode for *Out and About with Matthew Irving* consisted of him sitting in the middle of a pride of lions, the lions resting and barely acknowledging his presence. The premiere episode was a massive success, causing Animal Planet to order a full first season, along with a second.

It was during his second season that he met his wife, Cassandra Jimenez, a biologist Matt interviewed on an episode while a sedated jaguar laid between them. The beautiful cat puffed with its powerful lungs as Cassandra blushed, while Matt wooed her with his southern charm. In the following weeks, fans of the show were fascinated by the on-screen chemistry between the two, and were hopeful for a behind-the-scenes romance. Which wasn't that far-fetched. Matt and Cassandra indeed fell for each other. Cassandra Jimenez was a wildlife biologist for a zoo in Nuevo Leon, but she was originally from Monterey, Mexico. Matt Irving purposely kept his show in Mexico for a few months, having her guest-star every other episode. So much so that Animal Planet offered her a spot in Matt's show, with the insistence from Matt.

It was in the third season premiere that Matt proposed to her, skyrocketing the ratings of the show for the remainder of the season. They were soulmates, on and off screen. Matt and Cassandra did everything together, traveled around the world, meeting and educating their fans about nature. They were inseparable, their love for wildlife making their bond stronger with each endeavor. During an episode on Indian elephants in season four, Cassandra revealed to both Matt and the fans that she was pregnant. Once more, the show kept skyrocketing its own ratings, making it the number one show in only two years.

After they both took a few months off the show for the birth of their daughter, Anika, the show returned completely revamped, with its new name *Out with the Irvings.* The following years were among the most successful of all, and each family member had their own role and segment on the show. The episodes had a basic outline: the start would be Matt showing off the animal, standing incredibly close to it with his camera crew, remarking about their behaviors, and do's and don'ts. The second third of the episode would be Cassandra talking about the physiology while it was sedated. And the last third, which quickly became a fan favorite, a young Anika playing with the younger offspring of said species. Young Anika's ability to make quirky jokes and appeal to younger audiences created such a fan craze and rapport, that Animal Planet ordered four more seasons in advance. The show did indeed run for four more seasons, and the show grew just as Anika did over the years.

However, tragedy was around the corner, and it was a gradual decline between Matt and Cassandra that most believe was the cause of the incident. Fans noticed in a couple episodes that Cassandra was a bit more cautious and wary of standing so close to animals with her daughter. Matt never seemed to change his behavior with wildlife but Cassandra was a bit more protective of Anika. It was always the same thing. Cassandra would express a concern and Matt would shrug it off, assuring that things would be fine.

On a gloomy and rainy day in the amazon rainforest was when the dreaded incident occurred. The episode was about Irving talking about all kinds of wildlife in the rainforest. At one point, Matt spotted a jaguar roaming through the jungle. Matt approached it with Anika, while trying to get a good camera shot with them both. All witness testimonies had different events to describe, but they all had the same common theme. The jaguar lunged at Matt and Anika, but Cassandra interceded before it reached them. The jaguar mauled and killed Cassandra Irving, leaving both Matt and Anika devastated for years to come.

The show fell apart. Animal Planet claimed that Matt decided to take a sabbatical, but the truth was the magic of the show was gone. It felt empty, the chemistry and fun gone from it forever. By this point, the Irvings had known the Burnses for years, and Anika, being a little older now, chose to stay with them more often than with her father. Their own relationship deteriorated over time, Anika choosing her own path and purposely ignoring her father's limelight. Eventually, Matt convinced Animal Planet to allow him to revive his old show, with him as a leading man. Anika found it insulting that he continued his show as if nothing had ever happened, and even more insulting that fans accepted it immediately.

Anika's resentment and contempt did not fade over the years, and she carries it even now.

"Having second thoughts?" Burns asks her.

"And thirds, and fourths," she replies.

"Technically you don't have to talk to him at all during our time there."

"I hope not, but that's impossible," she says, leaning back in her seat.

"You know, I should mention I don't plan on being a referee while we're there."

"I'm an adult, Bill, and hopefully so is he," she says. "Wake me up when we get there." Anika leans her head back and closes her eyes. Burns knows she doesn't usually sleep much, which explains the bags under her eyes. Burns turns his head and sees Lucy buckling herself into her seat.

"How are you, Lucy?" Burns asks.

She adjusts her glasses resting on the brim of her nose. "Fine, a little tired, didn't really sleep last night."

"I don't think any of us did. We're all a bit nervous," Burns says, "You think it'll take long to identify the creature?"

"Hard to say, depends on the level of detail of the footage and photos we obtain. I've done identification before, but it was all fossilized so it's a bit easier to examine."

"Rough estimate?"

"Maybe a week, perhaps a little more."

"Hmm, I know you gave the general information during the briefing, but do you have any theories of your own?"

"Not at the moment, the evidence doesn't suggest anything... definitive. Well, except for the bite marks, at least we know it's a carnivore."

"Yeah," Burns mumbles, "At least."

"How long is this flight again?"

"*Long.* Best to find something to do, even if it's sleep," Burns says, nodding his head toward Anika, who is fast asleep with her head slouched to the side. Lucy pulls her laptop out of her backpack that she placed by her feet, and then some headphones.

"What'll it be? Show? Movie?" Burns asks her.

"Unfinished dig site reports for the museum, maybe a movie later if I'm bored," she says, putting the laptop on her lap.

"Yeah, just stay away from any dinosaur related movie," Burns says, leaning back in his own seat, "Otherwise you won't sleep at all."

Lucy giggles to herself as Burns closes his eyes. She thinks to herself that nothing could possibly scare her about seeing a dinosaur.

Lucy finishes up her reports after an hour. The entire time, she could hear Burns and Anika snoring, and the indistinct conversations between Matt and the marines. Burns snores like an 80-year-old man, while Anika snores like a puppy. Lucy grabs her headphones, plugs them in, and then opens her browser. She has heard of all the shows that some of the team members star in, but she has never watched any of them. Why would she? She's always more interested in dinosaurs and rarely ever cares about current ecosystems.

But she likes Burns, and Matt is charming, although she's a little unsure about Anika, but she seems polite for the most part. She types in Burns's name in the search bar, and clicks enter. *William Burns: Wildlife Conservationist & Biologist.* There are pictures, clips, and a brief biography on Wikipedia as the first results. She clicks on a video clip. The browser buffers and then plays a video with low quality, It's clearly an old video as even Burns looks significantly younger. Burns stares into a handheld camera, a herd of buffalo in the background grazing in a field on a northwestern peninsula. Burns seems to be keeping his distance, about a hundred feet away.

"These buffalo, known as the Plains bison, have roamed the American west for decades," Burns says in a soft voice. "They are a subspecies of the common American bison, and were at one point endangered, with a population of less than six hundred in the entire world. A lot of what went into their endangerment, came from private ranches here in Montana in the late 1800s."

Lucy clicks the back arrow on her browser, and then scrolls some more, looking for a more recent clip. She sees one that looks more like the Burns she knows now, and she clicks on that one.

"Look at that beauty," Burns says, pointing at a rhinoceros, again about a hundred feet away. "The black rhino has been on the endangered species list since the late '90s. Their population dropped about ninety percent between the 1960s and '90s. Poaching is a major contributor to their drop in population."

Lucy clicks on a suggested video under the one she's watching, and it plays another video of Burns, sitting in a little hut in the jungle. This time, he's talking about the Amur leopards, another endangered species. That looks to be the underlying topic in his show, endangered animals, their history, and how to protect them. Burns is always talking to the viewer in a soft voice. He's cautious with a good distance so as to not frighten or instigate the animal.

Lucy gets curious and types another name in the search bar: Matthew Irving. The first thing that pops up is a headshot of him. *Matthew Arthur Irving*, the short description at the top says, 'Television Personality', not wildlife biologist, or conservationist like Burns. She scrolls down and clicks on a video, and immediately, it is wildly different from Burns's show. Matt sits close to a frightening tiger; he isn't more than a few feet away from it.

"Tigers are very prominent here in India, they're smart and agile hunters, and oftentimes their prey has no idea where the tiger was hiding," Matt says. The tiger huffs at Matt, but he just smiles and holds his hand up to the tiger. "Oh, pipe down, it's all good here, buddy." Matt looks at the camera. "He likes me, he just seems to be in a grumpy mood today. Isn't that right buddy?" Matt says to the tiger. The tiger bellows loudly in response. Matt just chuckles. "Yeah he is, it's why I'm not super close to him."

Jesus, Lucy thinks, *he's okay being that close to a tiger?* This makes Lucy even more curious. She clicks on more suggested Matthew Irving videos. She watches one where he's next to a ten-foot crocodile, the crocodile slowly moving and snapping its jaws at Matt. Matt is laughing while he talks to the viewer, and he looks as if he's taunting the reptile. Lucy clicks on another video, but this one seems older, Matt looks younger, his hair shorter. He's riding an African elephant, and there's a little girl with pigtails in his arms. Another woman stands close to the elephant, looking up at them both, smiling.

"Come on, Ani, look at the camera, say 'bye from the Irvings', go on," Matt says. The little girl, about six or seven years old, smiles and waves her small hand.

"Bye from the Irvings!" she says in a sweet voice. Matt

then waves his hand at the camera, and the woman standing next to the elephant turns and waves at the camera too. Lucy knows the little girl is obviously Anika Irving, but she notices a resemblance between her and the woman. Could she be her mother? Lucy clicks the back arrow a few times to get to the search results page. She clicks on the Wikipedia page on Matthew. She continues to read the page until she sees a name, *Cassandra Irving (formerly Cassandra Jimenez)*. The name is highlighted blue as it's a hyperlink. Lucy clicks on it. She's taken to Cassandra's Wikipedia page, a single picture of her smiling in the right corner with generalized information under it. Brown hair, green eyes, big energetic smile, she definitely looks like Anika, if she ever smiled. She skims the general information: Wildlife Biologist, born October 27, 1976, place of birth, Monterey, Mexico, *deceased January 3, 2003*.

Deceased? How? Lucy lets her morbid curiosity take over. She scrolls farther down the Wikipedia page, past the career segment, and stops at the one labeled "Death".

Cassandra Irving, age 27, died on January 3rd, 2003, after a fatal jaguar attack while filming an episode of Out with the Irvings. *The jaguar's fierce attack caused severe injuries to her neck. EMS was called but Cassandra succumbed to her wounds before they could reach her. Her husband and co-star, Matt Irving, refused to track down and kill the animal, calling the incident a 'freak accident'. A private funeral service was held on January 18, 2003, where the only attendees were Cassandra's sister, Natalia Jimenez, and Bill and Addie Burns from* Saving Our Planet.

All of this was both intriguing and extremely heartbreaking to Lucy. So Anika's not 'strange' like Kit had mentioned to her a day before. Anika is broken, probably traumatized by the loss of her mother. Just like Burns, who lost his wife to cancer. Maybe that's why they're so close?

Burns gives a loud snort and wakes up. He looks around,

dazed. Lucy quickly closes all the tabs on her browser. Maybe she should leave this alone. So she pulls up the streaming service and clicks play on a movie.

INTO THE FRAY

"Ani."

Her eyes haven't yet adjusted to the dark. At the moment, she can only feel the warm breeze of the African air. Anika blinks and focuses her sight until she can see the African savannah, the moonlight illuminating the plains of long grass in the distance.

"Ani."

She turns her head and sees her mom, Cassandra, sitting next to her, holding a pair of night vision binoculars. They're both sitting in a Land Rover, Cassandra watching the plains in the distance, a short smile on her face.

"Ani, can you see them?"

Anika looks at the plains again. She sees a herd of gazelles, grazing in the long grass. Their dark brown bodies peeking from over the tall yellow grass.

"The gazelles?" Anika asks.

"No, Ani, keep looking."

Anika looks again. She squints her eyes, trying to concentrate them, trying to see what her mom is seeing. She sees a shadow, a line in the long grass moving toward the herd of gazelles.

"Something in the grass?"

"Not just something, Ani, look again."

Anika looks again, feeling frustrated, but this time it's a

little clearer. There are multiple shadows moving toward the herd. They're hidden under the grass, slowly trickling their way to the gazelles. Hunting behavior. Something is hunting them. The gazelles bob their heads, looking around. The gazelles stand perfectly still, listening, scanning the horizon for predators. Unbeknownst to them, the shadows are already too close to evade.

"What's hunting them?" Anika asks.

Cassandra reaches over and puts the night vision binoculars over her eyes. Her mother's sweet smell puts Anika's frustration at ease. Anika peers through the night vision binoculars, and it all becomes clearer than before. She sees glowing eyes in the grass, lurking, determined and strategic toward the gazelles. Anika recognizes the hunting patterns, and the movements, they're lions.

"Lions?"

"Yes, Ani."

In an instant, the lions leap forward, catching one of the gazelles before it has a chance to react. The rest converge on the gazelle, who slowly tries to free itself from the powerful jaws. The lions proceed to tear into the gazelle, under the long grass, the whining of the gazelle eventually stopping. There was no sound in their stalking, no communication between the pride of lions. Anika can't fathom how on earth they were so coordinated.

"How do they know?" Anika asks, looking up at her mother.

"Know what?"

"To move like that, how do they plan it?" Anika says, looking back at the savannah.

"They don't, they communicate with their eyes, Ani. Any noise can give them away, so they trust each other's eyes. It's all there, all that needs to be said."

"They can do that?"

"Yes, Ani, it's part of their instinct, just like the gazelles looking around. They knew something was wrong, but couldn't see anything. They didn't trust their instinct, Ani, but the lions did, that's why they won."

Cassandra puts the binoculars in the seat next to her, then gently rubs Anika's head with her fingers. Anika gives a small, comforted smile; she's missed her mother's touch for so long. Cassandra's voice is soft and soothing to Anika's ears; she's singing as she runs her fingers through Anika's hair.

"Ani."

Anika looks up at her mother again.

"Ani."

"I'm here, Mom."

"Ani."

"I'm right here."

"Ani."

Anika jolts awake in her seat. She looks around, she's still on the jet. Lucy is looking out of the small window at the landscape below. She sees her father, Matt, for once sitting quietly in his seat. Kit, JJ, and the film crew sit silently too, looking restless and tired from sitting in this jet for so long. And then she sees Burns, sitting across from her, holding a book, a face of concern directed at Anika.

"Bad dream?" Burns asks.

Anika settles in her seat and exhales her tension. "A good one, actually, should've let me sleep longer," Anika says.

"Longer? We're already landing."

"They didn't stop to refuel?"

Burns smiles. "Twice, once in San Francisco and then Sydney."

"Shit."

"I figure you don't get much sleep in Iceland?"

"No."

Anika adjusts her seat forward, and looks out of the window.

"What was your dream?" Burns asks her.

"How far from Hobart did you say?" Anika asks, ignoring his question.

"Almost a couple hours."

Burns is used to Anika's evasive maneuvers. He has watched Anika grow up, but ever since losing her mother, she became closed off. Everyone assumes because she spends a lot of time with Burns, that he must know everything. They couldn't be more wrong. Anika doesn't really talk about herself and her wellbeing. Yes, she shows concern for Burns and cares about him, but she rarely ever tells anyone what she's feeling.

"Think we're ready?" Anika asks.

"We have to, too late to turn back now."

Anika watches as the airport runway in Hobart slowly becomes closer to the jet. They're finally landing.

The jet sits in a hangar at Hobart International Airport, with everyone on the jet having the same idea once they exit the luxurious tube. They all give a big stretch, and look glad to finally be standing upright after twenty-six hours. The jet landed and then rolled to a private hangar separate from the rest of the terminals. Anika sees a large cargo plane, sitting in the same hangar, three Ford F-350s sitting in front of the cargo plane, all a strange shade of green.

"There's our ride, courtesy of Valtech Industries," Burns says. He walks toward Anika while carrying his duffel bag.

"I know, he has the logo on the doors. Why are the logos purple?" Anika says.

"You got me."

"I thought he wanted discretion."

"He's a capitalist, Ani, he wants everyone to know who he is."

Anika shakes her head. She will never relate, or understand the need for proving who you are. Both Burns and Anika make their way to the trucks, some film crew already putting their bags in the pickup beds, or at least attempting to, since every pickup bed is packed full of supplies for the trip. Matt is helping the crew, while Kit and JJ put their own backpacks and weapon crates into another. Kit and JJ packed light, their backpacks slipped right into the truck's pickup bed. Lucy hands her own backpack to Kit, who then puts it into the truck somehow.

"Come on, Ani. You ride with me," Burns says.

Burns and Anika find their way to the truck. Burns hands his duffel bag to Kit, who tries to find a place for it. Anika is only carrying her backpack. She doesn't have many belongings and usually doesn't carry much luggage. Kit offers to put it in somewhere but Anika just tells him she'll carry it in the passenger cabin.

"Alright, Kit is driving, Anika and Lucy with us. Already talked to Matt and JJ, Matt will drive one and JJ the other, the crew can find a way to fit into the trucks," Burns says.

Anika feels a bit relieved. It's one thing to be in the same plane as Matt, but another to be in the same car. Burns gets into the passenger seat while Kit waits for the other two trucks to be ready to move. Anika and Lucy enter the back two seats. There's an empty seat between them, which would've probably been filled by Valente. Anika sees Kit give a thumbs up to the other trucks, then step into the driver seat. He switches the ignition and the vehicle rumbles to life.

"Let's go make history," Kit says, as he drives out of the private hangar. The convoy of upgraded pick-ups move past the airport hangars, following the marked routes in the runways for the exit. The trucks run smoothly, gray metal bars bolted and covering all the windows except the windshield. Anika notices they're significantly wider than the ones she saw before. Maybe she made Ward nervous enough that he changed them. The pick-up beds have a canopy that's larger than the ones you would normally see on a truck. They're slightly taller on the back end to make more space for cargo.

And all the space is used to its entirety, as the supplies, equipment and luggage make no sound as the truck moves around. The cargo is squeezed in place, unable to physically move. Valente certainly gave them enough resources for a month.

The Ford steers through the streets of Hobart, Kit driving and constantly glancing at the GPS for directions. Burns sits in the passenger seat, with Anika and Lucy in the back seats, all of them quiet for a few minutes now. Since they were all stuck inside a plane for a day, being stuck inside a car now is not at all relaxing. Anika stares out the window of the Ford; she can see the city of Hobart through the metal bars. Buildings, homes, and marinas with yachts, all of this will be gone in a bit, the last remnants of civilization, before they make their way into the bushes. Anika has never been to Tasmania. The last time she was ever near here was Papua New Guinea. Her family was filming an episode on Cassowaries.

Interestingly enough, Cassowaries are the only animal Matt keeps a good distance from. Their powerful talons, accompanied by erratic and unpredictable behavior keep Matt Irving a good distance away. The thought always brings some comfort to Anika. Those creatures intimidate her father into common sense.

Australia and Tasmania are home to some of the strangest and most dangerous creatures in the world. It makes sense to Anika that a species of dinosaurs somehow miraculously survived in Tasmania. The Thylacine, or Tasmanian tiger, is only speculated to be extinct, as the Tasmanian wilderness is so vast and dense that it is risky to go too far into it. It's not surprising that no one has seen the hidden species of dinosaur until now. The thought suddenly occurs again to Anika. Have there really been no sightings until now?

"Bill, I have a question," Anika asks.

"Shoot," Burns responds.

"How far did you and Valente look into all of this?"

"What do you mean?"

"Has anyone ever seen these animals? Encountered or even attacked?"

Kit finds the thought interesting; he interjects, "I've been wondering that myself, I mean, we're looking for a dinosaur, supposedly hidden deep in the woods, that no one has seen for centuries, until now apparently. No one has ever seen one?"

"Tasmania is a very... *compressed* kind of wilderness. Incredibly easy to get lost in. It's nowhere near like the desert or jungles you've probably been in. But to answer your questions, yes, there was one guy. Someone had a lead on a local seeing a tiger when we were filming. I interviewed him," Burns says.

"What did he say?"

Burns is sitting in a chair, writing down notes into a small notepad. He then pulls out a map from his backpack next to him. He unfolds the map and hands it to an older man, who is sitting next to him. They both sit in front of a small trailer home, junk and appliances scattered around the home. The obvious home of a hoarder, who cares more about smoking cigarettes and tossing them into the overflowing bucket of cigarette butts than cleaning his home. The man is in his late 60s, with long gray hair and a beard, wearing a tank top and shorts. He's smoking a cigarette now, just as Burns hands him the unfolded map.

"Alright, Wiley, where exactly did you see this?" Burns asks him.

Wiley grabs the map, looks it over, and scoffs. "Christ, mate, ya couldn't get an older map, could ya?" Wiley says in his thick tazzie accent.

Burns doesn't acknowledge Wiley's remark. He ignores it as Burns has been dealing with Wiley's attitude for a while now. Wiley takes another glance at the map. He leans in closer to it and points to a certain spot. "Out here, about five miles east of Tarraleah. Came real close to the city, but like I said before, I didn't get a good look, I just said the tail looked weird compared to a dog."

Burns writes it down in his notepad, "Weird how?"

"I don't know, just weird. Not like a dog, ya know?"

Burns puts the notepad in his pocket. Wiley hands the map back to him, and Burns starts to fold it up. "Thanks Wiley. You've been a great help." Burns stands up. He's done with this man. He looks to be slightly irritated. Wiley may not have been very cooperative.

"Ya know anything about lizards?"

Burns stops. He turns to face the old man again. "Why do you ask?"

"I got a story for ya, if you're willing to listen."

Burns doesn't really feel like listening to Wiley anymore. Every time he talks, he goes on a long rant and never actually says anything important. But for whatever reason, Burns agrees with a cold sigh. "Sure, Wiley."

Wiley sucks in from his cigarette, and then blows a cloud of smoke from his nostrils. "About a week ago, a Tuesday I'd say, Reggie brought me something strange," Wiley says.

"Reggie?"

"My dog, mate. Reggie," Wiley says, pointing to a Pitbull laying on the grass a few feet away. The dog bobs its head at the sound of its name. Burns nods his head for Wiley to continue. "Tuesdays are my days off, I usually start drinking at noon or so. I sit outside and just relax or listen to some tunes. I let Reggie run around the bush, he's a big dog and knows how to take care of himself so I don't really worry. Anyways, that day, I see Reggie come out of the woods, blood on his jaws. I said, 'Ah shit Reggie's gone and fought some dingo again'. I got worried and was just about to grab some alcohol and bandages when I got a better look. As he got closer I noticed he was actually fine. Blood wasn't his, mate, but he had something in his mouth. He strolled over with that cocky little walk he does when he's proud of himself, and dropped something in my hand. I held it, it was warm and wet with blood. It was about the length of my palm. A tiny skull with some flesh on it, fresh, it looked like a bird's head."

Wiley sucks in some more on his cigarette, reminiscing. "Seems Reggie went at it with some bird. Which is weird because Reggie ain't smart enough or fast enough to catch a bird, ya know? Guess he got it pretty good cause it was mostly a skull. But I held it up to my face and thought it was strange because its beak didn't look like any bird I've seen before."

Wiley lets out a short, old-man laugh before he continues, "Imagine my surprise when I opened up its beaks to see two rows of tiny white teeth. I've never seen anything like it. I passed my thumb over the teeth, and little red lines cut into my thumb. Shiny, fuckin' razor-sharp teeth. *Blimey*, I looked at it again and realized it wasn't a beak, but a snout, like a lizard. But if it was a lizard, why did it have feathers on its head?"

Wiley stares at Burns for a few seconds, like he's expecting a round of applause over his stellar story. Burns's face doesn't change; he still looks as annoyed as before.

"Well, mate? Whatcha think?" Wiley nudges.

"Do you still have it?"

"Have what?"

"The bird head."

"Ah no, mate, it smelled like shit so I threw it away. It fuckin' reeked, mate."

Burns finds it amusing, the thought of Wiley finding something 'stinky' in this god-awful mess he calls home. This whole area reeks of piss and cigarettes.

"Ya find this funny, don't ya?" Wiley says sternly.

Burns hasn't noticed he was smirking, so he quickly brushes it off. "It just sounds crazy, is all. Probably just some bird."

"I'm telling ya, not a fuckin' bird."

"Then what?"

"Do I look like a fuckin' scientist?"

"Alright," Burns says, calming him down, "I wouldn't know what to tell you without looking at it, you should've kept it."

"Yeah, sure mate. Well if Reggie ever brings me another head, I'll fuckin' mail it to ya, how's that?"

This conversation is over. Burns just turns around and he walks away, not bothering to acknowledge Wiley's last remark.

"Ya only hear what you wanna hear, eh? *Fuckin' useless pricks.*"

"Is that the only sighting you've heard of?" Anika asks after hearing Burns's story.

"So far, yes. Me and Valente were out here, talking to a lot of townsfolk, hunters, and even park rangers. Nothing turned up. These creatures are well hidden, either they're very deep into the bush, or avoid people quite well," Burns explains.

"Did you ever go back to talk to this 'Wiley' guy?"

"I tried. Wouldn't see me, he wasn't a 'people' person to begin with. We had to bribe him with beer the first time around. Valente felt there was no use, he didn't have much to tell us anyways. We did a search around his property, like the surrounding forest, and found nothing. Me and Valente agreed to let it go for the time being."

"We should visit him," Anika says.

"We could, it'd be a start. It's been a while since we last talked to him, maybe he's cooled off by now."

Lucy has her own question that she's been waiting to ask. "Why did he say he threw the tiny skull away?"

"Said it smelled bad," Burns responds, "Which makes sense, when I encountered it, there was a strong stench that accompanied the creature."

"You told me it smelled like a chemical," Anika says.

"Sort of, chemicals have a distinct smell but there are factors that make it obvious. For starters, you might feel tingling in your nostrils or throat when you breathe it in. This smell, from what I remember, had no such effect."

"You couldn't guess what the scent was like? Any similarities?" Anika asks.

"I tried to find similarities, we've been around all kinds of animals for a long time, and eventually you learn to categorize them in your head. I know you do this too. Big felines, like lions, tigers, cheetahs, all have a unique musky scent, since they tend to spend a lot of time licking their fur. They also tend to mark their territories with urine, so there's that too. Big mammals like deer or elk, also have the urine and musk smell, but with a kind of leaf or heavy foliage scent. Reptiles like crocodiles or alligators, even Komodo dragons, have a swampy, almost fishlike smell. Like I said, you learn to categorize as most are generally similar. All carnivores after a fresh kill tend to have the same scent of blood and flesh for a bit. Even if they all have different scents, depending on their species and habitats, they all have a natural, ecological scent. But not this creature, there was not a trace of anything natural in its scent. The smell was putrid, it felt unnatural, pharmacological is the only way I can describe it."

Anika can see the logic in Burns's explanation, so does Lucy, but Kit wears a confused frown. He's not sure what any of this means, or why it's relevant to the expedition. Anika can see Kit's bewilderment through the rearview mirror. "You know, just like human beings having different natural scents to themselves individually, animals have individual scents too. I would imagine these creatures, even if they are prehistoric, are no different. That's why it stood out to Bill. Humans are just not used to dinosaur scent; humans and dinosaurs have never co-existed. The planet has changed a lot in millions of years. Things were very different back then," Anika says to Kit, hoping it'll clear it up.

"Oh, okay," Kit says, "God, this all seems so weird to me, had you told me in basic training that in six years, I'd be part of a team that rediscovers dinosaurs, I'd think you were crazy."

"Maybe we are crazy, and just dumb enough to do this anyways," Anika says.

"You don't think this is a good idea?" Kit asks. It's the first time he's heard of someone being skeptical about the expedition.

"I think it's dangerous' we're in the process of trying to find a species that somehow survived an *extinction event*," Anika says. "Anything that can survive that has to have some thick skin."

The thought lights up Kit's face, as if he's been waiting to ask his own questions. "Wait a minute, I've been meaning to ask, how'd you think they survived this long?"

"I don't know. I've read a lot of books these past few days. There's so many theories about that era, the most common I saw was the asteroid," Anika says. She looks at Lucy and nudges her. "Lucy, think you can elaborate?"

Lucy has been waiting for her moment in this conversation. "I've been wondering that myself too, how they survived. And yes, the most common theory is the asteroid impact, a meteor about five or six miles in diameter struck earth and delivered roughly seventy-two teratonnes of energy. It's theorized that it caused massive earthquakes that lasted for months, and these aren't small earthquakes like we're used to. Huge, devastating earthquakes that reshaped the earth and killed off anything that moved. Now, there are other theories too, like constant volcanic activity around the globe, or something as simple as climate change. But I honestly think they shouldn't be individual theories, because it makes more sense that they are all a part of the asteroid impact, like residual effects. It wouldn't be far-fetched to theorize that an amalgamation of all these factors contributed to their extinction. The earth itself became a destructive force as it evolved into a completely different version."

"Survival of the fittest," Burns adds.

"Yeah, that had to be a big factor. Their ability to adapt to the new environment and keep reproduction at a sustainable pace. And not to mention surviving earth in the process of terraforming itself had to have passed down some incredible survival traits," Lucy says.

"Yeah, incredible," Anika says.

"And through all that, they survived," Kit says, "Wild, just wild. They just survived in a small pocket of earth like that one movie. God, I can't remember the name, I used to watch it as a kid."

"Jurassic Park?" Burns says.

"No, no, it was older, way older," Kit says, "It had real clunky stop motion."

"The Lost World," Lucy says, "I used to watch it too. Yeah, it's kind of like that if you really think about it."

"Yeah, never in a hundred years did I think I would be doing this. 'Kenneth Kitsap, dinosaur hunter'," he says with a chuckle. "Somehow this is more wild than Afghanistan."

"Is that where you toured?" Anika asks, eager to change the subject.

"Yep, three tours, and this last one was the craziest. It was when we pulled out of Afghanistan."

"Shit, that wasn't that long ago," Anika says.

"No it was not, wild shit, real wild," Kit says. He notices everyone's demeanor has changed at the mention of his military service. "Sorry, I didn't mean to bring it up. All this talk about 'surviving' reminded me of it. The shit people will do to try to survive. I can't even think of the shit these dinosaurs had to do to stay alive."

"In humans, survival is unnatural, chaotic, and deemed unethical. In animals, it's normal," Burns says.

"You know, I always hated the term 'acted like an animal'. Animals don't do bad shit 'cause they want to, they do it 'cause it's part of their survival. It's why I work for Valtech. If I'm gonna do something with my skillset, it's to help our environment, our home."

Burns nods his head and agrees, it's why Burns liked

Kit in the first place. Both Burns and Valente handpicked the team for the expedition. Burns knew Ward kept a lot of people employed with military service backgrounds, so it wasn't hard. Still, Burns had insisted to Valente that they interview the potential candidates, to see what their strengths, weaknesses, and intentions are. They interviewed everybody who had applied for the expedition, but no one had any idea what the expedition was for. Which was another concern Valente brought up. If they went through the process and picked the best candidates, there was the possibility that they back out once they learned of the details.

But Burns knew how to read people. It's the one good thing he has kept from his time as a first responder. He could tell who was going to be calm and collected, and who was going to panic in a tense situation. Burns was aware of Kit's service record, as it stood out from the others; Kit had one purple heart, and one medal of honor. Kit might've only done three tours, but it looked like trouble always seemed to find him. And even if he was always in the wrong place at the wrong time, Burns found it admirable that Kit's focus was to save lives.

During the interview, Burns let Kit talk about his life and service record. Burns knew that the best way to see someone was to let them describe themselves. Kit had a normal life, grew up well, went to school, and once he graduated, he followed in his father's footsteps by enlisting in the marines. He did three tours in Afghanistan. During his first tour, his unit was caught in an ambush. The way Kit described it, the leading Humvee in his convoy driving over a mine, killing everyone inside instantly. They immediately started taking sniper fire from a nearby city, pinning the convoy in place. Kit was the one to take charge, despite his rank. He found a way to move toward the destroyed Humvee and search for survivors. There was none, but Kit still pulled out all of his fallen brothers, and carried them to another Humvee. After the matter was resolved, Kit's bravery didn't go unnoticed, and that was when he received the medal of honor.

On his second tour, Kit was caught in a hectic gunfight between his unit and insurgents attempting to retake a city. The city was lost, and his unit was forced to pull back, during which Kit was wounded. Kit had a gunshot in his abdomen, and even though it hurt more than anything, Kit still managed to carry another wounded marine to safety. That earned him his purple heart, and a trip back home to his family. But Kit declined his trip home. He wanted to stay and could not think of a good reason to leave his unit behind. In his third tour, when he witnessed the fall of Afghanistan, Kit was at an airfield waiting for extraction.

He watched as hundreds of people climbed the fences and attempted to find a way out of the country. He watched as they trampled over each other, and tossed their infants over the walls, all for survival. Amidst the chaos was where Kit decided he would no longer continue his military career. Burns noticed that there was a hidden melancholy in Kit's eyes as he explained his last tour. While Kit described his service record, Burns also noticed Kit was incredibly thorough, hardworking, and concentrated on safety above all else. Which is how Burns knew he was the perfect candidate for the team.

The truck comes to an intersection, the road directly in front of them no longer surrounded by human structures, the road leading into the rest Tasmania has to offer.

"Once more into the fray, huh?" Burns says to Kit.

"Fuckin' A," Kit says.

The truck moves forward on the road leading into mother nature itself.

ALAMO

The truck convoy moves farther and farther into the Tasmanian wilderness, the roads becoming more narrow and unpaved. The dirt roads become windier, the surrounding forest dense, making it hard to see what's around the next bend in the road. The tall trees tower over the roads as they drive through them, the ferns and bushes brushing against the sides of the trucks as if the vegetation is slowly trying to overtake the man-made road. Kit, being in the lead truck, slows down a bit, as the roads sometimes overlook ravines and hillsides. Kit can only imagine what it's like driving at night on these roads, no amount of high beams would see through this forest. Kit has never seen this kind of terrain before, and he can finally see what Burns was talking about when he said it was easy to get lost here. The terrain is uneven, with ferns and thickets covering the floor and protruding tree roots. Aside from Hobart, the island Tasmania seems to be just a massive, unconquered forest.

From the Iraqi sun at high noon, to the squelching fever of the Afghan roads that Kit is used to, all he can think about is at least the humidity is manageable. And at least there are no mines or IEDs to worry about, no incoming sniper fire, no locals flailing AKs from behind cover. Just chaperone the film crew, keep them from wandering off, and keep them from getting mauled by a big lizard. Even with how ridiculous that sounds, it's still as exciting to Kit than another deployment. He feels as if he's on an episode with his childhood hero, Steve Irwin. Kit watched him in the late 90s, every Saturday morning. For a while in his early years, he wanted to be like him, roam the world while learning and meeting wild animals. But that world of wonder left Kit's life when Steve Irwin tragically died. Kit left that avenue alone, instead, he enlisted years later to help with the global war on terror like many of his friends in Park City, Utah.

But life has a funny way of bringing you back to your childhood dreams, doesn't it? Kit smiles at that thought, not even minding the bumpy dirt roads anymore. They've been driving on these dirt roads for roughly an hour, the Ford's GPS still marking forty minutes left on their drive. Everyone on board is mostly silent, with the occasional small talk between them. Kit is the one to usually break the silence with a random question or conversation starter. Anika can tell that Kit is not used to silence, or at least to being alone. She imagines that Kit was probably always communicating with his unit and couldn't sit still on his own. Anika doesn't mind it, Kit's a decent guy. He's funny and not intimidated by dark subject matter. Kit quickly grows on Anika; at least there's one other person she can potentially trust.

Lucy doesn't talk much, and it's not like they don't try to involve her in the conversations. She just seems reserved and not at all interested in topics she knows nothing about. Anika respects her reserved demeanor, but perhaps she should stay at the HQ instead of joining anyone in the field. Lucy's inattention to the conversations of Anika's and Burns's work can make her a liability in the field. Paleontologists dig up fossils and study dinosaurs in the comfort of their museums, no need to change that anytime soon.

The dirt road eventually opens into a clearing of a forest, a small gas station and convenience store sitting on the side of the road. Burns immediately recognizes the gas station.

"Finally," Burns says, "Pull over, we'll take a small break, let people use the bathroom. We're not far now."

Kit nods and pulls the truck into the empty spaces of the

gas station. He shifts the truck in park, and then watches in the side mirror as the other trucks follow behind him. Burns steps out of the truck, and stretches his limbs with a relaxed sigh. Anika steps out to join Burns who is about to enter the convenience store.

"Should I top it off?" Kit asks Burns, inquiring about the truck's fuel levels. Burns nods to Kit as he holds the door open for Anika.

The gas station is small, with only two rows of food in the middle and one single beverage cooler in the corner. While Anika and Burns are both inside the gas station, Anika wanders to look around the store for granola bars, and maybe a Coke. Burns goes straight for the cashier, a woman in her 40s, reading a magazine.

"Mr. Burns, it's been a while," the woman says.

"Tanya, how are you?" Burns asks.

"Fine, fine, back again for the tazzie tiger?" she asks.

"Something like that... have you seen Wiley?"

The woman shakes her head. "Not for a good minute, saw him a month back maybe, bought about four gallons of gasoline. Haven't seen him since."

"Gas? I thought he didn't own a car."

"He doesn't, rode in here on that fuckin' bike, bought gas, and rolled on outta here."

"He didn't say what the gas was for?" Burns asks with a confused frown.

"Nah, didn't ask either, you know how he is, he'd have told me to fuck off."

Burns nods, the information puzzling to him, Wiley never leaves his part of the forest, and Burns can't think of a good reason for him needing gas. Anika walks up behind Burns, holding a can of soda and a bag of jerky.

"Do you take dollars?" Anika asks Tanya. Tanya nods and holds out her hand. She doesn't even tell Anika what the total is. Anika pulls a twenty from her pocket and hands it to Tanya. She takes the twenty and puts it in her register. She doesn't give any change and just goes back to her conversation with Burns.

"You know he was just fuckin' with you, right?" Tanya asks Burns.

"What about?" Burns says.

"Seeing a tiger, all bullshit, Wiley never gets that close to the city. Fucker just wanted free beer."

Burns gives an exasperated sigh. He's contemplating the idea that Wiley may have bullshitted the story about the bird head too. Burns turns around and nods at Anika to get going. They both exit the store. Matt and some of the film crew are stretching while standing next to their truck. JJ is still inside, waiting. Lucy hasn't bothered to look up from her phone the entire time. Kit is leaning up against the truck, his eyes lost in the trees above. He looks away as Burns and Anika start to enter the truck.

"Ready?" Kit asks.

"We have one more stop I want to make," Burns says.

"I doubt he'll return the scammed beer," Anika says to Burns while opening her passenger door.

"What're you talking about?" Kit asks.

"We'll tell you on the way there," Anika says to Kit, who just shrugs and steps into the driver seat.

The Ford rumbles to life and the convoy is on the move again. Burns gives Kit verbal instructions to Wiley's place as they're unable to find it on the GPS. Anika explains the story to Kit about Wiley. Kit chuckles, finding the beer scam amusing. Wiley's place isn't far from the gas station, but it turns out to be difficult to bring the trucks close to the home. Kit pushes the truck as far as he can, the tires spinning in the loose soil and foliage. Burns explains that it's better to wait there, and he and Anika will go see what's up with Wiley. Burns and Anika are on their way when they hear hurried steps behind them. They turn to see Matt catching up with them both.

"What was this fella's name again?" Matt asks.

"Wiley," Burns responds.

"You think he has more to say?"

"I think he has some explaining to do."

"About what?"

"His bullshit story," Burns says with a sincere tone.

Burns turns and continues to walk, Anika following with Matt closely behind. They walk through what was once a gravel driveway, grass and ferns sprouting all over the place. The crunching of the gravel beneath their feet covers most of the silence between the three as they walk. Anika has no idea what Burns is expecting to find, or if he's genuinely on his way to sucker punch the guy. The soft wind sways the tall trees, the clicking of the leaves bumping into one another. Eventually, the sight of a small trailer home can be seen through the vegetation. They pick up the pace. They walk past a single bicycle, old and rusted, and a broken basket on the front.

Just before they reach the clearing where the trailer home sits, they step over a rough piece of grass. Burns stops in his tracks. No, not rough. He kneels down to take a closer look at the grassy ground. The grass and dirt look burnt, charred, the soil looks greasy. Burns follows the trail of burnt grass with his gaze; the charred grass is seemingly in an irregular line. The line looks like it's meant to encircle the trailer home in the clearing. Anika has already gotten ahead of Burns and followed around the trailer home, pacing the burnt line.

"Now we know what he used the gas for," Anika says.

"Why would he burn it like this?" Burns asks as he stands up. Anika just shakes her head—she had no idea.

Matt is already at the trailer home, looking through the windows, searching for signs of life. The small home is barren, cluttered kitchen counters and boxes of belongings scattered throughout the home. The lights are off, the sun shining through the windows as Matt peers in, trying to find Wiley. He turns around to face Burns and Anika and shakes his head. Wiley's not home.

"Wiley!" Burns yells out, hoping for a response. The soft wind moving the forest around them gives no valuable response. Matt looks around the property, specifically the burnt line circling the clearing.

"Nah, he's long gone, Bill," Matt says, "I'm thinkin' this was the alamo, the last stand."

"Last stand?" Burns asks.

"Yep, maybe your dinos got a bit frisky with your only witness," Matt says, scanning the forest one more time.

"I don't know about that," Anika says, "I've walked the perimeter, no other tracks, traces, or remains anywhere."

"Maybe he just left?" Matt suggests.

"No, the guy is unemployed, he's got nowhere to go," Burns says.

Matt sighs. "Damn, really wanted to interview this guy on tape. Well, at any rate, I reckon we come back another day, we're wasting daylight."

Matt starts to walk back down the gravel road toward the convoy, away from the empty trailer home. Burns just shakes his head in disbelief. He hoped to get some more answers from Wiley, and maybe a few heated words too. He just turns around and starts to head back himself. Anika looks at the burnt grass one more time. Matt is right—whatever happened here, gas was poured around this property, and then lit. If there's one thing most animals have in common, it's their wariness of fire. The circle of gasoline was made for the purpose of home defense, and the home owner's disappearance does not make things easier to accept.

As Anika walks back down the gravel road toward the vehicles, she can't help but feel every fiber of her being begging her to leave. Her stomach, chest, and head all carry a weight of restlessness, a weight of preemptive paranoia. She lets her mind convince her, or at least tries to, that there are no tracks or any evidence of an attack. There is the possibility that the Wiley made it, or held off his attackers. Or the possibility that he was just a raving drunk playing with gasoline. But every theory is immediately shot down by her instincts, telling her not to ignore them. And just before she reaches the vehicles parked at the end of the gravel road, the wind gives one final flourish. It shoves a subtle putrid scent into Anika's nose, a harsh and aggressive scent that reminds her of ammonia, or maybe bleach. Anika stops in her tracks and turns to look around the woods, the wind just silently blowing while nothing can be seen in this dense forest.

Anika sighs and steps into the truck.

The convoy finally makes its way onto a paved driveway veering off the main dirt road. The driveway has a clean, neat, and sleek-looking pavement. It looks brand-new. The Fords roll onto the paved driveway, the bumping of the passengers inside stops, and the ride is finally smooth again. Kit can't help but notice that it looks odd that the main road is just dirt and this particular driveway is paved.

"The cement looks new," Kit finally mentions.

"That's because Valente had it built for us," Burns says.

"Built? No shit?"

"No shit, just wait till you see the house."

Just as Burns says that, the driveway curves, and the forest opens up, revealing a massive property. The trees and foliage have been cleared out to make room for the house sitting in the middle of it. The house is about twenty feet in height, about forty feet in length, and the width is almost equal to the length. The walls of the house are dark brown with a smooth look, logs on top of logs, made to look like a cabin or a lodge. The windows have a protective caging on the outside, bars about four inches thick. The roof is gable like any normal house, with a single satellite on top pointing at the sky above the forest. A double door sits in the middle of the bottom floor, clearly the entrance. Kit stops the truck in front of a stack of unused logs sitting in the front yard. The other trucks proceed to park behind Kit in a line.

"Can't help but think this house looks out of place out here," Kit says.

"Forrest is used to a certain kind of luxury. Ever been to his home?" Burns asks.

Kit shakes his head.

"It's up in Camano Island, it looks just like this. It's got the whole *outdoorsy* lodge-look to it."

Kit just shakes his head. It must be nice to have that kind of money. Kit puts the vehicle in park and switches off the ignition. He steps out of the truck and he looks around. The lodge has a beautiful dark wood porch. Sitting over the double door entrance is a set of heavy floodlights, pointing out into the forest.

Kit begins to help get some luggage out of the pick-up bed, Anika and Lucy helping as well. Anika glimpses over to the other vehicles. She finally gets a good look at the film crew. They're all unloading their camera equipment, large cases of film and computers. She recognizes everyone involved; they used to be part of the old show back then. There's Marcus Frink, a professional editor, Matt always likes to edit on the go so he can get his episodes out fast. There's Zeke Barnhart, a very opinionated unit cameraman.

There's Megan Polevoy. She's the series producer who only ever listens to Matt. Anika always had a sneaking suspicion she has a crush on her father all these years. Then there's Mike, the boom mic operator, and that's as far as Anika knows him. She never learned his name or even what he sounds like. Mike just always nods.

Matt walks past Anika with his rucksack on his back and duffel bag over his shoulder. He walks right up the front porch steps and pulls a set of keys out of his pocket. Matt unlocks the front entrance to the lodge, and opens the double doors. The film crew follows closely behind. Anika can hear Matt talking in his showman voice and then start laughing. Anika gives Burns a look, at which Burns just shakes his head and makes his way inside the lodge.

When Anika steps inside, the first thing she sees is the lavish look of the living room. Four sets of couches sitting in front of a fireplace. There's a kitchen to the right of the living room, two smooth granite counter islands with stovetops. A single refrigerator separates rows of cabinets, all made of a mahogany wood finish. There's a staircase sitting in between the living room and the kitchen, the stairs leading up to the top floor. The whole inside of the lodge smells like sweet wood.

"Come on," Burns says to Anika, "Let's find our rooms."

Anika sighs and calmly goes upstairs with Burns.

THE SAGAN STANDARD

Anika could hear Matt from downstairs, his playlist called 'Golden Oldies' blasting throughout the lodge. His loud but signature southern drawl telling stories as if he's next to the campfire, with the chattering and giggling of his audience. Matt has a story for every occasion, stories of his life, each as wild as the last. His audience often feels warm and entranced by the life Matt has led up until this point, but Anika always hates the fact that nobody ever seems to notice his anecdotes are all close calls with dangerous wildlife. A wildlife biologist shouldn't have that many close calls in their career, but then again, Matt really isn't one, as he never went to school for what he's passionate about.

Then again, if you ask Anika, she'll tell you that what Matt is actually passionate about, is his viewership. Never in his life has Matt Irving done something that hasn't benefited him in any way. Anika always refers to the simplest circumstance to describe what she means about her father. A couple years after he rebooted his show on Animal Planet, Matt traveled to the jungles of India to talk about a specific species of lemurs that were in danger of losing their habitat due to deforestation. Matt explained on camera that a company focused on tourism was the culprit, and they were deforesting in order to build more hotels. However during shooting, Matt and his camera crew stayed at a hotel only thirty minutes away.

A hotel owned by the very company he was supposedly scolding on his show. It's not like they didn't know. Animal Planet has the ample resources to find that information, as

Burns has done so himself various times in his career. Anika always explains that Matt just doesn't ever seem to practice what he preaches. To be honest, had the hotel chain asked Matt to cut out their company name, Anika is sure Matt's first question would have been "In return for what?" Which is why she is doing her very best to stay away from Matt, and if she could, make sure everyone in the field does the right thing by ignoring his advice.

Anika hears a slight knock on her door. She turns her head to see Burns standing in the doorway. "You're my roommate, no need to knock, Bill."

"Just being polite, are you coming?"

"To what? His red-carpet dinner?"

"Yes, Ani."

"No, thank you."

"Ani, I'd like you to eat something," Burns pushes.

"I don't really feel like listening to him blabber on about bullshit."

"Would you rather he fill their heads with said bullshit?" Burns says.

"So you're asking me to argue with him?"

"If I contradict him, he'll fire back and make a big thing. If it's coming from you however…"

Anika scoffs. "You really are asking me to argue with him."

"I'm asking you to help me get people in the right mindset, you know how serious this is."

Anika sighs.

"Ani, I'll be there with you."

Anika puts her hands on her hips and nods her head at Burns. Burns smiles, and signals her with his hand to follow him downstairs.

There are two tables in the common area, both big enough to seat around seven people. Matt is standing in the kitchen with Kit, both talking and watching the large pot on the stove. Lucy sits at one of the tables, reading a book while taking notes in a spiral notebook. JJ sits in a corner of the house, looking out the window, either daydreaming or just blankly staring out the window—it's starting to get dark. The rest of the film crew is scattered throughout the common area, either talking, eating, or unpacking their equipment.

Anika and Burns make their way from the bottom of the stairs to the table where Lucy is sitting. Lucy doesn't look away from her book when they both slide a chair back to sit down.

"Bill, Anika, y'all hungry? These cabinets are stocked with food, and Kit and I here took it upon ourselves to make some spaghetti," Matt says.

Anika just sits down; Burns looks over at her after sitting down himself. She nods her head. Burns holds up two fingers indicating two plates of food. Matt gives Burns a thumbs up and continues talking to Kit while he starts serving plates of food.

"Lucy, are you eating?" Burns asks.

"I don't really eat after five p.m.," she replies.

Matt hands plates to Kit, and Kit starts to hand them to those eating at the table.

"What about him?" Matt asks Kit, referring to JJ.

"He only eats once a day. He's done for the night," Kit says.

Matt just nods his head and finally turns off the stove. He takes his own plate and strolls over to the table to take a seat. "I swear, y'all haven't tried my new recipe for this. I got it last year while filming in Naples. Spaghetti has never tasted so good," Matt says after taking a seat.

Kit twirls some pasta onto his fork and takes a bite. He nods his head in agreement to the recipe.

"Good, ain't it? A little extra spice adds some spunk to it," Matt says, taking a bite.

Everyone takes a moment to dig into their dinner. Burns just eats and is glad to see Anika eating. Anika can't tell the difference between Matt's recipe and something from Walmart.

"So, what y'all think of this house?" Matt asks.

"It's nuts, Valente and Ward built it?" Kit says.

"Them and their crew. I think they finished it last month," Matt says.

"I don't think I've ever been in a place as nice as this," Kit adds..

"It'll certainly make it easier to spend time here," Burns adds.

There's another moment of just eating food, but Matt looks up at Anika and waits for her to lock eyes with him. Once she does, he says: "So, Anika, what have you been up to lately?"

Anika is about to put a forkful of spaghetti in her mouth when she feels Burns tap her boot. *Socialize, Ani*, she can almost hear him say in his head. Anika gives in to the question.

"I've been studying wolves in Iceland for the institute," Anika answers bluntly.

Matt raises an eyebrow. "Iceland? There are no wolves in Iceland," he says with a smirk.

"There never have been, until now. That's why I'm studying them."

"Huh," Matt says, his face genuinely intrigued. "How'd that happen?"

"No one has a clue," Anika explains. "A few years ago, hunters and even locals started reporting finding an exorbitant amount of reindeer carcasses. At first, people just thought it may have been a polar bear, but some remains were found too close to the cities. That, and these carcasses were almost stripped to the bone. They were eaten clean—polar bears don't usually eat an entire carcass like that. Eventually, there were reports of what looked like wolves lurking about. The institute received a call from the Icelandic government, and they sent me, along with a couple other biologists. I was so sure it was all a hoax. It took us about a week to finally spot one."

Matt leans in at the table. "Thrilling. Absolutely thrilling. What species?"

"Timber wolves," Anika says, then she finally takes the forkful of spaghetti.

"Timber wolves? That far up?" Matt says, mesmerized.

Anika nods. "The Icelandic government had no clue how or why they were there." Anika says while chewing. "At first, me and my partners thought the government or some other entity had introduced them to this habitat, but no, everyone was as surprised as we were."

"How do they fit in? They gotta be invasive in some way, right?"

"Not at all. Quite the opposite actually. I've been studying them for nearly a couple years now. When we first found them, they were one pack of about eight members. We expected them to flourish in the environment, but they haven't."

"So they haven't adapted well?"

Anika smiles. She's forgotten her disdain for her father and let herself go in her passion for her work. "In a *prey*-rich environment like that? There's no way they wouldn't adapt," Anika says, twirling her fork in her spaghetti. "Their pack hasn't increased in size by much; it's stayed mostly the same for almost two years now. Which is really interesting, because if they did increase by too much, they almost certainly would be invasive."

Matt finally erases his amazement and his face changes to confusion. "Hold on," Matt says. "That doesn't make any goddamn sense, how would they not increase their pack size?"

"That's the question, isn't it?"

Kit hasn't touched his food, fully attentive to Anika's conversation. "You almost make it sound like they're regulating their reproductive rates."

Anika points at Kit and nods at his comment. "See, at face value, that sounds like the exact reason why. However, if you steer in that direction, the second question is: why? Why keep their pack size in check?"

"To refrain from being invasive?" Kit says in a speculative tone.

"Exactly, to me that's indicative that ecosystems have almost a utilitarian system of functionality. Increasing their pack size would eventually cause a drought in prey in their new habitat, creating an imbalance."

"How? How would they know to do that?" Kit asks.

Burns jumps into the conversation. "There's a theory that some species are more intelligent and aware of their habitat function. Thus keeping their own species in check to make sure they continue to thrive. A lot of animals actually do this for different reasons, the most common one is photoperiodic control. Animals and plants might avoid reproducing during harsher times of the year."

"Exactly," Anika continues, "See, I have several videos of the alpha of this pack pushing back at other males come mating season. Which looks like the alpha is keeping an eye on pack size, but even then, at one point a female finally got pregnant.

Usually a female gives birth to a litter of about six pups, can you guess how many she had?"

Kit shakes his head.

"Two."

Kit raises his eyebrows, entranced by the conversation.

"There was a biologist in the 1950s," Burns adds, "His name was David Lack, had his own theory about reproduction, in birds specifically. It was later called the 'Lack Clutch' theory. He claimed that sometimes animals had fewer offspring than their physiological limit. The size of each species of bird had been adapted to match with the largest number of young for which they can provide enough food for. They do all this presumably for the good of the species," Burns says.

"For the good of the species," Anika says, "that'd be the only reason why these wolves are keeping their pack size low. Increasing their size would create a need to hunt more food, which would greatly diminish the food population, which in turn would eventually affect the pack directly."

Matt finally gives up. He was curious at first but he finds this preposterous. "You lost me, Anika. Animals ain't that smart," Matt says.

Anika's subtle smirk fades away. "Well, not consciously, no. I don't think they might even be aware that they're doing it, or why."

"Then why?" Kit asks.

"They're somehow connected to their ecosystem. Like I said before, they have a system that guides them. Keeps them from being a danger to their current habitat," Anika says.

"Uh-huh, well then, how do you explain other ecosystems where some species are invasive? I understand the point you're getting at, the theory that nature is in control of all wildlife, unanimously. But what about the instances where a species becomes too dense and destroys their habitat? What then?" Matt pushes.

"They're actively denying their programming, straying away from their purpose and directives. Apex predators do it all the time, it usually tends to happen when they-"

Matt cuts off Anika. "Hold on there, kid. I know exactly what you're about to get into, I read your paper when it was published. This 'apex theory' of yours, in my opinion, doesn't hold as much water as you think. I've been to countless countries with different species and each had the same reason as to why a predator became invasive. They just don't belong, and because of this, other third parties, *humans*, had to deal with them to restore balance. That is why after all these years, I firmly believe that human beings were meant to keep this planet in check. We are at the top of the food chain, we help keep our surrounding ecosystems from getting too wild. The problem is, we became too advanced as a species and started focusing on menial things that don't really matter too much in hindsight. I mean, hell, Bill is doing his part too, I know you agree with this."

Burns just stares at Matt as he explains his own opinion, and yes, Burns does agree to a certain point. Burns believes Matt's own theories could have more facts if he actually gathered evidence during his expeditions, rather than gathering what Matt calls 'cool footage'.

"I agree with the fact that one of our duties is to protect our environment, but I don't think we are at the top of the food chain. Not in the slightest. We'd like to think we are, but ultimately what makes us think we are is our adaptability," Burns says.

"I completely agree with that," Kit says. "But not so much so that we are great at adapting to a new environment, more like we are good at adapting our environment to us."

"What do you mean by that?" Matt asks, caught off-guard

by Kit's comment.

"I mean, in the military, you see these super fucked up places where people somehow live and you don't understand how it happened. But there were times when we visited a village or a forest of some kind, and years later when we returned, it's vastly different than before. I totally understand what you guys mean when you mention a balance in an environment. But with human intervention, it can be either a hit or miss in my opinion. We can either change something for the good, or for the worst," Kit explains.

"Usually for the worst..." Anika adds.

"Yeah, absolutely a lot of that in the middle east... hey what's this apex theory he mentioned about you?" Kit asks Anika.

Before Anika can answer, Matt holds up his hand, waving away her potential explanation. "Just her own theory about why sometimes apex predators pop up in random ecosystems. Which, by the way, your theory would be more prominent if you had evidence of it happening on more than one occasion. So far, you only have the timber wolves in Iceland, which could easily be explained by some forced migration. Timber wolves are mostly native to Canada, not that far of a walk to Iceland.".

"Over water?" Anika pushes back.

"Then they stowed away on a ship. It happens more often than you think."

Anika doesn't say a word. Matt has the ability to find a reason that best suits him to ignore facts.

"You got a good eye, Anika, but I think you're steering in the wrong direction," Matt says, taking another bite of food. "Animals will do what they can to survive, but there is a limit to their methods. It's all about instinct, not intelligence, and that's for about ninety percent of the animal kingdom."

This is the first time Kit has noticed a shred of ignorance

from Matt. He shrugs off a rather important conversation like it's nothing.

"You really got in too deep with this theory of yours," Matt continues. "I'm not sure where you picked up this idea. You've been around a bit, you've seen all kinds of behaviors, I know you have. Animals ain't smart enough to do stuff like that, let alone be conscious of their habitat. It's a basic animal instinct. Remember the story of that horse in the 1900s or so? They really thought that damn horse knew math. Add, subtract, multiply, the works. They were so damn sure of it, until what?"

Anika doesn't say a word.

"Don't worry, I'll remind you. The horse didn't know math. It just knew how to read the electromyographies of its owner. It could sense the behavioral anticipation. It knew the number its owner wanted when it was 'counting'. See? Animals aren't smart, they're just finely tuned to pick up behaviors and energies from other species. Which is why your theory isn't as plausible as you think."

"You didn't even read the damn paper, did you?" Burns says.

"Of course I did."

"Then you would know that she never claimed that animals were intelligent. Her claims go far beyond that," Burns adds.

"At any rate," Matt says, waving away the thought. "I don't see any logic in her theory, that's all." Matt turns to Lucy. "Which reminds me, Ms. Benitez, I've been meaning to pick your brain, how do you figure in all this?"

Lucy bobs her head, not understanding what Matt wants from her.

"These dinosaurs, tell me about them, ecosystems and all," Matt says.

Lucy put the book in her hands down on the table. She pauses, as for a split second she forgets Matt wasn't in their truck earlier that day during this same explanation. "Not unlike most animals now, I would assume. They lived all around the globe, in various habitats and environments. Of course, climate and terrains were different millions of years ago, but fossils have all been found in packs of good size and health. Same goes for the predators that were loners. They had a good population size. There really have only been a few countries where no fossils have been found, the middle east, parts of Australia, and well, here in Tasmania," Lucy says.

Anika drowns out the rest of the conversation. Lucy goes on to repeat a lot of what she has said before. Matt is supposedly attentive to every word she says. He always has an attention span for anything that benefits him. Which is why he shut Anika down. He showed interest in her work, and then saw no need for her input. Matt is here to become more iconic with this discovery, and that's the end of it.

Anika saw Burns looking at her, his eyes apologizing for Matt's rude behavior. Anika just shrugged, what did it matter? Anika ended up finishing her meal, washing her plate, and made her way back upstairs to bed.

INTRODUCTION: TAKE ONE

Anika and Burns wake up around the same time, due to the chattering of the other crew downstairs, which is loud enough to be heard around the entire lodge. Burns walks into the bathroom in their room and starts to wash his face with cold water. Anika rubs her eyes as she sits on the side of her bed, yawning and wondering if she still wants to be a part of this. She spent all night thinking about their conversation at dinner. Matt listened to everyone's input and still managed to make it about himself. The only reason that kept her from walking away was Burns. She couldn't fathom the idea of leaving him there alone with Matt. Anika puts her hair up in a ponytail. She grabs her jacket from her bag and makes her way downstairs.

The crew is wide awake, to put it lightly. Most munch on their food, which consists of wrapped sandwiches, granola bars, and MREs. Other crew are inspecting their camera gear and getting ready to film. Anika walks past Kit and JJ, who are both sitting on stools in the kitchen area.

"Never thought I'd eat MREs again in my life," Kit says.

"I have a ton of granola and protein bars in my bag upstairs, you're welcome to any of them," Anika says as she puts on her jacket.

"Might take you up on that," Kit says.

"Same goes for you, JJ, unless you like MREs," Anika jokes.

"*Fuck. No.*" JJ utters.

Anika couldn't help but smirk at JJ's comment. She was

scanning the room once more as she made her way to the front door, some of the crew was missing, along with Matt. Maybe they weren't awake yet? Anika opens the front door, ready to take in some fresh air, she steps out and is met with Zeke the cameraman. He had his finger up against his lips, shushing her.

Matt stands a few feet away in the clearing in front of the lodge, the forest behind him. Two cameras are on stands at different angles, while Mike, the boom mic operator, stands in between them. Lucy is standing on the porch along with Anika, watching them film Matt, fascinated at the behind-the-scenes look of a wildlife show.

Matt is in the middle of a monologue to the camera. "... vastly different from anything I've done before. Than *anyone* has ever done before. Ladies, gentlemen, what if I told you, a completely different world lived beyond these trees," Matt says in a calm voice as he holds his arm up at the trees. "A world... so exotic, so superb, a world that has remained hidden from the public eye for *millions of years*?"

Matt moves closer to the trees; the boom mic inches closer to Matt's head.

"Not that long ago, a long-time friend of mine, made a startling discovery right here in Tasmania. While studying the local wildlife, our good friend Bill Burns came across something so unbelievable, *words* would not do it justice. I will play this footage for you, dear viewer, and you will see the reason for this special event on Animal Planet. So, without further ado..." Matt waves away to the viewer, like he's pulling back the curtain.

"Alright," Zeke, the cameraman, says, "We're good."

"Cool, I actually might redo that intro later, but I like it. It seems natural, what do y'all think?" Matt says. His crew along with Lucy give him either a nod or a thumbs up. Anika remains neutral in her expression.

"Anika... you want to do the next segment with me?" Matt asks her.

Anika shakes her head.

"Come on, it'll be like old times..."

"No."

Matt sighs. "Well alright, then."

Matt signals the crew to move closer to the forest with him. Matt walks them to the closest tree and then crouches in front of it. Zeke and Mike move the camera stands closer to where Matt is crouching. Matt instructs them on where to place the cameras. "I want to do this next one like this. Folks will be on the edge of their seats. I want to be sitting with them. Y'all ready?" Matt asks.

Zeke adjusts the angles while kneeling on the soft ground in front of Matt, while the boom mic operator remains standing. He moves the mic closer to Matt's head. Matt clears his throat and says "testing". The operator gives him a nod.

"Alright Matt," Zeke says, "Ready in three, two, one..."

Matt's face changes to an energetic but welcoming demeanor, his eyes showing the viewer that he's just as surprised as they are. "Crazy, ain't it? I can't tell you how many times I have watched that clip, and every time my heart skips a beat. I know what you're thinking, how could it be real? Well... how could it not? We all know our pal Bill has never lied to us. He's the most steady guy I know, and believe me, he's here with me now. What we have gathered here for, is to search and locate a living, breathing dinosaur. A species thought to be extinct, here in Tasmania. Stay tuned with us, dear viewers, and be a part of this moment. A moment in history, where the old will join the new." Matt holds up the index finger on each hand. "A moment, where two worlds separated by periods in time, collide together." Matt moves his index fingers on an imaginary line to meet in the middle.

He continues, "I said I know what y'all might be thinking, but I also know what you're feeling. The same thing I've been feeling everyday while we prepared for this expedition. That feeling that flutters your stomach with butterflies and pumps your heart with adrenaline. The need for adventure, the need to put your doubts away and jump in feet first to prove it yourself. So come on y'all, jump in with me." He gives a warming smile and reaches his hand out to the camera, inviting the viewer to join him.

"We're good," Zeke says.

"Hell yeah, I ain't changing that one," Matt says with a smile. Matt stands up and walks to his crew. "Show me, I want to see it.".

Lucy looks over at Anika, with an admiring smirk on Lucy's face. It happens every time, Anika knows it, and she doesn't blame them. Anika isn't afraid to admit it. Matt certainly knows how to use his charm and demeanor to capture your attention. He's very skilled in getting the audience pumped up for whatever he has coming next.

The front door opens behind Anika, and Burns steps out with Kit. They both are wearing their jackets and hiking gear, and Burns has his small backpack slung over one shoulder.

"What's going on out here?" Kit asks.

"Filming an introduction, I think," Lucy replies.

Kit nods his head. "When are we heading out?" he asks Burns.

"Soon as we have a good idea of where we're going. Go ahead and grab one of those rifles. I'll talk to Matt and see what's what," Burns says to Kit.

Kit gave nod again and began stepping off the porch toward the parked trucks in the driveway. Burns looked at Anika and signaled her to follow him. They made their way to Matt, who was chuckling as he rewatched the footage he just filmed.

"Matt, are you ready to head out?" Burns asks him.

"Hell yeah, I'm ready. This is your domain, Bill, where are we off to?" Matt said as he looked away from the footage.

Burns reached into his jacket and pulled out a small GPS, he switched it on. He navigated through the menu until a map appeared on the screen. The map had an arrow indicating their current location, and there were six dots creating a line heading due northeast. "These dots are as far as we originally followed that night in the video. About a 40-minute walk, I say we head that direction, set up a couple trail cameras along the way, and once we reach that point, we'll set up some more cameras with bait" Burns said.

"Sounds like a plan, once we get there we can... HEY! What the hell are you doing?" Matt suddenly yells in one direction. Everyone outside looks at what Matt is yelling about. Kit is standing next to the pick-up bed of one of the trucks. He's holding one of the elephant rifles and is in the process of loading the rounds. Kit stares back in confusion at Matt's sudden outburst.

"You brought hunting rifles? What the hell's the matter with you?" Matt sneers.

"I ordered them," Burns says.

"You? Why?" Matt says, the charm in his voice completely gone.

"Matt... they're carnivores," Burns says.

"I don't give a shit. I'm not bringing any of those guns with us," Matt says.

"Do you really want to go out there without any fucking protection?" Anika snaps.

"I've done it before, Christ almighty, you guys have too. Did your balls drop off?" Matt snaps back.

"Matt, this seems more dangerous..." Burns says, trying to

inject reason.

"I got a can of bear spray in my bag, I got plenty if y'all want one. But there is no way in hell we are going out there with even the possibility we could shoot one because we're scared. We're here to observe and document, not interfere," Matt says. Matt's not budging, but neither are Burns or Anika. They all stand for a second, not willing to let any of this go. Anika is staring into Matt's ignorant eyes when Kit breaks the silence.

"What about if I bring one of the dart guns? I could stow the rifle on my back," Kit asks.

"No stowing, I'll carry the rifle myself," Burns says.

Matt frowns, but then he looks around at everyone's scornful expressions, then he slowly nods his head. "I'm cool with that. But I don't want you to use that thing, ever," he says. Anika shakes her head; she can't believe Matt will never see reason. Burns then nods in agreement; he walks over and takes the .375 rifle from Kit. He disengages the safety and does a brass check. After confirming there is a round in the chamber, he slides the bolt forward. Kit then digs into his pocket and hands him the extra rounds. Burns puts them in his jacket pocket, and turns around, ready to move.

Matt ignores the scornful looks from Anika and Burns. Burns just looks back at Kit. Burns nods his head in the direction of the Ford pick-ups, and Kit strolls over and opens the canopy door. He rustles around until he pulls out one of the Dan Inject Model JM air rifles. Kit holds it up and inspects it, then pulls out a separate case from the pick-up bed. The case is small, about the size of a fanny pack. It has a carry handle and a carrying strap.

"Load it up, Kit," Matt says, "It's got a little screw at the end of the stock."

Kit inspects the air rifle again. He finds the screw Matt is referring to and unscrews it. It reveals a small opening in the rifle's stock that looks to be in line with the barrel.

"Take a dart out of the pack and slide it in there" Matt says, "When you open the case, it should be one of the darts with the pink tailpiece. That's a sedative, the ones with the blue tailpiece are the counter sedatives."

Kit opens the case and grabs one of the tranquilizer darts. It's about eight inches long, with a hypodermic needle tip and a pink fibrous tailpiece on the other tip. Kit inserts it in the rifle and screws the stock cap back on.

"Bingo, you're ready to work," Matt says in a joyful tone.

Kit sighs. In his peripheral vision, he sees Anika watching him. He knows what she's thinking. He looks at her and then lifts his shirt with his right hand. He shows her a single holster in his waistband on his right hip. Anika sees a pistol handle sticking out. Kit grabs the handle to show her the weapon, a small snub-nosed revolver, a Taurus model 605.

Kit smiles at her then slips it back in the holster. He puts his finger to his lips, telling her to keep quiet about it. That puts Anika a little at ease; she doesn't know much about guns but it's better than Kit carrying nothing.

Lucy stands on the porch watching the whole commotion. They are barely a day in and they're already butting heads. Is it going to be like this the entire time? And they're supposed to be out here for a month? She reminds herself that the length of their stay would depend on how long it takes her to determine the species. She'd have to work hard to find it in a timely manner. After watching Kit load a single hypodermic needle into the dart gun, she can't help but wonder if the needle would even penetrate a giant lizard's skin.

She also can't help but be glad that she isn't going out there by herself.

MANEATERS

Ward sits in the passenger seat as Valente drives through the crowded city that is Seattle, toward their destination. Shortly after the cargo and passenger plane lifts off for Tasmania, Valente and Ward make their way to the Municipal Court of Seattle. The only thought on Valente's mind is the first night in Tasmania he was looking forward to. The idea of preparing for such an expedition, coming up with a game plan, barely getting enough sleep because of the anticipation. But now he's not there; now he has to resolve this matter in the court before joining his team.

Valente keeps his mouth shut on the drive there. He knows himself and his few flaws. Valente often snaps at his friends when he has a lot on his mind. And he respects Ward too much to talk down to him like that simply because he's frustrated. Valente glances at Ward. He's fiddling with his necktie, attempting to get it to look right in the car's sun visor mirror. Ward also hasn't said a word in about twenty minutes, but occasionally he hears Ward grunt at his dissatisfaction with the necktie arrangement.

"You really didn't have any of those clip-on ties?" Ward finally asks.

"Nobody wears clip-ons anymore, Lee."

"I find that hard to believe. Do I really have to be there for this?"

"Yes you do, you are the co-owner. By the way, don't wear this hat in there."

Ward frowns as he takes the trucker hat off. "I wear a hat cause I don't like anyone looking at my bald head."

"It's either this or shave, Lee."

"Fat fucking chance of that," Ward says as he rubs his beard. "So what's going on today?"

"They're going to reiterate the charges, the nature of them, and who pressed the charges in the first place. They're also going to tell us our court date and ask us how we plead."

"Complete bullshit. I honestly can't think of any other reason to sue us. It has to be because of the expedition."

"The other charges don't make sense. Withholding information is one thing, but how could we have done the other charges?"

Ward knew Valente was right, the other charges didn't really make sense if it was because of the expedition. Ward decided to let it go, and to wait to see the truth behind all of this. Ward took off his glasses and rubbed the top of his nose. He put his glasses back on and then looked up at the city. He watched the high-rises in Seattle get closer and closer, he hated the city, especially Seattle. It was a special kind of trash, in Ward's opinion, and he had always begged Valente to move the company to Oregon or Idaho. Valente never saw any logical reason to do that, he liked the engineering hangar a little too much.

Eventually, Valente pulled into the parking garage for the municipal court, found a space to park, and then made their way towards the court building. Valente's mind stopped wandering for a brief moment, as he found Ward in a suit a bit amusing. He'd never thought he'd see Ward in a suit. Valente always figured if he ever got married, that Ward would just show up in jeans and a flannel to his wedding. Valente couldn't help but compare Ward to a child wearing a suit that was too big for him.

"The fuck are you smiling at?" Ward asks as he walks beside him.

"Nothing."

"It's my bald head, isn't it?"

"Don't worry about it."

Ward and Valente enter the courthouse. They pass through the security checkpoint where they put their belongings in a plastic tray, and then through the metal detectors. Valente passes through without a problem, but the metal detector goes off when Ward steps through. The security guards give him a look.

"Got a metal strip in my forearm... you know what? Just frisk me," Ward says to them. One of the security guards decides to frisk Ward. He pats him down and then grabs his wand from his belt. The guard moves the wand around Ward's body. It beeps when he moves it over Ward's left forearm.

"Is that where the metal strip is, sir?" the guard asks.

"Yes," Ward replies.

The guard finally lets Ward through. Ward starts to grab his belongings from the plastic tray while Valente waits for him. Once Ward has grabbed his things, they both start walking through the courthouse.

"When'd you break your arm?" Valente asks curiously.

"Somalia, 1991," Ward says in a somber tone.

Valente decided not to pry, bringing that up right now while Ward was already stressed was not a good idea. Valente kept to himself while they walked through the busy hallways of the courthouse. Eventually they found the right section for their case. They informed one of the receptionists of their arrival, and they were instructed to sit and wait for their preliminary hearing to start. The receptionist had handed a set of stapled papers to Valente. He flipped through them as they waited in the lobby.

"What're you looking at?" Ward asks, uneasy.

"Looking at the charges again, and I'm trying to find who pressed them in the first place. They should be in here somewhere," Valente says.

It's the second to last page where he sees a single name in the middle of the page; *Intecon Construction LLC.*

"Intecon Construction," Valente mutters.

"Who's that?"

"No idea. You've never heard of them? Not even before I came on?"

Ward shakes his head. "No. Never heard of them."

"Well, they've heard of us. And it's not a mistake, They named Valtech Industries specifically," Valente says. He's nothing short of baffled.

He's positive Valtech has never had any dealings with Intecon, so could it be a scam? Valente quickly turned that notion down. It would be extremely idiotic to try and do that in a municipal court. Withholding evidence, property damage. Perhaps a project Valtech had done became faulty? Valente despised the idea, as he considered his and Ward's work solid, but he entertained the theory for a moment. A project became faulty. It damaged property, recklessly endangered people, and in some way, Intecon feels Valtech withheld evidence. Evidence of what though? Faulty materials? No... it couldn't be that. He and Ward would've heard of it by now. At any rate, if they hadn't heard of Intecon before, then they must be owned by someone else, another parent company. Perhaps the preliminary hearing or even discovery will yield those answers.

"Anything ring a bell?" Ward asks. He's been watching Valente's face jump through the hoops of potential possibilities.

"Maybe, but nothing that sounds plausible enough," Valente says, as he leans back in his chair, still thinking to himself.

Valente and Ward both remain seated in silence for a few minutes in the lobby, both men confused and slightly anxious. Ward hates government buildings and just wants to go home. Valente wants to get this ordeal over with and join his team in Tasmania. Now that he really thinks about it, Valente finds it odd that the court date for their first appearance is so early. The court summons was given to him only a day in advance. Valente has never heard of court dates being so quick. Perhaps they had a difficult time getting a hold of him? Valente does like to stay busy.

"Valtech Industries, Docket 113097," the receptionist calls out.

Valente and Ward stood up from their chairs. They walked forward until the receptionist let them through to the courtroom. The courtroom was large, but it was empty, only the judge, the bailiff, and three other men in suits were in the room. The judge, an older woman in her 50s, sat in her chair in the center of the room. The bailiff stood next to the judge, and the three men were standing at a table in front of the judge. These men were from Intecon or at least representing them. Valente didn't recognize any of them, neither did Ward.

The three men, all of them ranging from late 40s to late 50s, stood and watched as Valente and Ward made their way to their defendant table. Valente examined them, tailored three-piece suits from Brooks Brothers, one had a Rolex watch, another had a Maxwell Scott briefcase. Valente recognized all of these things. Whoever Intecon is, they are not a random construction company. Ward and Valente arrived at their defendant table. The judge looked down at a stack of papers in her hand. Valente was waiting for the judge's formal introduction from the bailiff, but it never came. They all stood in silence while the judge read through the papers, until she put them down and looked at Ward and Valente.

"Valtech Industries?" the judge asks.

"Yes, your honor," Valente answers.

"Are you his legal counsel?" the judge asks Valente, referring to Ward.

"No, your honor. We are co-owners of Valtech."

"And your legal counsel?"

"Representing myself, your honor."

The judge just stares for a moment. She then looks at the papers in front of her once more. "Intecon Construction LLC, you are accusing the defendant of withholding evidence, property damage, and reckless endangerment. Valtech Industries, do you understand these charges?" the judge asks.

"We do, your honor," Valente says.

"How do you plead?" the judge asks.

"Not guilty, your honor."

The judge doesn't look up from the papers. She seems indirect and distracted. "The plaintiffs have agreed to a formal meeting between you and them, before we move forward with a trial date. You will meet with them in a conference room down the hall and then reconvene here. That'll be all," the judge says.

That'll be all? What the hell is all this? Has the judicial system changed in the last ten years? This is nothing like the process that he studied for years in Harvard. No, the law hasn't changed. Valente trusts his instinct that something is wrong with all this. The judge stands up from her chair and walks into her office in the back. The three plaintiffs start to walk out of the courtroom, presumably to the conference room.

"What now?" Ward asks.

"I have no idea, Lee. But something is really wrong."

"No, I got the gist of that. What's the meeting for?"

"I don't know, none of this makes any sense."

Valente and Ward exit the courtroom.

The conference room was small. The three plaintiffs each took seats at the end of a long table. A single projector sat on a book in the middle of the table. It whirred as the men adjusted in their seats. Valente and Ward both sat down on the other end of the table, their seats closer to the door. That's the only comfort Ward took in all this: at least the exit was close by.

"Hello gentlemen. My name is Richard Stein, and these are my colleagues, Peter Landa and Charles Rosley," Stein says, his voice soft but frank. Landa and Rosley don't bother to say a word to them.

Stein was balding and had wrinkly eyes and a small nose. He looks like he was in his mid-50s. Landa seemed the youngest, with combed gray hair and thick eyebrows. And Rosley looked the oldest, with a wide face and even wider glasses. Rosely sat in between Stein and Landa. All three of them had a specific look about them, high-classed and connected. They reminded Valente of all the "guest speakers" at Harvard during the class lectures. Pretentious lawyers who spent the better part of an afternoon boasting about their firm. Valente never liked any of those speakers. He always noticed they spent a third of their lecture talking about themselves before saying anything of importance.

"Are you legal counsel for Intecon?" Valente asks Stein.

"We all are. Intecon hired our firm. Stein & Associates," Stein answers.

Valente nods his head. "And what is the purpose of this

meeting?"

Rosley leans forward. "Intecon is open to an arrangement for a settlement instead of a trial. They have an offer for you."

"Settlement? Already?"

"Yes, Mr. Valente. We could settle it today if we needed to."

Incredibly odd, all of it really, Valente thinks.

"What is the reason Intecon is suing us?" Valente asks.

Landa stands up from his chair and reaches forward to the projector. He grabs a remote sitting next to it on the table.

"We'll inform you right now," Landa says. He sits down after acquiring the projector remote and clicks a single button. The projector illuminates a picture on the wall. It's a blank screen with a 'play' symbol on it. "However, Intecon and its parent company have instructed us to show you this video before anything else," Landa says.

A parent company. Valente was right.

"What's the parent company? I'm currently at a loss, I've never heard of Intecon," Valente says.

"RV Analytics," Stein replies.

Valente has never heard of that company either. He glances at Ward, who has an equally confused look on his face. Ward has never heard of RV Analytics either.

"I can see you're confused, but our client assured us that this video would clear it all up for you," Stein says. Landa clicks another button on the remote, and the video commences. Valente notices Stein, Rosley, and Landa all turn away from the video instead of watching alongside them. What are they about to see?

The video flips from a gray blank screen to a large face, a man wearing a facemask and glasses. He appears to be adjusting the camera, he then steps back, and reveals he's standing in what looks like a morgue. The man is wearing a lab coat and scrubs, latex gloves on his hands, and a plastic apron around his waist. He steps to the left, revealing a table behind him horizontal to the camera.

A corpse lays on the table.

The corpse looks like it was torn to shreds, bits of bone protruding and flesh missing. The corpse's skin is pale and purple around the wounds. The face missing the lower jaw, the lips and nose missing from the corpse. The sudden image startles both Ward and Valente. Now they know why the lawyers chose to look away.

"Today is March 4th, 2024. I'm Dr. Gene Hogan from the coroner's office of the Magistrate Court of Tasmania," the man says, a heavy Tasmanian accent in his voice. Hearing the word *Tasmania* causes Ward to plant his face in his hands, but Valente keeps watching, unyielded.

"What we have here today, is a victim of a gruesome animal attack that happened two days ago at a construction site close to Queenstown. Victim is a 35-year-old male, approximately six feet tall, *heavy on the approximately*. Parts of his lower legs are missing, so it's just an estimate," Hogan says. Hogan moves around the table toward the legs of the corpse. He lifts the left leg for the camera. The foot is gone at the ankle, the ivory-colored stump bulging, long gashes on the thigh separating the skin and muscle from the bone underneath.

"Left and right foot are completely severed, severe lacerations and deep trauma on both thighs," Hogan says. He puts the leg down and moves to the abdomen. The stomach is gone. There is no skin and muscle, or entrails, the only thing holding the top of the body and the bottom together is the spine. "Lower abdomen looks like it was torn into, severe trauma with multiple organs missing, intestines and stomach lining basically gone."

Hogan moves to the left, toward the corpse's upper body. He lifts the right arm, bicep and parts of the forearm, slashed but mostly intact. The skin doesn't look pale; it looked dark yellow, especially along the open breaks in the skin. The muscle tissue looks bloated and stiff.

"Hand is missing on the right arm, but the hand is intact on the left arm as you can see. These cuts on the forearm look like defensive wounds. These cuts are clean, with no jagged tears that would indicate separate or numerous attacks. It was done in one swift move. Whatever did this, it has the vigor and dexterity to cut as deep as the bone with one movement."

Hogan puts the right arm down and finally moves to the head of the corpse.

"Once more, severe trauma to the face, mandible missing as well as the decedent's nose. Multiple lacerations all around the cranium, both frontal and zygomatic parts seem to have taken the brunt of the attack." Hogan stops. He takes a loud and clear deep breath. He looks over the body once more before looking at the camera.

"I've seen murders more humane than this. Now, I'm no pathologist, but my assumption is that the victim was incapacitated, then it started with his feet. The stump on both ankles indicate that the feet were twisted and popped off. Then the rest of the attack ensued. Now, as far as I know, there is no predator in Tasmania big enough to inflict this kind of damage on a human being. First thing anyone would suggest is maybe a saltwater crocodile, but they don't eat like this, and there's no evidence of a death roll. And I've never heard of there ever being any crocodile in Tasmania. Certainly not a cassowary. They usually just kick their opponent continuously with their talons and couldn't create lacerations this deep."

Hogan holds out his arm, pointing at the abdomen. His mouth opens but he is at a loss for words. He scoffs. "I've honestly got no clue, not one, on how this happened, on *what* could have done this. But then again, that's not my job, is it?" Hogan says. He steps back from the body and crosses his arms. "Per usual, I will continue the autopsy and send my findings to the chief examiner. Expect to have them later today. My advice, call someone with experience in wildlife, professional hunters or wildlife consultants. Otherwise you'll never know how this happened, or if it will continue."

The video pauses.

Valente looked at the lawyers, all three of them still turned around, facing away from the image on the screen. He takes a glance at Ward, who is still glued to the screen. He notices Ward is squinting through his glasses. Ward leans forward a little more, then leans back and gives Valente a strange look. Ward has noticed something, something Valente is not seeing.

"Mr. Valente, I hope you can see the importance of the matter. This is one of many construction workers lost to a dangerous animal in the wilds of Tasmania. Intecon was informed that Valtech Engineering was aware of the dangerous wildlife. Aware for quite some time and purposely withheld that information, which would have been vital to prevent further attacks and loss of life. Not only have their employees' lives been constantly endangered, but it has put a halt to their work causing significant financial damage to their company," Stein explains.

Valente says nothing, neither does Ward. Landa switches off the projector with the remote, and the lawyers turn to Valente and Ward. "We could go to trial, yes, or we could settle it right now. Intecon has a list of demands, and if they are met, they will drop the charges," Rosley adds.

"Demands?" Valente finally says.

Landa hands Stein a piece of paper. Stein skims it over and then proceeds to read it aloud. "All physical evidence is to be handed over to Intecon Construction LLC. Any and all witnesses to the evidence brought forward are to sign NDA agreements. Cash settlement of 13.5 million dollars for the damages done to Intecon Construction LLC and its parent company, RV Analytics."

"Evidence?" Ward asks.

"Evidence of the wildlife that is causing the damages," Stein clarifies.

"And what exactly will they do with the evidence?" Valente snaps.

"That is up to Intecon, and not your concern. But you've seen the video, likely they will use the information you have to put a stop to the animal," Stein says.

Valente opens his mouth to retort, but he can't think of anything logical. His gaze darts from each lawyer to the next. They just sit still with unsympathetic eyes. Ward can almost feel the heat coming off of Valente's body, the anger that every once in a while slips. Ward quickly intercedes to make sure Valente doesn't say or do anything stupid in a government building.

"Could we take the day to talk this over with my colleague?" Ward asks.

Stein turns his head to look at Landa and Rosley. They don't say a word but all agree with each other. "Take two days, consider the settlement. We'll be waiting for a response in a timely manner," Stein says. The lawyers get out of their chairs and proceed to leave the conference room, leaving Ward and Valente to ruminate in their mixed feelings.

Valente and Ward finally step out into the lobby. Valente's face is furious. He can't stand the fact that his first expedition, his first project ever, is slipping through his fingers. Ward takes off his glasses and rubs his eyes. He then pats Valente on the back. Valente's body is stiff with rage and frustration. Ward knows exactly what's going on in his head. Valente very rarely gets stumped about what to do next.

"I don't think there's much we can do here," Ward says.

"It'll clean us out," Valente says. "The cash settlement, even if I find a way to negotiate it down, it'll most likely bankrupt Valtech. And the expedition is moot."

"Speaking of which. We should call them, let them know that the animal has attacked humans. Maybe bring them back."

"Bring them back?"

"Forrest, you saw the video. They're extremely dangerous, ferocious, and the lawyers say it's happened to more than one construction worker... well... supposedly."

Valente catches Ward's casual remark. "What do you mean 'supposedly'?"

Ward leans in closer to Valente so the lawyers can't hear them. "The body in the video... he had scrapes and bruises on his elbow."

Valente doesn't say anything, confused.

"In the military, there's certain things that give away an individual's job other than their rank. The body was sun-bleached, dirty and mud-crusted pants, and had a scraped-up elbow. He looked more like a soldier, or a hunter."

"A soldier or a hunter? They said he was a construction worker."

"It's probably nothing... just a hunch really."

"We should get going, and think about our next move before we do anything at all," Valente says.

Valente takes a glance at the lawyers talking to each other. He notices there's no longer three. A fourth member has joined them and has his back turned to them. Another lawyer perhaps? Colleague? Or maybe an employee of Intecon? Valente watches them talk to each other, hoping the fourth man turns around so he can potentially recognize him. Or put a face to whoever has laid this shitstorm onto...

The man turns around. Valente's shoulders tense up as he looks over the man's face.

The man casually strolls toward them. He stops a few feet from Ward and Valente. A wiry man in his late 50s, lavish and skillfully tailored three-piece suit, carefully combed thin gray hair, pilot-framed glasses over his sincere green eyes. The man extends his hand toward Ward, and Ward out of habit shakes the man's hand.

"Rafe Valente," he says. "Pleasure to finally meet you, Mr. Ward."

Ward is caught off-guard after hearing the man's name. Valente stays still, star-struck. Rafe's smile is wide, but there seems to be nothing behind it. Same goes for the rest of Rafe's face, an empty shell meant specifically for the corporate world. Rafe finally lets go of Ward's hand after the long handshake. Rafe turns his green eyes to Valente, scanning him from top to bottom.

"Son, you look well," Rafe says, his voice monotone and soothing. "You know, I'll admit, I was worried you would be struggling when you bought into this company of yours. But look at you," Rafe pats his son on the shoulder, "You seem to have done well. Nice suit too, haven't lost your touch when it comes to fashion, I like it."

"What are you doing here?" Valente asks.

"Well, that's the unfortunate thing. See, here I am mentioning your successful business venture, when I have to make a substantial dent into it in the next couple days," Rafe says.

Valente and Ward don't say a word.

"RV Analytics? 'Rafe Valente Analytics'? That's one of my smaller companies, which owns several construction companies," Rafe says. "I'm here 'cause, well... you know. No need to reiterate anything, you must still be soaking it all in."

"You're suing me?" Valente says in a defeated tone.

"Forrest, things happen, out of our control, unfortunately. And I have to take care of my employees," Rafe says.

"You have construction companies out in Tasmania?" Valente asks.

"I have them everywhere. They build hospitals, warehouses, fleet services, wherever they're needed, really," Rafe says, then looks at Ward. "I've been trying to expand and diversify Valente Pharmaceuticals globally. I'm sure you guys can understand."

"Okay, and why do you need my evidence? I mean, you're asking my company to sign NDAs after handing it over," Valente presses.

"Not just your company, anyone who has come in contact or is aware of the evidence you are withholding," Rafe explains. "It's a maneater, Forrest, it needs to be put down, whatever it is."

Valente's demeanor seems to be charging up, soon to reach its limit and explode. Rafe notices and his smile gets wider. "Oh, don't get your panties in a bunch," Rafe says, as he gives Valente a playful pat on the arm. "Lighten up, take these two days I'm giving you, come to your senses. No need to go to court and make it *worse*. It's only a settlement and a couple of papers to sign. Your company will be A-okay."

Valente chooses to remain silent. He has nothing to say to his taunting father. Rafe once again notices the stubbornness emanating from his son. "Lee," Rafe says, turning his attention to Ward. "Please, use these two days to talk this over with my son. Make him see reason, accept the deal."

Rafe turns around to walk away from them both, but then glances back at Ward.

"Try and stay healthy, Lee. And see to it my son does too."

Rafe strolls away from them both. He reaches his lawyers and they all start to walk down the courthouse hallway. Valente breathes out a shuddering, rageful breath. He moves forward and sits in one of the chairs in the hallway. Ward can hear Valente muttering under his breath. *Fuck, fuck, fuck.*

"He couldn't have come straight to you? Just right out of the gate with the lawsuit?" Ward asks.

"You don't know him, there's no negotiating, no leeway, nothing," Valente mutters

"What the hell do you mean?"

"He knows exactly what the settlement will do to me. To us. It doesn't matter if we take it or not, either way he's going to leave us with nothing."

Ward puts his hands on his hips, taking it all in.

"How does he know?" Valente mutters.

"What?"

"How does he know about the evidence? How does he know we have anything to do with his 'maneater'?"

Ward just shrugs.

"Someone talked. Someone had to." Valente says. He takes a moment to sharpen his mind, then a thought occurs to him. "He's lying."

"Lying about what?"

"Taking care of his employees. He couldn't give a shit about their wellbeing."

"Forrest, he said he's building things. He could just be concerned about his investments."

"No, that's not it," Valente says. "He also doesn't give a shit about building hospitals or warehouses. There's something else to this. What is he doing in Tasmania?"

All of Valente's remarks about Rafe make Ward cautiously curious about their validity.

"Is your father *really* how you describe him?" Ward asks.

"Like everything you could hate in a human being? Valente says without skipping a beat. "And the most taunting smile anyone could carry."

"Yeah, no, I definitely noticed that," Ward says with a sigh. "What now?"

Valente straightens his body in the chair, a plan finally formulating in his head. "We're flying out there to Tasmania," Valente says. "I want to talk to Dr. Hogan, maybe get the full story. And then I want to find out what my dad is actually doing out there."

Ward nods his head in agreement, and they both start to make their way through the courthouse.

TRACKWAY

Kit was slowly walking through the dense forest that is Tasmania, carefully maneuvering through the ferns and bushes, watching his step. The tall Blackwood trees created a crowded feeling for the biologists and camera crew as they trekked through the wilderness. They all walked in a single file line, Matt and Burns at the very front with the GPS, Anika behind them, and a single cameraman. Kit was at the very end of the line of explorers, the Dan Inject JM air rifle in his hands.

The rifle was light, significantly lighter than the Ruger Guide chambered in .375 he was originally going to carry. Kit could kind of understand Matt's position on why he didn't want to bring the hunting rifles. If their purpose is to document the animal in order to protect its life, bringing a lethal weapon begs the question as to why try in the first place?

Still, Kit remembers the briefing clear as day. These are potentially dangerous creatures. Lucy Benitez was very clear and thorough. Even if it was all speculation up to this point, there was no other indication that it wasn't carnivorous. Kit fully understood the other side of the argument about the hunting rifles, but Kit didn't know who was right, or who to agree with. Things were definitely easier to decide in the military. There were orders from a superior, and there was no questioning involved.

Still, even then, Kit prefers being here than in Afghanistan.

Kit almost loses his footing as he's walking. His foot slips on a moist tree root but he catches himself before toppling over. *Christ*, he thinks to himself, *this terrain is much weirder than any other place I've deployed to.* Kit has been to Afghanistan, Iraq, Japan, Germany, England, and one very short trip to South America. Kit is an explorer; he likes the outdoors. While everyone else was in a German or English bar on their weekend, Kit was in the nearby nature trail. His favorite so far was the Japanese peninsula close to Kyoto. The cherry blossoms made him feel serene as he walked by them. He wondered if all the samurai back then felt the same way.

Kit sees the cameraman slip in front of him, landing on his knee.

"Whoa, you good?" Kit asks.

The cameraman just grunts and stands back up, and completely ignores Kit's concern. The cameraman continues to walk, but Kit notices Anika lets the cameraman walk past her. Anika waits for Kit to catch up to her. "The guy seems tense," Kit says, referring to the rude cameraman.

"Zeke hates the outdoors," Anika says. She turns to walk alongside Kit.

"Has he worked with Matt before?" Kit asks.

"For about ten years."

"He's been working on a nature show for ten years and he still hates being outside?" Kit asks.

"He sure knows how to pick them, huh?"

Kit chuckles, and he almost slips again. "This place is so goddamn..."

"Uneven?"

"Yep, that's how I'd describe it."

"This entire island is like that. I've only been here twice in my life and my only advice is to mind your footing and keep your eyes peeled."

"For the dinosaur?"

"No, for the other *real* creatures that live here. Like tiger snakes and copperheads, they can be easily instigated."

"Real?" Kit says. "You don't think this dinosaur is real?"

"I'm hoping it isn't."

"Why is that?"

"Because then everything will go back to normal," Anika says. "You know nothing will be the same if it is real, right?"

"How do you figure that?"

Anika shakes her head. "We're out here to find evidence so that we can protect it, but it won't matter, it really won't. Not only will every scientist from every country rush down here, but every other maniac that wants attention will do so too. My father says we'd be 'observing not interfering', but that's not possible. Not only are we putting ourselves in danger, but also this habitat and the animal itself. Think about it, Kit. After we show the world that this animal exists, and everyone comes rushing down to study it, how long before someone gets hurt? Or worse? Do you know what happens to a predator after it kills a human?"

Kit's face is blank.

"It's declared a maneater, and maneaters have to be killed. Because unfortunately, once a predator learns that humans are easy prey, there's no going back. It has to be put down," Anika explains.

Kit shakes his head. "Man, you are not at all like Forrest described you."

"Oh yeah? How'd he describe me?"

"Stubborn. But I don't think you are, at least not without reason. I think I agree with you about being out here," Kit says. "So why are we out there then? By your logic, shouldn't we have left these animals alone?"

"We're humoring your boss, Valente, and the 'master

outdoorsman' up front," Anika says, referring to Matt. "See, they both took a side on a topic that's nothing but gray area. To be honest, Bill and I are here for the same reason, to keep an eye on this project to make sure things don't get too invasive."

Took a side on a topic that's nothing but gray area. Kit doesn't know if he finds that admirable or foolish. Kit very much agrees with Anika. He wasn't sure about her at first, as she can come across as odd. But Anika seems like one of the few people on this expedition who isn't blind to reason or other points of view. Kit is reminded of the conversation at dinner the night before. He was fascinated by Anika's explanation of the wolves in Iceland, only for Matt to shut it down and change the topic. "I'd rather stick with you from now on," Kit says. "And Mr. Burns."

Anika is glad to hear that. "We'll never ignore your opinion, or concern. If you have something to say, we'd like you to tell us."

Kit nods. "Thank you, that means a whole lot."

"Can the same be said about JJ?" Anika asks as casually as she can.

"Cause he doesn't talk? Yeah, don't worry about him, he's a no-nonsense kind of guy."

"How well do you know him?"

"Well," Kit says with a sigh. "I did carry him out of a firefight in Afghanistan."

"Oh, sorry, I didn't mean to imply..."

"No worries. It's understandable, a guy is too quiet and people start to wonder. But like I said, he's steady, he'll have your back. The only thing you might have to watch out for is his leg."

"What about his leg?" Anika asks.

"Prosthetic," Kit says. He then notices Anika's sudden

bewildered look. "Hard to tell, isn't it? His right leg is a prosthetic, just below the knee. Got torn off by a sniper round. It's why I had to carry him out. JJ's too proud, he won't tell anyone, let alone acknowledge that you noticed it. I'd rather you know now, and it's better if you don't mention it."

"Noted," Anika says.

The group stops at the front, Matt and Burns turn back to face everyone else. "This is it," Burns says. "This is as far as we ever followed."

They stand in an incredibly irregular part of the forest, the foliage substantially thicker and the terrain bumpy with burrowing tree roots. Burns takes off his rucksack and places it on the ground. He opens one of the zippers and pulls out a trail camera. The camera is about the size of a smartphone, except it's a little bulkier. Burns undoes the strap on the back of the camera, and then looks around the forest.

"What do you think? Hundred-yard radius?" Matt asks Burns.

"Give or take. Leave them here for the night, come back the next morning and check up on them," Burns adds.

"Next morning? You want to wait an entire 24 hours?" Matt asks.

"Would you like to come get these in the dark? *Out here*?" Burns presses.

Matt shakes his head. "Tomorrow morning sounds fine." Even Matt knows better than to meddle with the Tasmanian wilderness at night. Matt also takes off his small rucksack and begins to pull out his own trail cameras, as does Anika. Kit and the cameraman, Zeke, watch the three wildlife experts start to walk in separate directions. They each take the trail camera's elastic strap, and put it around the trunk of a tree, securing it with a heavy-duty Velcro strip. Kit gets closer to Anika and decides to follow her as she walks to another tree several yards away, a second trail camera in her hand.

"How do these work?" Kit asks her, curiously.

"They're motion activated," Anika replies as she fastens the second camera on another tree trunk. "It's got night vision too."

"Does it have like, live feed?"

"Up to a certain range, and we're well out of it out here. We have to come back and retrieve the SD card to see what it picked up. It's also battery-powered, so we have to watch out for that too."

Kit just nods, satisfied with the response. He follows Anika toward another tree, a third trail camera in her hands. Anika is talking as she walks. "Don't bother trying to use that air rifle too, that's if things get dangerous."

"Do the sedatives take too long to take effect?" Kit speculates.

"Even fast acting sedatives take about five to eight minutes," Anika says, "That, and an air rifle's range is only good for about fifty yards. You really want to be that close to the animal we're looking for?"

"No, I do not," Kit says. Kit turns his head slightly as he hears Matt speaking to the cameraman.

"Hold it here, Zeke, that's... right there," Matt says as the cameraman positions the camera close to Matt. Matt holds up one of the trail cameras, showing it to the potential audience. "These babies have always been my most trusted ally in all of my expeditions," Matt says. "Tactacam game cameras, long battery life, night vision-"

"What's he doing?" Kit asks Anika.

"Product placement," Anika mutters.

Kit scoffs.

"That should be good," Anika says. "Like Bill said, we'll come back tomorrow, we can head back now."

"That's it?" Kit asks.

"Yep, that's the gist of it."

"What do we do for the rest of the day?"

"For starters, we try not to get cabin fever," Anika says with a smirk.

"Ha," Kit says in a sarcastic tone. "You're hilarious."

Anika and Kit make their way back to meet with the others. Matt seems to have finished up his segment on trail cameras. Matt picks up his rucksack and puts it on his back. "Is that it?" Matt asks.

Anika just nods to him in response. She picks up her own rucksack but then looks around before putting it on. "Where's Bill?" she asks. They all look around. Burns is nowhere in sight. "Bill?" Anika calls out again.

Everyone rotated their gaze around; there is no response.

"For god's sake, Bill?!" Anika calls out, starting to panic.

Everyone looks around and behind trees, moving in the vicinity, calling for Burns. Anika loops around a tree and sees him standing a few feet away, motionless, still. Out of habit, Anika scans her surroundings, looking for any signs of danger. When bumping into a wild animal, the most common response among biologists was to stand still and remain quiet, so as not to startle the animal. Anika sees nothing around her, but Burns remains stationary where he's standing. He appears to be looking down at his feet. Anika slowly approaches him. She can hear him exhaling, his breath shaky, nervous. As she slowly gets closer to Burns, she can hear his fingers squeezing the elephant rifle in his hands.

This unsettles Anika even more. She's only a few inches away from Burns when she sees what he's looking at. The sight before her sends her blood rushing, and she's caught in the same trance as Burns. Shortly after, the rest of the group finds them both, and joins them in the stricken behavior.

On the damp, cold ground before them, is a footprint in the mud, as fresh as it can get, perfectly preserved and complete. Three toes, each a little over a foot in length, about five inches wide. From the top of the left toe and the top of the right toe, the footprint measures two feet wide. Three distinct circles hover over each toe, the circles eight centimeters in diameter.

Nobody talks; nobody dares to break the silence.

They all stare at the frightening print in the mud, wide but limber, heavy and detailed. It looks like a bird track, an enormous bird track. There's a long moment where no one says a word; no one has anything to say. While the moment persists for several seconds that feel like minutes, eventually, it's Kit who breaks the silence.

"Well," Kit says, "At least we know the video wasn't bullshit."

PHASE TWO

"The opposing apex species does not need higher population numbers or even faster reproductive rates. Instead, it simply needs to be more effective in not only eradicating the invasive species but doing so in a way that prevents it from being eradicated itself."

- Excerpts from *"The Apex Theory: An In-Depth Analysis of Apex Predators in Arbitrary Environments."*. Published in the *Journal of Wildlife Biology*, submitted by Dr. Anika Irving, PhD.

FISHER'S FUNDAMENTAL THEOREM

"Well it's definitely not a dromaeosaurid," Lucy says, her voice giddy as she examines the pictures of the footprint on Zeke's camera. "Three toes, each of them clawed and similar to one another. Dromaeosaurids usually have a curved claw on the inside toe."

Anika sat on the couch next to Burns, both of them still edgy after seeing the footprint in the mud. They had made their way back after seeing it, in complete silence, while Matt had argued why they had to leave. But to his dismay, he was outvoted to come back.

"Look at the details," Matt added. "You can see the kind of pattern its skin has, so fascinating, we really should have cast it."

"Not to mention the dimensions of it," Lucy says. "Look at the lengths of each toe."

Matt glanced over and saw Anika and Burns sitting on the couch, ever so silent, watching him and Lucy banter about the picture. "What's up with you guys? Ain't this incredible or what?" Matt asks.

"Not really, no," Kit says from the other side of the room. "I think the sheer size of the trackway has put the real weight of the situation into perspective."

"Weight of the situation? What the hell are you talking about?" Matt says.

"Lucy," Anika's voice is sharp. "If you were to estimate the body proportions to fit the size of the track?"

"Hmm. Well..." Lucy theorizes for a moment.

"Big enough," Burns says before letting Lucy give an estimate. "The track was as big as a juvenile elephant."

Matt scoffs. "I don't believe it, your balls really did drop off. You can't tell me you're scared?"

"The fact that you aren't just shows your naiveté. This is not some juvenile or small animal we are pursuing out there. Certainly not the same one we saw in the video," Burns says.

"Horseshit, we all knew the risk. That video is months old, ain't no way you didn't expect it to get bigger," Matt argues. "Even so, what's your plan now? Calling it quits a day into it? Jesus Christ, Bill, since when do you spook so easy?"

"Fuck off, Matt, this isn't some random episode on lions or goddamn crocodiles. I don't need Lucy or anyone to tell me that that fucking thing out there is huge, *and* we don't know a damn thing about it. And I'm not spooked, Matthew, I'm cautious. Cautious and very fucking sincere at the moment," Burns snaps.

Matt finds it painfully amusing. He sits down, smirking in disbelief, shaking his head. Anika recognizes the smirk all too well, so does Burns.

"Hey, Dad?" Anika says softly. Matt's smirk fades. He hasn't heard his daughter call him 'Dad' in years. When Anika sees that she has Matt's full attention, she lets him have it. "We don't give a shit about your show, or your fucking plans," Anika says sharply. "There's no amount of wild bullshit we are willing to put up with. It stops here."

"What?"

"We're calling you out. We are no longer putting up with your ignorance. There is real danger here, very real. And moving forward without addressing it will be nothing short of reckless," Burns says, his voice stern.

"Calling me out, huh? And what exactly am I doing here that you 'are done putting up with'?" Matt says, his words sound defeated. Anika struck him where it hurts by calling him *Dad* to get his attention.

"We almost went out there unarmed," Anika says.

"Almost? I seem to clearly remember Bill carrying a big ass elephant gun," Matt retorts.

"We had to outvote you to do that, *again*. That shouldn't be a goddamn requirement every time we go out. We should be able to bring whatever the hell we need to stay safe out there," Anika says.

"We have the dart guns too, with top shelf sedatives. Not to mention the two marines we brought along for security," Matt says.

"Lots of good we'll do if they get mauled because the sedatives took too long to take effect," Burns says. "We brought those guns to ensure safety, to have a chance to not only protect ourselves, but this project as well."

"We've all been around animals for years, hell, *decades*," Matt is more argumentative. "How many times did y'all go out armed with nothing other than bear spray? Whatever happens, we can handle it, they're just animals with basic animal instincts."

"There is nothing to indicate that these animals will behave in the same manner as anything we've seen before," Anika explains. "We know nothing about their instinctual behaviors or intelligence for that matter. All we do know without a doubt is that it is a predator, with never-before-studied hunting patterns. How could you possibly expect to predict their behavior in the field? There is only one reason you've been able to go out with your can of bear spray: you are working off the back of countless wildlife consultants and biologists who have studied those species' behaviors for years."

"Even so," Burns adds before Matt can interject. "Accidents happen all the time in the field. Knowing the behavior of an animal to a tee doesn't guarantee your safety."

"Jesus Christ," Matt is exasperated. His face says it all, frowning at the preposterous argument being made. Not only are they insulting his character, but everything he has ever learned over the years. "Even if we don't know everything about an animal, we can learn, can't we? We can learn to anticipate its behavior, that's what we're here for, to study it."

Burns shakes his head. "You're not getting the point, the issue is inexperience in this subject brings unpredictability, and poses a concern for safety."

Matt's demeanor is bullheaded. "We can prevent accidents, and we don't need-"

"Prevent accidents?" Anika snaps as loudly as she can. "This is exactly what you sounded like when Mom died. Fuck's sake, haven't changed a goddamn bit."

The room is more silent than before. The dark subject is better not interrupted. Matt has an astonished but disturbed look on his face. It's a subject he would've never brought up. "You, of all people talking about *preventing accidents*," Anika says, each word like a sharp knife. "How many times were you warned about that jaguar? By the local natives and the crew?"

Matt says nothing, but no one else dares to utter a word either. This is between Anika and Matt. "How many times were you warned?" Anika presses again; she's expecting an answer.

"They were just locals and crew-"

"One of those crew was *your wife*," Anika's voice is furious. "*She told you so* many times. She told me to stay away and to stay away from you. You know that's the last thing she ever said to me? *To stay away from you*, because you kept trying to have me on camera alongside you while we followed that fucking jaguar."

"Anika," Matt is stunned but needs to defend himself. "We've been around jaguars before, this one was no different."

"Oh, it was very different. And you knew it was too. We weren't following it, it was following us. The locals told us that three people had disappeared while strolling at night just days before. But no, you played it cool, *cool as the breeze*, like your goddamn motto," Anika says, her eyes intense. "You know, I often wonder what would've happened if I had listened to Mom and let you approach that thing by yourself."

"It was never supposed to happen, Anika. To this day, I don't understand why it happened. Predators sense fear, and I had none, so it had no reason to-"

"*Matthew,*" Burns finally interjects, his voice disappointed. "This belief is not mutual, you can't trust a predator just cause you think it knows you're not afraid of it. I mean, *Jesus*, Matthew, you're walking on the same path as Timothy Treadwell and you don't even see it."

"Leave *Treadwell* out of this," Matt says.

"He knew it too, you know," Anika says. "We all saw his last video entry before that bear killed him. His usual charm was gone, he knew something was up, and he foolishly decided to ignore his instinct. Just like you..."

Matt doesn't know what to say, or how else to defend himself.

"And then what came after," Anika starts. "You refused to hunt it down, and kill it. How'd you describe it? 'Freak accident'? Oh right, 'we can't hurt it, the animal is innocent'. Took a page out of Siegfried and Roy's, didn't you?"

"Is that why you've had this disdain toward me all these years? Because I didn't want any more bloodshed?" Matt asks.

Anika closes her eyes, trying to refrain from bursting into a yelling contest. Instead, she composes herself, and chooses her words as carefully as she can. "You wanted to keep the footage, that's why," Anika says through her teeth. "That's why I hate your fucking guts."

Matt says nothing.

"What?" Burns asks, turning his head toward Anika, but she doesn't look away from her father.

"He wanted to keep the footage," Anika replies to Burns. "Keep the episode with Mom's death, he was going to air it on TV."

Burns didn't know. He never knew. He turns his even more disappointed gaze to Matt. "What the fuck?" Burns mumbles, the undertone in his words echoing fury. "Tell me it isn't true."

Matt clears his throat, then decides to speak. "Our purpose was to teach the public what the job is like-"

"You wanted to air it. You wanted people to not only see her getting killed, but hear her *screams*," Anika says. "The same screams I hear every other night."

"Anika, what we need-"

Burns cuts off Matt again. "Matthew, you wanted to air the goddamn footage of Cassie *dying*?!"

Matt chooses to remain silent; his eyes have a hint of melancholy. Burns breathes in a heavy and angry breath. He stands up from the couch, hands on his hips. He's trying to remain composed, refraining from bursting out in fury like his body wants him to, which would only lower the group's morale.

"No more bullshit. Anybody here that is going to be heading out there with us can make up your own minds and decide," Burns says. "No one here has to go out there with him, much less unarmed. Don't feel pressured, nobody here wants to get hurt, so make the decision that doesn't."

The room is quiet, but they understand.

"Bill," Matt says. "I only want-"

Burns raises up his hand. "I don't want to hear it. As a matter of fact, stay away from me for the rest of our stay here."

Burns walks away from the living room.

Anika has stepped out onto the porch, in desperate need of fresh air. Doing her best to relieve the tension in her shoulders and arms. Christ, she could go for a drink right about now. She hears the front door open behind her, and Kit steps out and strolls toward her, his boots thumping on the hard wood porch. She doesn't mind Kit, but she wants some alone time. She doesn't bother to acknowledge his presence; she's hoping he'll get the message and leave her alone.

"Probably a dumb question, but are you alright?" Kit asks.

Anika shakes her head. "No need to worry, I'm used to his bullshit by now."

"Yeah, I noticed. I always got the vibe he kind of talked out of his ass."

Anika scoffs. "All the time."

"Yeah," Kit says. He takes a moment to work up the bravery to ask a question. "Did he really refuse to kill the jaguar?"

"Yes, he did. But don't worry, Bill told me a few years ago that Bill flew out there and killed the animal only a couple days after the incident."

"Mr. Burns killed it?"

"That he did. He's not about the bullshit, as you've noticed. Still though, to this day that's the only predator he's ever killed in his life."

"Hmm. That's heavy," Kit says. "I like Mr. Burns, I can tell he's stable."

"He's the only person I've trusted my whole life."

"Seems like you guys are pretty close," Kit says.

"I owe a lot to him. He practically raised me during a hard time in my life," Anika says, her words laced with a somber tone. "After my mother died, I didn't really want to be home. I was nine years old. I also didn't want to be anywhere near my dad or his show. I moved in with Bill and his wife, Addie. I was in shambles, and to tell you the truth, Bill and Addie were the reason I never went insane. I was so broken, and I could've easily fallen into drug addiction or something, like every other child star."

"That was kind of them, to take you in like that. Usually that's not how the story goes," Kit says.

"I was really lucky. Bill and Addie were everything I needed; they were so kind to me," Anika continues. "Bill was the realist, always asking me to be prudent and never compromise my character. Addie was so sweet with me. She was the dreamer, and told me to follow what my heart thought was important. So I did. I went back to school and learned what I wanted to learn. I went to a university and majored in wildlife studies and biology. I got my PhD and got hired by a university."

"You still liked animals, even after what happened?" Kit asks.

Anika sighs. "In the end, I did it for my mom. She was one of the best biologists I had ever known. Despite earning her fame on my dad's show, she never really cared for an audience. She just loved wildlife. Always told me to find the beauty in our world, because one day it would all be gone."

"So is that what you do now? Appreciate the beauty of our world?" Kit asks.

"Yes, to better understand how nature works as a whole."

"With wolves specifically?"

"I am studying wolves now, but they weren't specifically my focus. My specific focus was social systems in pack hunters. I was always fascinated by how animals behaved and communicated in their packs. How these social systems were different from each species depending on territory or mating systems. Lions, hyenas, wolves, wild dogs, coyotes, any predator with complex socialization."

Kit looks around the dark forest, pitch black, the porch lights only seem to illuminate a few hundred yards. "Can I ask you something?" Kit says.

"Sure."

"You know, all this talk about science and wildlife…"

"Is it giving you a headache yet?"

"No, god no. I find it all fascinating," Kit says. "I don't really keep up with any of this, so I get really curious. Last night, they mentioned you wrote a paper?"

"For a wildlife biology journal. The theory I explore is about why apex predators sometimes appear in different habitats. Call it 'The Apex Theory'."

"Could you… tell me about it?" Kit asks with a smile.

Anika takes a deep breath, fully ready to delve into another topic to ease her mind.

"It's a theory I realized while studying the timber wolves in Iceland," Anika explains. "Like you heard last night, timber wolves are not native to Iceland. Why they were there was anyone's guess. I took the assignment as another job, but it really intrigued me to the point where I could not wait to go back. See, not only was the Icelandic government especially alarmed about their appearance, but the locals as well. The livestock occupation makes up about eighty percent of Iceland's economy. So we assumed that the wolves would have eventually started to attack the cattle or sheep, which would cause problems to the agricultural economy. After months of monitoring them, it turns out the wolves were only specifically targeting the reindeer population. And interestingly enough, the livestock business was already struggling even before the wolves arrived; the local farmers were already losing cattle due to a shortage of grazing fields because of the reindeer."

"The reindeer? They were becoming invasive?" Kit crosses his arms, fascinated.

"The reindeer population had, for whatever reason, grown exponentially in the last four years. Once the wolves arrived, the reindeer population started to gradually decline, minimizing their invasive effect. Naturally, the Icelandic government and the locals were thrilled, but it begs the question: how did the wolves get there? Why were they there? They seemed to have shown up just in time before the reindeer destroyed their habitat. And believe me, I did my research, nobody on that entire continent had the means, or the funding to introduce these timber wolf species. And even if they did, you can't teach wolves to specifically target reindeer."

"So I started to theorize," Anika continues, "what if ecosystems find a unified way to deal with an invasive species? I mean sure, at the moment I have data for only one circumstance, but I have heard of it happening in other situations very recently. Just last year, I heard from an old colleague who had been keeping up with my research. They had encountered a very concerning species of locust in South America. This specific species had been causing severe economic and environmental issues. Only for a competing predator, in this case *hornets* not at all native to the continent, to begin to specifically target these locusts and thrive. These hornets didn't seem to touch any other sort of prey, to the layman it seemed to have it out for the locusts. I found it very intriguing, and eerily similar to my findings on the timber wolves. And just as I was formulating my possible theory, I met a biologist in passing at a conference the university had some time ago. They had explained that there were reported sightings of what looked like *hyenas in Texas*."

"Hyenas?" Kit asks, "That can't be."

"The university I work for has decided to send a team out there sometime next month," Anika says. "These supposed hyenas are only targeting the feral hogs out there, and again, the hogs have become invasive."

Kit takes a breath, taking it all in. "I'm seeing a pattern here," he says.

"Exactly, my question is: is it a new phenomenon?" Anika says. "Or has it been happening for quite some time? Arguments or counterpoints for each possibility are as plausible as the last. If it's new, what's there to prove that it hasn't happened in the past? After I published my paper, I was in Nairobi, accompanying some colleagues when I ran into a game warden named Forsing. He was an old friend of my mother, and he had read my paper. He genuinely believed my theory to be newly discovered but not a completely new process. His family lineage traced back as far as the 1800s in east Africa. Some of his older ancestors were witnesses to the 'maneaters of Tsavo' incident. Are you familiar with this?"

"Is that the movie with Val Kilmer and Michael Douglas?"

Anika smiles. "Yes, interestingly enough, that is one of the few movies that is mostly accurate to the events it's portraying. Anyways, two lions were targeting the workers in Tsavo as they attempted to extend the railway and build a bridge over a river. This happened for almost a year; people died or disappeared every other night. The workers believed they were ghosts of medicine men who came back to punish them. The British government just believed that they were only 'maneaters', predators that have learned that humans are significantly easier prey. But this game warden told me his ancestors had been living in east Africa for some time even before they attempted to extend the railway. They had witnessed the extent of the habitat fragmentation as the railroad expanded. Forsing's ancestors believed the lions were attempting to bring back balance in some ingenious and malicious way."

"What do you believe?" Kit asks, absorbed in the topic. "You said it yourself, there are valid reasons to believe one side of an argument or the other."

Anika looks at him, and she shrugs. "My theory is based on patterns, that's all I really did. I just recognized the patterns that were similar in each case, and created my theory around that. You know, before my mom passed away, she was starting to teach me these little sayings she found interesting. Eponymous laws, like Murphy's law or Occam's razor. She gifted me a book on all of them for one of my birthdays. When I was looking at these patterns in these different but somehow similar ecosystems, I applied Gall's law. 'A complex system that works is consistently found to have evolved from a simple system that worked'. A simple system, or rather, a *simple process*, because what do you do when an invasive species is ruining the balance of an ecosystem?"

Kit is attentive.

"You bring about a competing species, a species that can easily dwindle the numbers of the invasive species without needing the higher population. What better than an apex predator? A predator with no predators of their own, a species at the top of their trophic level?"

"You think ecosystems are doing this on their own?" Kit asks. "Nature just… picks a predator?"

"Simple, but ingenious. And to answer your question from before, I do believe that is what is occurring. And to contradict the argument as to why it hasn't happened before, think of this: when most think of evolution, they think of individual species adapting to new environments or conditions to survive. Changing their behaviors and even their basic structure to better adhere and survive. But what about nature as a whole?"

Kit bobs his head.

"Nature, not in the general sense of individual species, but as a whole network of ecosystems working together. Could nature evolve its own techniques for survival? If we think of nature as a unified entity, it all makes more sense. It is evolving, discovering new ways to deal with problems on its own."

"How could that be possible? How could it be smart enough to do that?" Kit asks.

"Not smart, no. Orgel's second rule," Anika says. "The process of natural selection is not itself intelligent, but that the products of evolution are ingenious."

"That's... a lot. A whole lot to take into consideration," Kit says. "Now I really wish I brought my cigarettes."

"I've been thinking about this for so long now, it's a part of my life," Anika says. "No matter how many people dispel my theory, I really think there's some weight to it."

"So why are you here? Not to overstep, but it seems like this situation is hurtful to your mental health. Being around this again, it looks like it affects you a great deal."

"Kit, I'm going to take a gamble that you're one of the good ones on this expedition. So I'm going to tell you something I haven't told anyone just yet."

Kit's face is sincere; he feels nothing other than pure support for Anika.

"Valente asked me to come along for a chance at genuine scientific discovery, and I agreed. Bill asked me to keep an eye on my dad while on this expedition, and I agreed. But none of those were my true intentions, not really. To be honest, I knew I had to come the moment Valente showed me the footage," Anika says, her face sullen. Anika turns to Kit and looks him in the eyes.

"What we are looking for out here, is the most dangerous and distinct predator no human has ever seen."

There is nothing but silence from Kit.

"We talked about it yesterday, how they could have survived, how and why no one has seen one until now," Anika says. "I have an alternative theory."

"You think nature put them here."

Anika nods. She takes a moment before continuing the conversation, trying to figure out a way to explain it to Kit. "You know, there are over a hundred different species of animals on this island," Anika says. "Yet, none of them are capable of competing with this predator at their own trophic level."

"Trophic level? I'm not familiar with the term," Kit asks.

"The position of an animal in the food chain. What I'm saying is that no other species on this island is capable of competing with this predator. All the animals on this island are quite small, the tallest could be a cassowary, an emu, about two or three feet tall. So if my theory is to be believed, who would this apex predator be in response to?"

Kit knows, but he's not saying it out loud.

"They're here for us, humans." Anika says. "It's the simplest answer, and the one that makes the most sense. Because a track of that size, *a predator* of that size, does not and cannot sustain its existence solely on the prey native to Tasmania."

Kit sighs through his nose. "Fuck me."

"It's just a theory."

"I know, but it makes sense to me," Kit says. "If you're right, then what do we do?"

"Hope that I'm wrong."

"I mean, realistically, what should we do?"

"What every other species does to survive against a predator," Anika says. "Run and hide, or kill it before it kills you."

"Wouldn't the smart thing be to just leave?"

"It would, but I guess my one flaw right now is that I have to see this for myself, a chance to prove my theory, and to see why these dinosaurs are here in the first place," Anika says.

Kit thinks to himself for a moment. He then shakes his head. "Hold on a second, your theory suggests that nature somehow brings apex predators in response to an invasive species. That's the gist of it, right?"

"Yes."

"And you have a different theory as to why these dinosaurs are here, on this island. Your theory suggests that the reason no one has seen one until now, is because nature put the dinosaurs here."

"Correct."

"Nature's response to an invasive species, possibly humans."

Anika nods.

Kit frowns. "Well then, what's going on here that would warrant that kind of response?"

Anika shrugs. "I don't know. This is my first time here in Tasmania in years. I wouldn't know."

"Hmm, well," Kit considers some more. "No offense, but I hope you're wrong. I hope they've just been in a 'lost world' all this time."

"I do, too."

"Well then, good talk, I probably won't sleep."

"Sorry."

"Don't worry about it. I'm going to head inside, all this talk is making me reconsider my 'fresh air' breaks. You coming?"

"I'll be inside soon," Anika says. "Need a bit more time to cool off."

"Right, don't... uh... don't stay out here too long. For safety."

Anika nods, and Kit gives Anika a friendly pat on the back, and turns around, strolling toward the front door. Kit opened the doors and stepped inside. Anika heard the door close shut behind her. All she could hear now was the muffled conversations from inside the lodge and her own breathing. The forest trees swayed back and forth, the gusts of wind starting to settle for the night. Anika sighed, staring out at the dark, unconquered wilderness before her, wondering to herself why she didn't just leave. Kit was right. The logical thing would be to leave this island and never come back. But she couldn't, Anika had to see; she had to know what the truth was.

Eventually, Anika decided to call it night, and stepped inside the lodge.

CAUSE & EFFECT

"Ani, look up."

Anika looks up from the journal in her lap. There was a worn-out pencil in her hand, her drawing of a small elephant only halfway done. She was sitting in a Range Rover, the rover sitting on a hill overlooking the African savannah. As Anika looked up, the sun glared in her face. She held her hand up to block the sunlight, only for a shadow to block the sun for her instead. Cassandra Irving was standing on her front seat, leaning against the caged canopy of the roofless rover.

"Mom?" Anika asks.

"Look at the way Hekima is moving, tell me what you see," Cassandra says.

Anika turned her head. She looked out of her back passenger window. In the distance, lumbering along the Serengeti, was an elephant. Tall, bulky, with tusks on the edges of its mouth, it's a female elephant. Her giant ears flopping back and forth as she walked, the sign of a content pachyderm.

"She's walking slow?" Anika asks.

"Slower than usual. Tell me why."

Anika looked at the cow elephant again, examining it intensely. As the elephant moved, Anika noticed its pace, its eyes leveled at the horizon. It was walking slow, cautious but somehow weighted. Weighted, like it was carrying additional weight it wasn't used to. The elephant slowly moved its head from right to left, watching its surroundings closely. Anika recognized the behavior. She then quickly examined the animal's belly. The belly is drooping and round, more so than usual.

"Wow," Anika says, her eyes lighting up. "Is Hekima pregnant?"

"*Que niña tan lista*," Cassandra mumbles with a smile. "Smart girl, yes, she is pregnant. I noticed it yesterday."

Anika watches the pachyderm lumber along, its content ears now seeming happier than before. "She looks happy," Anika adds.

"Because she is. This would be her first calf in almost a decade."

"Dec- decade?" Anika stammers.

"Ten years, Ani."

"Oh," Anika says. "Why did she take so long?"

"She had a calf once, just before I met your dad," Cassandra says, her tone suddenly grim. "She lost it to a crocodile. They were crossing the marshes and the calf stumbled."

"Oh no."

"*Pobrecita*," Cassandra says. "She was so sad for a long time. I really thought she would die of a broken heart. But she didn't; she made it through a tough time. And now she's here, pregnant again. It's why she looks so happy. It's also why she's walking so slow."

"She's being careful."

"Good, Ani, good. Yes, she's being very careful," Cassandra says. "It's why we're not as close as we usually are. It's why she charged at Alec and Warsami's rover yesterday. She's very protective right now."

"She's scared of losing another baby," Anika adds.

"Yes," Cassandra says. "Remember this, Ani, animals are always the most dangerous when they're protecting their babies."

Anika smiles at her mom. "Even you?" she asks.

"Yes, Ani," Cassandra replies as she watches the elephant walk and then trumpet. "Even me."

Anika jolts awake once more, this time in the small bed of her room at the lodge. She took deep breaths as she blinked, trying to adjust her sight to the dark room. The room wasn't completely dark; the dim sunlight of dawn creeped in through the curtains over the window. Anika stretched in her bed, her bones quietly cracking. She felt the back of her t-shirt damp with sweat.

She sighed and then sat up in bed. She stretched her back as she reached forward as far as she could, her fingertips moving past her toes. She felt her back slowly release the tension she acquired over her vivid dream.

What's unusual is the type of dreams she's been having. It was another pleasant one, a good memory of her mother. Usually, every other night was a nightmare of some sort. Either sounds, like screams, or flashes of traumatic images. Her mother's terrified eyes staring up into the sky as she was dying from the jaguar attack. Her father's hands keeping pressure on her mother's neck, the blood trickling through his fingers and soaking his skin.

Anika shook the thought away. No need to remind herself of her hideous nightmares. She would take the win. At least these new dreams were fond memories.

Anika swung her legs around the bed, placing her feet on

the cold wooden floor. She yawned and then glanced over at Burns's bed. It was empty. Anika glanced at her watch, 6:53 a.m. Burns had always been an early riser, which he tried to teach Anika when she was living in his home. It worked in its own way. Anika always seemed to wake up before her alarm in the morning. Although most of the time, Anika found it quite irritating, especially when she didn't get enough sleep to begin with.

Anika slid out her hiking boots from under her bed. She slipped them on and then stood up. On her way out of her room, she grabbed her jacket sitting on the office chair. She put on the jacket as she walked down the steps of the staircase. She could hear Burns's voice; it was stern like always. He seemed intrigued by something. As Anika turned the corner, she saw Matt standing next to Burns, both of them intently examining one of the laptops.

"You're awake, I was about to come get you," Burns says.

"What's going on?" Anika asks.

"Something really weird, none of us have a clue what we're looking at," Matt says.

Burns sighs. "I went out a couple hours ago."

"By yourself?" Anika asks.

"No, not to where we left our trail cameras yesterday. I went back to Wiley's place," Burns says.

"For what?"

"Try my luck again, I guess. I took another look with JJ, and we found these," Burns says, pointing to three trail cameras sitting on the desk next to the laptop. Anika leans forward and examines the trail cameras. They're a different brand than the ones they brought. They look grimy and corroded, which means they have been out in the elements for some time. Anika picks up one of them. She opens the outer protective cover, only to find a single piece of masking tape on the inside under the lens. The masking tape has a name scribbled in sharpie: *N. Gagnon.*

"Who's N. Gagnon?" Anika asks.

"No clue," Burns says.

"Did they catch anything?" Anika asks.

"That's what we're looking at." Burns ushers her to take a look at the laptop screen. It's a single image of a cassowary, with a gray play button icon directly on top of it. *Wait, a cassowary?*

"A cassowary? In Tasmania?" Anika asks.

"That's not even the weirdest part," Burns says. He presses the play icon over the image.

The video starts playing. A cassowary, four feet tall, a terrifying bird of prey that normally walks with an aura of unpredictability. But it's not walking. It's limping, its left leg deformed at the foot. Its clawed talons are bloated, and its skin brittle. The emu's normally feathered body now has almost bare patches of skin, with tiny featherless shafts. Its left wing is drooping, the bones visible against the skin of the frail body. The camera lens follows the cassowary in a panoramic shot until it goes out of frame and is caught by a different trail camera. Burns plays another video. The cassowary then suddenly wails as it walks past the camera. The skin under its eyes is drooping, making it seem like the bird has suffered a stroke.

The cameras continue to capture the bird. It wails again, struggling to walk. The cassowary eventually disappears into the foliage of the forest. The video footage comes to a halt.

Burns then rewinds the footage and pauses it on the clearest frame of the emu.

"What happened to it?" Anika asks, her voice soft.

"I don't know," Burns responds. "I've seen all kinds of sicknesses or reactions to chemicals in animals. I have never seen anything like that."

"Is there any more footage?" Anika asks.

"No."

"What happened then?" she mumbles. "What is a cassowary doing all the way out here?"

Anika stares blankly for a second. Burns shakes his head. "This is getting weirder by the second. I'm starting to think we shouldn't even go out," Burns says.

"Now hold on just a minute-" Matt says.

"It looked like it was having a reaction, or an illness," Burns says. "Don't be stupid, Matt, you've seen sick animals before. Have you ever seen an animal like that?"

Matt shakes his head again. "Well..."

"We should be more careful."

"In what sense?"

"Cassowaries aren't native to Tasmania," Anika says. "And, come to think of it, have you seen any other wildlife at all?"

Burns and Matt finally realize.

"I've been to Tasmania a total of three times, the only things I remember are the disparity of the species here," she says. "Something is wrong, very wrong. These animals we are looking for could be having some kind of effect on the habitat."

"Effect?" Matt challenges. "The theory is that they've been here the whole time."

"Have they? And tell me how the cassowaries got here too."

"Here we go again-"

"Quiet, take the evidence without theorizing," Burns says. "The emu is not okay, something is clearly wrong. We have to accept the fact there may be other risks."

"Then what would be the precautions?" Matt asks.

"Quick trips, no leaving the lodge for unnecessary tasks," Burns says.

Matt gasps. He waves his hands and walks away. Burns turns to Anika, his eyes gleaming with concern. "You don't have to go out today if you don't want to," he says to her.

"I don't want to," Anika says. "But I have to do my fair share of work, so I'll go out. It'll be quick, no unnecessary tasks."

Burns looks at her again, like a father sending his child out to war. *"Be careful,"* Burns says. "Any problems, you come right back."

Anika nods and walks away to grab her gear. While she prepares along with JJ and Zeke the cameraman, she feels a new sense of dread coupled with morbid curiosity. What was going on with the emu? Why was it deformed? Anika has her own theory as to why, but she will keep it to herself for now. Her theory might be hard to prove, but that's her new mission.

To find out exactly what these dinosaurs mean to Tasmania.

WILDERNESS

Anika was dredging along through the wilds of Tasmania. All she could wonder while hiking through the compressed vegetation was if her theory about apex species was correct. The footage of the emu had left her shocked, and it had left her contemplating the reason for the animal's deformities. Was there in fact something lurking here that did not exist before? Were these animals indeed not part of the ecosystem and were now having an effect? Had they been put here just as her theory had predicted? She did not know the correct answer; all that she knew is that she felt even more unsure than before.

And she wasn't just talking about the dinosaurs. She's also surprised to see Cassowaries in Tasmania. Where did they come from? Is anyone aware of them? Has anyone reported their existence? The fact that they found a trail camera brings up more questions. Were the trail cameras for the purpose of studying the Cassowaries, or the undiscovered prehistoric animals? Who is 'N. Gagnon'? Anika will make sure to find this person the first chance she gets. Because as of right now, there are two non-native species living in these woods, and her Apex Theory is all she can think of.

But what can she do? Even if she was right, what could the rest of the group do if they believed her? Her theory explores the possibility that animals at the top of their food chain are placed in parts of the world for the sole purpose of eradicating an invasive species. If her theory was correct, who's the invasive species in this scenario? Nothing comforted her, not even the thought that someone as solid as Burns had her back. Not even the acknowledging nod that Kit had given her right as she finished watching the footage of the emu. Still, what does it matter? She was out here, and she had to accept her situation and adapt to it.

As she walked past a tree, she noticed that JJ was walking right beside her. He wasn't in line anymore with Zeke right behind him. She turned to JJ with weary eyes to ask him a question. "What do you think of all this?" Anika asks. "I haven't really had any time to ask you anything since we started the expedition."

JJ didn't look away from where he was walking but he did answer the question in a very straightforward style. "Well," he says. "It's certainly not Afghanistan, and it's certainly not Iraq, but I could get used to it. I like the outdoors. I don't like being cooped up inside. Especially with all those film crew who won't stop talking."

Anika smiled. Well, at least there was one similarity between her and JJ. "You know, I like to address things as they come to me," Anika says. "You don't really talk much, and I don't mind it. I really don't. But whenever I'm on an expedition, I like to know all of the points of view in the room, especially from the quiet ones."

Again, without looking away from where he was going, JJ responded. "I think the idea of discovering something extinct is exhilarating to a lot of people, but not to me. The only reason I agreed to do this was because I wanted to feel like I was at war again."

Anika's smile faded for a second. She tilts her head just slightly so that she could see JJ's face. JJ noticed Anika's sudden shift; he noticed that she wasn't quite comfortable all of a sudden with his comment, and how bad it can seem to say that you wanted to be 'at war'.

"Look," JJ says. "I'm not some PTSD whack job, okay? I'm not looking for some kind of thrill-seeking adventure or whatever the fuck you think. I just don't like being inside. I don't like sitting in an office. I don't like sitting in a booth. I like to be outside moving around with a rifle in my hands feeling like I'm doing something."

"I understand, I could never work in an office either."

"Still though," JJ says. "I know it's a crazy thing to say out loud. But I like your attitude, so I'm hoping that you will keep this to yourself. I'm not a very open person to begin with, but I know that you are of good character, and I appreciate your honesty with me."

Anika turns a corner around a tree. She almost slips but JJ catches her by the arm. He gives her a nod. "Thank you," Anika says, "and don't worry, your secret is safe with me."

"It's not a secret," JJ says. "It's just a trait, is all. It doesn't make me as a whole. I just want you to understand my motivations."

"Well not to worry," Anika says. "I'm only here to prove my own research paper correct, or incorrect for that matter. And to be honest with you, I really hope it's incorrect."

JJ smirks for the first time in the entire trip here, his face changing from its usual baseline behavior. "You know, your dad, the other day, he kind of interrupted you," JJ says. "You did mention something about some paper that you wrote, give me the cliff notes of it just so I understand why you're out here."

"It's about apex species," Anika says. "You understand the basic structure of the wildlife right?"

"Yes, I understand the basics, for God's sake. I went the

fucking school," JJ says.

"All right, all right. I'll stop treating you like a child," Anika says. "I believe that sometimes nature will pick an apex predator, and put them into an ecosystem where an invasive species is destroying it."

JJ frowns. "An apex species?" JJ clears his throat. "You think nature just picks a random fucking predator, to do what? To deal with an invasive species?"

"Not random, no," Anika says. "I think it picks a specific species, a likely contender, suited enough to properly deal with the invasive species. That's as simple as it can get. Obviously my paper makes it seem more complex but that's the basic gist of it."

"Well, why didn't you just say that when your dad interrupted you the other night?" JJ says. "You know, to give us some context."

"Because you don't just interrupt my dad," Anika says. "He loves having a challenging personality. He won't just let things go. He would have argued with me and kept shutting me down."

"You really should set some boundaries," JJ says.

"Oh yeah, *boundaries*, definitely would have never thought to do that," Anika says. "I've tried, believe me. I've tried but the case is he'll never listen. That's what he does, he only ever listens to himself. He loves the sound of his voice and he'll never give that up. What else do you expect from a celebrity?"

JJ is about to answer Anika's question when they hear Zeke from behind them shuffle forward quickly to join in on the conversation. "He's a celebrity with two decades worth of experience," Zeke says. "Have a little respect for a legend."

Anika snorts a laugh. "*Legend*? Is that how you would describe him? He's basically a cult leader with a nature show. He'll never listen to anybody else's input. Not even to save a life. I remember you, Zeke, you've been with my dad's production team for a long time, but you weren't there when my mom died. If you had seen the way he had acted before the accident, you would have never stuck around with him this long."

Zeke just chuckles. "Man, you are as snarky as your father says you were."

Anika wants to retort. She wants to argue with him. She wants to argue with Zeke, the fucking cameraman, but JJ interrupts. "You know, we were having a private conversation. I don't exactly remember inviting you to join in," JJ snaps.

"I work for the man," Zeke says. "I'm not just going to let you berate him while I'm standing in front of you."

"Behind us," JJ says. "You were standing behind us."

"Don't be such a fucking child," Zeke says. "Have some respect for the man. He might make you famous."

"Famous?" JJ says suddenly. "Do you really think being famous is all it's cracked up to be?"

JJ stops walking. He turns around swiftly to face Zeke. He wants him to see the sudden anger in his eyes. "You know, I had my fifteen seconds of fame," JJ says. "It happened when I walked back through that fucking airport, after I came back from deployment. After I returned without my fucking leg. I listened to all the claps, that goddamn useless applause. All the hooting and hollering from everybody in that airport. Let me tell you it's nothing special, you feel nothing but hollow."

Zeke just stares blankly, not knowing what to say. Zeke only then takes a quick glance at the rifle in JJ's hands, and decides it's best not to antagonize the marine with a gun. Especially after his remark of wanting to be 'at war' again. And especially after Zeke locks eyes with JJ and notices he does not lose the intensity in his gaze.

Anika notices JJ is going to continue to stare at Zeke until he responds, but Zeke isn't going to respond. How can he? What can he say? Anika knows she has to cut off the conversation, so they can get back to the case in point, to the mission. She pats JJ on the shoulder. "We really should get going. We don't want to lose daylight and we don't want to get stuck out here at night. Let's just go do what we were going to do, set up the cameras and head back to base. I don't want to be out here and run into something."

Without looking away from Zeke, JJ just nods, then turns around and walks in the same direction that they were walking before. Zeke wants comfort, but he gets none from Anika. She just looks away, and she continues to walk into the forest right behind JJ.

"All right," Anika says. "I think this is far enough, we're only about two miles ahead from where we were yesterday. This should be a good spot to set up our new trail cameras. We'll double back and pick up the ones from last night on our way back."

Anika kneeled down. She took off her backpack and pulled out a couple of trail cameras. JJ did the same. He slung the rifle over his shoulder and he pulled out three trail cameras. Zeke just gawked vacantly at both of them, holding the camera in his hand, unsure of what to do in the moment.

"Are you going to help? Or are you just going to stand there like a fucking idiot?" JJ asks.

JJ is a very aggressive human being, but not without reason. He opened himself to be vulnerable to Anika, so that she can understand his motivations, so that she can trust him. But instead of leaving them alone and respecting his privacy, Zeke decided to jump in and give his own opinion. Which made JJ upset, and turned Zeke into his enemy for the time being. Anika has seen this behavior before. Burns used to do the same thing, but Burns is a bit more subtle. He would just stop talking to you. He would never outwardly challenge you just like JJ just did.

"Let's just get this over with," Anika says. "We have quite a hike back and I really want to take a shower."

JJ stands up. "Fine. Where do I put these cameras, just any tree?"

"Yeah, just any tree," Anika says. "Just make sure they're evenly spread out. You don't want them too close to each other, you want to cover a good section of the forest."

JJ nodded. He left his backpack where it was sitting on the floor, and he walked around the foliage holding the three trail cameras in his hands. He picked his first tree and he put it on, then he picked a second and a third. Anika did the same with both of her cameras, until all the cameras were spread evenly out in a hundred-yard radius. JJ picked up his backpack off the damp ground.

"I guess that's it then, huh? There's not much to it?" JJ asks.

"That's about ninety percent of wildlife biology," Anika says. "You just kind of set up bullshit cameras, and then just sit and wait for the rest of the day."

"So how do you all pick the spots to put up these cameras? Just at random?" JJ asks.

"Normally, no," Anika replies. "We usually put them up

where we know the animal spends its time. Close to its den, or a game trail, or even breeding grounds. In this case however..."

"We don't know a damn thing about these animals," JJ says.

"Exactly."

"At least I got a good workout in for my calf," JJ says. "And my quad, or *quads*, sorry. I keep forgetting I'm only missing one calf."

Anika can't help but chuckle. JJ chuckles too. And again, it's the first time she sees JJ be something else other than stoic. "All right, let's head back now, I don't like being out here," Anika says.

"Why don't you like being out here?" JJ asks. "I think it's a nice enough forest."

"It's just really dense. I like to see where I'm going," Anika says. "It's a nice forest, but stand long enough out here, and you'll feel cooped up. Plus, you know, there's a fucking dinosaur around here somewhere."

"Hey, were you serious about the emu? Do you really think the dinosaur had some effect on it and that's why it was fucked up like that?" JJ asks.

"I don't know what to think," Anika says. "I just know that it's not a good idea to be out here for too long, otherwise we're going to find out real fast what the effects really are."

"You know, after what you just told me about your apex conundrum, I would have a different guess to what happened to that bird," JJ says.

"Oh?" Anika says, bewildered.

JJ snorts. "You're a scientist. You really didn't even think of it, did you?"

"Think of what?"

JJ smiles and shrugs at the same time. "Your theory, does it ever explore how the animals get there? The apex ones?"

"No."

"So you just assumed they magically appeared out of thin air?" JJ asks.

"No, I didn't. I assumed a kind of forced migration," Anika says.

"Maybe, who knows? Or maybe... They did what every other animal has done since the beginning of time. They evol-"

"Holy shit! Guys!" they hear Zeke yell out.

Both Anika and JJ turn their heads, searching for Zeke and where his voice is coming from. They see him about a few hundred yards away from them both. He's facing away, looking behind some bushes, pointing his camera frantically trying to get a good shot of something. "Oh shit," JJ says, quickly grabbing his rifle from his shoulder and holding it in his hands firmly. "Zeke, don't fuck around, don't go anywhere without us. I'm here for your protection," JJ snaps.

"Come look," Zeke says. "For god's sake, just come look."

Both Anika and JJ hurry over to Zeke's position. When they reach him, they stand behind him and both peek over his shoulders, looking at what Zeke is looking at. In a small clearing surrounded by vegetation, are two distinct mounds of dirt. Buried in the dirt mounds, there are multiple elongated, oval white shapes. They're protruding out of the dirt mounds, some of them broken, shattered.

"Holy shit," JJ says. "Is this what I think it is?"

Anika doesn't look away. She knows the answer. She feels her heart beating out of her chest. "Yeah," she says. "I think it's a dinosaur nest."

ORGEL'S FIRST RULE

The cargo hold opens just as the hangar crew puts chocks under the wheels of the giant Dreamlifter. The sunlight finally glared through as the cargo hold door touched the concrete, creating a ramp for its passengers. Ward and Valente sat next to each other. They've been sitting in these small and unpleasant seats for almost twenty hours. The cargo freighter was not luxurious in any way. They're mostly used for military applications. The seats were rigid and nonadjustable, sitting at a 90-degree angle with thick straps to use as seatbelts. Valentewas uncomfortable the entire time, but not Ward. As a matter of fact, he slept the entire time. Valente often looked over to his friend as he sat slouched and snored for the entire flight. Valente didn't dare wake him; he knows Ward has been working hard these past few days.

Valente unbuckled his seat belt and stood up. He stretched his arms and legs, feeling relieved. Valente reached down to the seat next to him and picked up his jacket. He slipped it on, a green BAERSkin waterproof jacket with a purple Valtech logo on the breast pocket. He then decided to give Ward a friendly kick to his boot. Ward stopped snoring and slowly looked up at Valente.

"We're here," Valente said to him.

Ward looked around with his tired eyes, blinking to get used to the sunlight. "Already?" Ward said with a yawn.

"You're right, it's only been eighteen hours," Valente responded.

Ward unbuckled his own seatbelt and finally stood up, his back cracking as he stretched. Ward was wearing his trucker hat, black jean jacket, and tan cargo pants. He looked around, getting acquainted with the cargo freighter.

"Come on, help me with these straps," Valente said. Valente moved toward the back of the cargo plane, his leather work boots squidging on the steel floor. On the front end closer to the cockpit, there's an olive-green Toyota 4Runner strapped down to the floor. All-terrain tires, thick brush guards, a roof rack with rear-window exterior storage, and a bright red Fuel Pax was attached to one side of the Toyota. Valente started to remove the straps that were snug around the tires.

"Easy with the strap buckles. I don't want to chip the paint," Ward said to Valente.

"I'm not going to scratch your truck, Lee."

Ward followed. He helped remove the straps from his SUV. When they finished, they both stepped inside the Toyota. Ward slid the key into the ignition and turned it. The Toyota roared to life, then Ward drove the vehicle forward slowly out of the cargo plane. The gloomy day in southern Tasmania makes its presence known, as some rain is already starting to sprinkle.

"Were you able to reach them?" Ward asks.

"I called one of the ranger stations before we left and asked them to transmit a message to them," Valente replied.

"Do you know if they got a response? Did they acknowledge?"

"I don't know. I can call the ranger station again later today."

Ward shook his head. "I can't believe we can't reach them directly."

"They're miles into the national park. The radio dish you

installed on the roof can only reach the ranger stations, and it depends on the weather. Which I'm hoping doesn't get any worse," Valente said as he leaned forward, looking at the clouds.

"We really sent them out there with nothing, didn't we? A lot of good those air rifles are going to do in the wild with those man-killers."

"They're not completely defenseless," Valente says.

"What do you mean?"

"Bill ordered rifles, I think three of them."

"What kind of rifles?"

"Hunting rifles, elephant guns as far as I know. I was skeptical about buying them but it seemed to give Bill peace of mind."

"Do they have those with them now?"

"As far as I know."

"Good," Ward says, his words softer with relief. "At least someone's thinking ahead."

"We planned this as best as we could, Lee. We planned for every contingency."

Ward drives around the airport hangars, following the arrows on the pavement leading to the exit. "Did you ever plan for them to be hostile?" Ward asks.

"We planned for them to be predators, carnivores."

"A man-killer is much more different than a regular carnivore, Forrest. Even I know that."

"I don't believe it's ever the animal's fault. When they resort to killing humans, it's usually because the humans were pushing into their territory," Valente says.

Ward waves his finger at Valente. "Either way, the point still stands. They are *man-killers*. You think I wasn't paying attention when we took that safari in Tanzania? The guide told us that once a predator has a taste for human flesh, once they see how easy it is to hunt a human, there's no turning back."

"And what do you suggest we do? Let them kill the animals? They are the greatest scientific discovery in the last century."

"Leave it to someone else," Ward scorns. "They may be a great discovery, but you don't have to be involved. Take it from me, Forrest, sometimes it's best to not have been involved in the first place."

"What the hell do you mean 'don't get involved'?"

Ward swings his head around. "Because when things go to shit, the last place you'll want to be is in the middle of it, with your name smeared all over it," Ward hisses. "And the only goddamn reason I'm here is because you don't have the sense to watch your own back."

"Why do you think I'm here if not to watch my own back?"

"I don't think you're here for the right reasons."

"Oh please, enlighten me, Lee. Tell me what the fuck I'm doing here."

"You're protecting your investment."

Valente scoffs. "Bullshit, Lee."

"Not quite. You're here to see what your dad's up to. You're worried he's going to jeopardize the biggest investment of your life," Ward says bluntly. "You're doing a lot of things but not necessarily for the right reasons."

Ward stops the Toyota at a large chain-link gate. He waves at the man in the security booth adjacent to the gate. The man in the booth opens the gate. Ward keeps the truck idle as the gate slowly opens.

"Right reasons? You don't think I have good intentions?" Valente asks.

"No, no, the opposite," Ward replies. He drives the vehicle past the gate after it opens, and then pulls over to the side of the road before continuing on. "I'm sure you have good intentions, but ultimately, you are not doing this for the right reasons. I mean, think about it with the information you were given. Your father is suing you and the first thing you do is fly down here to see what he's up to. What about the expedition team? I mean, hell, provided with the information that these animals have already killed people, the sensible thing to do was to pull them out immediately. But you didn't, you're confident that they have what they need and they can deal with it. Or let's go farther back to when you were first introduced to the animal in the footage. Sure, the goal of the expedition is to protect these animals, but that wasn't your first thought, was it? Your first thought was to strike up a deal with the Animal Planet exec's before moving on to the expedition phase."

Valente is silent.

"If you really cared about the animal's wellbeing, wouldn't it make more sense that you document the proper evidence without showing it to the world?" Ward explains. "Instead, here you are, hiring the biggest nature TV star and sending him out to somehow glorify your achievement. You want your name all over it. You want Valtech all over the news and history books. For the same reason you stamped the damn logo on your shirts, jackets, cars, and planes. You're a capitalist; you want everyone to see what you've done with a hefty price tag."

Valente shakes his head. "How long have you been practicing that spiel?"

"*Fuck's sake,*" Ward mumbles. "Moral of the story: stop cutting corners and face the reality of your goals. And for fuck's sake, try doing something for once that in some way doesn't benefit you."

Valente shakes his head in defiance at his friend's advice. Ward points at the road in front of them.

"Where to?" Ward asks.

"Dr. Hogan."

Ward scoffs. "Shouldn't we check up on the group first?"

"They'll get the message, Lee."

Ward's advice seems to have fallen on deaf ears. Ward chooses not to say anything anymore. Valente is clearly a brick wall in this conversation. Valente pulls up the GPS on his phone.

"The website said the coroner's office is located inside the magistrate court," Valente says.

Ward sighs bitterly. He pulls the Toyota forward and turns left at the main road. He followed the GPS in Valente's hand for a while. The city of Hobart was gloomy under today's weather, and everything seemed lifeless. There were very few cars on the roads and very few pedestrians strolling around. Ward drove on while Valente stared blankly out of the window.

Eventually, the Toyota found itself in the magistrate court parking lot. It was nearly empty, only a few cars in the entire lot. Ward parked the SUV. They both stepped out of the vehicle and made their way to the main entrance. The building was a low-cut brick building, a single faded bronze plaque next to the revolving door. The plaque reads: *Magistrate Court of Tasmania.*

Ward and Valente both enter through the revolving door. There was no lobby or reception desk, instead there was a single bathroom and another plastic plaque on the wall. The plastic plaque had all of the offices listed inside the court, their room numbers next to each one. Valente scanned the list until he saw it, *City Coroner's Office: Room 128*. They both walked down the hallways of the magistrate court. Following the bright green arrows on the walls, which have room numbers painted over them.

Ward and Valente followed the arrows until they came upon a hallway intersection. To the right, the arrows say:

Rooms 115-125. To the left, the arrows say: *Rooms 126-130.* They both turned left and walked down the hallway. Ward and Valente, at some point, pass a woman in a skirt, reading the papers in her hand intently as she walks, paying no attention to them both. They finally came up to the door in the hallway marked *Room 128, City Coroner's Office.*

Ward turned the handle and opened the thin wooden door, and they stepped inside. The main room looked like a small lobby, two separate rooms in each far corner. A single person sat at a desk typing on their computer, a man in his 30s. The man looked up at Ward and Valente.

"Help you folks?" the man asks.

"We're looking for Dr. Hogan," Valente replies.

The man doesn't skip a beat. "Gene!" he calls out. "It's for you."

From one of the rooms, Ward and Valente hear the creak of an office chair as someone stands up. A burly man in his mid-forties steps out, white hair and silver goatee. Wire framed glasses over his hazel eyes. He carries a tired posture on his shoulders.

"I'm Hogan, who are you?" Hogan says

"I'm Forrest Valente, this is LeeWard. We need to speak with you," Valente says.

"Never heard of either of you," Hogan says.

"Well, no, we were hoping-"

"Yeah, yeah, *talk.* About what?" Hogan snaps.

Valente sighs. "We saw your video. The autopsy on the construction worker from Queenstown."

Hogan freezes. He doesn't say a word. Before he decides to talk, Hogan scans Ward and Valente from top to bottom. "Are you journalists?" Hogan asks.

"No, not journalists," Valente says.

"Hunters?"

"Not that either."

"Then what the bloody hell are you?"

Ward shrugs. "To be blunt, engineers."

Hogan thinks it's a joke. He smirks but Ward's serious face tells him it's the truth. Hogan shakes his head at the notion of engineers. "God help me," Hogan mumbles to himself. "Why didn't I take the job in Sydney?"

Valente steps forward. "Dr. Hogan, if you could-"

Hogan holds up his hand. "Do you smoke? I need a smoke," he says to them. Hogan walks toward Ward and Valente. "Follow me," Hogan says, herding them out of the door. Ward and Valente follow Hogan toward an employee exit down the hall. "I swear, it's all bullshit. I ought to quit and leave their workload in the wind," Hogan mumbles as he walks. "I ask for answers and they send me engineers, God help us all."

Ward and Valente step out with Hogan, the fresh morning wind brushing their faces. Hogan takes a pack of cigarettes out of his breast pocket, and he puts one in his lips. He then holds out his hand and offers a cigarette to them both. Valente shakes his head. "You're gonna need one, trust me," Hogan says.

Valente shakes his head once more, but Ward does take a cigarette. Hogan puts the pack back in his pocket and pulls out a lighter. He lights his cigarette and then Ward's. He finally looks up at them both, inhaling a cloud of smoke. "Tell me, why are two engineers asking about something no one wants to talk about?" Hogan says. He exhales the smoke at the end of his question.

"We want to know what happened to the construction worker," Valente says. "What happened with the investigation?

What the outcome was, what you know. We looked online and found nothing about it, no reports to match the autopsy video."

"Why would I tell you all that?" Hogan snaps.

"I understand if it's still part of an ongoing investigation, but if could get more info-"

"Damn right, it's an ongoing investigation," Hogan says. "And you're 'engineers', not police."

Valente doesn't know what to say. He's stumped on how to work his way around the stubborn coroner. Ward sees his friend's stumped demeanor and decides to step in. Ward simply exhales his cigarette smoke. "We sent a group of biologists out here, people we consider friends, to look for... *something*. We think this is the same animal that killed the construction worker."

Hogan sighs at the explanation, his demeanor too tired to contest. "*Killing* is putting it lightly," Hogan says, referring to the construction worker. "And you sent how many poor souls in pursuit of this thing?"

Ward doesn't acknowledge the question, "We're concerned about this whole thing. We were just hoping for more details."

"Details, hmm," Hogan says. "The details are, we don't have a damn clue what's going on. That construction worker case went nowhere, as far as I know. If you saw the autopsy video, I'm assuming you saw my suggestion for a wildlife expert to take a look. That we did, we got a herpetologist out here, a crocodile expert. Mate took one look and said he knew fuck all."

"And what? That was it?" Valente asks.

"Unfortunately, it wasn't," Hogan says. "You see, I think there's something fishy going on here in Hobart. There's probably a reason why you didn't find any reports online."

"What do you mean?" Ward asks.

Hogan shifts in his posture. "Truth be told, no one is seeing the patterns, or just not listening at all. Over the past couple months, I've heard of multiple reports of missing people. Mostly from family or friends. They drive all the way down here to Hobart to report them. But nothing can be done. This is Tasmania, things happen often. Either to those that aren't careful or just plain bad luck. Police don't send out search parties; they send out hunters or consultants. Frankly, no one's properly equipped or willing to go out deep into the forest to look for missing people. Going out means potentially getting lost yourself."

"That being said," Hogan continues. "People going missing is not a new phenomenon. And that's not even counting all those rural areas up north, where there's no contact and no way of reporting missing folks. Missing people in Tasmania would mean nothing if it weren't for the other occurrences."

"Occurrences?" Valente asks.

"At first, it was just a couple of victims. Police reports stated they were from a construction site in Queenstown," Hogan replies. "Mutilated and mauled corpses—both went missing during their shift at the construction site. They were found about two miles south of the site. No witnesses, no other evidence as to what killed those workers. Police left it at that; of course they would. But then people started going missing every week. One or two at a time. And not just construction workers, other civilians, poor souls walking home from work. Remains started being brought into the morgue. Each equally mangled if not more than the last. In total, there must've been ten or eleven victims I examined. There were some missing folks who were never seen or heard of again. Honestly, it got to the point where I preferred that they weren't found. I hated examining those victims, and I hated even more bringing in their family to identify what was left of their loved one."

"What happened? They had to have investigated, right?"

Ward asks.

"To a certain extent," Hogan says solemnly. "We made our reports of these incidents to our higher ups, and so did they. Police here are vastly different, our goddamn court judge lives in Melbourne and rarely ever comes down here. Even then, they eventually sent some help down here. Three experts, two professional hunters and one field biologist from the University of Sydney. I met them in passing, they were very eager to get started on their work."

Hogan inhales a long drag from his cigarette. He then coughs at the bad inhale.

"What happened? What were their findings?" Valente asks.

"I would assume their findings were more than they bargained for. Nobody ever saw them again."

"Anybody tried to look for them?"

"Who would we send? They were the cavalry."

"So what happened after?"

Hogan sighs. "I did the only thing I could. You know, I like my sleep, I get very upset if I lose my sleep. So after countless sleepless nights, I decided to put on my foot-soldier shoes and go take a look myself. I drove down to this construction site. I didn't care if there was the possibility of me getting mauled. I needed to see for myself."

"And?"

"There is no construction site in Queenstown. And it's not just the address being rubbish, the whole site doesn't exist."

Valente bobs his head. "So where were the construction workers coming from?"

"Your guess is as good as mine," Hogan says. "I had hit a dead end, and the bodies were still coming in. There was nothing much for me to do then, no one else to fuss to. Bodies have since slowed down now, last one I saw was two weeks ago."

Hogan puts out his cigarette on the brick wall behind him. He flicks the cigarette butt into a nearby garbage can. "As much as we fussed here at the magistrate court, in the end, we got nothing," Hogan says. "We did everything we could to get more help, more resources, hell, any answers for God's sake. But nothing happened, just empty promises. I can tell by the looks on your faces. I know exactly what you're thinking. How come you or the general public hasn't heard of this? Excellent question. You have to wonder why no news of this has even reached outside of Tasmania. But as you've heard, it's not for lack of trying."

"You think someone is deliberately keeping this quiet?"

"It's the only possibility," Hogan says. "Money can make anything happen. Anything."

"What would be the reason to cover this up? I honestly can't think of anything logical," Valente says.

"I certainly can," Hogan says with a smirk. "See, I sometimes get a lot of downtime here. And with that and my persevering attitude, I got very curious. So I ran a tox screen and some blood tests. There was nothing much out of the ordinary. But one day, I decided to take a look at a blood sample under a microscope."

Hogan reaches for his breast pocket, pulling out the pack of cigarettes for a second time. "I'm not much of a molecular biologist," Hogan says, opening the pack of cigarettes and pulling another one out. "But I know the basics, I have a master's in forensic science. I know serology like the back of my hand. I noticed something really extraordinary under the microscope that day. Possibly the answer to my very question about why things are quiet around here."

Ward and Valente let the man speak, waiting for him to reveal the information.

"One of the victims had a severe gene mutation. Some of his blood cells were dividing wildly. It was spreading all over his body," Hogan says. "But here's the kicker, I noticed that the animal's saliva had complex and reactive DNA properties. It had an effect on the victim's blood."

"Was it causing the victim's blood cells to divide?" Valente asks.

"No, no. You're misunderstanding me," Hogan says. "The victim already had a cell gene mutation prior to being killed. What I'm saying is that the animal's DNA cells in its saliva were destroying the mutated cells."

Valente's jaw drops; he blinks. "Wait a minute," he says. "You don't mean..."

"*Cancer cells*," Hogan says, smiling. "The saliva was eradicating the cancer cells."

BRIFFAULT'S LAW

Anika, JJ, and Zeke are standing at the edge of a small nesting ground. They cannot believe their eyes. There are eggshells shattered all over the place but they aren't white. They're slightly dirty, old, and decrepit. But you can still count the bottom side of the eggshells, since they're still buried in the wet dirt. There are at least ten of them. Ten eggshells and two nests, about four or five in each if you take an estimate.

"How do you know it's a dinosaur nest?" JJ asks.

"I've never seen any eggs or nests that look like this, ever," Anika whispers.

"Jesus," JJ mumbles. He holds the rifle tightly in his hands.

"Two adults," Anika says. "Or maybe even four adults, if you include their mates."

"Four adult motherfucking dinosaurs," JJ whispers. "And we're now standing in their nesting grounds. Do you think these dinosaurs like to move ahead or do they stay in one place?"

"I don't know anything about dinosaurs," Anika says. "But I do know animals that lay eggs, and most of them, if not all, are very protective of their nesting grounds. And by that logic, they wouldn't mov., They'd only leave their nest to go hunting and then they come right back."

"So?" JJ says. "Should we be standing here?"

"No," Anika says, quickly realizing. "We shouldn't be standing here. We need to go right now."

"Let's get out of here then," JJ says.

And just as Anika and JJ both try to turn around, they see Zeke take a step forward. Zeke is holding the camera confidently in his hands, bending over, shoving the lens into the nest. "Zeke," JJ says. "We're fucking leaving."

Zeke doesn't respond. He continues to roam around the nest, trying to get a good angle on them. "We're out here to observe and document," Zeke finally says. "I have to get some footage."

"Zeke," Anika whispers through her teeth. "*Let's go.*"

Zeke's not listening. He keeps the camera close to the nest of eggs, filming them. He moves the camera around the nesting grounds, taking it all in for the footage. JJ has had enough of it. He stomps forward, ready to grab Zeke and yank him away, when suddenly, they hear something whistle. A bird whistle, and then a squeak. JJ stops moving and turns to look back at Anika. Anika has never heard bird sounds like that in Tasmania before.

Suddenly, a small creature walks through the foliage to their right. In an instant, the animal is there. Anika's mind is unable to properly process what she's seeing. She only sees the outline and the colors. Dark brown leather-like skin, with even darker feathers on its head, neck, spine, and tail. The animal is about three feet tall, and it lumbers along into the nesting grounds, rubbing its snout with its small arms, unaware of the humans present.

Until it looks up. The animal freezes, and so does everyone else. The animal doesn't move; it just stands there, blinking. The animal moves its eyes from left to right, looking for intention from the towering humans. Anika and JJ both know they need to step away immediately, slowly and quietly. Zeke then takes two steps toward the animal, holding the camera forward. "*Zeke,*" Anika whispers through her teeth again. "*Stop.*"

The small animal then takes two frightened steps backward, and wails as loudly as it can.

Shit.

Shit.

The animal continues to wail. It lowers its head and body close to the ground, like a frightened deer fawn trying to stay alive. Anika turns around and begins to move away from the wailing creature, and JJ starts to follow her. "What about the dumbass?" JJ asks behind her, referring to Zeke.

"He wants to stay and meet his parents, let him. Let's haul ass, *now*," Anika replies.

Anika and JJ brush past the heavy foliage surrounding the nesting grounds. Pushing the thick bush branches and ferns away from their face as they hurriedly move through. As they both moved away, they hear the wailing creature suddenly stop. The forest becomes soundless again. Both Anika and JJ stop in their tracks, listening. All they can hear is the wind moving through the forest. They can't hear anything else, not the animal and certainly not Zeke...

The forest suddenly erupts into deep, rumbling hooting coming from every direction. Anika and JJ frantically look around, trying to catch a glimpse of what can possibly be making those unearthly noises. The hooting starts in one direction, stops, and then starts in another. Becoming louder and louder each time. But they can see nothing, the thick underbrush blanketing their ability to see past three feet.

"*Oh fuck*," JJ says. "What do we do?"

Anika grabs JJ by his rucksack. "We have to leave now."

Anika tugs at JJ until they're moving again, the incessant hooting becoming more frequent. Anika doesn't even bother to look if they're heading in the right direction toward the lodge. She just wants to get away from this wicked place. They finally come upon a small clearing, and they quickly move across when Anika slips on some mud. She falls to her knees, and JJ stops to help her up from the ground, but then...

JJ stops in his tracks. Anika looks up at him, his body frozen. Anika looks around, to see what has stopped JJ from moving. To their left next to a bush, a small animal similar to the one at the nest stands, watching. It bobs its head, and chirps. Anika stands up from the mud, and then the animal squawks. They hear rustling in the foliage, and a second small animal emerges from the tree line. The animal squawks again, and then a third and fourth animal emerge around Anika and JJ. Suddenly they're all squawking, and more animals join their friends. In total, about ten small animals surround JJ and Anika in the clearing, forming a circle.

They all stand watching their intruders, each examining Anika and JJ, but they don't move any closer. JJ grips the rifle in his hands. He puts it to his shoulder and looks down the scope. "What's the plan, scientist?" JJ whispers.

Anika tries to put logic to the situation, while trying to keep calm. "They're not attacking. They're infants. Either they're unsure of how to proceed, or they're waiting for something else."

"Parents?"

"Probably," Anika says, her voice shaky.

JJ tries to keep his breathing calm. "I can shoot one, scatter them away."

"Killing one might scare them, or might instigate them to attack."

"Fucking Christ, we're wasting time."

"Okay, okay," Anika says. She quickly comes up with a plan. "That looks like a heavy rifle, heavy bullets too, right?"

"Yes."

"Okay, it should be pretty loud. So you fire a round to scare them, and if it works, we haul ass."

"And if not?"

Anika sneers. "Then we have to kill one."

That's as good as it gets, JJ thinks. "Okay. Ready?"

"Ready."

JJ raises the rifle and points the barrel up in the air, but then Zeke bursts through the foliage. He's yelling at the top of his lungs. "Get back! Back!" Zeke yells. He's waving the camera at the animals. "What the fuck? You left me?!"

Zeke has agitated the animals. Some of them begin to wail in unison.

"Shut up, shut the fuck up!" Zeke yells at the animals.

"Zeke! Stop!" Anika yells.

All of a sudden, a long, guttural and continuous screech, similar to an eagle, silences the wailing. The eagle screech is deafening, and it goes on for seconds. It echoes into the forest. Anika covers her ears, but the screech doesn't stop. How can one animal go on for this long?

"What the hell is that?!" JJ says as he tries to cover his own ears.

The screeching stopped, and the forest became silent once more. The infant animals were no longer wailing, or moving. Anika was just about to tell JJ what to do when the most terrifying creature they had ever seen stepped out of the foliage.

An enormous dinosaur emerged from the forest. It slowly stepped past the small animals and confidently lumbered toward the humans. It stood at about seven feet tall, from the tip of its snout to the end of its tail, it measured almost ten feet. Its skin is layered dark brown leather speckled in dark orange spots. All of its feathers are combed back like any other bird. The feathers ran from the top of its head, along the top of the neck, and the spinal column to the end of its tail. The feathers are also dark and spotted orange. Anika stared at the animal's appendages, strong muscles holding its long and clawed three-fingered forearms. Its thighs and calves looked impressive and swift. It stepped forward with its mighty taloned feet. Anika could not believe her eyes; her mind could not process that what was before her was real.

"*Anika...*" JJ said, his words whispering but his inflection screaming *help*.

"Kneel," Anika responded. She let her wildlife instinct take over.

"Kneel?" JJ whispered again.

"Don't be a threat. Make yourself seem smaller," Anika whispered back.

"But I can shoot it."

"Oh yeah? Do you have enough bullets for all of these? *Kneel.*"

Zeke was already kneeling down. Anika followed, and JJ reluctantly did so as well. The giant animal stepped forward a couple more steps and then stopped. It was only a few feet from them when it dropped its head downward to be at eye level with the humans. Its snout was about two feet long, less than a foot wide. Its nostrils flared as it huffed while it scanned them. Anika noticed that it didn't move its entire head like most predators when it was looking at something, instead it moved only its eyes like a person would. It moved its eyes over Anika, then JJ, and then Zeke; its eyes had a dark purple iris wrapped around its pupil. It wriggled its clawed fingers as it examined the humans, balling up the fingers almost making a fist. The next thing Anika noticed was its teeth, only the top row visible like an alligator, the teeth ivory yellow and sharp.

When the animal was satisfied, it lifted its head up to its usual height. It then arched its head and neck back, opened its jaws slightly, and crowed like a bird. The crow echoed through the forest, as it was surprisingly loud. The animal then positioned its head and neck back to normal, and it continued to stare at the humans.

What was it doing? What was it waiting for?

Anika then saw Zeke trying to slowly creep away from the situation; the mighty beast was not impressed. It stepped to the side to cut him off and face Zeke directly. Zeke looked up into its eyes. And just as he did, the beast opened its jaws and began to screech again. It was louder than before, incredibly thunderous, progressively getting louder and higher pitched as it continued. Zeke, Anika, and JJ held their ears in fright, the screeching like needles in their eardrums. When the beast stopped screeching, it just stared at Zeke. No words needed to be said; it wanted Zeke to stop moving. Anika put her hands down from her ears, the screeching leaving her dazed from the high decibels. She shook her head, shaking the daze off.

Through the ringing in their ears, they heard another crowing sound coming from behind them. They all turned around to see another dinosaur, as tall and as frightening as the first, slowly moving toward them from the forest. It was exactly identical to the first, a twin of the beast keeping the humans in place. It moved around the terrified humans until it was standing next to the other beast. Anika noticed that it actually wasn't as tall as the other dinosaur. It looked like it was a few inches shorter than its twin. The two beasts then suddenly crowed to each other, the younglings around them just watching. Anika noticed immediately that the slightly bigger one was the alpha; its demeanor showed no signs of fear. There was pure confidence in its stature. The slightly smaller one was clearly the beta of the pack. It would lower its head just slightly, in respect to the alpha.

"Scientist," JJ whispered through his teeth. "What now?"

"*Quiet.*"

Anika examined the situation as best as she could, but the truth was: she could see no way out. They were surrounded by about ten younglings, the cubs all seemingly faster and more agile than them, not possible to outrun. JJ carried a bolt action hunting rifle, with not enough ammunition to stop all of them. Firing a round as a warning shot had an equal chance of startling the pack, making them more aggressive. Killing the alpha would potentially disperse or confuse the pack, but Anika could tell there is something wrong with the twin beasts. They weren't moving. The twins would occasionally bob their heads back and forth, looking at them and then each other. The alpha made a sound like a cackle, the beta then looked at Anika and the group, and probed them all intently.

The beta then took two aggressive steps towards the humans, but the irritated snarl of the alpha stopped it in its tracks. The beta looked back, its shoulders loosening, its head lowered. The beta crows and growls softly at the alpha, and in response the alpha growls through its teeth. The beta then cackles a little louder. It almost looked like pleading.

The alpha just kept its gaze toward its twin, unyielded. It then hissed and crackled.

Were they... talking to each other?

Anika could hear Zeke silently sobbing behind her, scared out of his mind. Anika looked back at him. He's still holding the camera, filming. Anika shushed him. He needed to stay still and quiet. The beta had made a move toward them but the alpha stopped it. A clear indication of control. For now, Anika guessed no violence would occur without the alpha's approval. The alpha did not want to attack the humans, yet. They were still alive, and as long as there weren't any rapid movements or anything that looked like a threat or challenge, they would remain alive. Anika perused the younglings. They patted their feet in the dirt as they stood, almost like flamingos. Their behavior wasn't erratic, but they did seem anxious. The fact that they didn't move gave more indication that they were waiting for a decision.

What would it be? She's seen similar behavior in other packs like gorillas or wolves. Usually the alpha would challenge the threat to determine if they would leave or submit. The animals moved their heads like a bird, but their eyes were reptilian. The alpha's dark purple eyes carried nothing behind them. When she compared them to crocodiles, their behavior made only a little sense. If she saw them as cold and calculating, then their movement was only being studied. Crocodiles were always mistaken for being intelligent, but the truth was that they were just really good at pattern recognition. And crocodiles never waited to attack with their prey this dead to rights.

Anika heard a click.

She turned her head to see JJ holding the rifle, slowly raising it to his eyes. JJ had flipped off the safety and was getting ready to fire. "No... stop..." Anika whispers.

JJ wasn't listening. He put the Leupold scope to his eyesight. Anika turned her head to see what the alpha and beta were doing. They were no longer communicating. They were silently observing her. They had seen the shift in body language; they knew something was wrong. Anika had to do something. She wasn't sure what needed to happen, but she knew antagonizing them wouldn't help. Anika turned her head back and slowly waved her hands at JJ, trying to get into his line of sight. Just as she did this, JJ fired.

The rifle cracked like a low deafening whip. She felt the bullet whiz past the side of her head. The .375 H&H magnum bullet took a small chunk of skin off of the alpha's right shoulder, grazing its skin. It didn't yelp or snarl, or make any sound to acknowledge the pain. Instead, it jerked its head around, blinking, confused by the attack. Anika just stared at JJ, her ears ringing. She watched as JJ slid the bolt back to rack in another round.

His eyes grew wide open. They're filled with terror. He looked like he was yelling at her to move, but she couldn't hear it. A rush of warmth flew past her. In her peripheral, she saw a large shape lunge forward and past her body. The alpha had darted forward with shocking speed. She saw the alpha send JJ flying backward. The alpha had used its weight to tackle JJ with immense force. Anika saw the rifle fly out of JJ's hands and topple to the ground.

The ringing in her ear stopped, and she could hear Zeke screaming as he watched the beast overpower JJ. The alpha held JJ down with its mighty talons, its claws digging into his chest. JJ swung his arms at the beast. The beast caught one of JJ's arms in its jaws, and clamped down, snapping his ulna and radius like twigs. JJ howled. The beast opened its jaws, letting JJ's arm slump to the ground. It then stepped off JJ, grabbed him by the shoulder, and flipped him onto his stomach. The beast handled JJ like a weightless ragdoll. JJ was still screaming in pain, when the alpha stepped on his back, holding him down again, pressing JJ's face and stomach into the dirt.

Anika couldn't snap out of it. She was terrified; she didn't know what to do, what to think. The only logical thing she could think of, was to lunge for the rifle and blow her own head off.

JJ's screaming became a bit quieter as he was pressed into the dirt and struggled to breathe. The alpha wasn't moving. It wasn't hurting JJ anymore. Instead, it was holding him down, waiting, Anika looked up at the alpha, against her own judgement, and locked eyes with it. It was looking into her eyes, like it had been waiting for her to look at it. Tiny streams of blood trickled down from the bullet graze on its shoulder. The animal just stared, then bobbed its head slightly. It examined its wound. The alpha growled, and then swung its gaze back to Anika. Its eyes staring directly forward, on either side of its snout. It was unlike anything Anika had ever seen.

"Anika... what do... I do?" JJ mumbled from under the creature.

Anika couldn't speak; she couldn't move. There was nothing she could say to JJ.

Anika then heard a sudden set of running footsteps. Zeke had made a run for it. But the beta was ready for it. Zeke didn't make it five feet before the beta caught him. It grabbed Zeke by the shoulder with its jaws and jerked its head back, sending Zeke flying through the air. He landed on the dirt with a thud, the wind knocked out of him as he didn't even scream. Zeke caught his breath and was about to try his escape again when the beta lunged forward again. It used its claws to tear into Zeke's stomach. It cut open his flesh like paper. Blood and coils of entrails spilling as the smell of warm iron filled the air. Anika saw Zeke's face; he wasn't screaming. He didn't make any sound. Zeke had a surprised look on his face as he died, like he didn't believe what was happening. It only took a few seconds for Zeke's eyes to appear lifeless.

Anika looked away and locked eyes with the alpha holding JJ once more. It was still looking at her. Its eyes squinted as it watched Anika's reaction to Zeke's death. JJ had seen the whole thing. He struggled to breath with the weight of the beast on his back, and attempted to speak again.

"Anika... just promise me you'll kill one... before they get you..." JJ mumbled.

The alpha swung its head down, grabbed JJ's ear with its teeth, and peeled it off with such ease that it looked like a sticky note coming off of JJ's head. JJ grunted in pain, trying to keep himself together, unwilling to die screaming or begging for his life.

The beta moved away from Zeke's mutilated body, blood dripping from its jaws as it walked. The beta moved in closer to where the alpha was. It rattled its head, shaking the sticky blood off its feathers. The alpha then crowed once more, this time a command to its cubs. The cubs darted forward to Zeke's body. The cubs tore into Zeke's body like starved and vicious creatures, swallowing chunks of flesh whole like a crocodile would.

Anika looked away from the sight, her mind giving her flashes of her mother's death. Anika then caught a glance of the rifle laying in the dirt, a few feet away from her. She thought about scrambling for it, but then the beta darted forward. It stood over the rifle, glaring at her as menacingly as it could. Anika was shocked. The beta had recognized her sudden discovery of the weapon, and stopped her before she could make a move. The beta dropped its head down and picked up the rifle in its jaws. Anika followed the rifle with her eyes as it ascended to the beta's height.

The beta then started to rattle its head again, but not like before. This time, it was because of the *force* it was using in its jaws. It was clamping down as hard as it could on the rifle, its teeth sinking into the sleek wood of the elephant gun. Anika watched as the elephant rifle slowly bent out of shape, the animal's powerful jaws somehow curving *steel*. The beta then opened its jaws, and the rifle tumbled out of its mouth.

The alpha crowed again. Anika turned to see the alpha sneering at her. It bent its head down and grabbed JJ's right ankle. Just like a bird would, it twisted JJ's ankle and popped off his foot. JJ tried to hold in his pain, but he screamed through his teeth.

"Motherfucker! You fucking piece of-" JJ mumbled in agony.

The alpha tossed JJ's severed foot at Anika, which bounces on the dirt in front of her. Anika had tears running down her face. She then noticed JJ was staring right at her.

"*Psycho motherfucker*," JJ says. "Just don't look, Anika, I think it's what it wants…"

The alpha then swung its head down and clamped its jaws on JJ's head. The ivory yellow teeth sinking into the temples of JJ's head. Just before the alpha finally kills JJ, JJ says: *"Just get this over with."*

The alpha tore off JJ's head in one swift move, bright red blood gushing from JJ's decapitated neck. Anika wanted to look away, but she was frozen in terror. She saw as JJ's face went pale after being decapitated, his eyes rolling back into his head. The alpha tossed JJ's head at Anika again, the head rolling toward her after hitting the dirt.

The dinosaur finally stepped off of JJ's now lifeless body. It clumped forward toward Anika. As its talons squelched in the wet dirt, it gave a quick crow, a command to its cubs. Some of the cubs that didn't get to feed on Zeke's body darted toward JJ's. They began to feed on JJ's headless corpse, tearing into his thick jacket ravenously. The alpha stepped toward Anika and then stopped, glaring at her. It drooped its head down to be at eye level with her, to examine the petrified and hopeless expression on her face. Anika could smell JJ's blood and the animal's hot breath as it stood only a few feet away. The stinging smell of ammonia emanating from the animal, its natural scent upsetting to the human senses.

Burns was right to be afraid, and all Anika could think about was why she let her morbid curiosity win her over. Why did she ever agree to come? Why did she ever risk her life to prove a theory nobody believed? The alpha opened its jaws wide. Anika could see the animal's dark red tongue and slimy membranes of its oral cavity.

This is it. She was going to die. Anika closed her eyes and her last hope was that her death was quick.

But then a very distinct animal call emerged from the forest, a similar sound to these dinosaurs but slightly deeper. Anika had her eyes closed but she heard the alpha's jaws clamp together suddenly. Anika peeked through her eyelids.

She sees the alpha and the beta now alert and tense. They were scanning the forest, looking for something. Then, without any other indication, another dinosaur marched out of the foliage.

It was another adult, about six feet tall, seven feet long, and it carried a sneering look on its snout. It had almost the same discernible features as the alpha and beta, but with a few key differences. Its body configuration was wider, its snout covered in scarred claw marks. Its leather-like skin was a dark dirty green speckled with brown spots, and its feathers dark brown with yellow spots. And as the animal walked by Anika, she noticed that it did not even acknowledge her presence. Anika followed up its neck with her eyes, a short mane of smaller feathers that wrapped its neck up to its chin. The maned dinosaur had its eyesight directed at the alpha, its gaze intense and foreboding. It almost seemed... *defiant*. The maned dinosaur continued its stride in an unyielded manner, and it was then that Anika recognized the behavior she was witnessing.

She had witnessed behavior like this in several other species, in lions, elephants, and hyenas. It was a *matriarchal pride*. The alpha and the beta were the females, the maned dinosaur probably a male. In matriarchal social systems, males are not part of the pack. Which is why the male didn't seem to have an ounce of respect for the alpha, even as the terrifying alpha hissed in contempt.

The beta stepped in front of the alpha when the male was only a couple feet away. The beta snarled, protecting its alpha. The alpha then snarled too, but at the beta, making it cower to the side. The alpha can clearly take care of itself. The alpha got very close to the male, attempting to scare him off with its stare. But it still did not yield. The alpha snarled again, and then rammed its head toward the male, striking it in the neck. The male stepped back and roared, the deep growl suddenly frightening the cubs.

The alpha had enough of it. It charged at the male in full force. The male seemed to have expected as much, as it rolled on its back and used its legs to send the alpha flying over him. The alpha landed on the dirt hard, its failed attack noticed by the beta. The beta charged too, all while the male was still getting to its feet. The beta pounced onto the male, digging its talons and claws into its back. The male roared at the pain, stood up, and turned its neck around to grab the beta. The male clamped its wide jaws onto the beta's leg, and yanked. The male is incredibly strong, as it pulled the beta off its back with ease.

In the meantime, the alpha had gotten to its feet. It charged forward just as the male had gotten the beta off its back. The male must have seen the alpha during the scuffle. The male used its jaws and grabbed the beta by the snout. It swung its body around and sent the beta flying toward the alpha, toppling the alpha backward again.

Anika saw her chance. She didn't care what the fight was about or who would win. The animals were busy. She quickly stood up and fled into the foliage, her blood racing at the sudden surge of fight-or-flight. She ran as fast as she could, hearing the fighting dinosaurs behind her become more faint until all she could hear was the sound of her feet running in the dirt.

MURPHY'S LAW

The day of the incident in South America, Burns and his wife, Addie, weren't far from the production team. Burns and Addie weren't making an appearance on Out with the Irvings, but they had accompanied them to their shooting location. They had done it many times before. They were like a family; they liked to stick together most of the time. While they were both strolling around Manaus talking to the locals, they received an emergency call from the Irvings editor. Something had happened, but there were no details, only that there was an attack and that Anika was taken to a hospital. There were no other details on Matt or Cassandra.

Burns remembers rushing into the emergency room of Hospital Santo Alberto. The hot, humid, old and decrepit hospital building in a city surrounded by jungle. He remembers the scratched-up tiles that covered the floor as he and his wife Addie hurried through the hallways. The indistinct chatter of the nurses and ER doctors was all too familiar to Burns. His time as a paramedic left certain smells and sounds of a hospital ingrained in his mind. He never once thought he would ever have to step into an emergency room again.

"Bill, through here," Addie said to him. She pointed to a board on the hospital hallway's wall, labeled 'ala pediátrica'. Addie was somewhat fluent in Portuguese, but even Burns knew that word indicated the pediatric wing. He and Addie continued to hurry through the hallways, until they reached another reception office full of nurses. Addie walked up to the desk and began asking in Portuguese. Burns looked around the pediatric ward, peeking inside every room from where he was standing, searching. Addie finally turned around from the nurse, and she signaled Burns to follow her.

"Nurse said room four," Addie said to him.

Burns followed her, scanning each room number until they both saw number four. They slid the glass door open and pushed the curtain aside. Sitting on the bed by herself was Anika. At the time she was only nine years old, her dark brown hair in a ponytail, her face small and innocent. Burns and Addie both went to her and stood beside the bed, but Anika didn't look at them. She was just staring forward at the blank wall in front of her.

"Ani, sweetie," Addie said, her words soft. "Hey, let me look at you."

Anika finally moved her eyes toward Addie. Anika instantly recognized Addie's warm hazel eyes and dark hair. Anika didn't say anything; she didn't smile or frown. She just looked at Addie, her face empty. Addie reached out and touched Anika's face. Her hands were warm and tender. Addie brushed Anika's hair over her ear, hoping for any reaction from Anika. It was then that she noticed specks of blood on Anika's ears.

Addie turned to her husband. "Can you get me a wet paper towel, anything like that?"

Burns stood up and looked around the hospital room. He found a small plastic dispenser for wet wipes and took a couple. He handed them to Addie. "Did the nurse say anything else?" Burns asked.

"No, she didn't say much other than that they cleaned her up and are checking her for infections," Addie said while wiping Anika's ear.

"Infections?" Burns whispered.

Addie held up the wet wipe, showing Burns the smeared dark blood. Burns understood. Unfortunately, he had seen it and done it too many times as a paramedic. The process was called *decon*. Whenever a patient's skin was soaked or peppered in someone else's blood, the medics had to clean the blood away from the victim's face to ensure they weren't contaminated. It's probably why they were testing Anika for infections. The fact that they had deconned Anika means she had been covered in blood.

"Baby," Addie said to Anika. "Where's your mom and dad?"

Anika didn't say a word; she just continued to stare and blink. "Hey," Addie said softly, ensuring that she didn't agitate the little girl. "Are you hurt? How do you feel?"

Anika remained silent. Addie scanned Anika's body, looking for injuries, any indication of why she was at the hospital. "She's not hurt, Bill," Addie said.

"I know, but she's unresponsive. Shock, maybe," Burns said.

"Can you stay with her?" Addie asked. "I'm going to ask around and see if Matt and Cassie are here somewhere."

Addie stood up, but just as she did, Anika looked up at her and spoke. "Dead," Anika said, her words blank like her gaze.

"What?" Addie asked her. She leaned back down into Anika.

"Mom is dead," Anika said.

Burns's and Addie's faces sank; they went pale. "Jesus," Burns mumbled.

"It... It tore out her neck," Anika said.

Burns took action. He sat down beside her and held her

hand. "Don't think about that right now, okay?" Burns said to her. "Just breathe, kiddo." He turned to Addie. "Go ask around for Matt."

"He left me here," Anika said again.

"Who did?" Addie asked.

"Dad," Anika said. Matt was alive, but if he was hurt too, neither of them knew. "Don't look for him," Anika muttered.

"What was that, sweetie?" Addie asked her.

"Don't look for him. I don't want him here."

"Why not, sweetie?" Addie asked, her voice concerned.

"Because Mom told me to stay away from him," Anika said. "I didn't listen, and now she's dead."

There was a definite sincerity and emptiness in Anika's voice. From that day, she never went back to being the extroverted little girl who loved animals. Instead, she became a quiet, reserved, and at times, hollow human being. Burns and Addie took her in. There was no custody battle or even a request. Matt just walked away after the funeral and secluded himself for months. They never heard from him; he never called or contacted Burns and Addie about Anika. A year later, Matt resurfaced, his show back on air. Burns was furious, claiming he would 'break his face' if he ever crossed paths with him. Addie simply told her husband to let it go; she kept her main focus on Anika's health.

Both Burns and Addie tried for a long time to keep Anika safe and healthy while giving her the freedom to choose her own path. But Anika's response was always the same, a clear and monotone "I don't know" whenever they asked her what she wanted. Her passion was gone; her will to do anything for herself was dead.

But Burns and Addie persevered; not once did they give up on Anika. Their devotion to Anika's health was relentless, so much so that they gave up the scheduling of their own show. It didn't seem like it at first, but they were raising Anika as their own. Slowly inching her to open up more after her traumatic experience. Burns always had an idea of what Addie was trying to teach her. While it seemed like Addie was keeping her up with her wildlife projects, what Addie was really doing was making sure that all of Anika's memories of her mother weren't tainted forever.

Burns, on the other hand, focused his attention on making sure she could take care of herself. Burns often worried about what Anika would do when she was on her own again. So in response, Burns taught her all of his knowledge on surviving in the wild, as well as all of his medical knowledge. Constant lessons accompanied by real world practical scenarios only strengthened Anika's will to move on. Eventually, Anika grew up into a sturdy, prudent, and well-educated young woman.

Which is why Burns is now staring out of the window of the lodge, feeling uneasy.

"It's been three hours. They should've been back by now," Burns says, staring out of the barred window close to the front doors.

"It's roughly a two-hour hike back, give them some time, Bill," Matt says. Matt is sitting next to his editor on the couch, the editor cutting away at the footage they had so far.

"Matt, I don't think she'd take this long to get back. I know her."

"Chill out, Bill. She'll be back in no time."

Burns scrunches up his nose, refraining from snapping at Matt once more. It has been increasingly difficult to keep away from him, but despite the size of the lodge, it feels small with all the people here. Burns turns away from the window. He paces back to the kitchen and grabs a water bottle from inside the fridge. He twists the cap off and takes a swig.

His stomach feels uneasy, and the water doesn't seem to help. Burns has this habit of feeling sick whenever he feels something is wrong. He first picked up on this habit during his time as a first responder. Just hearing vague details of their next call on dispatch always screamed trouble. He feels the same way now, his bones aching, his hands trembling. He knows something is wrong. The last time Burns had these feelings was when he drove Addie to the doctor's office. The very same day, she was diagnosed with cancer.

Burns hears someone walk up behind him. He turns to see Kit standing close to him.

"You good?" Kit asks.

"No, not really," Burns responds.

"Feel sick?" Kit asks.

"No. Well, yes, but not like that," Burns says, shaking his head. "When you were in the service, did you ever feel strange before something went wrong? You know like... am I making sense here?"

"Before shit hit the fan?" Kit asks.

Burns waves his hands. "Forget it, I'm sorry. I know I'm not making sense."

"Don't be sorry, I know what you mean," Kit says. "I would get a weird taste in my mouth, like ash or iron. Shit always went sideways after. Wish I would've spoken up in any of those times."

"Really?"

"Yes, so if you have something to say, tell me," Kit says firmly.

"I know Anika," Burns says. "I know how long it would've taken her to get where she was going, roughly. She would never stop to explore, she's goal-oriented. Onceshe put up those trail cameras, she would've come right back. If she's not back yet, then maybe..."

"Something's impeding her from making it back."

Burns nods sternly.

"Have you tried her radio?" Kit asks.

"I was about to."

Burns and Kit walk towards the northeast corner of the ground floor of the lodge. They reach the table with the CB radio setup. Burns picks up the handset and tunes the radio to Anika's last frequency. Burns then stops before speaking into it.

"What's wrong?" Kit asks.

"What if I put her in danger by doing this?" Burns says, his words laced with concern.

"Let me see," Kit says, holding his hand out. Burns hands him the radio handset. "My unit used to do this all the time if we were worried about giving someone away during radio silence."

Kit holds up the handset to his ear. He taps the dispatch button a couple times and waits. The radio just crackles, no response. Kit tries again; he taps it three times this time. No response. "Could just be out of range," Kit suggests.

Burns grunts in disagreement.

"Yeah, I don't think so either," Kit says. He puts the handset down and looks at Burns. "Want to do something about it?".

"Yes, I do."

"Good, I'm coming with you," Kit says. He steps to the side and starts to make his way to his couch in the other corner of the first floor. Burns follows him. He notices Kit kneel down and slide out a black gun case from under the couch.

"You have it inside the house?" Burns asks.

"Once we saw that trackway yesterday..," Kit says while he opens the gun case, revealing the scoped elephant gun. "There was no way I was going to sit in this house unarmed."

Burns feels proud. He's glad he brought Kit onto the team. Kit holds up the rifle in his hands, and he pulls the bolt back, glancing at the 270 grain round inside. After making a brass check, he slides the bolt back and stands up.

"Plus, that ashy taste feeling I mentioned? I've been feeling that since we got here, to be honest," Kit says. "The last time I felt that was in Afghanistan, since then, I can't sleep without a rifle by my side."

Kit turns to Burns, ready to go. "Alright, how do you want to do this?" he asks.

"I'll go grab my backpack, we'll follow the GPS to where she says she was going, after that-"

"Bill! Come quick!" Matt yells out. Burns and Kit hurry over to Matt, who's standing next to Lucy, both hunched over, looking at the computer screen.

"What's wrong?" Burns asks.

"Look! Look!" Matt says, moving away from the screen, letting Burns take a look. "Play it again, play it, Lucy."

Burns and Kit hunch over. Lucy has the Tactacam app pulled up on the screen. There's a recorded video ready to play. Lucy clicks play on the video. "Motion sensors picked this up ten minutes ago, look," Matt says.

The video starts playing. It's the forest only a mile away. Suddenly, a dark shape steps into view, a small three-foot dinosaur, lumbering along. It walks toward the camera and then past it, its small snout just barely scraping by the camera lens. The dinosaur can be seen clear as day. The video then pauses, and Lucy turns around to Burns and Kit. "Can you believe it?" Lucy says, her face stricken with intrigue and joy. But Burns and Kit feel no such joy; their newly found goal has just gotten more difficult to achieve.

"How'd you get this?" Burns asks.

"Uh, the trail cameras. What do you mean how?" Matt replies.

"The ones we put up yesterday?" Burns asks, "I thought we were out of range."

"Apparently not, not if we sit close to this window. Mind you, it did take nearly an hour to download this video from this range. But it was worth it. They're so close to us!" Matt says. "We can finally get started on our work. How thrilling!"

"You've been sitting on this information for a goddamn hour?" Burns snaps.

Matt rolls his eyes. "What's the problem now?"

"Anika's not back yet," Burns snapped. "She went out four hours ago to retrieve the SD cards."

"Still on about that?" Matt says. "She'll be back soon. She's probably out there right now, with the dinosaurs. *The dinosaurs*, Bill."

"Why isn't she back, Matthew? Suppose she ran into these things already?"

"Last I checked she had a fightin' marine with her," Matt

says in a joking manner, but Burns didn't laugh, neither did Kit. Matt noticed Burns's and Kit's angry demeanor. "Bill, she has JJ with her, he's carrying a goddamn rifle."

"Fuck this, it's pointless with you, Matthew, every damn time," Burns says. He turned to walk away. "I'm grabbing my backpack. I'll be with you in a second," Burns says to Kit.

"Oh, for God's sake, Bill-" Matt was saying.

"No," Burns snapped again. "Not again, once more you fail to see… No, you *ignore the possibility* of real danger. It's right here, here, Matthew. Your daughter is smart, she would've hauled ass back here the moment she saw those things. The fact that she isn't here means something's wrong. I'm going out there, to save your daughter, and my friend.

Burns finally turned away and hurried upstairs to grab his backpack. He grabbed it and thought to himself that he would grab the shotgun from the truck as well. Burns no longer cared about the objective of the expedition. He knew it in his gut, something was wrong. Anika was in trouble, and he would not hesitate to put the animal down. In Burns's opinion, Anika Irving was the only tie to the human world he had left. The only good reminder of his late wife Addie. More often than not, Burns would look into Anika's eyes and see remnants of Addie's energy and prudence.

Burns swung the backpack over his shoulders, and then he grabbed a single handheld radio and GPS from his nightstand and stuffed them in his jacket pocket. Burns suddenly heard Kit's voice echoing from downstairs. His voice had gone up an octave. Kit was arguing with someone. Burns didn't have to even guess who he was arguing with. Burns hurried downstairs. He was about to tell Matt to stay out of their way, but Matt wasn't there. He saw Kit standing there as the front doors swung shut. Kit looked up to the stairs and saw Burns hurrying down.

"Where the hell is Matt?" Burns asks.

"He grabbed his handheld camera," Kit says. "He went outside with it, I tried to tell him."

"He did what?" Burns snapped. "By himself? Why didn't you stop him?"

"What was I supposed to do? Hit him in the head with my rifle?" Kit is exasperated.

Burns sighed angrily through gritted teeth. "That motherfucker will never learn. Animal Planet proudly presents: *Matthew fucking Irving!*"

MASTER OUTDOORSMAN

Matt jogs through the forest, his boots squelching through the thick mud on the ground. Matt holds the dart gun firmly in his hands, keeping it from bouncing as it hangs around his shoulder in the sling. As soon as the opportunity arises, he jumps at it. There's a dinosaur, a prehistoric animal thought to be extinct, alive and close. Nobody on earth can pass up the opportunity to see one in the flesh. Matt was envious when he first saw the footage of Burns with the small animal. Matt asked so many questions; he wanted to know as much as he could from Burns.

But Burns always shrugged him off, refusing to go into detail about his experience. In fact, Matt noticed that Burns seemed to dread talking about the experience entirely. Why on earth would he? How could he be so close to the greatest discovery in history and be full of dread? *Not me*, Matt thinks, *I'm always first in line to see an animal face to face.*

Matt stopped for a brief moment. He looked around the forest. He was trying to find his bearings, glancing in every direction. Shit, he should've grabbed a GPS. Nah, he thought, he didn't need it. He could handle himself. There was still plenty of daylight out here to show the way. Matt eventually just picked a direction and started his jog again. All he could hear was the sound of his boots hitting the ground as he hurried through the foliage. The forest was unusually quiet, but it didn't matter. All the more reason to believe the animals were out here, waiting to be spotted.

Something caught Matt's eye, and he came to stop, his boots sliding in the mud. He saw the three Tactacam trail cameras strapped on the trees. It was the ones he had placed before anyone had woken up this morning. He had placed them only a few minutes from the lodge. He wanted to see if the animals ever came this close. These ones haven't caught anything unfortunately, but seeing them meant he was heading in the right direction. *There we go*, he thought, *now we're getting somewhere.* Matt looked around the foliage, but he couldn't see any signs of life. He then looked around the base of the trees with the cameras, scanning for tracks in the wet dirt.

Bingo, there was a set of tracks in the mud. He kneeled down to inspect them. They were three-fingered animal tracks, very similar to ostriches. These had to be the dinosaurs', which means he was right. They did come close to the lodge. Matt examined the tracks, and all of them were heading in one direction, to the west. Matt checked the dart gun in his hands. He opened the port and saw a single dart round inside. Locked and loaded, he stood up, and slowly began to follow the tracks.

"That son of a bitch. I swear I'm gonna hit him when I find him," Burns says. Burns was adjusting his backpack straps as he strolled toward the front door. Kit was already at the door, waiting, the elephant rifle in his hands.

"*Cowboy shit*," Kit says, shaking his head. "Just running off like that."

"Unfortunately, it's nothing new. I've been dealing with his shit for years now," Burns says. He grabbed a set of keys from the rack next to the front door. "But this time, he's pushing it."

"Why'd he run off this time? His daughter or the dinosaur?" Kit asks.

"He wanted to air the footage of his wife dying," Burns reminds him. "Take a guess."

Kit shook his head again. Burns turned to Lucy and the rest of the group.

"Lucy, keep the doors locked and no one goes outside," Burns says, his voice sharp. "If you don't hear from us, or we're not back in two hours, call for help."

"Who do I call?" Lucy asks.

"Ranger stations, Valente, anyone at this point," Burns replied.

Burns finally opened the front door and stepped outside with Kit. He walked toward the lead Ford pickup. "I'm grabbing the shotgun," Burns says.

"You know how to use it?" Kit asks.

Burns held up the key fob in his hand. "Of course, I do." He clicked the unlock button. The Ford parked behind the lead beeped open. "Shit, I grabbed the wrong keys," Burns says.

"Wait here," Kit says. He jogged back to the front door. He knocked and the door opened. Without stepping in, Kit reached inside to the key rack. He pulled his arm out and held up the other key fob, clicking the unlock button.

The third vehicle beeped as it unlocked, wrong one again.

"Grab the other key, wrong one," Burns yelled out to Kit. Kit reached in the doorway again. He felt around and then decided to peek his head in instead. Kit then looked back at Burns from the doorway.

"There's no other keys," Kit yelled back.

"What?" Burns mumbled. He reached into his pockets and felt around. No other keys in his pocket either. He looked up in Kit's direction. Kit had his head inside the doorway, but Burns could hear him talking to someone inside. Kit then stepped back and the door closed behind him. He walked toward Burns.

"No one has the other keys," Kit says.

"Did JJ take them?" Burns asks. "He did grab the other rifle this morning."

"No, I saw him put the keys back."

"Well, Anika certainly doesn't have them."

They both suddenly realized the answer to their question. Kit walked to the lead Ford and peeked inside the pick-up canopy. "The air rifle case is open," Kit says.

"Matthew," Burns mumbled mid-sigh.

"I could try to break the window if you want."

"None of us will be able to reach through the bars."

"Shit."

"We ought to leave him out there by himself, selfish bastard," Burns says.

"As much as I'd like to, it's against my nature to leave anyone behind," Kit says.

"I know. I wasn't being serious, just wishful thinking," Burns says to him. "Either way, we're going to have to get his ass. And from there, we'll go for Anika and the rest. You up for it?"

"Yes, sir."

Burns nodded and grabbed the GPS from his pocket. Kit stepped up close to Burns, and reaching behind his hip, he pulled his revolver with the holster and gives it to Burns. "Take this," Kit says.

"How many guns do you have on you?" Burns says, taking the holstered Taurus revolver.

"Wasn't planning on bringing it. I just forgot I had it until it was too late," Kit says. "I only have the chambered rounds, no other ammo, so take careful shots."

Burns nodded and stuffed the holster in his waistband at his 3 o'clock.

"I'll take point," Kit says, walking past Burns. "Let's go get our team."

Matt slowly crept through the ferns, still following the tracks as best as he could. Matt was very lucky that the tracks were easy to follow, because he's never been a good tracker to begin with. For working in the wild as long as he did, he never did get around to get proper terrain training. Even then, he always felt he didn't need it. He always seemed to find his way around.

Matt stepped over a downed tree, his eyes scanning the dense forest. He looked down at the dirt again, but he didn't see any more trackway. He looked around; no more tracks anywhere. He glanced back at the log he stepped over. There were tracks leading up to the log. So the animal hopped up on the log and either went left or right.

Damn, he was going to have to take a gamble. Matt turned left and continued in that direction. He moved in a crouched position, being as silent as he could. He had done this countless times before. He had stalked animals before with a guide in Kenya. Usually to sedate them for his segments on the show. But this time he had no guide; he was on his own.

It didn't matter. Matt was going to sedate one. He could do it on his own. His plan was to sedate it and bring it back to the lodge. Once there, he was going to set up the collapsable cage he had brought with him. They'd put the animal in the cage, have Lucy identify it, take a blood sample, and then film a segment for the show. Afterward, they'd let the animal scurry back to the forest.

Matt hadn't told anyone about the cage he had brought. Why would he? Everyone had been so combative with him for the last few days. He couldn't be honest with them anymore. The world needed to see these animals, alive and up close. Otherwise, their discovery would have no credibility. Matt understands that better than anyone; he's not doing all of this only for the world to reject it. People were going to see how magnificent these creatures are.

Matt heard a chirp. He stopped for a second and listened closely. He heard more chirps. Not agitated chirps, but passive. At least, they sounded passive. Matt changed his stance to a crouch. He slowly snuck forward. The chirping becomes slightly louder with each step. Matt stopped moving and stayed as still as he could. About forty yards away, there was a small animal, standing up against a tree. It's a dinosaur, almost four feet tall. It's leaning up against the base of the tree, its slender clawed arms rubbing its snout. It seemed to be fixated on the rubbing.

Matt watched the dinosaur, feeling his stomach flutter with butterflies. *Why didn't you tell me, Bill*, he thought to himself, *that how beautiful these animals are?* The animal's skin was a dark color that almost made it blend in with the vegetation behind it. The only reason it wasn't completely camouflaged was because it was moving its arms.

Matt slowly raised the dart rifle. He, he aimed down the small holographic sight, placing the red dot directly over the animal's left shoulder. Matt inhaled, held his breath, and pulled the trigger. The dart rifle had no recoil and made very little noise. All that was heard was the click of the trigger pull.

The air rifle shot out a single dart, sending it flying toward the dinosaur.

The small dart struck the dinosaur right where Matt had aimed it. But the dart didn't penetrate fully. The dart's sharp end only seemed to have gone in a couple millimeters. It just hung loosely from the animal's thick hide. The cub swung its head around and examined the dart, confused. Matt exhaled, readying for another shot, but then the cub looked up and saw him immediately. The cub decided to wail in fear, calling for help. Matt opened the air rifle, pulled out a dart, and held it in his hand.

"Guess we're doing this the hard way," Matt mumbled to himself. He dropped the air rifle and sprinted forward at the cub, his hand raised, holding the dart like a knife.

The cub continued to wail, but in short bursts, surprised by the sudden charge from the human. When Matt was only a couple of feet away, the cub snapped its head forward and hissed, standing its ground. The cub snapped its jaws at Matt. He jerked back, keeping his distance. Matt inched his hand forward, and the cub snapped its jaws again. Matt felt a sense of familiarity—crocodiles would do the same thing. They would snap their jaws and inch forward every time, but rarely ever do a full-on attack.

Matt felt safe, even if the animal kept on wailing as loud as it could. He taunted the animal once more, waving his hands at it to get it to snap at him. Once the animal did, Matt stepped to the side instead of jerking back. He grabbed the cub by the top of its snout with his free hand and swung it forward. The cub yipped as it was shocked to have been outsmarted by a larger animal. Matt put his arm around the cub's neck and kneeled down. He tightened his grip around the cub's neck, trying to get the animal to settle.

The cub continued to wail, almost begging for mercy in its whimpers. Matt held the animal tight to his body, constantly bobbing his face back and forth, dodging the cubs' defensive bites. Matt then swung his free arm around, dart in his hand. He shushed the animal. "Don't make this harder, buddy," he whispered as he brought his hand around to stick the dart in the animal. He stabs the dart over the cub's left shoulder, — he was waiting for the opportunity in between defensive bites to jam the dart in. Suddenly, he heard a hooting noise behind him. Matt moves his head slightly only to see a shape pounce onto his back.

He felt something grip the back of his jacket and the weight of something sitting on his back.

He felt a sharp pain on his shoulder, accompanied by a rageful growling. Matt let the cub in his hands go and stood up, shaking his body. The weight on his back suddenly faded. He had shaken whatever had pounced on him. He quickly turned to face his attacker. He saw another cub, head hunched down, hissing in contempt at Matt.

Matt touched his shoulder. He felt the jagged cuts in his jacket were warm with blood. He then heard the other cub behind him, the one he let go, start to hiss as well. Matt realized he still held the dart in his hand, so he quickly shook off the pain. He watched as the two cubs circled him, hissing menacingly.

"I'm waiting for ya," Matt says. "You don't scare me."

Matt then suddenly heard a third hissing sound, from above him. Matt glanced up and saw a third cub, holding itself up in one of the trees, its arms gripping the soft bark with its claws. The cub jumped off the tree, pouncing at Matt. But Matt was quick on his feet. He rolled out of the way before the third cub landed on him. It landed and clumsily toppled forward. It then stood up and turned its attention at Matt, who was already on his feet.

"Tried to jump me, didn't ya?" Matt says with a smile. *"Cheeky fucker."*

All three cubs then hissed in unison, and again began to slowly circle Matt. He calmly turned his body, trying to keep his back away from the animals. Matt found it amusing that they were attempting to intimidate him. Matt yelled back his own attempted snarl at the animals, trying to frighten them. But they didn't falter. They were not afraid of Matt in the slightest.

Okay, Matt thought, *this might be bad.*

One of the animals picked up its pace and circled until it was at Matthew's back. It took the opportunity and bolted forward. Matt swung around with his hands raised. The animal caught Matt's left forearm in its jaws. It clamped down just as Matt swung a punch. He gasped in pain and tried to pull his arm back. But he couldn't. It was latched onto his forearm with its sharp teeth. Matt instinctively tried to swing a kick at the cub biting his forearm.

That was a mistake. By focusing on the animal biting his arm, he neglected the other two cubs. The others saw their opportunity and darted forward. One of them grabbed Matt by the leg before he could deliver a kick. The cub sunk its teeth into Matt's ankle and pulled backward. Matt kept his balance, just barely, as two cubs were tugging his body in opposite directions. He powered through the pains in his forearm and ankle. He was just about to try another defensive maneuver when the third cub pounced on his back.

Between the tugging and the dinosaur on his back, Matt collapsed onto the dirt. He swung his free arm wildly, trying to defend himself. The cub on his back snapped a bite at his shoulder again, tugging at his jacket, trying to tear through. Matt felt a rush of adrenaline. He suddenly swung his other foot and kicked the cub holding his ankle. The heel of his boot struck the cub in the nose, and the cub on his ankle let go, retreating with a snort. He then managed to get to his knees and shook his body hard. Sending the cub on his back staggering off onto the dirt floor.

He was almost free. He turned his attention to the cub still latched onto his forearm. He tugged as hard as he could and pulled the animal closer to him. He swung the dart in his hand and jammed it right into the cub's neck. Matt felt the needle finally break the skin, the dart sinking all the way in. The cub whimpered and opened its jaws. It staggered backward, clawing at the dart in its neck. The cub took out the dart and turned to hiss at Matt.

Matt scrambled to his feet, his body in pain from the animals' attacks. He saw the three cubs snarl at him, starting their circling behavior again, poised to attack. Matt recognized this kind of behavior. He saw it in wolves, hyenas, and African wild dogs. They would keep picking at him. They would tire him out, little by little, until his stamina was gone. Then he won't be able to defend himself, and they'd eat at their leisure. Matt knew this as the animals continued to circle him, the young cubs full of energy. The second attack from the cubs was imminent, Matt could feel it. He readied himself, waiting for one of them to charge.

The forest air suddenly cracked, a deafening sound echoing through the trees. Matt turned to see Burns and Kit running toward him, Kit holding a rifle. The cubs became startled by the rifle shot, and once they saw Burns and Kit, they quickly scampered away into the foliage. Matt put his hands on his knees, relieved as he gasped for air. Burns and Kit reached Matt. Kit slid back the bolt, sending the hot casing tumbling out. He racked in another round and then leaned over to pick up the spent casing from the mud.

"Just in the nick of time," Matt says, catching his breath. "I really thought they had me there for a sec-"

Matt suddenly staggered backward. Burns had sent a well-placed haymaker toward Matt's jaw, striking Matt in the face. Burns's knuckles cracked as they struck the jawline. Kit saw it happen, but he decided not to interfere. Matt caught his balance after the punch. He held his jaw and looked up at Burns. "If I had any sensibilities I would-"

"If you had any," Burns interrupted. "You would keep your goddamn mouth shut."

Matt scoffed. "What are we doing here, Bill? Are we studying these animals? Or are we cowering in our fortress?"

"Didn't look much like studying, I just saved your ass," Burns says.

Matt gasped. "Oh please, I was-"

"*I saved you.*"

Matt smiled. "Yeah, you kinda did."

Kit shakes his head at Matt's smile. The man cannot seem to take anything seriously. He was almost mauled by three dinosaurs and he's still somehow wearing a smile. Kit thought either the man was in shock or insane.

"Let me take a look at those wounds," Burns says to Matt. He leaned in closer, his face close to the cuts on his shoulder. He then kneeled down and slipped off his backpack. He rummaged around until he saw a small roll of bandages. He gave it to Matt. Matt took the roll of bandages. "Wrap up your arm and leg for now. We'll patch you up properly at the lodge," Burns says.

"They don't hurt, no need to worry," Matt told him.

"They don't hurt now," Burns says. "But they definitely will later. You need to clean those wounds as soon as you can. Who knows what those animals have in their teeth."

"We'll have to escort him back," Kit reminded. "Chances are, they'll be back for him if they see him alone again."

"Christ," Burns growled. Kit was right. "Fine then, we'll get him back to the lodge. Then we'll double it back out here."

Matt frowned. "Whoa there, hold your horses, ain't no way I'm not coming with you."

"Fat chance of that," Burns says. "I don't want you anywhere near us."

"I came out here to look for my daughter, Bill," Matt says. "I'm coming with you."

Kit gasped. "You have a shitty poker face, by the way."

"Just, listen for a moment," Matt says. "I was just attacked, okay? I'll admit, they're a bit more aggressive than I anticipated. Let me come with. I can help."

Burns gave Matt a look, a disappointed frown. Kit was right. You could see right through Matt's bullshit almost immediately. Burns knew having Matt with them would be more of hindrance than actual help.

"We're wasting daylight," Kit says.

Burns sighed. He stepped forward, only inches away from Matt's face. "If you jeopardize us in any way, I swear, I won't save you again."

Matt has never liked being challenged, and this was the

first time Burns had ever threatened him in any way. Still, there would be no point in arguing with him right now. The animals' hostile behavior did make Matt reconsider that Anika might be in danger. Matt just nodded at Burns, acknowledging his ultimatum. Burns stepped back. He grabbed his backpack off the ground and slipped it on. He then pulled the GPS out of his pocket. He looked at it for a few seconds, then to their right. "We go that way," Burns says, pointing to their right. "We keep going until we find Anika. With any luck, we'll run into her."

"With any luck, the dinosaurs ran off that way," Matt says.

"Well then, same as before," Kit says. He walked forward past them both. "I'll take point, keep it tight, and let's not wander off. I'm talking to you, *Jack Hanna*."

Matt just smiled. They really didn't trust him. This was some team he had. Kit strolled through the forest, rifle raised, and Burns and Matt followed. As they walked, Burns couldn't help but notice they were walking right on top of fresh dinosaur tracks.

HUNTED

Anika didn't know how far or how long she had run. What she did know was that she had barely escaped from the vicious dinosaurs. The adrenaline had worn off just a bit, enough that her memories started to parade in her mind. The images of JJ and Zeke's demise seared into her brain. She should have done something. Anything to save their lives, but instead she froze.

Instead, she just watched in horror as they were torn apart. She had seen the extent of the animal's savagery. Their eating behavior was unlike anything she had ever seen. The alpha's need to tear into JJ, piece by piece. Nothing short of cruelty, the alpha waiting after every bite to make sure Anika was watching. Why did it do that? Is she right? Was it for the sake of being cruel that it slowly took JJ apart?

Anika learned over her life that no matter how violent or cruel an animal seems, there's never any malice behind it. It's a basic instinct, their predator-prey response. The only animals known to torture their prey are chimpanzees, and humans.

Regardless of what happened, she needs to stay alive as long as possible. Which seems improbable every second she runs. She reminds herself that she knows nothing about these animals. She doesn't know if they would attempt to follow Anika or leave her alone after she left their territory. She can still hear her boots squelching in the mud as she bolts through the forest. Her breath shallow and her lungs wheezing, her body desperately needs a break.

Anika decided to stop running, her lungs aching for rest and oxygen. She let her legs come to a stop, her boots sliding across the mud, almost toppling forward. Once she regained her balance, she bent over and put her hands on her knees, catching her breath. She tried to calm her breathing so she could listen to the forest. She listened closely, the leaves rustling in the wind and rain. The heavy rain pattering on the ferns and dirt. She could not hear anything, nothing at all that would indicate she was being followed. The only other thing she could hear was her heart pounding in her throat.

She is not being followed.

Unless they were excellent stalkers, already creeping up on her while she caught her breath. Seconds away from pouncing on her back to tear her apart like they did to Zeke and JJ. Anika quickly shook the thought away. She needed to keep her pessimism in check if she wanted to stay alive. She had to find her way back to the lodge and warn the others. She had to tell them that Zeke and JJ were not only dead, but that their corpses were unrecoverable. How could she find her way back? She didn't even know what direction she's running in. She has nothing on her, no tools at all. She dropped her backpack on the ground so that she could flee faster.

Anika then noticed the bulge in her right pocket, *the GPS*. She remembers she stuffed it in her pants pocket the last time she used it. So she wasn't completely screwed; she had increased her chances by about one percent. She quickly pulled it out and flipped it on, scanning the map. She saw the arrow indicator of her current position, and the red systematic line they had been following earlier. She had run southwest, diagonal from the lodge. The way back was northeast, but even then, it would still be almost a two-hour walk...

A loud hooting emanated from the forest behind her in the distance. Anika stood up, petrified. She looked around where she was, but she couldn't see anything. Nothing but trees and ferns as far as the eye could see. She could not see more than a few feet in front of her. The dinosaurs had an advantage. They could hide anywhere, stalk from anywhere.

Stop with those damn thoughts, get your shit together.

She then heard a second hooting, a response from another direction. It came from the forest to her right. They were communicating, and it confirmed that they were indeed following her. The hooting sounded far, but not by a lot. She had some time before they found her. Anika had to think of something quick. She thought about running, but she would not be able to keep it up for the almost two-hour hike back. Also, she remembered the terrifying speed of the animals. There was no point in running from a predator like this' she would just die tired. With predators like these, the smart thing to do was to evade them as best as she could and save her stamina.

Besides, running is what you do when a plan fails.

She heard more hooting, this time considerably closer. They were covering ground incredibly fast. She had no more time; she had to hide. Anika looked around. She needs to get out of sight, but where? She then heard another deep response to the hooting. It started as a screech and ended like a bark. The hooting went silent. Anika instantly knew it came from one of the adults. The presence of the adults helped Anika make up her mind. She looked at where she was standing, in the middle of a cluster of Huon pine trees. Tall, majestic but old trees that belonged to the old earth. The Huon pines were straight trunked, with erratic branches and drooping layers of green leaves.

She bolted for the nearest tree and began to climb. She felt the fragrant damp tree bark against her hands and face as she climbed as high as she could. Her hands slipped as well as her boots while climbing, but she didn't care. The instant fight-or-flight response gave her the stamina and will to keep going. She climbs, as high as she can, smaller branches and leaves scratching her face, ears, and neck as she makes her way up.

Eventually, she found herself in a position where she could climb no further. The branches were either fragile or out of reach. To climb higher meant more risk of plummeting down to the impending creatures below.

She was standing on a thick branch, about thirty feet in the air. The branch was sturdy enough to hold her weight. She pressed her back up against the tree, keeping her boots together on the branch, keeping herself perfectly vertical with the tree. If anything were to look up, hopefully she would be harder to spot. Hopefully, the constant rain would impede the animal's vision just enough to look past her. Just as she had this thought, she heard rustling from beneath her tree. She slowly peered down and saw a cub stepping into view. The small animal looked around, glancing in every direction.

Stand still.

It stepped forward a couple more steps, until it was directly under Anika. The cub just kept glancing in all directions, bobbing its head, confused. She could see the feathers on its head, which looked like they were moving. The feathers move up and down, either spiking its appearance or combing themselves nicely on the animal's head. The animal then hopped forward, playfully. It rustled through the nearby bushes. It was chirping and then squawking when it could not find anything. The cub seemed confused as it searched, as if it was unsure what to do next.

Anika then saw the alpha emerge from behind a bouquet of ferns. The terrifying adult dinosaur makes no noise as it approaches. And despite the colors on its scales and feathers, it blends in well to its surroundings. Anika watched as the alpha slowly stepped toward the confused cub and then nudged it with its snout. The cub turned its head around, squawking at the alpha. The cub still seemed bewildered, unsure of where to go. The alpha then lowers its head close to the ground and sniffs the dirt. It moved its nose around for a couple feet and then moved its head back upright. It crowed at the cub and then nudged it in a specific direction. The cub then scampered away, not even bothering to follow a scent trail.

The cubs don't know how to track. Anika almost felt relieved at the thought, but it quickly faded away when the alpha continued to sniff the dirt around the tree. *The cubs can't, but the adults can.*

How good are the creatures' predatory senses? She knew the answer to the question would determine her survival in the next few moments. Anika cupped her hands. She covered her nose and mouth, trying to keep her noise and scent at a minimum. The alpha sniffed the dirt and slowly crept forward, like a bloodhound following a trail. It kept following until it stopped. It snorted and picked up the scent again. Only to stop sniffing and snort in frustration. The animal seems to have lost its trail. Anika hoped the alpha didn't pick up her scent again and figure out that she had climbed a tree.

The alpha looks around some more, and then goes into the direction that it sent the cub in. It trudges along, its head up, probing and alert for any movement. As the alpha walks, it tends to the wounds on its neck and forearms. The slashes are still fresh from the scuffle with the male. Anika wonders if the beta is also stalking her elsewhere, or if the male was successful in its fight. Maybe she only has the alpha to worry about. Still, she will move forward on the assumption that there are four adult dinosaurs pursuing her.

Anika watched the alpha slowly disappear hundreds of feet away into the forest. Anika exhaled in relief, feeling incredibly lucky. She deduced that the only reason she wasn't spotted is because the animals probably haven't encountered any prey that can climb trees.

That could be her strategy. There were hundreds of trees in the Tasmanian forest. She had to be extra careful from now on though. If she's spotted climbing a tree, she can no longer hide in them. Unfortunately for her, the alpha had wandered away in the direction she needed to go. This was going to be really dicey. She would need to be as careful as possible.

I wonder if they double back? Could I safely follow from behind the animals without being spotted?

Anika peered around her tree, making sure there weren't any more animals searching for her. She didn't see anything, so she decided it was safe enough to climb down. She slowly crept off the branch she was on and started to climb down. It was much more difficult to get down, the slippery tree bark making it hard for her boots to get a grip. She finally made it to the bottom and looked around the base of the tree. She could only hear her breath and the rain. *God, the incessant damn rain.*

There was no sign of any life. She seemed to be alone for now. She took one step forward when she felt a rush of warm air brush her ponytail. She froze and slowly turned her head to look over her shoulder.

Behind Anika, standing next to the tree sneering at her, *was the male.*

ACTON'S DICTUM

Valente was bent over at the waist, his head between his knees, breathing in and out slowly. His mind was racing, his heart pumping out of his chest. There was a feeling of walls closing in on him, even though he was outside. The sun barely peeks through the clouds. "This is big," Ward says. "I mean, hell, if any of it is true, it's insane. Now the damn lawsuit makes sense. You're not the only one protecting an investment."

"I never thought it would be something this crazy," Valente says. "My father is nuts. This is the worst possible outcome we could have had."

Hogan just stared at both Valente and Ward, confused about whatever it was they were talking about. "What are you on about?" Hogan says. "Whose father are we talking about? What does that have to do with anything?"

"To give you some context," Ward says. "His father was suing us for being out here in the first place, something about reckless endangerment. Said he had a 'construction site' or 'owned a construction site' out here, so we came to see what it was."

"A construction site," Hogan says. "Well, doesn't that just piece together beautifully. And why is your father such an asshole?"

"To give you some more context," Ward says. "His father is Rafe Valente. He owns Valente Pharmaceuticals."

Hogan jerked his head back at the sudden information,

"Valente Pharmaceuticals?" Hogan asks. "Oh Lord, things just keep getting worse, *the* Valente Pharmaceuticals?"

"That's right," Ward says. "So you can imagine the kind of problems this is going to bring up for us now."

Valente finally stood up after catching his breath, but he kept his hands on his hips, thinking while looking off into the distance. "*Problems* don't even begin to describe our current situation," Valente says in a firm tone. "If what you've told us is true, Dr. Hogan, him acquiring the animal's DNA that produces these kinds of reactions for cancer patients, it does not bode well for the rest of the world. My father is the definition of corporate greed."

"Well, there's not much you can do about it now," Hogan says. "The cat's out of the bag. He probably has access to the animals and the saliva. But now, all of this makes more sense. Fucker's been keeping all the shit happening here hush-hush. No offense, mate, but your father is a *right asshole.*"

"Yeah," Ward says. "I was thinking that too, what could we possibly do? All we can do is cut short the expedition and head home. I mean, it's the most logical thing to do."

"I know it's the most logical thing to do," Valente says. "But I still want to look into this."

"What do you mean *look into this*?" Ward says angrily. "How else could we possibly look into this? We wouldn't know where to start. You really got to get your fucking priorities straight. There are people out there, our *friends*, that are in danger."

"Christ, I'm not naïve, Lee," Valente says. "I'm not ignoring the story that Dr. Hogan just told us. As a matter of fact, we're going to call the ranger stations right now and get somebody to go out there to check up on them as soon as we can."

Ward sneered at his friend. "It should be *us* driving out

there, Forrest, why are *we* not driving out there?"

"Because we're going to do both. We're going to make sure they are safe, and then we are going to figure out what my father is going to do with this discovery," Valente says. "Remember what you told me? To do something that for once didn't benefit me. Looking into what my father is doing does not benefit me at all."

Hogan shook his head. "Hold on. Hold on. You're not actually considering going up against Valente Pharma, are you?" Hogan scoffed and pulled out another cigarette. "You remember that story of that journalist a few years back? The one about the illegal test trials?"

Valente didn't say a word, and Hogan read his face like a book.

"Yeah, *you know*," Hogan says.

"What journalist?" Ward asks.

Hogan kept his stare with Valente. "Pretended to be a pharmacist of some kind, got into some lab in New York. Had footage showing illegal test trials on dogs, very awful stuff. Almost got it published, *almost*. What was it? Mercs for hire of some sort? Or was it the actual police?"

Valente says nothing.

"Either way, he died in a supposed gunfight. Funny, his friends don't remember him ever owning a gun," Hogan says.

Ward looked at his friend, annoyed that Valente never mentioned how dangerous his father was. Valente only sighed and gave Ward a short shrug.

"Oh fuck," Ward says. "So that shit about 'keeping you in good health' was a genuine fucking threat?"

"You've met him in person?" Hogan asks.

"In the flesh, dead-eyed scrawny motherfucker," Ward says.

Valente shook off the dread and looked at Ward. "We have to find the construction site".

"What?!" Ward snapped.

"Think of what he is doing," Valente says sternly. "He somehow discovered the animal, either before or after we did. If it was after, someone talked."

"Who gives a shit if someone talked-" Ward began to say.

"He knows. He knows we know," Valente says. "Whether we walk away or not. We are in it now. He will not stop, lawsuit or not, he is not done with us."

Ward just frowned.

"He has access to the animal. My father is not a scientist. There's no way he could have figured this out on his own. And I'm positive Dr. Hogan here didn't tell anyone about this".

"He's right," Hogan agreed.

"Transfer of materials," Valente says.

Ward sighed and rolled his eyes.

"What does that mean?" Hogan asks.

"We built a headquarters for our team, in the national park. We used a construction firm based out of Hobart. They helped facilitate the transfer of our materials and even provided vehicles and blueprints. Those victims you spoke of had to have been coming from somewhere. I guarantee you we can find the site, wherever it is," Valente says.

"Forrest," Ward says firmly.

"We can find it, Lee," Valente pleaded.

Ward sighed. That was not what he meant, and he didn't know how else to convince his friend otherwise. But what was the point in arguing? Whenever Valente got into doing something, there was hardly anything at all that could stop him. Ward gave his friend an angry look. "Okay, this is what we are going to do. For the sake of saving time," Ward says. "We are going to call the ranger station, and we are going to have them send everybody out there. And then we are going to call my colleague at the construction firm that we used to build the house, and I'm going to ask him nicely about where this construction site actually is."

Valente smiled. "See, I knew you knew what to do."

Ward shook his head. "Just remember if anything goes wrong, *you* suggested otherwise." Ward then turned to look at Dr. Hogan. "All right, Dr. Hogan, we're going to be heading out to go rile up some shit, if you know what I mean. I think it'd be safe for you to go home at some point. Lock yourself in and don't come out until we come back."

Dr. Hogan bobbed his head in a confused manner. "And if for whatever reason you don't come back?"

"Then you hope to God that they don't come after you too," Ward says.

"Jesus Christ mate, you Americans love the Clint Eastwood shit, huh? Well then, all right," Dr. Hogan says. "But do me a favor, if you do make it out of whatever you're about to do, fill me in, yeah? Oh, and one more thing."

Valente and Ward both nodded to Hogan.

"What animal is killing all these people?" Hogan asks. "It's not a fucking sasquatch, is it?"

"Nothing as crazy as that," Ward says. "It's a dinosaur."

Hogan couldn't help but laugh. He stopped cackling the moment he saw Ward was serious. Hogan simply shook his head and herded them both into the building. Valente and Ward shook Dr. Hogan's hand then parted ways. They maneuvered through the hallways once more to make it back to the entrance of the Magistrate Court of Tasmania. They exited the building and made their way quickly to the Toyota 4Runner parked in the mostly empty lot. They stepped inside quickly. Ward was driving once again while Valente pulled up his phone.

"What was the construction company we used again?" Valente asks.

"Birch Contracting," Ward says.

"Think they'll tell us what we need?"

"Positive, he will."

"You seem awfully confident."

"I served with him in the military. Jeff will tell us," Ward says.

Valente typed it into his phone. The search results came up with a 'Birch Contracting', with the main office only forty minutes away. Ward started to drive away while Valente pulled up the route to the contractor company. On the drive there, Valente used Ward's phone to dial for the ranger station that was in the national park. It took them a few phone calls to get them to finally answer, and when they did, Valente explained the situation to them.

Explaining to them the kind of danger the expedition team was in and the creatures they would encounter did not go well. It occurred to Ward that it was probably not the best idea, but at least they got the point across. They were exposed to dangerous wildlife. The park rangers, at first, being residents of the continent, were nonchalant about the matter. They assured them saying that they would make it out later this evening. Valente told them that this was life and death, that this was an emergency and they needed to head out there now. Again, the park rangers nonchalantly responded with: "Yeah, whatever, we'll get to it when we get to it. No worries, we'll check out your friends." And then, they hung up without letting Valente say anything more in response.

Valente shrugged in annoyance. "I'm not entirely sure they're going to do what we asked them to do. And not as expeditiously as we'd like. What should I do? Should I call them again and offer them money? To speed things up?"

Ward shook his head. "Just leave it alone. This business with the contractors shouldn't take long. Plus, I got a radio rigged up here in my truck, so hopefully wherever we go, we're in range of them. We can just call them over the radio and see what's going on. If they're smart, they've been staying indoors. And I trust Kit and JJ to keep shit in line."

"Maybe we'll finally know what my dad was building out here in the first place," Valente says.

"Yes," Ward says firmly. "I've been thinking about that myself since you mentioned it earlier. I wonder if whatever he's building out here was before or after he made this discovery? He seemed to be throwing a lot of bodies at the project, not willing to give up on it. I mean, what does he usually build? He builds hospitals or something?"

"That's what Wikipedia says he does," Valente says. "Truth be told, he's only really built three hospitals in the entire world. The rest of them he just bought and owned and says he built them. I know it for sure, I was there. He's quite the fucking liar if you ask me. That's one of the reasons I tend to stay away from him as much as I can. He has no sense of morality. He just wants to buy and buy more stuff, own more liquidation, be the richest man he can possibly be. All this stuff you hear about hospitals is just a ploy."

Ward chuckled. "Sounds like the apple didn't fall too far from the tree."

"Lee, I could do without the negative comments, for God's sake," Valente says. "We're on the same side. Don't you forget that I'm trying to figure this out so nobody else gets hurt. I know you think I don't have my priorities straight. I can see how you might feel that way, but you have to understand that something like this could greatly affect the world. Do you know the weight of what Dr. Hogan just told us? The animal's DNA has an effect on cancer cells. It eradicates them, essentially curing it. Do you know how big that is, Lee?"

"You know, maybe I'm being naïve, but a pharmaceutical company finding the cure for cancer does not seem like the end of the world."

"You're right, it's an incredibly naïve thought," Valente says, "You didn't grow up with him. You didn't let him try to raise you. Rafe Valente is one of the greediest humans you could possibly meet. And the only thing he loves more than money is violence. Do you know how many heads he has in his big-game hunting rooms across his *multiple* mansions? He kills because he can. He loves feeling in control of everything, and everyone. Him owning the cure for cancer? He's not the person who should own it. He's going to find a way to control the market, and in order to do that, he needs to control the source, and to control the source, take a guess what he needs to do?"

Ward sighed. "The source of this cure are the animals, the dinosaurs. Of course, he would need to keep them contained in some way so that he could extract their DNA."

"That's right," Valente says. "He's going to find a way to exploit these animals. Contrary to what you may believe about my character, Lee, I really do believe in what I do. I don't want anyone taking advantage of nature. The reason that I found this passion is because I grew up with someone who did nothing but take advantage. I want to stop that. I want to do my part, and this in no way benefits me, Lee. You have to understand that I want to do this because it's the right thing to do."

Ward turned a corner, the Toyota 4Runner going down an empty street before he spoke again. "If we're going to do this," Ward says grimly. "I hope you know what the implications of the situation are. I paid attention to the little journalist story Hogan told us. I hope you know how far we're going to have to take it."

"I know exactly how far we're going to have to take it," Valente says.

"Oh, do you?" Ward says. "Let's test that theory. I want you to open up the glove box and tell me what you see."

Valente didn't think anything of it. He reached forward to the glove box and he opened it. With his right hand, he pulled the glove box latch, and its compartment plopped open. There was a pair of sunglasses and an HK USP .45 ACP pistol in a leather Bianchi over the waistband holster. Just in that very moment, he knew what his friend Ward was talking about. If indeed his father was taking advantage of the cure for cancer, then he would have to bring the exploitation of these animals to light. He knew this for certain: Rafe Valente, owner of Valente Pharmaceuticals, *was not going to go down quietly*.

"That's how far we're going to have to take it," Ward says. "There's no other way around it. If it comes to that, let me take over. But when it comes to the talking and all the lawyer bullshit, you go right ahead, okay?"

Valente closed the glove box. "I understand, Lee. If it comes down to that, then this is your world, and you do what you think is best. Now let's go find this construction site and save our friends."

SEARCH PARTY

Kit trekked through the dense forest floor of the Tasmanian wilderness, with Burns and Matt following closely behind. Kit carefully minded his step, finding his footing a lot easier than before. His rain jacket constantly snagged on a variety of plants as he was walking. Some of them are different shades of green, most of them sending out thick layers of vertical branches. He was getting used to the terrain; he wasn't slipping as much as before. Even then, he was still feeling uneasy. The situation at hand made it difficult to contemplate anything else.

He was starting to see their expedition in a whole different perspective. When Valente had first shown him the footage of the dinosaur and explained the expedition, Kit had been ecstatic. It had been the most interesting mission he had ever heard of. For months, he could not wait to step foot into the world of explorers. Now that he was finally here, he couldn't help but feel disappointed. This was no ordinary mission. In fact, it seemed more complicated than anything he had ever done before.

They were only two days into this expedition and there were already missing team members. Not to mention the attack on Matt. *Christ*, he thought, *the attack those animals delivered*. Kit remembers jogging through the forest after he spotted Matt on the ground in the distance. The dinosaurs on his body, trying to tear him apart and kill him. The animals were pulling Matt's body in opposite directions, keeping him disoriented. Matt had barely scraped by with his life. Those animals seemed so vicious. Matt was incredibly lucky that they found him when they did.

These dinosaurs that they couldn't wait to see immediately became a dire threat. Kit felt that the charm of rediscovery was gone. Just like his time in the service. After his last tour, he just felt so disillusioned and so tired of fighting for what seemed like nothing at all. Now he felt he was stuck in another battlefield, where he once more didn't know what was right or wrong. But still, Kit somehow preferred a gunfight than whatever the hell this was. Even if nature was supposed to be impersonal, being torn apart seemed more personal than getting domed by a bullet.

"These animals are a bit nifty, aren't they?" Matt says.

"What the hell are you talking about?" Burns asks.

"I mean, they just attacked me out of the blue. I didn't really do anything to them. I just tried to tranquilize one of them," Matt says nonchalantly.

"Yes, and how exactly did you try to tranquilize them?" Burns asks, annoyed.

"All right, I'll admit I may have startled them a little bit," Matt says. "What I meant was that they seemed a little more aggressive than what I'm used to."

"A little more aggressive than what you're used to," Burns repeated. "And what exactly are you used to?"

"Well," Matt was starting to say, but Burns quickly interrupted.

"It was a rhetorical question. I know exactly what the hell you're talking about," Burns snapped. "You scared the shit out of these animals. I bet that's exactly what you did. I've seen you do it before. Hell, I saw you do it three years ago with some goddamn hyenas. These animals attacked because you instigated it, and I don't doubt that for a second."

"God, you know all this hostility toward me really has no end, does it?" Matt says. "And what? I'm supposed to spend a month out here with you guys? I don't know what your deal is with me. I'm just doing my job."

"You're a bull in a china shop, buddy," Kit added. "Ain't no way you consider what you would do a motherfucking job."

"At any rate," Matt says. "All I'll say is this. I'll admit these animals seem a bit more dangerous than I anticipated, and for that, just for you guys, I'll be a little more cautious. I'll try to keep my... *excitement* under control. I know y'all are worried about Anika and the rest. We'll find them, probably just a minor setback."

Burns chose not to retort or say anything. He always hated that he tried to take control like that. He would mess up a situation and then try and take accountability in the worst way possible. And then in the end, when everything ends, you realize his accountability actually meant nothing. Burns also especially hated that he tried to seem extremely positive, no matter the situation. Sure, Burns was hoping that nothing had happened to Anika, and he also hoped that Matt was right, that she had hit a minor setback with her group. But Matt's naive optimism was obnoxious, and Burns could not shake the uneasy feeling from his body. He knew something was wrong and he knew he had to find her.

"You know, I've been meaning to ask you, Mr. Burns," Kit says. "I don't know much about animals, but I saw the way they were attacking Matt. Did that seem at all similar to anything you've seen before? Any measure of familiarity so that you can perhaps predict their movement?"

Burns shook his head. "Not that I could see. I only saw glimpses of how they were attacking Matthew. From what I can tell, they're exceptionally good at being pack hunters. Did you see the way they were hopping around him, surrounding him, making his personal space smaller and smaller by the second? A lot of pack hunters do that. These ones seem to be especially skilled at rounding up prey. And our assumption is that they are only younglings, and they're already skilled in doing that. Who knows what the adults will be like."

"You've been around pack hunters much?" Kit asks.

"I have," Burns says.

"And what are you doing in that scenario, if you're surrounded?" Kit asks.

"Well," Burns says, "If you're in the odd situation where you only have about three or four animals surrounding you, you would stand your ground, and try not to run away. Try to make yourself seem as big as you can, and try to frighten them away. Try to make them think that killing you is not worth the risk. If you try to run away, they will only kill you quicker. It's what they do. They'll purposely try to lower your stamina so that you have nothing left to fight back with."

Kit had another question, but didn't know if he should ask it. He asks anyway: "And what do you do if it's more than three or four animals surrounding you?"

Burns sighed. "Try to kill as many as you can, and pray that it's over quickly. Because the thing is, most pack hunters I've seen don't really wait for you to die to start eating."

"Fuck, man," Kit says. "You really make me feel like I should have stayed home."

"We all should have stayed home," Burns says solemnly.

Kit decided not to say anything else. The conversation was making him queasy. He continued to walk behind Burns as he had the GPS and guided them through the forest. Matt was behind them both, but every once in a while, Kit would glance backward to make sure that he had not wandered off. Which didn't make sense, to any normal person, knowing the stakes of the current situation. Why would anyone wander off? Still, Kit had finally accepted that Matt Irving was not normal. He was just almost killed not twenty minutes ago. He could have been torn apart by a pack of ravenous dinosaurs had it not been for Kit and Burns. And yet here he was, defending himself as if he was innocent in the cause.

The man just would not take anything seriously, even when there was the implication that his own daughter was possibly in danger. Kit knew this type of people well. He would encounter them every once in a while, in his time in the military. Incredibly extroverted people, they would love nothing more than to be the center of attention. They had to be the center of attention, or else their life would not make sense to them. And because of their extroverted nature and their incessant need to be liked by everyone, they would often put themselves and others in situations that were not ideal.

Kit knew that these people existed everywhere, not just in the military. But these kinds of people were specifically dangerous in more extreme situations. Like the one they seem to find themselves in now. So Kit decided to keep an eye on him a lot more than anyone else on this expedition. Hell, a lot more than the actual film crew. Not once did he ever imagine that he would have to watch out for actual nature TV show stars, the people that have been doing this far longer than anyone else.

In the distance, they suddenly heard a deafening sound. It sounded like wailing, or howling. It continued and seemed to only come from one direction. Kit, Burns, and Matt all looked around, trying to find the source of the wailing. After a short while of listening to the sound, to the men, it almost seemed like a distant cry for help, but not human. Kit crouched just slightly, holding the rifle in his hands. He slowly put it to his shoulder, getting ready to fire at the first sign of trouble. He didn't know how animals worked exactly, but what was ingrained in his mind was the tactics used by his enemy while he was in the military. An abrupt cry for help usually meant an ambush. Burns turned his head slowly to face Kit, and then he pointed in a direction to their left.

"I think it's coming from just past those trees over there, about fifty yards away," Burns whispered. "How do you want to do this?"

"Okay," Kit whispered in response. "I'm going to fan out this way on the flank." He points to the left. "And I need you to stay close to this line right here facing the tree. As soon as I start moving in, you start moving in after me. Stay right on my heels but do not get closer to me. We need to stay spaced out. If something happens, it's a lot easier to be enclosed in an array of gunfire."

Burns looked around, and for some reason, he knew exactly what Kit was alluding to. Burns stayed where he was and nodded to Kit that he was ready. He held the revolver forward in his hands, his stance steady. Kit slowly started to fan around, going perpendicular to Burns, the rifle scope raised to his eyesight. Once he was about five meters away from Burns, he started to take a few steps forward, and once he did, he signaled Burns to start following him. Burns followed slowly, and he stayed right on the horizontal line to the tree.

They moved in slowly. The howling noise had been incessant at this point. It would stop and then start as if something was taking a breath after every howl. Burns and Kit took it step by step, holding the weapons in their hands tightly, scanning their surroundings, ready to pull the trigger. And that's when they finally saw it, just past the trees, hidden in an underbrush: a small dinosaur. It was wriggling around on the dirt, its feet kicking while it lay on its side. Its hands moving up and down on the dirt, creating waves. It looked like it was hurt, which was why it was wailing in the first place. It was indeed a cry for help, or so it looked like.

"I don't trust this one bit," Burns says quietly.

Kit breathed in. "I don't trust this either, Mr. Burns. Keep your weapon trained on this animal. I'm going to take a quick scan around the woods."

"We're all good around here," Matt says from behind them.

Kit had forgotten that Matt Irving was there, just behind them. "I don't trust your judgment," Kit whispered. "So I'm going to look around."

Kit slowly spun around, methodically trying to find any sign of trouble, any sign that looked like an ambush to them. He listened while he looked around, moving his eyes from fern to fern, bush to bush, tree to tree, looking for any sign of danger. There was nothing that he could see, nothing obvious to the eye. He finally turned around all the way back to face Burns, who still had his gun pointed right at the wailing dinosaur. "I think we're fine," Kit says to him.

"I want to move in to see what's wrong with it," Burns says.

"Are you sure that's a good idea?" Kit asks him.

"No, I don't think it's a good idea," Burns says. "But even if I'm cautious at the moment, I'm not cruel."

Kit had forgotten up until that very moment that Bill Burns

was in fact a wildlife conservationist. "Okay, you're clear to move in," Kit says to him.

Slowly, Burns took a few cautious steps forward toward the wailing animal. He kept the gun forward, clenched in his hands, ready to pull the trigger on the Taurus Model 605. Once he was close enough to be satisfied, Burns kneeled down to examine the animal. It was foaming at the mouth, and it seemed to be in some kind of muscular distress. After a closer look, Burns realized it wasn't wriggling its hands or moving its feet.

These movements were in fact muscle spasms. They were as recognizable in humans as they were in animals. Burns took his left hand off the grip of his gun, and while he kept the revolver hovered over the animal's head, ready to fire, he reached forward with his fingers and touched the animal's head. The small feathers on the animal's head were thick and matted. Even if these feathers were damp from the rain, Burns could still feel the warm skin under his fingers. The animal was warm-blooded.

The reptilian look of this dinosaur was very misleading. He placed his fingers on the top ridge of its brow and nudged the head toward him slowly so that he could get a good look at the eye. The yellow-colored iris of the dinosaur's eye was pointing upward, almost rolling into its head. The animal was having some kind of seizure. What could the animal be reacting to? What could have happened to it? Burns searched the rest of the animal's body. He saw nothing out of the ordinary. Nothing that could catch his eye as to what was going on with the animal.

Then he saw it. Because of his initial quick examination over the animal's body, he had almost missed it. There was a small red dot over the animal's left forearm. It didn't look like a cut. It looked like a vertical insertion of some kind. A puncture. Something was stung or stabbed into this animal's hide. If the animal was stung by something, what could it have been? It couldn't have been a snake bite. There was only one puncture wound. Burns eventually realized what he was looking at, and without looking up, he called out to Matt.

"Matt, did you hit this animal with a tranquilizer dart?" Burns asks.

"I tried to shoot it with the air rifle, but it didn't work," Matt answered.

"That's not what I asked you," Burns says. "I asked you if you hit this animal with a tranquilizer dart in any way shape or form?"

"Yes I did, eventually," Matt says triumphantly. "I was trying to sedate it."

"And how much of the sedative was plunged into it? Do you think it was the whole dose?" Burns asks.

"I don't know. I just remember hitting it with it, and then the animals attacked me. I don't know if the whole vial went into it," Matt says. "Why? Is that what's happening to it?"

"Yes," Burns says. "I think it's having a negative reaction. It's having a seizure. We might be looking at an overdose. You didn't happen to bring any counter sedatives with you, did you?"

"No, I just grabbed the air rifle with a couple of darts. I didn't think I'd need more than one," Matt says.

"Well, it seems like one was just too much. This animal is dying," Burns says.

"What do we do about the animal?" Kit asks anxiously. "It sounds like it's in pain, and it's calling out for help as far as I know. What do you think its parents are going to think when it sees us hovering over it as it's dying?"

Burns let go of the animal's head and he put his left hand back onto the pistol grip. "There's not much else we can do. We can try and carry it with us back to camp but-" Burns was saying.

"But what?" Matt says.

"But we have other priorities, like the safety of our team members," Burns says. "I want to help this animal, I really do, but we have a different priority at the moment."

"Sorry, are we just going to leave this animal here, by itself? Just screaming into the wind?" Kit says, there was a bit of panic in his voice.

"It's a bad situation," Burns says. "But we just have to accept it for how it is. We leave it behind and move away from it as quickly as possible. This is a young cub. Its parents will not be ecstatic to see us with their dead child. Bad comes to worse, we'll have to defend ourselves if that happens."

"Are we really going to shoot the adult if it comes at us?" Matt asks.

"Yes," Burns says. "Unfortunately, that is the consequence to your fucking action."

Matt opened his mouth to retort, but he was interrupted by the howling of the dinosaur. It's getting softer and softer, until it stops completely. The three men looked down at the dinosaur. Its eyes were not blinking; the animal was suddenly lifeless.

"Did it just die?" Kit asks.

Burns kneeled down again. He ran his hand down the dinosaur's neck onto the middle of its chest, feeling for a heartbeat. "I don't feel a heartbeat, no visible chest rise either," Burns says. He then poked at the animal's forearm with the muzzle of his revolver. The animal didn't move, it just remained still and stiff. "I think the animal's dead," Burns says sharply. "But at least the noise is down to a minimum. It'll decrease our chances of an unexpected visitor."

"That fucking sucked," Kit says, a touch of relief in his voice. "It got my adrenaline up and everything, but whatever, let's just move forward. Let's find JJ and Anika, and that fucking guy with the camera."

Burns didn't respond. He just kept staring at the animal. In short time working with Burns, Kit had learned one of his behavioral traits. Whenever Burns suddenly stopped being the voice of reason, that meant he was soaking in a piece of information. A detail of something he didn't like.

"What is it, Mr. Burns?" Kit asks quietly, fearing an answer.

Burns didn't respond. He just reached his free hand over the animal's jaws, and then he picked something out of the dinosaur's teeth. He held it up over his head to get a good look at it. It was a thin piece of cloth, dark in color.

"Is that a piece of my jacket?" Matt asks.

"Your jacket's olive green," Burns answered. "This isn't a piece of jacket, it's a piece of shirt, and it's blue."

Matt leaned his head in to take a good look at the piece of cloth in Burns's hand. And for a brief second, Kit and Burns both noticed Matt's usual chipper attitude and charisma abruptly fade from his face. "Jesus Christ," Matt mumbled. "It's a piece of Zeke's shirt."

"The cameraman," Kit says loudly.

"Yes," Matt says again. "It's a piece of his Led Zeppelin shirt."

Burns didn't react. His face didn't change nor his demeanor. He just tossed the piece of cloth aside and he stood up. "This changes things," Burns says, his voice even sharper than before. He was all business now. "We have to assume that the group has been attacked, that they are injured, or worse. First thing we need to do is regroup and secure the lodge. We then need to call the ranger station. We need to call for help and get people out here for a proper search party."

"Bill," Matt snapped. "You're not really proposing for us to go back and wait for fucking help? Are you?"

"It's the safest and most logical solution," Burns says. "We need bodies out here, *numbers*. Right now, it's just three guys with one fucking gun."

"You're holding a revolver in your hand," Matt says. "We have you and we have Kit holding the damn elephant gun. My daughter is out there, Bill, I'm not going back to the lodge. I'm going to stay out here and find her whether you like it or not."

Kit was unsure if Matt's sudden change in priorities was genuine, but he wanted to stay optimistic. Maybe the reality of the situation had finally sunk in.

"We can't help them right now," Burns says. "We don't have the correct ratio to do this properly. It's the same basic process for first responders. If something happens to us, who's going to call for help? Who's going to save us? Our main priority is to focus on our survival so that we can save them."

"William," Matt says firmly, his southern accent getting deeper. "I'm going to keep looking for my daughter. You can come with me or you can go back, but I am not coming out of this forest without her."

"Goddamn it," Burns is exasperated. "We are never going to be on the same page, are we? For god's sake, just listen to me for once."

"I'm afraid I agree with him, Mr. Burns," Kit says. "This is an exigent circumstance, there's going to be a lot of gray area on what is right or wrong. We need to make a decision, and we need to make it now. I'm more inclined to go out here with Matt."

Burns wanted to ponder the consequences, but he shook the thought away. Kit was right. They could not waste any more time. "No matter what happens from this point forward," Burns says. "We still have to call for help, we still have to let someone know what's going on because if something happens to us, then how will the rest of the group know?"

Kit took the initiative in the decision. "I could run back to the lodge. I could tell them to start calling the ranger station for help."

"Could you find your way back?" Burns asks.

"I have a GPS on me. I know how to use it. I can make my way back and then find you guys again," Kit says.

"And you're comfortable doing that?" Burns asks grimly. "Going out into the forest by yourself?"

Kit gasped. "I'll admit, this sounds like a bad horror movie decision, but what's the alternative?"

"All right then," Burns says. "You do that and make it back here as soon as you can. Me and Matthew are going to keep moving forward to find Anika. If anything happens, if you run into anything, it goes without saying *do not hesitate to save your fucking life.*"

Kit nodded and then quickly grabbed the GPS from his pocket. He turned around to find his bearings and started to head in the direction back to the lodge. "Stay frosty," Kit says to them as he walks away.

Burns watched Kit disappear into the foliage. He then turned and looked at Matt. "Do you have any weapons on you?"

Matt swung the rucksack off his back. He reached into his backpack and pulled out a can of bear spray. "See?" Matt says, "I'm not as reckless as you think."

"That's beside the point right now," Burn says. "Let's get a move on. Anika might not have much time."

Matt, for once in his life, didn't argue. Instead, he decided to follow Burns. Both men continued their way into the forest.

PREY

The male dinosaur was covered in slashes and fresh claw marks, but it paid no mind to the wounds. The wounds looked deep and dark in color. They were no longer actively bleeding but the rain trickled through, turning red in the process. Its feathered mane was peppered in dark blood. The male was staring at Anika, its bright purple eyes piercing through her. When she climbed down the tree, the animal had snuck up on her. She never heard it coming, and for a large creature, it was so unnervingly quiet. The male inhaled and exhaled heavily, an intimidation tactic against Anika.

But there was no need. Anika was already terrified. This time she could not see a way out; the animal had her dead to rights. The male took a step forward. Anika gulped\. The male's bloody appearance reminded her of JJ and Zeke's death. She was not ready; she didn't want to die like that. There was nothing she could do; she was now at the mercy of the animal. She slowly began to kneel, tears running down her horrified face. The male moved its head toward Anika's, getting as close as it can. Anika could smell the animal's breath: it was warm and stale.

The male sniffed around Anika's head, first her hair, then her forehead and face. The animal's thick and scaly skin was so close to Anika that she could see the clear, basketball-like texture. The animal then bumped her forehead with its snout and growled. It then stepped back from Anika finally. The animal snarled at her. Anika remained kneeled, waiting for the attack to ensue. The male snarled again, a bit louder. Anika raised her gaze up, and the animal just stared.

And it did nothing. It was standing there with its menacing stature. It didn't attack, didn't do anything at all. It growled at Anika suddenly, then bumped her harder with its snout. Anika was dumbfounded to say the least, her tears giving pause to their flow. The animal shook its head, the feathers on its mane sending sprinkles of rain. The male was apparently frustrated, and it snarled much louder than before. It then grabbed her by the shoulder with its jaws. There was no pain, however, its teeth went only as far as to firmly grasp her. The male pulled upward while holding her shoulder in its jaws. It yanked Anika to her feet and then let go of her shoulder.

And once more, the animal just blankly stared at her. For God's sake, what did it want? Anika's mind was racing. She had been expecting death and now she was more baffled than she'd ever been in her life. The male snarled once more and bumped her once more. Anika then noticed it wasn't bumping her. It was nudging her in a specific direction.

Anika took a few steps backward in the direction that animal nudged her in, not wanting to turn her back to an animal. The male didn't make any noise; it just watched. She stopped moving, the animal waited a few seconds, and then snarled at her again. Anika stayed motionless, testing the creature's intentions. The creature squinted its eyes and pushed her a lot harder than before.

The male wants her to walk; it wants her to move where it wants her to go.

Anika saw that the male was beginning to get increasingly frustrated. She decided to do what it wanted. She turned around and started to walk into the woods. The animal followed closely behind her.

Anika cautiously strolled in the dense woods of the

Tasmanian forest. Usually her focus would be on not slipping and hurting herself in this difficult terrain. Instead, she was preoccupied with the animal closely following behind her.

She could hear it lumbering along, its talons scraping the wooden roots every time they walked by a tree. She could feel the animal's every exhale, the hot breath stroking the back of her head. She had been walking with her head slightly tilted, keeping the animal in her peripheral view. Dreading the imminent attack from the male.

But why isn't the animal attacking? Why doesn't it kill her? Where's the animal taking her? These questions have been parading in Anika's mind for a while now. She tries to apply logic along with her wildlife knowledge, but nothing makes sense. There was clearly an issue between the alpha and the male, but what is the fight about? Territory rights? Did Anika get lucky and the male picked that precise moment to fight for territory?

That theory doesn't make a whole lot of sense, even if it's completely plausible. Is it about Anika? Not about her as an individual, but as prey? Anika has seen it countless times over her life; starving male lions would invade territories and fight a whole pride for the prize.

Anika quickly dispels that theory as well. The Male looks strong, its skin and body fat plump, a well-fed predator. A fight over feeding rights doesn't seem to hold any water. Anika didn't consider it to have been a mating ritual either. The fight was far too aggressive to have been about *that*. Maybe the fight altogether was just some unresolved issue from the past. Something Anika shouldn't have witnessed. It happens all the time, especially in primates. They have a tendency to hold grudges for a long time.

Even so, none of these possible theories gave an answer as to why or where this terrifying creature was escorting her. Maybe Anika was thinking too broadly. Perhaps it just wanted her away from the pack's territory so it could feast without any hindrance.

Jesus, how did the animal manage to sneak up on Anika? How had she not heard it? With its immense height and weight, how was it so silent until it was inches from Anika's back? Unless the animal was already there. Anika had noticed that the vibrant colors of the dinosaur's hide and feathers helped it blend in with the scrubs and banksias—flora native to Tasmania. The animal could have stood perfectly still and Anika could've missed the male completely as she climbed down the Huon pine.

Anika glanced over her shoulder a little too much, and the animal noticed. The male rammed her forward with its head. Anika almost tripped after the sudden force on her body. She gathered herself and continued to walk. A loud hooting resonated in the far distance. The pack was still searching for her. So much for her plan to hide in the trees, the male had clearly seen her climb down. She needed to find a new plan, but first things first, she needed to deal with the male. She needed to somehow get away from it before it changed attitude.

Like before, running would be foolish. If she chose to run, it would probably only trigger the predator's 'prey' response. Not to mention the animal could probably catch her fairly quickly. No, she needed to find a way to evade the animal and have it lose its trail. Putting her goal into words made it seem impossible. How could she possibly achieve it?

Anika wondered what would happen if she tried to move in a different direction. Was the animal smart enough to correct her? Or would it blindly follow? Anika decided to test her theory, because at this point, what else could she do?

Anika kept her steady walking pace, but slowly started to veer off to the right. Anika couldn't hear any sounds from the animal behind her. It didn't snarl or growl or anything. Maybe she could lead it to...

Suddenly, the animal darted around to her right and cut her off. It snarled and stomped its feet firmly in the dirt. Anika tested the animal further. She pretended to not understand what it wanted. So she continued to try and move east, but again the animal cut her off after a couple steps. The male pushed its snout in her face, the skin warm and damp from the rain. It growled under its breath, its intimidation tactic warning her to comply.

Anika slowly stepped back, trying not to instigate the animal further. She started to move back in the direction the animal wanted. In response, the male followed closely behind again. They were now back to square one. So the animal was smart enough to see what she was trying to do.

The male suddenly moved past Anika, its head raised, its nostrils flaring as it sniffed the air. The animal's lips suddenly curled, revealing its bottom row of teeth. It was getting ready for something. A set of hooting erupted from their left, and branches began to rustle. Anika's first thought was to make a run for it if another fight started.

But then the male swung its tail around, striking the back of Anika's calves. Sending her feet up and her body to the ground. She landed on her back, but she quickly gathered herself. She flipped herself onto her stomach and started to stand upright when the animal swung its tail down like a whip. The animal's tail struck her back hard, making Anika tumble to the floor again. The male then stepped on her back with its talons.

It had finally come. She was going to die. This is exactly how JJ found himself before he was torn apart. The thought, however, quickly faded as the animal swung its head down and hissed softly in her ear. It was then that Anika noticed the male's foot was not holding her down forcefully, instead, it was a bit gentle, its talons barely poking her jacket enough to where she could feel them.

Anika looked around from the ground, mud smearing against her cheek. A few hundred feet away, she saw two small taloned feet hidden in a bush. The male boldly snarled, and Anika heard a response from the cub in the bushes. The cub hissed defiantly at the male, confident in itself for whatever reason. The male raised its claws up into a fighting stance and snarled deeply again. This time, the cub slowly stepped back, cowering its head down, frightened.

The male kept its stance, waiting for the cub to leave. A crowing erupted from the forest. Anika by now knew the crow-like sound was a call from the alpha. The cub slowly turned around and hurried away from the male. The cub eventually disappeared into the underbrush. Anika felt the male slowly step off her back, and she carefully stood up.

The male had concealed her, that's what it seemed like at face value. It hid her from the pack and scared off the cub. Why on earth the animal had done this, she did not know.

The male stared at her for a moment and then started to walk away from her. Anika thought maybe the animal was finally leaving, but then it stopped and waved its tail in her face. Anika brushed the tail away in frustration. "I get it," she mumbled. "Follow."

She began to walk behind the animal, following it closely. The male kept its head up, alert for the pack. Why the animal had chosen to protect her was anyone's guess. Anika had given up trying to understand what the animal's intentions were.

Because in the end, at least she wasn't dead.

LODGE

Lucy Benitez was staring out of the window of the lodge, looking into the distance of the gloomy forest that was before her. She would scan the tree line, trying to find some evidence of life, any shadows or signs that the group was on their way back. But every time she scanned the tree line from left to right and right to left, she saw nothing. This was beginning to concern her. When she first agreed to go on this expedition, she fantasized about relationships that she would make along the way. She imagined finally taking credit for something ingrained in history.

A big discovery like this would have to bring people closer. Lucy was never good at making friends. She was always more of an introverted person. Often never leaving the museum, except every once in a while when she would go out to dig sites. Even then, in those dig site groups, she wasn't exactly very sociable. She's the kind of person to look at her job, focus on it, and just do it without any distraction. Not that she didn't like being social. She just never got around to it. She liked her work very much; she liked being out in the dirt searching for fossilized dinosaur bones.

Ever since she saw a little segment on the Discovery Channel about what paleontologists do, she fell in love with the idea of discovering ancient dinosaurs. Ancient reptiles and birds hidden in the rock just under her feet. From the moment she discovered her passion at eight years old, she knew what she was going to do for the rest of her life. But not once in her entire lifetime did she consider that she would be part of an expedition that would rediscover an extinct species of dinosaur. That never seemed like a possibility to a simple scientist like Lucy; it was a dream come true.

Still, she understood the constraints of the expedition. She understood the sheer reality of it. She knew that studying bones and studying live animals were two completely different things. She understood that she would practically be no help beyond identifying the specific species of dinosaur. But what did it matter? She would try to help as much as she could. But all the behaviors written in paleontology books about dinosaurs were all theoretical.

However, she wouldn't suggest that out loud to the group. She knew that the group consisted of very educated and very well-trained wildlife specialists. The last thing she wanted to do was get in their way during their work. She was going to silently observe. She would try and do her best to help whenever she could. And what would happen afterward? What would happen after their discovery was made public to the entire world? Would they attempt to study this animal further in the wild? Would it be considered an endangered species? To the point where they would be captured alive so that they could be safely monitored? Would they be put in an enclosed space, like countless other species, to be studied on how to help them move off the endangered list?

She didn't know, but she wondered if these dinosaurs were going to be allowed to be studied by paleontologists like her. She wondered if paleontologists were going to be considered unfit because of their inexperience in genuine wildlife settings.

There is no point in thinking about that right now. She had to live in the moment. She has to look at her situation just as she does every time when she looks at the bones in the grid. Just figure it out and document it along the way.

She scanned the tree line once more outside the lodge. She was hoping everyone was okay, because if there were no problems, it would mean that they could stay a little longer. She wanted to see the dinosaur; she wanted to see it in the flesh. She didn't care if it was from a distance or if it was up close, she wanted to see it moving. Running, feeding, and jumping. She wanted to *experience* the dinosaur. To stare directly into its eyes so that she could admire it. She wanted to see how close her theories have been her entire life. She wanted to know if all the books that she studied in college for her doctorate were as correct as everyone thought they were.

She didn't care if it was a carnivore. It didn't scare her. She knew that it was dangerous. You can still admire lions, can't you? You can know an animal is dangerous and still admire it from a safe distance. Even then, she understood some of the group's prudence toward this expedition. She understood why the wildlife biologists were wary. They were on the front lines, the ones who had to go out into the wild, into the potential danger. Into the potential risk of running into one of these animal's *face to face*. And if there's one theory about fossilized bones that every single paleontologist agrees on, it's that carnivores are indeed vicious predators.

Dinosaurs didn't have sharp claws, sharp teeth, or mighty talons on their feet for no reason at all. All of these tools, all of these weapons that these carnivores had were for a very specific reason. To hunt, to kill, to take down their prey as quickly as possible and to feast on them without any trouble at all. The thoughts that Lucy is currently having make her nervous. She just wanted the group to be okay; she wanted them to walk out of this tree line and explain some kind of misunderstanding. Sure, they had weapons, but how fast were these animals? How quickly could they kill someone? How could they hide? How would they hunt? She hadn't even identified the species yet. She didn't know if they in fact were pack hunters or if they were solitary animals.

Just as Lucy was having this thought, she saw a shadow in the distance. To the left, just behind where the convoy of Ford trucks were parked. She saw the shadow move alongside the convoy of trucks, following it to the porch. It looked like a man, a singular man, holding a rifle in his hands. It was one of the soldiers, Kit. She recognized him when she saw his beard in the porch light. She followed Kit with her eyes until he was at the door. She quickly scooted over to the door and unlocked it. She opened it, letting Kit step inside. He only peeked his head in. Kit's ball cap and his jacket, along with the scope of the rifle and the sleet wood stock were soaking wet with rain. She could smell the damp sweaty scent emanating from him

"Call the ranger station," Kit says in a hurried manner, his ball cap dripping water onto the floor below. "Call them and tell them to send everybody out here, we have problems."

"What kind of problems?" Lucy asks.

"Worst case scenario," Kit says. "Get on the radio. I need you to call the ranger station, tell them to send everyone they can out here. Police, rangers, medics, hell, even hunters if they have them, we need everyone out here, *pronto*."

"Okay, I can make the call to the ranger station. What are you going to do?" Lucy asks.

"I'm going to go back for Mr. Burns and Matt," Kit says. "I have to bring them back, they're in danger the longer I leave them out there."

"Did you find the others?" Lucy asks.

"We're working on that, just focus on calling the ranger station. The weather is a bit bad right now, reception might not be good, but I need you to keep trying until you reach somebody. Do not stop until you talk to someone, and let them know what's going on," Kit says. "And do me another favor. Once I leave, lock the door, and do not open it. No one leaves, no one comes in unless you know it's me and the others, okay?"

"Okay," Lucy says.

"Okay, and one last thing," Kit says. "After you establish contact with a ranger station, I need you to stand by the door and watch the window. Watch for us so that you can open the door when we come back. We might not have a lot of time."

Lucy frowned "Might not have a lot of time for what?"

"Don't worry about that right now," Kit says. "Now what did I just say?"

"Make the call, lock the door, wait by the door for you guys," Lucy repeated.

"Good," Kit says. "Now lock this door."

Kit stepped out from the doorway. Lucy closed the door and locked it. She turned around and headed for the table with the radio, adjacent to the kitchen area. She sat down at the little table and grabbed the radio. She put the handheld to her mouth, but then she stopped. How does she call the ranger station? In her time working around dig sites in the middle of the desert, Lucy had only been around radios just a few times. She's never actually used one. But she knew the basic idea of them, so she thought to herself for a second. In order for the radio to work, it has to be set to the right frequency, otherwise you won't be calling the right people.

The right frequency. Which one was the right frequency? The frequency for the ranger station. She looked around the desk and she saw a little booklet stacked next to some notebooks, and she grabbed it. She opened it up and flipped through the pages. She saw a series of numbers and a series of names for the numbers. One says 'Franklin-Gordon National Park Ranger Station frequency'.

That had to be the one. She remembers the name of the national park from the debriefing. She held the book in her hand and turned her attention to the radio on the desk. There were two knobs for the dials, one for the volume, one for the frequency. There is a digital display lit up in bright orange just above the dials; it reads a different frequency than the one in the booklet. She turned the dial for the frequency until she reached the number that matched the booklet for the ranger station. She then grabbed the handheld, and she held it up to her mouth. She squeezed the button on the left of the handheld, and she spoke.

"Hello, is this the Franklin-Gordon National Park Ranger Station? Hello? Is anybody there?"

She let go of the button and she listened. There was only static, no immediate response. She waited a few more seconds to see if there would be a response. Perhaps it would be a delayed response. Maybe the ranger wasn't at the desk but they did hear the call. After a few more seconds, there was still no response. Lucy clicked the button again on the handheld and she spoke again.

"Hello, this is the... uh... *the Valente expedition* in the National Park. Is this the ranger station? Pick up please, we need help."

Again, there is no response. She was just about to try again when she heard the static form a couple words that she could barely understand. "-anger station, --tify your-" the radio squelched.

Lucy clicked the button on the handheld again. "Hello, can you hear me? This is the Valente expedition. Is this the ranger station, hello?"

The radio squelched again and only a few sentences could be heard in the response. "Bad weather- -peat your last- -an't understand you."

Goddamn it, Lucy thought, *they can't understand what I'm saying, what do they mean about the bad weather, it's only raining?*

"We need help. This is the Valente expedition, please respond. Send help, send everyone," Lucy says into the mic again.

"-an't understand- damn thing- -epeat your last."

"Goddamn it," Lucy mumbled. This was clearly going to take forever. But she will keep trying, because all she can think about is the hidden panic in Kit's voice when he gave her the instructions.

SEARCH PARTY

Burns was moving fast through the wilderness. He was following the GPS in his hand, keeping a steady eye on the horizon with the revolver in his other hand. He had the hammer pulled back on the revolver. His finger is on the trigger, ready to pull it at any sign of trouble. Matt was unusually quiet, following closely behind him, his head on a swivel, looking for any signs of life, any signs of his daughter.

In high-stress situations, the usual advice was to think positive. But in Burns's case, and with his experience, the best thing to do was not think of any outcome at all. The best thing to do was manage it all—to manage your expectations. It was better to just go through the motions and not to expect anything in return. Going through the motions was something he had learned during his time as a medical responder. To think deeply about the situation or to create more unnecessary hope would only hinder their chances of rescue. It may seem like a pessimistic way, but that technique never failed him.

He knew that Anika was a capable human being. He had taught her everything that he knew about survival. But he didn't know how well she'd do under pressure. Despite her cynical attitude, Anika led a pretty stress-free life. The only thing that Burns was secretly hoping in his head, was that Anika had the ability to keep a level head. To think through the decisions and figure them out as smoothly as she could. That was all you could hope for whenever you were plunged into pure danger.

"What kind of behavior do you think these animals have in a pack?" Matt suddenly asks. "Do you think there's any way to try to anticipate their movements?"

"I have no idea," Burns replied. "Like I said before, I recognize some of the behavior, and I'm sure you did too. But so far, any speculation will mean nothing until we see their interactions with adults."

"I'd have to say their interactions with the adults are probably as good as it can be," Matt replied. "I mean, hell, it didn't take them long to overpower me. They had a process, they knew exactly what they were doing."

"Yes, they did," Burns says. "Which is why we should be extra careful and not take any chances."

"I'm sorry," Matt says. "Had I known things were going to be like this, I would not have left so suddenly."

"I don't want to talk about that right now," Burns says, a hint of disappointment in his voice. "Let's just keep moving, keep our attention high, and our noise at a minimum. We're in an alpha predator territory at the moment."

"You know, I've been thinking about that actually," Matt says. "Thinking about the track that we saw the other day, how big it was. A big animal like that, how does it feed itself?"

Burns frowned. "I don't understand your question, what do you mean *how does it feed itself*?"

"I mean, you are aware of the kind of species that live in Tasmania, right?" Matt says. "When it comes to carnivores and their sizes, usually carnivores don't go for prey smaller than their body proportions."

"You're wondering what it is that they prey on," Burns says.

"Is that right?"

"Precisely," Matt says. "What is it that they hunt out here? I mean, we saw that emu on the video. It looked sick but it didn't look wounded. It just looked deformed. And out here in Tasmania that emu is as big as animals can get. Everything else is smaller, birds, rodents, hell, even snakes or lizards. How does a big carnivorous predator manage to stay alive with the prey out here?"

"You seem to be excluding a certain species native to Tasmania," Burns says.

"What the hell are you talking about?" Matt asks.

"You're a smart enough man," Burns says sharply, "I'm sure you can figure it out."

Matt let his mind wander for a couple seconds, and then the answer came to him. "Human beings?" Matt asks.

"Bingo, Matthew," Burns says.

"If that were even true," Matt says. "We most certainly would have heard of these animals a long time ago."

"Don't be so sure," Burns says. "This country is a very isolated kind of island. A lot of people out here live in the middle of the bush, miles away from civilization."

"They would have reported it by now," Matthew insisted. "There just ain't no way."

"Oh yeah, because any form of technological communication works so well out here," Burns says. "Stop trying to feed off your own opinion. You know how big this forest is. It's incredibly easy for someone to die and no one to report them."

"Why are you always so goddamn negative?" Matt says. "If only you were just-"

A sudden movement about two-hundred feet ahead startled both of them. Some ferns rustled quite violently and then they stopped, as if something was hiding behind them and then scurried away. Burns crouched, and Matt did the same. Both men looked around in every direction, looking for any sign of danger.

"Did you see anything?" Matt whispered.

"No," Burns says, "Keep quiet."

They remained in their positions for more than a few seconds, just waiting and listening, scanning the wilderness around them. "Do you smell that?" Matt asks.

Burns didn't realize that he had been holding his breath the entire time. He exhaled through his mouth, and then he took a long breath in through his nose. The ammonia-like smell was putrid, intense. Burns recognized it all too well. The last time he had witnessed that kind of scent was months ago when he first encountered that creature. "It's from the dinosaur," Burns whispered. "It's the smell I told you about."

"So, are they around here somewhere?" Matt asks.

"Yes, they could be hiding just anywhere around here-"

A soft hooting emanated from one direction directly to the left of both men. It wasn't loud, but it wasn't soft enough that you couldn't hear it from a distance. To Burns, that sounded like an owl with a deeper tone. "I have never heard a sound like that," Matt whispered.

"I don't think anyone has for a million years," Burns whispered back. *"It's them."*

Just as Burns finished his sentence, another soft hooting came from directly to their right. And then it came from directly behind them, and then in front of them. Then there were so many hooting sounds from every direction that they couldn't tell how many there were in total, but it was definitely more than enough.

"How many rounds do you have in that revolver?" Matt asks.

"Six of them," Burns says, "Tell me that's a new can of bear spray."

"It's sort of new," Matt whispered. "I opened it four years ago. They're supposed to last for five, I think."

"We're about to find out," Burns says. "Because I think they got us surrounded."

CAT AND MOUSE

Anika cannot believe what she's doing. She's unable to put her current emotions into words. For whatever reason, she decided to follow a predatorial prehistoric dinosaur into the woods as if she's a lost duckling. She wanders behind the massive creature, watching as the male dinosaur constantly glances over its shoulder to ensure she was still following.

Just as she was doing a short while ago.

For reasons unknown, the male concealed her from the cubs and scared them away. Whether it was to protect her or to keep her as prey is anyone's guess. *Protect her*, what a silly notion. Why on earth would an oversized carnivorous bird protect her? It's obvious why it scared the cubs away. Stalking and killing prey is incredibly time-consuming. Often in the wild, predators have a harder time keeping their prize than hunting it. This 'I'll protect you from the others' shenanigans are starting to piss her off. Winning her favor might be this animal's way of getting a fresh meal undisturbed.

Which is why Anika has to quickly think of a way to lose the male before it finds a quiet place to feast. Anika has one advantage: the male has decided to trust the puny human being to follow it instead of doing the escorting as itself like earlier. The animal must be extremely confident in keeping its potential prey in check. The confidence is what Anika can use against it. She just needs to find a way to escape it without dying.

Escaping the male was only the start of her problems. There was a reason it was keeping her hidden. The pride of ravenous cubs led by matriarchal apex predators roamed this territory of Tasmania. They were cunning, extraordinarily lethal, and shockingly brutal with their prey. The images of JJ's and Zeke's death remind Anika to keep a close eye on the creature in front of her.

But keeping an eye on the male only further confused her. The deeper her theories went, the more confused she got. The animal didn't seem agitated or alert, or aggressive for that matter, at least not at the moment. Its behavior was nothing like Anika had ever seen in the animal kingdom. The animal didn't seem... *worried*. It was very calm, almost indifferent in its steps through the forest. Even with its constant glances back at Anika to see if she was still there. Anika had a theory that the animal felt it had gained her trust, and therefore trusted her to follow it.

There it was again, *trust*, another silly notion, another impossibility. How could a predator *trust* its prey? The truth was, it didn't. If anything, this was some ploy to gaslight her into following it to her death. Like a more vicious version of Stockholm syndrome, the human would *have* to trust its protector.

Trust among different species is not a distant hypothesis. Different species with different skills and abilities often stick together for better predator detection. Most notably in African mammals, like elephants stick close to zebras. Zebras have a keen sense of sight and hearing, while elephants are great at intimidating predators. It's part of a mutualistic relationship. Elephants and zebras benefit from each other's presence by working together to detect predators and survive.

But that concept is never defined as *trust* by biologists. It's more like a mutual working relationship.

Values, that was the better term. Animals use each other's values to survive. It's not really trust; they use each other for predator recognition. But even with that term making more sense, it does not help Anika understand her current predicament. What value could the male possibly have for her? None, nothing at all. Anika was grasping at random explanations. She knew the reality, the only possibility for this situation. The male would kill her eventually, because no matter how you try to bend the facts, you can't trust a predator.

You just can't. That's how horrifying accidents happen, and she has heard of too many. Timothy Treadwell, eaten alive by a grizzly because he thought bears would never hurt him, no matter how close he got. Sigmund and Freud, mauled by their supposed *pet tiger* during their act in Las Vegas. Cassandra Irving killed trying to save her daughter after her husband tried to approach a jaguar in the amazon jungle.

Yes, she had to put all her hopeful thoughts away. She had to stop thinking like her father. This animal was a predator, a carnivore, and its only goal was to kill and eat its prey. The sooner she accepted that reality, the better her chances for survival. First things first, she knows what will happen next. Unfortunately, she had to test the animal's intelligence again and see its reaction. Anika decided to stop walking, and she watched as the animal lumbered for a few steps and then stopped. It didn't turn its head, or even glance over its shoulder in her direction. It just huffed with its nose and then shook its head.

Anika didn't move; she didn't make a sound. She stayed where she was, her heart pounding in her chest. The animal then breathed in steadily and then breathed out. It slowly turned around to face her, its eyes beaming into hers. Anika had the momentary regret of testing the male again, forgetting how terrifying the animal was face-to-face.

Anika waited for a reaction from the animal. But the male just stared at her, and it did so for what seemed like a long time. Anika knew what was happening; the animal was waiting for her to make a move. It wanted to see what she intended to do. So Anika decided to do nothing, instead, she just stared back at the animal. Eventually, the animal broke the staring contest, and it growled at her.

No, not a growl. It was softer than that. It was almost like a purr, not aggressive in any way. It was almost as if the animal was nudging her, asking her what was going on. But again, Anika did nothing. She just continued to stand still where she was. Then the animal bobbed its head to the side. It began to sniff around into the air. It looked around at the shrubs and foliage.

The animal thought Anika was trying to tell it something, so it decided to look around for any threat. But there was none, and as soon as the animal realized it, the male growled at her just a little louder. This time, it did seem aggressive. The animal took a step forward toward Anika. But Anika remained still. She knew that the best thing to do if the animal was challenging her was to get on her knees like she did before, to submit.

But she chose not to; she wanted to survive and she was tired of playing games with this predator. She needed answers as to what it wanted to do with her. The animal then took another step toward her, and another. The animal's hot breath was getting closer to her. She could feel it up against her face. The animal stopped only a couple feet from her and turned its body around. It brushed its tail up against Anika's abdomen, back and forth. Once again, the animal was nudging her to follow it. Anika brushed the tail away; she was done playing games. *Make your move so I can make mine.*

The male then quickly swung around, pressed its snout up against her face, and snarled. Anika could feel the animal's teeth against her cheek. The animal's skin was thick and warm, even with the cold rain sliding off it. To any other person, this act of intimidation would have surely caused an involuntary bowel movement. But Anika stood her ground, even if this seemed like the worst idea. The animal continued to snarl and then stopped.

It took a step back, and the animal just stared at her again. The animal's bright yellow eyes moved over Anika's face and then her body. It was studying her; it was waiting for her to comply. Perhaps the animal is wondering if it's a delayed response. Once the animal has waited long enough and seen Anika continue to do nothing, it snorts at her. The snort makes a mist of cold breath, giving the impression of disapproval.

The animal then darted past Anika, swung its body around, and rammed Anika's back with its head. The male sent Anika tumbling forward, but Anika kept her balance and remained on her feet. She felt the animal ram her lower back again and heard the male snarl once more. Anika could sense the animal was growing frustrated, so she took some steps forward.

And the male started to follow closely behind, keeping an eye on her. Presumably to push her again should Anika chooses to stop. So Anika continued to walk, letting the animal escort her once more. Out of all this, the only fact that was very clear to Anika, was that the animal did not try to kill her. Big cats tend to sometimes play with their food, but after increasing frustration or escape attempts, they'll kill their prey.

The dinosaur did grow frustrated, but it did not kill her.

It didn't even harm her in any way. The animal seems very adamant to move her *somewhere*. Anika took a massive gamble with her life, but it pays off. Now she knew she could move in these dinosaur's territory unbothered. The male would scare away the cubs, and hopefully keep her concealed from the alpha and beta. Why the male had chosen to do this, or where it was taking her was still unknown. But what did it matter? Anika would remain alive for the time being, and when she saw her chance to escape, she would take it.

As she slowly walked with the dinosaur behind her, Anika wondered what was going on with everyone at the lodge. She was hoping they stayed indoors, that they didn't risk their lives to come find her. But she knew Burns. He would never be able to sit still with her missing out here. She knew he would rush out into the forest to find her. Even if Burns rushing out could save her life, she didn't want him to. Burns didn't deserve to get hurt. Anika cared that much about him. She considered him an honorable man, for never abandoning her, and for teaching her everything she knew.

Yet, there was the truth: he was an honorable man, and he would come looking for her. The only thing Anika hopes is that she finds him before these animals do. She hoped that she could save him.

The male suddenly growled softly Anika glanced over her shoulder and saw the animal had stopped. Anika stopped too. She slowly turned to face the male; it had its head down. It was alert. Something had caught its attention; its head was hunched forward close to its claws. The animal scanned intently, its eyes narrow, focused.

The forest was silent, Anika realized it, and remembered what that meant. They were here, the cubs or the alpha and beta. They were being hunted, so Anika began to look around too. She couldn't see anything, she couldn't hear anything. She quickly glanced over to the male; it seemed preoccupied in finding the threat. It was not paying attention to her, which hopefully meant it would keep its attention on the pack and not her. They were going to be attacked, and when they did, Anika would use the distraction to escape.

Anika heard one single sound. It sounded like a scrape, something against wood. She looked around and saw the nearest tree to her and the male. The male was nowhere near the tree or the roots. There was no way its talons could have...

She saw a dark shape fall toward them from the tree, something had jumped from the tree. The shape landed on the male, and the male hissed as it tumbled forward. The shape was the beta dinosaur. As it held down the male into the dirt, it snarled at her, jaws wide. It lunges at her. No, not lunges, the beta launches itself forward as the male heaves with its body. The beta's body struck Anika and she tumbled backward. The brunt of the force had struck Anika's solar plexus, and she gasped for air as she attempted to get to her feet.

When she stood up, she saw the beta was lunging forward toward Anika again. The male intervened before the devastating attack could reach Anika. The male tackled the beta only inches away from Anika's body. Both animals snarled and hissed as they rolled around on the forest ground. They clawed and bit at each other. The male then stopped the rolling and held the beta down with its claws. And for that brief second of control, it swung its powerful gaze at Anika and growled. It wasn't an aggressive growl, or an intimidating one, it rather seemed like a warning.

The male was warning her to flee.

Anika didn't hesitate. She turned around and bolted into the forest, once more leaving the two animals fighting behind her. The sounds of their vicious skirmish growing faint as she went deeper into the undergrowth. She then heard a crowing sound echoing in the forest canopy; the beta had made the call. They were coming. The rest would be here any second now. Anika had to make distance from the only hunters of the pack and then make herself scarce from the cubs.

She heard hooting in response to the call, and the responses sounded too close. Anika saw the nearest tree and darted toward it. Her plan was to climb it and evade the cubs by letting them pass her since tracking was not one of their strengths. She would then...

A cub burst out from behind some ferns, and it hissed at Anika, poised for an attack. Anika darted left, away from the cub. She had to create more distance now that she had been spotted. Her adrenaline was making her run as fast as she could. She could hear the cub behind her hoot into the forest sky, alerting the rest of the pack of her location. As she ran, she could hear the hooting continue to emanate from the woods, the pack responding to the calls again.

Suddenly, she could hear the hurried splashing of footsteps behind her. She was being pursued. She didn't know how many but definitely more than one. The footsteps behind her sounded light; it was possible she was being chased by the cubs. Anika knew the cubs were shorter, lighter, and probably more agile. They could catch up with her in an instant, or they were like any other young animal: clumsy. Anika began to run in zig-zag patterns, making erratic turns around eucalyptus and sassafras trees. Making more obstacles for her pursuers instead of fleeing in a straight line.

Anika could hear the cubs snarling, but rather than in hunger, it was in frustration. At some point, Anika glances over her shoulder just in time to see a cub fail to turn a corner around a tree and wipe out in the mud. It was working. Anika was right to assume the cubs would struggle to catch up with her. Anika didn't know how much longer she could keep up with her running, but at the moment, she could not feel her stamina depleting. Her adrenaline was at full throttle through her body. She could feel it in her fingers.

She then saw two more cubs burst out in front of her. They stood there hissing at her. Anika stopped in her tracks. She breathed in deep breaths. She wasn't tired in the slightest; she felt like she could run for miles. The reason Anika stopped was because she noticed something in the cubs. These ones in front of her right now didn't lunge forward to attack. In fact, they were both evenly spaced to each other, and both remained in their positions.

Anika recognized the behavior immediately; they were *herding* her. She had seen it while observing the wolves in Iceland. They were herding her toward the rest of the pack to further isolate her as prey. The blood rushing in Anika's veins gave her the energy she needed to make a decision. Anika realized the cubs were not confident on their own if they were purposely herding her to the rest of the pack. Anika charged toward the cubs instead of evading them. The cubs became agitated and hissed. Anika saw their frightened posture and took advantage of it.

She shoulder-charges both cubs, sending them flying backward in different directions. They yelped in fear of the sudden attack. Anika then continued to run, not letting any of the cubs push her in a different direction. In the distance, she saw something moving on the ground, something straight and chaotic. The sounds became clearer as she hurried toward it. It was the white water of river rapids. That was her chance, and that was probably the reason they were pushing her in a different direction. The animals were smart enough to know that they would lose her if she reached the river.

Anika was only ten feet away from the river when the beta jumped in front of her tracks. The beta snarled as Anika stopped and then crowed into the air. Anika heard hooting responses incredibly close to her. She glanced behind her and saw two cubs hop forward from the foliage and began moving in toward her. They had her surrounded; they had gotten to her just in time. The animals had won the game of cat and mouse. And as the beta and cubs moved in on her, Anika realized there was truly no way out.

It was game over.

Anika sighed, but she didn't feel scared. Her adrenaline would not allow her to. Instead, for whatever reason, she accepted her death and hoped that it would be quick. Anika stared at the beta in front of her, and she held her arms out. "Just fucking do it," she mumbled to the animal.

The beta stepped forward, its eyes locked onto hers, wriggling its clawed fingers as it readied for a fatal move. But then it stopped, and snarled again, but not at Anika. Something had caught its attention, something behind her. Anika turned her head to see the male sprinting forward, its jaws open and its claws up. The male was incredibly fast. Anika's body barely registered the force as the male rammed into her. Anika was suddenly flying in the air, and she saw the river barrelling toward her until it engulfed her in its cold embrace.

PREDATOR-PREY

Bill Burns and Matthew Irving both crouched with their backs to each other. They each scanned their surroundings, trying to see any signs of life as the entire forest was radiating in soft hooting noises. They couldn't see anything, and it certainly didn't help that it was now closer to dusk. The thick canopy of the forest trees didn't help. It made parts of the forest—about a hundred yards away—significantly darker. Burns held the revolver firmly in his hand, pointed at the forest, his arm now tired from holding a gun out for so long.

"It's a scare tactic," Burns says. "They're trying to frighten us, confuse us; they're trying to separate us."

"I can see that," Matt says. "What do you want to do?"

"Well, as logic serves," Burns says. "*If* they're trying to split us up, they might not be confident enough in taking us both on at the same time."

"All right, so what do we do?" Matt asks.

"I only have six rounds," Burns says. "And I'm willing to bet it won't be enough to kill these animals. At least not all of them. My suggestion is for us to keep moving forward, back-to-back like this. If one of them charges at us, you use that bear spray to keep them at bay. If they are a lot cockier than we think they are, then we resort to more lethal measures."

"That sounds like a plan, now which way are we moving?" Matt says.

"The same direction that we were going," Burns says. "But

we take it slow, we keep our head on a swivel, and we stay alert. Hopefully, soon enough, Kit will join us again with his rifle."

"You know, this is probably a bad time to mention this, but I remember reading somewhere that ducks have no reaction to pepper spray."

"What the hell are you talking about?" Burns asks.

"Well, that's the general debate about dinosaurs, right?" Matt says with a weird smile on his face.

"Are these dinosaurs' birds or are they reptiles?"

It finally dawned on Burns what Matt's point was. "Oh, for fuck's sake."

The hooting started to get progressively louder. It would start in one direction and then start in another. Both men kept their backs to each other, their weapons out in front of their faces, ready to defend themselves. Burns glanced at the GPS in his hand. "Just stay close to me," he says. "It's this way."

They took their movement step by step, being as cautious and attentive as they could. They inched closer and closer north, toward Anika's last location. They did it for about five minutes, until the hooting noise stopped suddenly. Both men stopped in their tracks. They scanned around the trees in the vegetation, looking for any signs of their potential attackers.

"What do we do?" Matt whispered.

"They've clearly given up trying to intimidate us," Burns says. "They're going to move on to the next best thing. Either they'll leave us alone or they'll try to attack."

Matt breathed in. "We need to stand our ground and fight them off. Any other movement we do might be seen as fleeing."

For once, Burns agreed with Matt. Any movement during an attack that wasn't a defense tactic would be seen as fleeing. It would only trigger an animal's predator-prey response. "Okay," Burns says. "We stand our ground."

Both men slowly bent their knees, but they did not crouch all the way. They went into a defensive stance and moved their head around, looking for the imminent attack. "It is way too goddamn quiet," Matt whispered. And just as he says this, they heard some bushes rattle to their left. Both men turned their heads to see the movement, but they only saw a small three-foot dinosaur charging toward them.

AMBUSH

After giving the instructions to Lucy at the lodge, Kit hurried to the last known location of Burns and Matt through the forest. Kit made sure to breathe in through his nose and exhale through his mouth as he jogged, trying to conserve stamina as much as he could. Even after leaving the military, Kit had made sure that he was in good athletic build, that his body had at least good strength and a good amount of cardio. But even running almost a mile a day didn't seem to help in this terrain. He often had to look where he was running as he felt he was going to trip at some point. The rain wasn't helping, and neither was the fact that it was almost dusk.

The only upside that he could see to his situation was that, for once in his life, his backpack wasn't as heavy as it usually was. As he was jogging and making his way back to the search party, he tried to have optimistic thoughts. He knew JJ; he had served with him on his last tour. Even though he was a pretty reserved guy, he was solid in his work. He always did what he was told, and he was a good team player. He never complained, and he never disobeyed orders. Which was more than he could say for some of his former unit members. He knew JJ wouldn't go out without fighting. What worried him the most about this debacle was Anika and the cameraman.

He hadn't known Anika for that long, but she seemed pretty steady herself. She was very cautious, and she would not let anybody turn away her concerns. That was always a good trait to have when you worked in a team, especially in dangerous situations. He then thought about the cameraman. He knew him even less. The only interactions that he saw of him at the cabin was with Matt, and he seemed as careless as the rest of the film crew. When he was filming one of the introductions with Matt the other day, Zeke had been munching on a granola bar. And without any care or regard for the rules given at the debriefing, he tossed the wrapper outside the lodge. Not in the trash bag or a garbage can, but on the ground outside. Zeke's inability to follow simple instructions made Kit immediately dislike him. This whole expedition was not to be taken lightly.

Kit's line of thought was suddenly interrupted. His body tensed up, the hair on the back of his neck standing up. Something was wrong, and although he did not know what it was, he knew his military sixth sense had gone off. Kit stopped and took a knee to catch his breath, and while he did, he looked around and tried to examine the situation. The forest was silent, *extremely silent*. He was not alone, that much he knew. He pressed the butt of the elephant gun up against his shoulder and raised the rifle to his eyes.

He looked around from his position, both eyes open, one looking through the scope and the other scanning at a regular distance. He then heard a noise; it sounded like a bird. It sounded slightly familiar; he could swear it almost sounded like an owl, but it wasn't. There was suddenly a putrid smell that upset his senses. It smelled unnatural, like a strong cleaning chemical smell. Kit couldn't quite put his finger on it. He had been in countless jungles and forests before, and he had never smelled something like that.

The bird sounds were soft at first. They stopped then started again, but this time a little louder. The bird sounded like it was coming from directly in front of him, but he could not see farther than fifty feet in front of him. Whatever was making this noise was flawlessly concealed in the vegetation. A second bird noise started, this time from his right. He swung his rifle around and again, he saw nothing. He alternated his searching gaze from his right to directly in front of him, looking for signs of life. And that's when he heard a third bird noise coming from directly behind him.

Ambush, he thought to himself.

He flipped his rifle's safety off, and he put his finger over the trigger. The bird noises suddenly stopped, and then in an abrupt manner, he heard a snarling bark. He heard rustling behind him, and he quickly turned his head to see a dinosaur charging at him. He swung the rifle around, found his target, and fired.

OLEORESIN CAPSICUM

Matt and Burns saw the three-foot dinosaur charging at them at full speed from the foliage. "Hey! Stop! Get back!" Matt yelled at the animal, but his attempt to startle it, as one would with other predators, didn't seem to work.

Making themselves look bigger and yelling as loudly as possible did not make the animal falter in its charge, so Matt quickly took action. He swung around the can of bear spray in his hand, lifted the safety cap on the handle with his thumb, and pressed the 'fire' button down. A stream of orange, oil-like liquid burst out toward the charging dinosaur, the concentrated capsaicin striking the animal right in its snout. The animal suddenly stopped in its tracks and started to yelp.

"Yes!" Matt yelled out. "Reptile eyes for the win!"

The animal scratched at its eyes and its snout with its clawed hands in panic after the sudden, irritating feeling in its eyes and mouth.

"Matthew!" Burns yelled.

Matt swung his head around to see a second dinosaur charging toward them from the bushes to their left. Matt gave another burst of capsaicin toward the animal. The stream of oily, orange liquid struck the animal in its chest, missing its eyes. Matt panicked. He frantically clicked the button again on the handle of the spray can. Another burst of liquid was sent spiralling out toward the animal. This time it struck it right in its eyes just as the animal was only a couple feet away. The animal stopped in its tracks and shrieked as loud as it could. The charging dinosaur had almost reached them, but in their complete focus on the animal charging at them, they neglected to look to their right. A third animal had charged almost at the same time as the second one.

Burns saw it too late in his peripheral vision. He tried to swing his handgun around but instead was met with almost a hundred pounds of feathers and scales. Burns tumbled to the ground, the animal toppling next to him. The animal had charged but apparently didn't really have a plan as to what it would do when it struck Burns. The animal quickly came to its feet. Burns was desperately trying to catch his breath. The animal was just about to pounce on Burns when Matthew shoved it away.

The animal hissed and turned its head toward Matthew and snapped its jaws making a clamping sound with its teeth. But Matt didn't let the attacking animals startle him. He simply pointed the can of bear spray at them and hit the animal right in the eyes. The dinosaur yelled, and it quickly crouched to the floor, trying to rub the orange liquid out of its eyes by rubbing its head on the ground. The animal then stood up quickly and darted away into the vegetation. Matt looked around; the other animals had done the same. They were gone. As Matt stood over Burns, he reached out with his free hand. He grabbed Burns by the elbow and yanked him up to his feet. Burns was taking in deep breaths and coughing up a storm from the mystified spray.

"That shit is fucking vile," Burns says, retching and coughing. "Are they gone?"

"I think so, that was a fucking close one, wasn't it?" Matt says, coughing.

"That was pure luck," Burns says out of breath, a small

string of saliva exiting his mouth from the spicy air. "We need to keep moving now."

Burns attempted to look around, his eyes wanting to squint from the pepper spray vapor in the air. He coughed, and it felt like his lungs were trying to close themselves.

"Let's move away from this area," Matt says, coughing. "Otherwise, this bear spray will handicap us too."

Matt and Burns started to slowly move away from the contaminated area, taking in deep breaths, trying to clear their lungs. That's when they heard an echoing crack coming from one side of the forest, and then another. It sounded like gunshots.

RETALIATION

Kit was on one of his knees, the elephant gun held out before him. He pulled the bolt back, sending a hot casing flying to the ground, and slid the bolt forward, chambering another round. Kit had already fired two rounds; the first one was at the charging animal from the bushes. He noticed that the animal ran in an almost zig-zag manner as it tried to approach him. Which is why he missed, but the deafening sound of the elephant gun seemed to have startled the animal for the moment. The animal darts left and runs back into one of the bushes.

Kit had quickly chambered a second round, and that's when the other attack came. It came from behind him. He heard the snarling at first, and then the running padded footsteps of the animal. He swung the rifle around and put the crosshairs right on the animal's sternum. But just before he pulled the trigger, he felt something pounce on his back. He had toppled forward, and unfortunately, he had fired at the same time. He felt something biting at his shoulder, a weight standing on his back. He then felt a sharp pain in his wrist as something began to tug at it.

Kit didn't panic. Instead, he took a deep breath and heaved up with his body. He sent the animal on his back flying off of him. When he looked up, he saw the other dinosaur with its jaws clenched around his wrist. He curled his free hand in a fist and punched the animal right in the eye. It yelped as it tumbled backward, letting go of his wrist. Kit quickly picked up the rifle and pulled the bolt back to chamber in a new round.

The animal's eyes widened, as if it recognized the weapon in Kit's hand. It darted off to the right as quickly as it could into the underbrush. Kit put the rifle to his shoulder, looking down the scope. He looked around the forest; it was silent again and he saw no other signs of danger. He continued to scan his surroundings carefully, ready to meet his attackers with gunfire once more. But the attack didn't come. Maybe the animals had given up for the time being.

Kit knows they will attack again. They will keep trying until they succeed. Kit thinks about their attacks. Every time they attack, it's a series of sounds around their prey, followed by silence, and then a bum rush from all sides. They just needed to do it enough times to get lucky, which is why Kit decided to go on the offensive. These fucking dinosaurs were not smarter than him. To Kit, they just acted like any other inexperienced fighting force. And to beat them, he had to turn the tables.

Kit took a knee and slid the rifle bolt back, the extractor sending the unspent round flying into Kit's hand. He slips the round into the rifle's fixed magazine, then fishes into his pocket for a few more fresh rounds of .375. He put two more into the magazine, then attempted to ghost-load the last round into the chamber by pushing the bolt forward while holding down the other rounds with his thumb. The rifle's capacity was three rounds, including the chambered round. But Kit had managed to fully load the rifle and add an extra one.

Kit doesn't decide to do this out of the blue, potentially creating a weapon jam. He has tested this technique while zeroing the rifles scope before they left the states. The only thing that bothers him and he wishes he had done differently is the rifle scope. With how close these animals have been getting, they should have mounted red dots or holographic sights instead of high-powered Leupold scopes. Even at the lowest zoom setting, all Kit can see while aiming at these cubs is a close-up of teeth and feathers.

Doesn't matter now. Kit has a plan, and he can still get it done with the gear he has. Kit can hear the cubs running around him in a circle, staying hidden in the scrubs and honey suckle banksias. They started their hooting again, like clockwork. Here they go again with their scare tactics. Kit simply flipped his baseball cap backward and got to work. He kept the rifle in the high-ready position and waited for the next step in the cubs' plan.

The hooting stopped, and that was Kit's queue. He stood up from his knee and pretended to flee in panic. That's when he heard one of the cubs take the bait and begin chasing him. Kit ran past a pandani tree and quickly sidestepped to his right, hiding quickly behind the tree. The cub briefly lost sight of him as it passed the tree. When the dinosaur cub finally spotted Kit, it was too late. Kit was inches away from the cub and had already swung the butt of the rifle on the cub's temple. The rifle butt knocked the cub unconscious. Kit then heard other cubs charging toward him. He turned around and faced them, *time to test how smart you are.*

Kit put his boot on the unconscious cub's neck and swung the rifle's barrel around, pointing it at the cub's head. To his surprise, the charging cubs stopped in their tracks when they saw him put the rifle barrel to the cub's head. Kit puffed his chest and gave them a menacing stare. The dinosaur cubs had amazing expressions in their eyes alone. Kit could tell they were instantly worried.

Oh yeah, they get the message. Kit could feel the dinosaur cub under his boot wake up and begin to whimper. He shoved the rifle barrel harder against the cub's head, and the cub began to whine. But Kit didn't break his gaze away from the other cubs, making sure they understood. Finally, Kit lifted his boot off the cub's neck, and as the dinosaur cub stood up, Kit gave it a hard kick in the ribs.

"Go on! Git!" he yelled.

He saw them scamper away, hoping they were now afraid of him after him turning the tables. Kit's left ear began to ring. He shook his head and dug his finger in to get the ringing to stop. For a moment, he felt dumb for not bringing hearing protection for the elephant rifle. But then again, he never actually expected to use it. When the ringing in his ear faded from the gunfire, he heard a voice crackling with static. He reached into his pocket and pulled out the small radio. "Are you there?" he heard Burns say. He was coughing.

"Yes, I can hear you," Kit says into the radio.

"We heard gunshots," Burns says. "Are you all right?"

"They tried to jump me just like they almost did with Matt," Kit says. "I think I scared them away."

"Yeah, we just got attacked too," Burns says. "I don't know how many of these young dinosaurs there are. Or how long they can keep this up. But our luck is going to run out."

"Are you guys okay?"

The radio crackled. "-mostly fine, we can still move."

"What do you want to do?" Kit asks.

"As much as it pains me to say it," Burns says as the radio crackles again. "We have to go back and regroup. We are not equipped for this."

Before responding, Kit gasped. "All right, I'll come to you, and then we can make our way back."

"No, you got the long-range weapon," Burns responded.

"You can cover our approach. I don't think you're far from us. The gunfire sounded close."

"Okay, I can do that," Kit says. "Then let's get on with it."

"Give us a call if you need help," Burns says.

"Copy that," Kit responded.

Kit put the radio back in his pocket. He pulled the bolt back on the rifle to make a brass check. There was a round in the chamber. So far, he has used up four rounds in total. They brought fifteen rounds for each weapon, which means for this particular elephant gun, he only has eleven rounds left. Five of those rounds were in the bottom-right pocket of his jacket. The remainder of them were in the rifle case in the back of one of the ford trucks. He had to use these bullets sparingly. He had to make sure that each trigger pulled met its target. He pushed the bolt back after making the brass check. He took a deep breath, his heart racing and his lungs pumping.

Burns was right. They were not equipped to deal with these animals, at least not at the moment. He never thought an animal would be able to overpower him. Just to think that these animals were able to easily outmaneuver him and bring him to the ground brought chills to his body. Yes, indeed, these attacks did feel more personal than getting domed by a bullet. Kit took a couple more deep breaths. When he finally felt a bit more sure of himself, he put the rifle to his shoulder. He grabbed the GPS from his jacket pocket. He found the way back to the lodge and started moving in that direction.

He knew his friends would be right on his heels, and Burns had asked him to cover their approach. He was going to do just that, and if these animals decided to test his patience once more...

Kit would simply give them a *good old marine ass-whooping*

again.

MAMMALS

Matthew Irving and Bill Burns were walking through the cold wilderness of Tasmania. The rain was not making it easy for them to make their way back. Both Burns and Matt really wanted to put the hood of their jacket on their heads, but they couldn't. To do so would mean handicapping themselves from their peripheral vision. The rain had also seemed to pick up its intensity, pattering down onto the forest a little more fiercely than before. So not only were both of their heads soaked in water, now they could barely hear the sounds of movement in the woodlands.

Burns held the revolver tightly in his hands, secretly hoping to himself that he would never have to fire the weapon. Burns let his mind meander back to the attack from before. To see the animal's shocking speed, ferocious tenacity, and their ability to learn and problem-solve staggered him. He also found it surprising that the bear spray worked on the animals. Matt had brought up the question earlier shortly before the attack. Would capsaicin have any effect on the dinosaurs? Matthew had said that he had learned somewhere that ducks had no effect or reaction to OC spray.

It wasn't just ducks. Burns knew that birds lack the pain receptors to react properly to capsaicinoids. So, because of that, Matthew had brought up the question if dinosaurs were in fact birds, or more closely related to reptiles. When the bear spray worked, Matthew had exclaimed 'reptile eyes for the win'.

Which made even less sense to Burns.

OC spray always has a reaction in mammals, with birds being the only exception. Reptiles were not mammals; they were cold-blooded. OC spray does not have any effect whatsoever, not on crocodiles, alligators, or even Komodo dragons.

So that brought up the speculation for Burns: if these animals had a reaction to the oleoresin capsicum, then what were they? They were not birds as they had a reaction, and they were not reptiles either. So what were these animals related to? Were they in fact just mammals, neither birds nor reptiles? Burns remembers touching the squirming animal earlier that was having the negative reaction to the sedative. When he touched its skin, it was surprisingly warm. It had not dawned on him until this moment that the animal was warm-blooded.

Had it not been for their current situation, Burns would have found this extremely fascinating. Every theory they have had on dinosaurs these past few centuries was completely wrong. Dinosaurs, at least this specific species, were warm-blooded mammals.

Matt broke the silence by suddenly speaking. "I'd love to know what you're thinking," he says to Burns.

"These dinosaurs are warm-blooded mammals," Burns simply says.

"What do you mean?" Matt asks.

"I mean, birds or reptiles aren't supposed to have a reaction to bear spray," Burns says. "Only mammals do. And when I touched that dinosaur earlier, it was warm, not cold-blooded."

Matt didn't respond for a few seconds, taking in the newly found information. "So dinosaurs are somehow closer related to lions or wolves then they are to ostriches and crocodiles?" Matt remarked.

"Seems that way," Burns says.

"Well, now hold on, there are warm-blooded reptiles in the world," Matt added.

"One single species," Burns says. "The Argentine tegu lizard, but they're only slightly warm-blooded during their reproductive periods. Other than that, it seems paleontology has been wrong from the get-go. By classifying the dinosaurs and comparing them to birds or reptiles based on their bone structure, they made the mistake of assuming them cold-blooded."

"Yes, it seems to contradict everything I've heard so far," Matt says. "And boy, are they a sight to see, aren't they? Scaled like a Komodo dragon but feathered like a cassowary. Who would have thought they were mammals?"

"My question for the moment," Burns says. "What kind of brain do they have? Birds are swift and instinctual, reptiles are cold and calculated. Do you think their brain is more mammalian than anything?"

"Mammalian brain on a dinosaur?"

"That's a scary fuckin thought," Burns mumbled.

"All I know," Matt says, "is that they're highly coordinated. And they can do so without the need of vocalization. You were right before, they were indeed trying to intimidate us and disperse us with their *hooting*. Once that stopped and they moved on to attacking us, did you hear any more noises?"

"No I did not," Burns says.

"Then they communicated with their eyes and movement," Matt says. "You don't just attack prey like that and get lucky. They can somehow see each other, even through this dense foliage."

"Their visual acuity must be tremendous," Burns says.

"My point exactly," Matt says. "I wonder if they can see us right now."

"Glass half full, Matthew," Burns says.

Matt chuckled to himself. "Well, look who's the optimist now."

Burns chuckled for a moment too, and for a couple seconds, he shared a moment with someone whom he trusted once. Despite everything that Matthew Irving is, it's easy to forget that he has been doing this for a long time, and he can recognize animal behavior quite well. If only he were like this all the time instead of his usual TV persona.

"You should check in on the marine," Matt says.

Burns nodded. He grabbed the radio from his jacket pocket and clicked the button. "Kit, radio check," Burns says into the radio.

"Loud and clear," Kit responded.

Burns put the radio back in his jacket pocket. He pulled out the GPS and examined their location. "We're not far now," Burns says. "Maybe twenty more minutes of this bullshit and we should be back at the lodge."

"With any luck," Matt says. "Someone was able to reach the ranger station, and there's help on the way."

"I certainly hope s-"

An ungodly sound emerged from the forest in the distance. It was an ear-piercing screech, getting progressively louder and louder as it continued. It must have gone on for about ten seconds. Burns and Matthew froze in their tracks, looking at each other, bewildered but concerned.

"Does that sound like a grieving parent to you?" Matt asks.

The radio in Burns's jacket pocket crackled. "Mommy's very angry," Kit's voice says through the radio static, his tone sarcastic. Burns handed the GPS to Matt and reached for the radio from his jacket. "I'd say so," Burns says into the radio. "Let's double-time it."

"Copy that," Kit responded.

Burns put the radio back in his pocket, and Matt handed the GPS back to him. Burns nodded to Matt, and they both started to jog a little faster through the woodlands. At this point, they did not seem to give much care to their step. The only thing on their mind was to make it back to the lodge before they were attacked again. The screeching sound that came emanating from the forest sounded angry and distraught.

The animal sound was a low rumbling. Burns and Matt knew that it could only come from a creature that was significantly bigger. Burns suddenly heard the radio in his jacket crackle. It sounded like Kit's voice calling out to him but he couldn't quite make out what he was saying. Burns put the GPS back into his pants pocket and reached upward to his jacket pocket to retrieve the radio.

But his hand did not reach the radio in time. Suddenly, Burns felt a weight strike him in the side of his ribs. He did not see it in his peripheral vision, it was so fast. It sent him flying to the side tumbling into Matthew, both of them toppling to the floor. Burns is caught so off-guard that he felt the revolver slip from his hands as he tumbled to the ground along with Matthew.

Matthew grunted a quick "Bill!" as he wondered why his friend had suddenly been sent flying toward him. After Burns hit the solid ground, the mud smearing his face, he instantly tried to catch his breath. He turned his head to see two small cubs standing right next to him.

Their jaws open, lips dripping with saliva, they're snarling at them. They were only about a foot away. Burns saw their posture change, and just before they pounced on him, he held up both of his hands to cover his face. He felt heavy jaws clamp down on his left forearm, the hot breathing of the animal's nose hitting him square in the forehead. He then felt the second set of teeth start tugging at his ankle, accompanied by rabid snarling. Burns did not scream for help, instead, he just took a brief moment to accept what was happening to him.

Even if Burns could feel the teeth slowly sinking into his flesh, he did not panic. With his free hand, he reached toward his right hip, and he grabbed the small five-inch survival knife he had in a sheath. He pulled it out and he swung it at the animal's snout that was staring at him right in the face. The knife slid right into the side of the animal's snout. He felt the knife slide all the way in until the animal's skin bumped into the handle. The animal opened its jaws and yelped, letting go of Burns's arm, surprised at the attack.

Then the animal did something unexpected. Before Burns could react, the animal gave a quick flick of its head. Like a dog flicking dirt or moisture off its head. The head flick made Burns lose grip of the knife handle. And when this happened, the animal lunged forward again with both of its claws instead of its teeth, and started to scratch at Burns's chest as if it was digging a hole into him.

This time, Burns grunts in pain; the claws on its arms are extremely sharp. The animal tore through the front of his jacket and T-shirt fairly quickly, its claws beginning to tear into the flesh of his chest. Burns screamed through gritted teeth, trying to push the animal away. Then suddenly he felt the animal's weight come off of him completely. He saw a quick flash of another human being tackle the animal right off of him.

It was Matthew.

Matt tackles the animal and begins to rain down punches. One of the animals was occupied for the moment. Burns quickly shook the pain away and turned his attention to the one tugging at his ankle. The animal had its head drooped down at his foot, its tail wagging up in the air. Burns was about to give it a forceful kick in the snout, when a low crack echoed through the forest.

The animal's torso suddenly burst open, blood spraying from one side and blood trickling from the other. The animal simply dropped to its side, its body suddenly stiff, its legs and forearms twitching in a final death rattle. The animal that Matthew was attempting to fist-fight suddenly wriggled out from under Matthew and darted into the forest. Matt stood up and looked around as he backed away toward Burns. Burns glanced around the forest; he saw nothing, no one. He looked down at his chest and saw that his jacket was slightly bloody. Matt turned around and looked at Burns who was still laying on the ground.

"Are you all right?" Matt asks.

"Mostly, it looks like you got him off me before these wounds became more than superficial," Burns says.

Matt then turned his attention to the dead animal at Burns's feet. "Looks like we got an angel on our shoulders," Matt says with a smile.

Burns looked around the woods again, until he heard his radio crackling in his jacket pocket. Burns attempted to get to his knees. He took a breath and fished the radio out of his pocket. He held the radio in his hands, dark blood dripping from his chest onto his hands and the radio. "Thanks for the save, Kit," he says into the radio.

"We need to keep moving," Kit says. "I'm positive they'll be back. These attacks are becoming more frequent."

"Copy that," Burns says into the radio.

He put the radio back in his pocket and tried to stand upright. His knees buckled from the pain. The claw marks on his chest, the teeth imprints on his left forearm, and the ankle injury made him feel weary. Matt leaned forward. He examined Burns's chest area. Jagged tears in his sternum and pectoral areas, and blood was trickling down his jacket.

"How are you going to walk?" Matt asks.

"My chest is on fire, my body wants to rest," Burns says.

"No can do," Matt says. "The animals will know you're hurt, keep moving."

Matt leaned forward and put Burns's arm over his shoulder, then put his hand on Burns's waist to help his friend walk. "Here brother, I got you," Matt says.

"Thank you," Burns says. "Don't forget the gun, and the bear spray, we need them."

Matt takes a quick glance around the ground. He picked up the can of bear spray and stuffed it in his cargo pants pocket. He then saw the revolver and picked it up. "I'm popping one of them if they attack us again," Matt says, holding the revolver in his hand.

"I'm glad we're finally on the same page," Burns says. Both men then slowly limped forward through the forest, heading back to the lodge.

GUNFIRE

"Were those gunshots?" Marcus, the editor asks.

Lucy Benitez was still sitting at the desk with the radio, desperately trying to get in contact with someone, just as Kit had instructed her. She turned her head to face Marcus. He was standing at a window near the front door, looking out into the forest. "No," Lucy says. "That's just thunder."

Marcus didn't respond. He just kept his gaze outside the window.

Lucy knew the truth; it wasn't thunder. Spending most of her childhood living in Juarez, she had grown accustomed to the sound of cracking gunfire in the distance. She had lied to the people in the room, but not without good reason. She remembers the times when she had to lie to her younger siblings. Though after the first couple of times when they heard the shootings, she had told her siblings the truth, and she immediately learned that sometimes telling the truth causes *panic*.

She remembers Kit's subtle nervous behavior when he gave her the directives to call for help. That accompanied with the gunshots, and the fact that Anika and her team were not back yet, indicated that the situation had gone to worse. There was no need to add mass panic to the mix.

She held the radio in her hand, the spiralled extension cord laying on her knees. She would continue to try until she reached someone, while keeping an eye on the rest of the film group. It was the least she could do. She knew there was trouble and she wanted to help.

Lucy hasn't been able to reach anybody just yet. She's been trying for the last forty minutes to get in contact with the ranger station. After the first fifteen minutes, it felt like the ranger station stopped trying to respond, and its pure static at the moment. She doesn't know how much of her information has reached them. God, why can't she reach them?

The steady drumming of rain on the roof gives her the answer. This rainstorm has picked up in the last hour. There's nothing she can do at the moment, except keep doing what Kit told her to do. "Hello," she says into the radio again. "This is the Valente expedition team. We need help."

The radio traffic is pure static, just as it has been for the past twenty minutes or so.

"*Chingada madre*," Lucy gets exasperated.

"You can't reach anyone?" Marcus says from the door.

"I think it's the storm," Lucy says. "I'm going to have to keep trying until I find someone."

"Wouldn't it be easier to grab one of the trucks and drive to the ranger station at this point?" Marcus asks.

"Do you know where the ranger station is, and how to get there?" Lucy asks.

"Well, no I don't," Marcus says. "Anyone who might is probably still out there."

"Then we just wait for them until they come back," Lucy says. "Until then, just stay put."

Lucy suddenly heard one more cracking gunshot. The chatter in the room fell silent.

"I don't think that's thunder," Marcus says.

"It's just thunder from the storm, quit worrying about it," Lucy says. She squeezed the button on the radio firmly. She called for help again and again. They needed to get someone out here to help, because there was something going on out there.

And it doesn't sound like an expedition anymore; it sounds like a war.

KIT

Kit is jogging through the dense forest, glancing at the GPS in his hand every now and then. He has to slow down his pace since dusk is almost over and the night is creeping in. It's significantly darker now, and it's harder to see where he's going. Every few hundred yards or so, Kit stops and looks in the direction of Burns and Matt, trying to find them on his scope. He's making sure that they're still following, that they're still okay. Kit can see them both slowly moving; both men are slightly obscured by the ferns through his scope. They seem to be doing fine. They look hurt but they're still moving.

Kit could feel the accumulated rain start to drip down onto his brows and eyes. He quickly brushed the rain away from his face, just then realizing that he had lost his ball cap while running. *Damn*, he thought, *that was my favorite ball cap*. It was from his favorite baseball team, the Tacoma Rainiers. He had been so focused on staying alive that he didn't notice he had lost his cap.

Suddenly, he heard a soft hooting coming from the forest. Kit stopped in his tracks; he knew the sound again and the meaning of it. Kit was about to be tested again. He gritted his teeth, and he took a knee, holding the rifle firmly to his shoulder.

He scanned the forest; he saw nothing. He then decided to find Matt and Burns on the rifle scope, but he couldn't see them. The hooting suddenly stopped, and then there was dead silence. Kit put the GPS in his pocket and swapped it for the radio. He held it up to his mouth, while his other hand held the rifle level to his eyes. "Mr. Burns, radio check," Kit says into the radio.

"Loud and clear buddy." It was Matt's voice. "We heard the animal calls too."

"Do you know where it came from?" Kit asks.

"It sounded distant from over here," Matt says. "It might be closer to where you are."

"Good," Kit says. "I'd rather keep it that way. I'm going to keep them interested. We're not far from the lodge."

"If you're confident enough, go ahead," Matt says. "We could certainly use the help. Just keep an eye out, these fuckers love to ambush."

"I've got the general idea of their methods," Kit says. "Stay frosty, keep moving."

"Roger that," Matt says.

Kit put the radio back in his pocket and again swapped it for the GPS. Kit slowly stood up as he started to scan his surroundings again, trying to find a target. He started to walk forward steadily, keeping an ear out for any sound that might give the dinosaurs away. He suddenly heard a bird chirp, but it wasn't high-pitched or jovial in the slightest. Kit knew instantly that it was coming from them. They were trying to curveball him, confuse him with a brand-new method of communication.

They knew he had become familiar with the hooting and the wailing from earlier. And he most certainly has an idea of their snarling and hissing when they were attacking. Now the animals seem like they are purposely trying to use a sound Kit hadn't heard before. Christ, *these fucking animals were smart.*

He felt nervous, which he hated as he rarely ever felt nervous. Even during combat when bullets were flying past his head and all he could hear from the insurgents was them screaming in their language, he'd never felt scared.

He was certainly in a world he did not understand, and he didn't want to. He needed to keep his mind levelled. There were people depending on him. He didn't like the fact that Matt and Burns were behind him and not in front. Kit had to leapfrog every few hundred yards to cover them as they moved. He had to get them to move past him; he had to protect his friends in the most logical way. God, the forest was so silent, he couldn't even hear any birds or insects anymore.

Wait, *the forest was silent.*

They were there, around him, Kit could sense it. But he kept moving, it didn't matter. The lodge was not far from them. He had to find a way to keep the animals at bay while they reached the lodge. He didn't know if the animals were smart enough to figure out they were close to home, but Kit wouldn't underestimate the creatures again. Kit decided he would have to distract the animals in some way.

He then quickly hopped over a burrowed Huon tree root. He stood there for a few seconds and listened, still nothing but silence. Kit was focused entirely on distracting the animals. It was against his own code to sit and do nothing while his friends were in potential danger. He knew Matt and Burns were hurt, and they wouldn't stand a chance if there was another attack.

He then hears the animals' soft hooting in the distance. They sounded like birds but not at all natural. The animal calls were not close to his location, which meant his assumption was right. They would attempt to attack Matt and Burns first. There was an attack coming; he knew it, so he had to do something *now.*

He slowly moved through the foliage, trying to be as silent as possible. He didn't know how good of hearing these creatures were, but either way, he avoided stepping on the wet mud or in the bushes to stay quiet. Kit figures out that if he stayed close to the trees and stepped on the roots, his footsteps made no noise. And the rain certainly helped mask his movement.

While he moved, Kit was hoping the other group was still alive. He was hoping they would enter the lodge and find Anika, JJ, and Zeke. But his mind could not let the situational logic slip away. He had seen the animals' attack methods. From what he could tell, the animals were about the size of a German shepherd. Not as big as the track they had found, but that didn't mean there wasn't a bigger one among them also. And even if these young animals weren't that big in size, it didn't mean they couldn't overwhelm you. Just like a pack of dogs, a pack of these young animals could easily take a human down. That much he had learned.

Kit brushed off those thoughts. He needed to keep his head in the game if he was going to help the others. He stopped a good distance away from the lodge, hidden in the rainy night amongst the ferns and bushes, crouched near a tree. Kit squeezed the rifle in his hands, thinking of a possible distraction for the animals. Using himself as bait would be foolish, but he still considered the option as a last resort. He'd rather go toe-to-toe with the animals himself than let anyone else do it. He felt confident enough that he'd stay alive. Kit took off his rucksack and opened the pockets. He found a bundled-up set of flares.

That could work. He pulled out the flares and took one out of the bundle after undoing the strap around them. He could toss one, he thought, out into one of the clearings. Either the animals will get curious and move toward it, or the animals will get afraid of it, and the group can follow the flares home. Or possibly, the animals will ignore the flares, and he will have to think of something else. If this doesn't work, then he will maybe find a more aggressive approach. Though he wasn't so sure about that. Burns wasn't firing the handgun he gave him, so maybe attacking the animals wasn't wise if they were keeping their distance. Still, Kit decided he would try the flares first and then find an alternative.

He took the flare in his hand and twisted the top off of it. He held it up, ready to toss it, when something caught his eye. In his peripheral vision, he saw something move on the tree he was crouched next to. Kit turned his head; he saw something pointy and scaly dangling vertically from the tree. He followed it up with his gaze only to see that it was a tail, and a massive dinosaur was holding itself up on the tree trunk, one with muscular arms and legs. The creature had its head turned to the side, looking down directly at Kit, its eyes glowing red from the flare.

And before Kit had a chance to react, the animal *jumped*.

CRUELTY

Matthew Irving had Burns's arm over his shoulder, and he's helping him walk alongside him. Burns held his chest, keeping pressure on his wounds with his jacket sleeve. Burns could already feel the sleeve begin to stick to his skin from soaked blood. He grunted after every step he took, the energy draining from him faster than his blood. Burns took it step by step, his feet wanting to give way every time.

They could see the illumination from the porch floodlights of the lodge in the distance. They were almost there. Matt peeked over his shoulder every other step, ensuring that they weren't being followed. The rain was pounding at this point, and the forest had become a cold, constant shower for every creature as dusk slowly seeped in. "Don't worry, brother," Matt says, struggling to keep Burns on his feet. "The lodge is right there, it's not far now."

"I got bit by a dinosaur again," Burns says, his West Virginia accent showing. "Tore my chest something fierce with their claws."

"How bad are the wounds?" Matt asks.

"Bad," Burns simply replied. "But they could be worse."

"Like you said, Bill," Matt remarked. "Glass half full. Come on, the porch is right there."

Burns and Matthew kept taking it step by step, slowly inching toward the lodge. They stepped onto the wooden porch, their boots squidging from the moisture. Burns almost slipped, but Matt had a good grip of him and kept Burns on his feet. "Bad choice of varnish," Burns grunted.

"I'll add it to the list of complaints for Valente," Matt says.

They reached the door. Matt extended a hand to knock on the door, but he wasn't able to. The door opened wide before his knuckles touched it. At the door was Marcus; he scanned their faces before moving on to their bodies, his eyes wide open when he saw Burns's chest and forearm.

"Oh my God," Marcus says.

"Just let us in," Burns snapped.

Marcus moved out of the way, and Matt and Burns made their way inside. They moved across the living room toward the nearest couch, their boots still squidging on the hardwood floor. Matt set Burns down on the end of the couch. Burns laid down onto the soft cushions. His damp clothes instantly imprint a wet shape on the cushions. Matt then hurried to the kitchen. There was a small cabinet labelled 'First Aid'. Matt flipped open the cabinet and grabbed the first-aid kit.

"Jesus Christ," Lucy says as she walks over to Burns on the couch. "Are you going to be all right?"

Burns had already begun to unbutton his shirt to take a look at the wounds. "It looks worse than it is," Burns says. "Believe me, I've seen worse. Nothing bandages and some peroxide won't fix. Were you able to get in contact with anyone?"

"I have been trying for the past hour," Lucy says. "I did reach someone the first couple times, but they couldn't hear me. I think the storm is messing up our reception here."

"Keep trying," Burns says. "Anika and the rest are out there. They might be in trouble."

Matt opens a separate cabinet, grabbing a bundle of dry

dish towels. Matt then walked back across the living room toward Burns holding the dish towels and first-aid kit in his hand. "Out here, in this forest, especially with this rain and the thunderstorm," Matt says. "It might be better to have someone drive to the nearest ranger station if we can't reach them. No use to keep trying with a useless radio."

"We thought about that too," Lucy says. "But nobody here knew how to get there. We were waiting for you."

"Either one of us can go," Burns says. "We'll probably just leave Kit here with you since he has the rifle and he's more qualified to shoot it."

"Is he right behind you guys?" Lucy asks.

"What the hell do you mean? Is he not here?" Burns snapped.

"No, I haven't seen him since he told me to make the radio call," Lucy says.

"Oh shit," Matt says. "He was in front of us, Bill, he should have made it here first."

"Fuck, *fuck*," Burns grunted as he stood up from the couch. "We have to go get him."

"You're hurt, Mr. Burns," Lucy says. "I think you should stay here and get bandaged up."

"You don't understand, Lucy," Burns says. "If Kit hasn't made it back yet, then he's definitely in trouble."

Burns fished the radio from out of his pocket. He put it up to his face as he walked toward the front door. "Kit, radio check," Burns says into the radio. There was no response, just static. Burns turned around and looked at Matt. "We need to go get him right now," Burns says to him.

Matt took one step forward but was interrupted by a

deafening screech. It sounded like the distinctive screech of a hawk barrelling down toward its prey. Only the screech was continuous and loud, echoing through the tall ceiling of the lodge. The screeching was coming from outside, and as soon as it stopped, they heard a man's voice calling for help. Burns and Matt hurried to the windows to look outside. They could only see a couple shadows about a hundred feet away from the porch. Burns leaned over to the light switches on the wall next to the door and turned on bright floodlights, which were positioned right on top of the front door outside. The floodlights illuminated as far as they needed to see.

And what they saw terrified every single person looking out that window.

It was a seven foot tall dinosaur, its muscled thighs and taloned feet holding down Kit into the dirt. The dinosaur had one of its clawed forearms holding down Kit's head. Kit was yelling for help, his voice frantic and terrified. "Good God," Matt mumbled to himself.

Burns didn't hesitate. Even if he was terrified and wounded, he knew he had to help. Burns quickly brushed aside his pain and emotions. "That fucking thing is going to kill him," Burns says quickly. "Do you have pepper spray?"

"Yes I do," Matt says.

"We have to get that fucking thing off of him right now," Burns says. "Lucy, we're going to open the door. Don't close it all the way. Just be ready, we might need to come in quick."

Matt handed Burns the revolver, and then Burns swung open the front door. Both Burns and Matt quickly stepped out of the door to face the mighty dinosaur.

But *mighty* was not the word that either of the men would have chosen to describe it. It was staring at both of them, its jaws wide open, dripping with strands of sticky saliva. The dinosaur didn't make a sound. It simply stood there, watching the two humans start to move toward it. It had damp spiky feathers on its head, the rain showing the men its muscular scaled body. The ridge over its eyeballs kept the dinosaur's eyes in shadows, the floodlights giving it a terrifying eyeshine. It looked like a crocodile out of water, standing on massive ostrich legs.

"Hit it with the spray," Burns whispered to Matt.

Matt slowly creeped forward, the can of bear spray in his hand. He then held his arm out, pointed the canister of bear spray, and fired a burst. The orange stream of oily capsaicin glided through the air. It was dead on target, the burst of spray hitting the dinosaur square in the eyes.

But nothing happened.

Matt knew that pepper spray usually had or could have a delayed reaction in some subjects. But they waited and waited, and the animal just blinked, wondering what it was that they had done to it. The animal then simply snarled at them.

"Fuck," Matt mumbled. "It didn't work. Do you want me to hit it again?"

Burns was done waiting and talking. He wasn't going to let Kit be terrified any longer. Burns took a knee and held out the Taurus 605 revolver in his hand, pointing it right at the animal. But once he did, the animal quickly drooped its head down and grabbed Kit by the temples of his head with its jaws. It began to wag its tail and snarl at Burns, the sudden reaction startled him.

Did it recognize the gun?

"For God's sake," Kit screamed. "Please do something."

Burns levelled the iron sights of the revolver. He adjusted his grip and then pulled the trigger. The revolver fired a single .357 magnum round. It flew through the air until it struck the animal straight on the shoulder. The animal snarled again, and with a petrifying ease, shrugged off the pain and began to squeeze Kit's head with its jaws. Kit began to howl like a scared child, his deafening screams cut short by his coughing as his lungs ran out of oxygen from screaming for so long.

"Oh fuck," Burns says.

While still holding Kit's head in its jaws, the animal began to claw away at Kit's back. Kit continued to scream and howl in pain, the long razor-sharp claws tearing through his clothes and the flesh of his back.

"Shoot that fucking thing again!" Matt yelled.

Burns fired two more consecutive shots; one missed, and the other grazed the animal's hide. Burns's hands were shaking. The animal was too far, and his heart was pumping while his fingers were cold. Burns knew right then and there; there was nothing they could do. The animal continued to tear into Kit's back, specks of blood flying up onto its forearms. Matt held up the bear spray in his hand and continued to fire short bursts of orange pepper spray. The bursts of pepper spray struck the animal in the face, and some of it leaked onto Kit's head, but it had no effect. They were helpless to do anything. They could then hear the dinosaur's claws begin to scrape against something on Kit's back. Just then they realized it had torn through Kit's flesh and reached his rib cage.

"Bill, fire the goddamn gun!" Matt was yelling. "I'm out of spray!"

But Burns was not responding. He was shocked. His eyes were wide as he watched Kit being torn apart. He let his morbid pessimism return from his past as a paramedic. Kit was too far gone. Even if the animal was stopped, Kit would still die from his wounds.

Then the animal growled one more time, and after it did, it effortlessly tore Kit's head off his body. Both Burns and Matt watched as Kit abruptly stopped screaming, and the dinosaur held his head in its jaws. Kit's decapitated head blinked for a few more seconds, his face still in terror. His eyes looked around, taking in what had just happened to him right before his life went out. The dinosaur tossed the head at them both, and the head rolled toward their feet.

Burns glanced down at Kit's head. He noticed his lips were still moving, but there was no sound coming from them. He then felt Matt grab him by his jacket and yank Burns back toward the front door. Burns looked up and saw the dinosaur charging toward them at full speed. Burns was then tossed onto the floor inside the lodge, and he watched the door close swiftly in front of him.

PHASE THREE

"*The invasive species struggles to remain relevant in the current ecosystem. While the opposing species manages to keep succeeding in decreasing their numbers. The invasive species will not survive, as they will always underestimate the competing apex species. They will underestimate how fast, how much stronger, and how far they are willing to go to restore balance in their ecosystem.*"

- Excerpts from "*The Apex Theory: An In-Depth Analysis of Apex Predators in Arbitrary Environments*". Published in the *Journal of Wildlife Biology*, submitted by Dr. Anika Irving, PhD.

LODGE

Burns was on the living room floor, his elbows propping him up as he watched Matt frantically lock the front door. Burns could see Matt talking, but he couldn't hear anything. Burns looked around the room and saw the many faces of the crew. All of them with different reactions, different emotions. There was fear, shock, and disgust, and some of the faces were talking too. But he couldn't hear anything; he could see all of their lips moving, much like Kit's decapitated head. Burns felt something strike his arm, and he turned to see Matthew Irving hitting him on the arm. His face was frantic. He could tell he was yelling and his hands were shaking. Burns could see-

"Goddamn it! Snap the hell out of it!"

Burns finally heard Matt's voice. Matt then struck him in the arm again. "Bill!" Matt yelled. "Get your ass up!"

Burns stood up, trying to keep his balance as his head felt light. Matt grabbed him by the arm and pulled him toward the nearest window. Burns made a quick glance toward Lucy Benitez. She was bent at the waist, her head between her knees, hands covering her mouth. "Pay attention!" Matt yelled.

"To what?" Burns asks.

Matt took a brief second. He realized his friend may have blacked out. Burns was not in a good mental state. Matt grabbed him by the shoulders and shook him hard. "The goddamn dinosaur, Bill!" Matt snapped. "Our problems ain't over just yet."

Burns lazily stood up, his thoughts firing in every direction

in his head. *The dinosaur*, Matt had said, a concept so wild only a few hours ago. And now it was real, and it had killed more than one person. No, not killed, *murdered* with cruel savagery. Burns limped forward to the window, the injuries on his chest and his arm feeling like they were on fire.

He looked out of the window, the bright floodlights over the porch illuminating only about forty feet. But it was enough to see the dinosaur—the tall, menacing, and blood-soaked dinosaur standing at the edge of the forest, sneering at them. Burns could've sworn he had last seen it charging, but the dinosaur didn't move. It looked like a statue. It only continued to stare at the lodge, the floodlights still giving it a terrifying eye shine, its reptilian eyes studying its prey with calculated thoughts.

He could hear Matt breathing heavily. Burns glanced over at his friend, and he saw him brushing away the fog created by his breath from the windowpane. Matt was scared. Burns had never seen Matt scared, not since…

"What do you think it's doing?" Matt asks.

Burns looked back outside the window toward the dinosaur. "I don't know what to think," Burns says simply.

"It's just looking at us," Matt says, "It's not moving."

"I can see that," Burns says. "I don't think there's any use in trying to understand what its next move is."

Matt took a breath to say something else, but he didn't say anything. Probably because the dinosaur took one simple step forward. And then another, and another step. It was starting to make its way toward the door. "*Oh shit*," Matt says. "*Oh fuck.*"

Burns didn't say a word. He just continued to watch the animal make its way toward the front entrance of the lodge. Matt glanced at the door. He gave the doors a tug. They were locked tight. But that wasn't what he was feeling for. Matt gave a soft knock to the wood. The doors didn't feel thick. Matt had no doubt that this animal could easily tear this door down if it wanted to.

"We need to move fast," Matt says, "Come on, Bill, help me."

"Help you do what," Burns says.

Matt was already moving toward the living room. "Barricade this door, we have to do it. It's going to try to get in," Matt says as he was trying to push one of the couches toward the door. The couch was moving, sliding against the floor but not as quick as he wanted. "Come on, Bill, snap out of it!" Matt yelled, his voice strained from pushing. Burns moved forward and he started to tug on the couch, even if his injuries were blaring with pain. They moved the couch firmly up against the door.

"Help me grab another one," Matt says. Both men went to the living room again, but this time with the help of Marcus and some other crew members. They moved the second and third couch up against the door, and they pushed as firmly as they could. When Matt was satisfied with their makeshift barricade, he moved toward the window to see what the dinosaur was doing.

Just as he looked outside the window, he saw the dinosaur take one step onto the porch. Its footsteps are completely silent against the porch's hardwood flooring. The dinosaur paid no mind to the humans looking at it through the glass window. Instead, it walked straight toward the door and then stopped when it was only a foot away. The predator drooped its head down to examine the door. It sniffed at the wood, then the handles, and then toward the edges of the door. Matt could smell the stale warm stench of the animal's every exhale as it studied the front doors.

The dinosaur then branded the top of its head, then slowly put the top of its skull up against the door and started to *slowly push.* Burns and Matt saw the double doors start to move slowly inward, pushing the couches up against the floors effortlessly. Burns and Matt quickly moved away from the windows and up against the couches to make some sort of resistance against the dinosaur. The pushing then stopped, and Marcus was already looking outside the window.

"What is it doing?" Matt asks.

"I don't know what it's doing," Marcus says.

Matt quickly darted toward the window again and he peeked outside. Only to find the dinosaur staring right at him through the glass window. The predator's eyes were a sight to see, full of rage and lifeless at the same time. Matt could smell the blood on its snout through the door. He could see bits of flesh and skin dangling from its teeth. Matt couldn't look away, instead, he watched as the dinosaur leaned its head forward and put its teeth around the metal bars covering the window. It firmly grasped one of the bars and gave it a tug. The metal bars didn't move, as they were not only bolted but welded onto the outside of the window. The animal let go of the bars and took a step back, but it still didn't make a single sound.

It just looked around the outside of the porch. Matt could get a sense that the animal was studying the structure, trying to find a way in, some kind of weakness. And then in an instant, the animal effortlessly hopped up onto the wood awning covering part of the porch. Everyone inside the lodge could hear the animal clawing at the hardwood of the outside of the lodge as it was climbing its walls.

"Are all the windows barred on the top floor?" Matt asks.

"They are," Burns says.

"Are there any more doors up top? Any more entrances? Anything?" Matt asks frantically.

"I don't think so," Burns says. "There's just a back door, but it's a steel door, and it's not a double door."

They could hear the loud clumping of the claws on top of the roof as the animal slowly moved, the roof creaking and bending at the weight of the animal. "How sturdy do you think this roof is?" Matt asks.

"That'll depend on the craftsmanship of our engineers," Burns says.

"It's studying this place," Matt says, "It's going to pick at every wall and every corner until it finds a way in."

Lucy had finally come to her senses. She took a step next to Matt while she was staring at the roof. "What do we do now then?" Lucy asks.

"Keep trying on the radio," Matt tells her. "You have to keep trying until you reach somebody, because as of right now, we are stuck here."

"I haven't been able to reach anybody on the radio," Lucy says, "But I can keep trying."

"That's about as much as we can do, Lucy," Matt says, "Try other frequencies, don't just try the ranger station. Maybe we can reach someone else, and they can call for help for us."

Lucy didn't hesitate. She turned around and rushed toward the radio. Matt, Burns, and the rest of the crew members continued to stare at the ceiling as they heard the dinosaur moving on the roof. The thing on Matt's mind was that the dinosaur made absolutely no noise when it stepped onto the porch. It was incredibly light-footed. But as it was walking on the roof, it gave the sense that the beast was exceptionally heavy as well. *God*, he thought, *Kit had no chance to get out from under the dinosaur.*

"Do we have any more weapons in the house?" Matt asks.

"No, the rest of them are in the truck outside," Burns answered bluntly. "But it doesn't matter. The only weapon that's left is a shotgun that I brought, and it's in the truck that we can't get to. Do you really think you can outrun this dinosaur to the damn truck?"

"We got to think of something else because I'm getting the sense that this damn dino is relentless," Matt says.

The creaking on the roof stopped. Everybody stood in silence, waiting for another movement. Waiting for another sound that would give away the dinosaur's position or intention. The dinosaur had stopped moving and they didn't know why. They suddenly heard scraping up against the roof, but the scraping wasn't claws frantically trying to find a way in. No, it was the beast slowly dragging its claws across one direction of the roof as a way of *instilling fear*.

"Same thing as the cubs in the woods," Matt says, "Trying to frighten us. Get us to make a wrong move or something. Get us to exit the house. My guess is it's going to be taunting us from every which way it can to get us to leave."

Burns took a deep breath. "Which means we have some time. It'll try to get us out of here the easy way before it moves on to something more... *difficult*. We have some time before it actually tries to break in here."

"Why is it so focused on us?" Matt asks, "Do you really think it's going to try and find a way in? It's not just going to leave when it realizes it can't?"

"I don't give a shit why it's focused on us," Burns says, "It's here and it's not leaving, that much is clear. We should prepare for the worst. We should try to blockade every entrance and every window in this entire lodge. Lucy, whatever you do, do not give up on the radio. That is our only way out of here as far as we know."

"Well, didn't Forrest say he would meet us here at some point?" Matt asks.

"He said he might in a few days," Burn says, "Do you think we'll last a few days? I don't think we'll last a few hours."

Right as Burns finished the sentence, they heard the screeching from the dinosaur on the roof. The loud and continuous, ungodly screaming of the dinosaur made everyone contemplate their chances of survival inside the lodge. "Yeah," Burns says to himself. "This fucking thing isn't going to give up, let's get to work, *now*."

FAITH IN A PREDATOR

Anika crept slowly through the forest, the hood of her jacket up as the rain pattered onto her head. She rubbed her hands together, trying to create warmth as she couldn't feel her fingers anymore. She took a long deep breath, trying to keep breathing steady as the mist of her cold breath exited her nose and mouth. She snuck through the ferns and the foliage, keeping her head down so as to keep her concealed in the vegetation. She looked around every once in a while, looking for a threat. Sure, the rain would mask her movement through the woods, but it worked both ways with a potential predator.

She came to a point in the woods where the density of the foliage had decreased. She saw the vegetation was a little lower, and it would be more difficult to walk in her current stance. She would have to crawl through the low flora if she wanted to get to the next area of the forest. Before she moved forward, she looked around one last time. She focused her hearing, trying to find any relevant sound. The only thing she could hear was the rain coming down on the leaves and the ferns. Other than that, she saw nothing and she heard nothing. But she had made a mistake. What she didn't see was the dark shape climbing down the tree behind her. The shape then suddenly grabbed her and yanked her off her feet, back into its arms.

"You're dead," the person says. Anika exhaled. She cussed up a storm as she stood up and the arms let her go. She turned around to see Burns in full hunting camouflage gear, his head completely soaked from the rain. Burns stood up, his height towering over a much younger, less cynical, fresh-faced Anika.

"What was your mistake?" Burns says. "Go on and tell me why you're dead."

Anika sighed, her frustration radiating from her body. "I didn't check the damn trees," Anika says.

"That's right," Burns says. "You were too busy looking for a cursorial predator, that you failed to look for the ambush predator."

"The only ambush predators out here are mountain lions," Anika says. "And they've never been spotted in this part of Washington state."

"Yeah, they're not now," Burns says. "But they could be. Very well could be. What have I been teaching you this entire time? What is the main thing that I've been teaching you?"

Anika gave a blank stare, but not because she didn't know. She had just repeated it so many times that it had become annoying that he would have to ask.

"Don't give me that damn look of yours," Burns says, "I want to hear you say it."

"The worst is inevitable," Anika says.

"That's right," Burns says/ "When you are out here, you have to watch out for everything. Assume the worst, because it is inevitable, and it is going to happen. The sooner you accept that, the easier it will be to stay alive. Out of all the different types of predators in the world, whether it be opportunistic or cursorial, ambush are the worst of them all, in my opinion. They won't make a sound, they'll just stalk you as long as they need to, and they will attack you when you least expect it. By the time you finally see it, it's already too late. Most of the ambush predators in the world spend their time hiding in the damn trees. Leopards, mountain lions."

Anika interrupted "Jaguars."

"That's right," Burns says.

"Is that why you're teaching me all this shit," Anika says, irritated, "so I don't get killed by a fucking jaguar?"

"I'm teaching you all of this shit so you can stay alive," Burns says. "So you don't make any more damn mistakes. You want to follow in your mother's footsteps and be a wildlife biologist? That's fine, go right ahead, but I'll be damned if I don't teach you something that can save yourself one day."

"That's a little on the nose, don't you think?" Anika asks. "I mean, teaching me to avoid jaguars, that's like, is it some kind of therapy tactic? I mean, shit, I think my actual shrink is a lot more subtle than that."

"Anika," Burns says in that tone. Anika suddenly stopped talking and became very attentive; she recognized that tone in Burns's voice. "Do you know how your mom died?" Burns asks her.

"What are you talking about?" Anika says.

"In the literal specific sense." Burns says. "Do you know exactly how she died?"

"No, I don't remember much from that day and never really looked into it," Anika says.

"I do. I know exactly how she died," Burns says, his voice stiff. "You know, I never saw a point in telling you, but I guess I'm going to now. That day, there was a camera rolling. I don't think you remember but there was a camera set up not too far from where she died. As your father approached this jaguar with you alongside him, the animal suddenly vanished in front of his eyes. He didn't see it, but after several watch-throughs of the footage, I saw it. The jaguar silently and effortlessly made its way around you both and up a tree that was only about fifty feet away. You weren't following the animal; it was leading you both away, and your father was too fucking stupid to see it. But your mom did. Your mom saw it immediately, that's why she ran forward. And the moment she ran toward you guys, the animal jumped from the fucking tree. That's how she died. The moment I saw that footage; all I could think of was that nobody else ever had to see it. So I had it destroyed, and I planned to keep it to myself for the rest of my life. But now that I see your goddamn incompetence walking through these woods as if nothing is ever going to happen, I decided I should lay this bomb on top of you. You think what I'm teaching you is shit? I'm teaching you to be as smart as your mom and not to be as fucking stupid and ignorant as your dad."

Anika was in shock. She was shivering, but not because she was freezing in the rain. She was shocked at Burns's current demeanor. She knew Burns was a tough guy, but as she stared at him right now, standing in the rain, completely indifferent to the freezing temperatures and the rain pounding on his head, he almost seemed like a Terminator, like a very dangerous man.

"What's the matter?" Burns says, breaking the silence. "No rude or witty comeback?"

"How did you beat it?" Anika asks in an apologetic tone.

Burns sighed. He took a step forward and put a hand on her shoulder, reminding her that he can be as loving as he can be cold. "You know the term 'if it ain't broke, don't fix it'?" Burns says. "I figured the jaguar would keep using this method. I went out there and tracked the jaguar, and I let it do the same thing it did to your father. I let it think it was luring me away to my death. And when it finally disappeared from my sight, I took an educated guess as to which tree it was going to lunge from. When it did, I already had my rifle set up on him, and I pulled the trigger as many times as I could. That's how I killed it. I let it hunt me first; made it think it had me and then turned the tables. I think that's the only way with an ambush predator."

Anika was in shivers, but she managed to nod at him in understanding.

"All right, then, kiddo," Burns says. "Let's get out of this rain and go get something hot to drink."

Anika could feel something slightly warm and slimy touch her fingers. She wiggled her fingers only for the creature to poke her hand again. She felt something flat and soft wrap around her index finger, and Anika felt it tickle. Anika jolted awake suddenly, coughing up balls of spit and water from her lungs. She opened her eyes slowly, or at least she tried to. Her left eye wouldn't open for some reason. The left side of her face was pressed against something cold and mushy. She lifted her head up and realized that she was face-first in wet mud. She feels her entire body is damp and her feet are freezing.

She slowly turned her head to look at her feet and saw that they were still in the moving water. It seems the river had tossed her to the shore. *Jesus Christ, it's a miracle I didn't drown*, she thought. She turned her head toward her right hand and saw a small shape near her fingers. She could barely make out the shape, but she recognized it when she heard it purr softly. It was a platypus, nudging her fingers. She pulled her hand away from the platypus, and she watched it lumber away. The platypus went to the edge of the river and hopped into it, disappearing under the surface. Anika snorted a quick laugh. Earlier, she was knocked out by one of nature's weirdest creations, and now she was woken up by one.

Anika pressed her hands firmly against the wet mud and tried to push her body off the ground like she was doing a push-up. Her hands went deeper and deeper into the mud as the weight of her body lifted from the shore of the river. Her muscles and bones ached, and her skin shivered from the chilling grip of the freezing water. She pushed her knees up as soon as her elbows locked tight, finally pulling her feet out of the water. She put her knees under herself and balanced her body on them.

As she lifted her head up right, she could feel it swaying back and forth, dizzy from the close encounters to death these past few hours. She took some deep breaths, trying to nudge away the light-headed feeling in her head. She looked around her, images of white dots bouncing back and forth in her corneas as her eyesight adjusted. She saw nothing in front of her; the forest was almost completely dark; the sun was almost gone. She knew the dark would give her more chances of concealment, but then, again she didn't know if these animals that were hunting her had exceptional night acuity. The dark could very well be more of an advantage to her current enemies.

Today had been nothing but a difficult day for her; nothing but pure luck and chance had kept her alive. Even though she knew her chances were slim to none for surviving, she tried to stay focused. She couldn't quite open her left eye because of the mud on her face, so she sluggishly turned her body around to face the river. She put her hands in the cold water, and she washed the mud away from her palms and fingers.

Once her hands were sufficiently clean, she took a scoop of water and put it up to her face. She smeared the mud away so that she could open both of her eyes completely. She then shook her head and coughed a couple times. She needed to get her bearings, because her next order of business was to get back to the lodge in one piece.

She slowly inched away from the side of the river, put her hand in her jacket pocket, and found that the GPS was still inside. She pulled out the small GPS only to find that it was shattered and the screen was lifeless. Even if the handheld GPS was waterproof, no doubt the cracked screen had let in the water that made it die. Well, that was no use now. Still, she stuffed it back in her pocket. Burns had taught her to never throw away any piece of equipment even if you think it's useless. Some of its components may become handy at some point.

She patted the rest of the pockets on her jacket and on her khaki pants; she had no other equipment on her. Except for the small survival knife in its sheath that she carried strapped to the back of her belt. It was a Gerber Strongarm four-inch fixed blade. She had been carrying it for six years now. She had only a single weapon, but it was better than nothing. She could maybe use that survival knife to make something that could help her. The idea of reverting to sticks and stones sounded stupid, but it was what Burns had taught her. Any weapon or tool is better than nothing when you're on your own and being hunted. She then remembered to look at both of her wrists. On her right hand, she had her digital watch, which was still in working order, but that wasn't what was important.

Her watch was a Timex, the Expedition Tide-Temp-*Compass* model. Which meant the watch had a separate dial that functioned as a compass. She finally realized it; she had a potential way of navigating back to the lodge. Now was the chance to see if these compasses on the watches actually work. She looked at her other wrist, and she saw that she still had her olive green paracord bracelet that she always wears, and her mother's elephant hair bracelet. Burns is always adamant that she carries a paracord bracelet with her. *You never know when you might need some sturdy rope to fasten something.* Anika was finally glad she paid attention to all those lessons, because now she was getting somewhere.

To anyone else, the minimal amount of gear that she was carrying would have made them lose hope, but it gave Anika the confidence she needed. She could make it back; there was a chance she could stay alive and she could save her friends. She could save Burns and keep them from leaving the lodge to try and find her. She would fight, she would do whatever she could to stay alive, and she would not let any of them down.

She remembers the face that JJ had as he was dying under that dinosaur. He would not die begging or screaming for his life. He would die trying to fight whatever was trying to kill him.

Now Anika would do the same. Even if these animals were terrifying and exceptional predators, she would be a thorn in their side before she died. She stood up and looked around, looking for any thick branches on the ground that looked sturdy enough to be a weapon. She looked around for almost five minutes, keeping her face close to the ground as she grasped around with her hands because of how dark the forest was. She finally found one, a thick branch from a Huon pine that was mostly straight. She put it on the ground, then put the heel of her boot in the middle of it and pressed down on it. The stick would barely bend. It could take a lot of weight before breaking; it was just what she needed. She took her knife out from the sheath and slowly started to carve pieces of it away, sharpening the end of it.

She remembers all those times that Burns taught her these lessons. At the time, she thought he was crazy. She thought Burns had seen too many Arnold Schwarzenegger movies, and that these skills would never be of any use. But they didn't feel stupid now as she sharpened the branch of the tree. She felt the conviction inside her grow; she wanted to live. She scraped and she scraped with her Gerber fixed blade, shaving small strips of branch away little by little, creating a sturdy spear-like weapon.

She was almost done with it after scraping away at the branch for minutes. But then she heard a loud rustle in the bushes to her right. She quickly got to her feet and put herself in a fighting stance, ready to shove the spear in her hands forward.

She saw a shadow slowly emerge from behind a tree. It was the male dinosaur; it slowly stepped forward, its eyes shining like white dots. The male stared directly into her eyes, and when it was only a few feet away, it stopped. Then it didn't move, didn't make any noise. It just stared at her, something the male seems to do out of force of habit.

How the hell did this animal keep finding her? Why was it so good at spotting her and then sneaking up on her? Not understanding the dinosaur's intentions was making Anika increasingly frustrated. What was it doing? Why does it just stand there all the time?

"What?" Anika says to it in an irritated tone.

The male bobbed its head slightly at the noise the human just made. It obviously didn't understand what she was saying, but Anika was hoping it would understand her demeanor, her body language.

The animal slowly stepped forward again, and for some reason, Anika decided to let it get very close to her. The animal was less than a few inches away from her face; she could feel its hot breath up against her forehead. The only thing that Anika was thinking was, if the dinosaur decided to test her, she would plunge not only the spear, but the fixed blade into its neck. The male just sniffed around her body, drooping its head, looking for something on her body. The animal then saw the large gash on her right shoulder. It poked at her shoulder with its snout, and she winced in pain. And it seems the animal noticed that she was in pain, almost as if that's what it was trying to determine.

The male, in a split second, opened its jaws and rolled its tongue out of its mouth. It dragged the sticky and warm tongue across the wound on her shoulder. Anika grew disgusted in an instant; she backed away from it, feeling foolish. She had just let the dinosaur take a taste of her as if they were in a cartoon. But then the animal slowly backed away from her and continued to stare. Anika's eyes suddenly began to water; the pain in her shoulder was abruptly *relieved*. She exhaled a long breath, feeling incredibly comfortable in an instant. She looked at the male, surprised, unsure if the animal did what she thought it just did.

The animal then made a noise that she hadn't heard it make before. It gave a slow, soft purr that seemed to come through its nose. It then nudged at her shoulder once more, and this time, she felt no pain, and she didn't wince at all. She glanced at her right shoulder. The gash was still there but it seemed that the pain had been *numbed*.

The animal's saliva numbed her injury.

The male seems to be aware that it did, and the nudge and purr was its way of asking her if it had worked. Whatever question she had before, whatever concern she had about the dinosaur's intentions, this seemed more like an act of peace than anything else it had done before.

She felt stupid for having this thought, but she needed to reciprocate. She needed to show that she was also at peace with it. She slowly put the knife away, back in the sheath, and with her right hand, she reached forward to touch the animal. The male didn't move, instead, it just stared at her and watched with glaring eyes as her hand firmly touched the animal snout. She kept her hand on the animal's warm snout for a few seconds, and then she withdrew her hand slowly.

The animal purred through its nostrils again in response.

Either this was the biggest mistake of her life, or this was the biggest discovery of her life. The male was the most... unbothered animal she had ever met. Its stoic demeanor gave Anika a bit more confidence in her survival. Just as she was having this thought, Anika and the male heard a loud screeching. It was from the other dinosaurs in the forest. They were still hunting, and they were hellbent on finding her. She then looked at the male again, searching around the forest until it found Anika's gaze. In that moment, she realized she had to do the one thing she had decided she would never do.

Anika had to take a page out of her father's book and *put her faith in a predator.*

DEFORESTATION

Valente crouched next to a large, sunbaked boulder in the middle of the African bush. He wiped the hot sweat off his forehead, trying to keep it from seeping into his eyelids. He looked around the African bush in the distance, great plains of long yellow grass with patches of Mopane trees. The African bush was amazingly quiet at the moment, which is why he hated being there. He hated being out in the sun this long, being in the middle of nowhere, sweating his ass off through his safari gear. He hated not knowing what was lurking in the long grass just a few hundred yards to his right. He suddenly heard a loud trumpeting in the distance.

"There he is," someone whispered to Valente.

From behind Valente, someone stepped forward and crouched next to him. While looking out into the African plains, Rafe also wiped the sweat off his forehead. He then used the sweat on his palm to slick his hair back over his head; there was a subtle smile on his face.

"Yeah, he's around here," Rafe whispered. "He's going to show his face sooner or later."

"How much longer are we going to be out here?" Valente asks his father.

"Oh, don't worry about it," Rafe whispered back nonchalantly. "We're in the home stretch now, we've caught up to him."

Valente just sighed. He took out a small rag from his pants pocket and wiped the sweat from the back of his neck. "We've been out here for *four hours.* I could swear I heard lions bellowing not far behind us," Valente whispered.

Rafe's smile grew wider. He didn't take his eyes off the African bush in front of him. "I don't think you've ever learned the point of all this," Rafe says. "It's being part of it all, part of the food chain, the way we were meant to be. Trust me, every kind of predator would have a piece of us if we let them. But we won't, because we can beat them. They're not better than us. See, it's not the acting of killing, it's the game of stalking, and *winning* that I enjoy so much. Everything that leads up to the very moment before I pull the trigger on my rifle. That's what makes the prize worth it. And look at that, right on schedule."

Rafe points north, and Valente looks once more into the African flats and sees a six-ton bull elephant wander away from behind a tree. "Eyes on the prize, my boy," Rafe whispered. Rafe stared at the elephant with a sneering smile; there was almost a look of lust in his eyes. Rafe then did something unexpectedly, something Valente had never seen his father do while hunting. With his green piercing eyes, he looked away from his prey and looked at his own son.

"I want you to shoot it," Rafe whispered.

"What?"

Rafe didn't repeat himself. He knew his son heard him. He simply gripped the rifle in his hands and casually handed it over to his son. Valente hesitated. The only reason he had come along on this hunting trip was to make sure that his father didn't die alone out here. It was not until Rafe's smile slowly started to fade away that Valente decided to take the rifle from his hands. Valente handled the heavy rifle in his hands, the Sabatti double-barrel elephant rifle chambered in .500 Nitro Express.

"Go on," Rafe says. "Just like I taught you. Rifle butt against your shoulder. Easy breathing. Sight picture right under your target. Let his heart be the lollipop."

Valente obliged, and against his own good judgment, he lined up the rifle sights on the African elephant wandering across the plains, its giant gray ears flapping back and forth. Valente took some deep breaths as he tried to keep the rifle steady in his hands. He put the elephant rifle's iron sights right where the pachyderm's heart would be. Valente took a final deep breath, and on his exhale, he pulled the first trigger. The elephant rifle burst like an artillery cannon, sending a single .570 grain nitro express round flying toward the African bull elephant.

The elephant collapsed onto the yellow grass.

Rafe just chuckled. "Good shot," he says. "But you need some more target practice."

"What do you mean?" Valente asks as he rubs his sore shoulder and collar bone.

"Come on," Rafe says. "I'll show you." Rafe stood up from his crouching position and casually started to stroll over toward the downed elephant. Valente decided to follow. They both walked a full forty yards before they reached the downed elephant in the grass.

Valente was only a few feet away when he realized that it was still alive.

"Look," Rafe says. "You hit it square in the head. Weren't you aiming for his heart?"

Valente was speechless. The animal's legs were shaking, twitching. The animal was suffering.

"Forrest."

"Yeah, I was aiming for his heart," Valente finally responded.

"Jesus," Rafe says, chuckling. "Talk about *Kentucky windage*."

Valente didn't say another word. He simply watched as the elephant lay there, helpless. There was blood trickling from the entry wound on the elephant's head, its breath raspy; it was struggling to breathe. Blood was spurting from its mouth every time it groaned. The animal was in pain, suffering, all because he was at the hands of an amateur hunter like Valente.

"You know, most people think its brain is all the way forward, over its eyes, but really, it's in between its ears," Rafe says, examining the entry wound. "I really thought you were aiming for his head. Oh, well. You still got the one barrel left in your rifle. Go on, put another round on its head and finish the deal."

Valente knew it was the right thing to do, but he didn't want to. He didn't want to pull another trigger on this gun again. Still, he raised the rifle toward the animal's head. To defy his father was to create all sorts of problems on their way home, and he would never hear the end of it. Just as he lined up the iron sights onto the elephant's head, the elephant turned its eye to look directly at Valente. And at that very moment before he pulled the trigger, Valente felt a sense of immeasurable sorrow in his heart. It is almost as if he could feel the animal's emotions in his own being.

A force of nature powerless to move and yet powerless to die.

Then Valente pulled the trigger and put the animal out of its misery. And it was on the journey back home with his father's prize that Valente finally decided that he would find a way out from under his father's wing.

Valente was gazing out of the window while he sat in the passenger seat, the GPS in his hand, guiding Ward as he drove around Tasmania onto their next location. "You want to give the radio one more try?" Ward asks.

Valente grabbed the handset from the CB radio. He clicked the receiver button and spoke into the handset. "This is Forest

Valente. Is anybody there? Can anybody hear me? Over." There was just static, no response. "Hello, this is Forrest Valente, Matt, Bill, Dr. Irving, is anybody there?"

Again, there was no response, nothing but static coming from the handset.

Ward gasped. "Had to be raining, and they had to be in the middle of the fucking woods."

"I'm sure they're fine," Valente reiterated. "We built that lodge to be a damn fortress."

"Let's hope you're right," Ward says. "God, I've been thinking, did any of our workers die?"

"What are you talking about?"

"When we had the lodge built, I wonder if any of our workers died. We hired locally, remember?" Ward asks.

"I don't know. I don't think so."

"Lemme guess, never bothered to ask, huh?" Ward says. The lack of response from Valente was enough to answer his question. "How far away are we?"

"Just a couple more minutes. Should be at the end of this street," Valente says as he glances at the GPS in his hand.

When they reached the end of the block, they saw a large sign attached to a chain-link fence. It read 'Burch Contracting & Surplus'.

"Yeah, this is the place. Let's hope he's here," Ward says. They pulled into the small construction complex and went to the far warehouse at the end. They pulled into a parking spot next to a sign on the wall which read 'Main Office'. Ward switched off his 4Runner, and both men stepped out of the vehicle. Ward held the door open for the main office to Valente, and they both walked inside.

There was a small reception counter and a room in the back. No one was there, or at least no one they could see. Ward walked up to the counter, a single bell sitting on top of it. He pushed the button on top and rang the bell. A man in his late 40s walked up to the counter. He was skinny with a stern face and a short droopy mustache.

"Well shit, Lee," the man says. "How much did they pay you to get you to come all the way out here?"

"Not nearly enough, Andrew," Ward responded with a smile. "How you doing, brother?"

"Just peachy. Guys, I'm not gonna lie, I'm so alone out here. You're the first people I've seen in a long time," Andrew says in a hurry, his voice and demeanor showing he may have had way too many energy drinks. "What brings you out here?"

"We had a couple questions that we were hoping you could answer," Ward says. "Do you know anything about a construction site around here where people keep getting mauled?"

Andrew's enthusiasm for seeing his friends suddenly faded, and he rolled his eyes. "Oh fuck, Lee," Andrew is exasperated. "You're going to ask me about that? You can talk to me about anything, literally anything. Why not ask about the New York Giants? You know, something conversation worthy?"

"Giants are doing terribly, like they do every year," Ward says. "Drewski, you know what we're talking about, don't you?"

"Yes, I do," Andrew says. "And let me tell you, I really think you should stay out of this one."

"Afraid we can't, Drewski," Ward says. "We need to know as much as you know. There's a lot at stake. People's lives are in danger."

Andrew groaned. "If I answer your question, just make sure you don't repeat it to anybody else, or at least don't tell them where it came from."

"Why do you say that?" Valente asks. "Have you been

threatened?"

"Yes and no," Andrew responded. "Every single laborer that has gone out there, from what I've heard, has been made to sign an NDA. A really heavy, dangerous-sounding NDA."

"Did you sign one?" Ward asks

"Yeah, I did," Andrew responded.

"So you've been out there?" Valente asks.

"No, I haven't been out there personally, but I did oversee the transfer of materials for whatever it is they're building out there," Andrew says. "They asked for a lot of shit, like truly, a lot of random shit."

"Transfer of materials," Ward repeated. "That must mean they gave you a copy of the blueprints, didn't they?"

"They did," Andrew says. "Guys, guys... wait until you see these fucking plans."

Andrew signaled them both to follow him to the office in the back. All three men stepped inside the office, and Andrew signaled them again to take a seat next to his desk. Andrew walked over to a medium-sized safe in the corner. He plugged some numbers in, opened it, and pulled out a roll of blueprints. Andrew put them on his desk and unrolled one for them to see.

"Go on, take a look," Andrew says as he picks up a can of Redbull from his desk. "I want to know your thoughts on this."

This was exactly what they were looking for. Both Valente and Ward looked over the blueprints in front of them. They were construction plans for massive buildings, countless structures stretched out for a few miles. It almost looked like a complete city. There were plans for hotels, restaurants, pool sides, plans for paving streets and main roads. At first, it looked like a resort of some kind, but then, there were also blueprints for medical buildings like hospitals, or infirmaries.

"These medical buildings you see there are last minute

additions, by the way. They weren't in the original plans. I don't understand the need for them. We have perfectly good hospitals in Hobart," Andrew added while taking a sip of his Redbull.

"What the hell is all this?" Ward asks. "Is he building a vacation resort out here? I mean, I'm no rich guy but I would never come all the way out here for a vacation."

"I don't think it's a vacation resort," Valente says. "That wouldn't explain the medical buildings over here on the far left. And that certainly wouldn't explain this large open field out here. Look at it. It looks like an empty field double the size of the whole complex. It's almost the size of three football fields. And it seems like it was intentionally left blank. No building blueprints anywhere in this area. But then again, look at this around it, tall and massive steel fencing all along the perimeter. Why would he need that?"

"You know," Andrew says. "I'm glad you noticed that little patch of area, because I have an idea what it is that they're doing over there. See, my company can get a lot of materials, whether they are regular or custom-made. Either way, they have to come through me, and I ship it out to them. I kept one of them just in case, but somebody ordered a decent amount of warning signs to be placed along the steel fence. I got curious, so I kept one to myself."

Andrew turned around and reopened the safe. He took out a small sign and placed it on the table. It was about two feet wide and one foot in length. A white sign with bright red lettering that read: *Caution: Live Animals and Live Fire Beyond This Point.*

"There's no fucking way," Ward says. "There's just no fucking way."

"You know, I met the guy that's building this place a few months back," Andrew says. "Scary looking fucker, beady eyes, very expensive-looking suit. You know, I had no idea what this little land was for, but when I saw him, it all made sense to me.

Rich people get up to all sorts of shit. My guess is, that little place over here is some kind of big-game hunting grounds. Or some kind of Hunger-Games shit. Wild stuff, real wild stuff. I mean, any person with money could most certainly ship out all kinds of exotic animals: lions, tigers, elephants, fucking crocodiles, whatever they want."

"Or maybe something that looks like a crocodile," Valente mumbled. He looked over to Ward. "Think about it, Lee," Valente says to him. "So you get sick, you get cancer, leukemia or whatever, but you have all the money in the world. One day, you get a brochure. It promises some kind of weekend excursion. You come all the way out here, get yourself a nice little room in a hotel. It's got fancy restaurants next to it, a pool, a fucking golf course. And then in the middle of all that, they walk you over to the treatment center. Can you guess what it might be for?"

Ward just stayed silent.

"Then after, they give you *your treatment*," Valente continued. "If you happen to be an avid big-game hunter, well, look at this. They got some hunting grounds with some very dangerous brand-new predators for you to have a go at."

Once more, Ward didn't say a single word in response. He simply stared at the blueprints in front of him, piecing all the information in his head. Valente had the suspicion that he was skimming the plans in order to find an alternative explanation, but it seems Ward didn't find any. Instead, Ward took off his glasses and rubbed his eyes.

"That's pretty thin," Ward says.

"What's the alternative?" Valente responded.

Andrew was looking at both of the men, confused. "What treatment are you talking about?" he asks.

"Believe me, brother," Ward says. "You're better off not knowing."

"Christ, is it that bad?" Andrew replied.

"Yes, it is," Ward answered. He put his glasses back on and looked at Valente. "What can we even do now?"

"What do you mean?" Valente asks.

"You want to do something about this?" Ward asks. "Make up your mind before I change mine."

Valente didn't hesitate. "Drewksi, do you happen to know where this construction site is exactly?"

"Oh buddy," Andrew says. "This has a bad idea written all over it. Maybe just stay and watch the Giant's game with me."

"Just tell us where it is."

Andrew put his Redbull down and reached over to the right of his desk, from where he pulled open a drawer. He takes out a package of sticky notes and a pen out of his shirt's breast pocket. He started to write down an address. He then took the sticky note off and he gave it to them.

"You know the address by memory?" Valente asks.

"I've sent a lot of workers to this location," Andrew says. "I know exactly where it is. It used to be a lumber mill. Who knows what it is now and how far they've gotten into this project. I haven't been there myself."

"Let's head out," Valente says. He then turned around and started walking toward the door. Ward stayed in the office and leaned in to whisper something. "If I were you, I'd lay low," Ward says to him. "Things could get heavy."

"What kind of heavy?" Andrew says.

"Starting to feel like *Mogadishu* or *Fallujah*. Shit's fucked, and we're already ten blocks in too far to turn around."

Andrew was startled by the metaphor and sudden flash of his and Ward's past. Andrew just nodded. "Stay frosty, brother."

"Actually, one more thing," Ward says. "You wouldn't happen to be able to reach the ranger station to the national park, would you?"

"You mean by phone or by radio?" Andrew asks. "I don't know if you remember. But when we built that lodge for you guys out there, the only way to reach the ranger station was radio. We don't really have any telephone lines all the way up there. Or cell reception for that matter."

"All right, then, like I said. Take it easy, brother," Ward says, and he finally walked out of the office. Both men exited back through the front entrance. They opened the doors to the Toyota 4Runner and stepped inside. "Let's go ahead and drive out there and see what the deal is," Ward says as he backs out of the parking spot. "What's your plan? How are we going to do this?"

Valente was already inputting the address into his phone's GPS. "We take pictures of everything," Valente says. "The whole construction site, as much as we can. Then bring it to the attention of the authorities, post it online, whatever. Everyone will hopefully make such a ruckus of it online that he won't have anywhere to hide his bullshit."

"What about our lawsuit?" Ward asks.

"Hopefully, we can get Dr. Hogan and your friend Andrew Burch to testify for us. They're exceptionally credible witnesses. And maybe, they'll know other people who would want to testify too. Maybe the families of the victims. We got to do this right. We can't let him get away with it."

"Well, that's it then."

Valente mounted the GPS onto the dashboard so Ward could see where he was going. Valente, without hesitating, grabbed the handset of the CB radio. He began to call for the ranger station more frequently. He would do this for about an hour.

The GPS eventually led them both to a forest road. It showed they had about three miles down this forest road before they reached their destination. Ward turned the 4Runner onto the narrow dirt road and took it slow. As they drove, they noticed the tree line surrounding the forest road was thick with plant life. The heavy rain made it difficult to see more than ten feet in front of them, even with the Toyota's high beams switched on.

"We need to make this quick," Ward says. "It will be completely dark soon."

"Are you sure we're on the right road?" Valente asks, his voice getting a little antsy.

"This is the right road," Ward says. "Says we'll be there in about a minute and a half."

"I don't see any structures or buildings whatsoever," Valente says.

"You spoke too soon," Ward says. "Look."

At the end of the road, there was a large gate with unfinished fencing around it. The fencing has the impression that it was supposed to go around the entire complex, but it had missing sections. Both men peered through the windshield into the security guard shack next to the gate. They saw no one standing there; the shack looked empty.

"As far as I see there's no security," Ward says. "Let's see if we can get that gate open."

Ward pulled up in front of the gate and stopped the vehicle. He and Valente stepped out of the 4Runner, and both approached the gate. As they peered inside the gate, they stopped in their tracks. Both men were instantly in shock at what they were seeing directly in front of them.

"Oh, my God," Valente says. *"Dad, what are you doing?"*

In front of them, beyond the gate, there were miles and

miles of the Tasmanian forest *gone*. The hundreds of logs of cut down Huon pine and Pandani trees discarded around the complex like nothing. It looked like a massive grave site of deforestation. The buildings in the distance had stacks that were puking black smoke.

"Your father did all of this?" Ward asks.

"Yes," Valente says without skipping a beat. "If we let him keep going, he'll make it much worse. Come on, help me with the gate. We're not done yet."

HERRERASAURUS ISCHIGUALASTENSIS

Lucy Benitez leaned in close to the almost complete skeleton of a dinosaur in front of her. Her eyes are inches away from the skeleton as she slowly brushes away the soil and dust in its cracks. She held a small toothbrush in her hand, which she would constantly dip in a solvent material to polish and remove grime at the same time. She did it carefully and methodically, her hands being as steady as a surgeon.

All of her co-workers at the museum seemed to hate this part of the job for some reason. They all preferred to be out there in the sun, excavating for fossils in the middle of nowhere. They liked to feel like the real paleontologists they read about or saw in a documentary. Close to the ground, digging for ancient beasts in a dried-up riverbed millions of years old. But when it came to actually polishing the skeletons that they had recovered, Lucy was always the only volunteer. She didn't mind this task; she loved every aspect of her job. Ever since she moved away from home, she didn't have much of a home life, so she didn't mind the extra overtime.

At the moment, she was at the eastern side of the museum. This part of the museum was the detailing section for newly recovered fossils. The entire room was filled with both equipment for polishing up fossils, as well as fragile fossils that have been encased in clay. There were also a couple of shelves with some bones that haven't been placed in any encasement. Fossils that were deemed too incomplete to put into a museum diorama.

The door to this particular room suddenly opens behind Lucy. Lucy turned her head to see her co-worker, Dexter, entering the room. Dexter and Lucy had started working at the museum around the same time. Dexter was great with his hands and even better with any kind of machinery in the field. The 29-year-old master excavator moved around the fossil that Lucy was finishing up. He leaned over and examined it with amazement.

"I can't believe we found this almost complete," Dexter says. "How many bones in total?"

"249," Lucy responded.

"And how many are missing?" Dexter asks.

Lucy smiled. "Assumed about fifty."

"That is just amazing," Dexter says. "This will be the most complete skeleton we have in the entire museum. And we're the ones who found it." Dexter was grinning as he was walking around the table, examining every piece of bone. He went from its tail all the way to the animal's snout. Dexter leans close to the giant skull, examining the razor-sharp teeth.

"Herrerasaurus," Dexter mumbled. "What was the rest of its name?"

"*Herrerasaurus Ischigualastensis*," Lucy says. "Although it will be a completely different species. Since we found it in Canada, not the Ischigualasto Formation."

"That's just beautiful," Dexter says. "You know, they're having the unveiling ceremony in about three weeks?"

"I know. I got the email too," Lucy says.

"Are you going?" Dexter asks. "I mean, you have to. You're part of the team. It's going to be a pretty big event."

"Why would I want to go?" Lucy says. "So I can watch Director Monson take credit for all of it again, just like he did the last time?"

"Oh, come on, Lucy," Dexter says, "it wasn't that bad."

"He has never mentioned any of us at these unveilings. You know he doesn't. He just takes credit for all of it. He doesn't even put our names on the plaques in the museum."

"Now, come on, Lucy, you wouldn't at least want to go with me?" Dexter says. "Just so at least I don't go alone."

And there it was, Lucy thought, the main reason that she stayed away from all of her co-workers as much as she could. All of her coworkers were mostly men with the exception of her and another woman named Loreen. Loreen was a 54-year-old paleontologist who loved to micromanage everything and everyone, so naturally everybody stayed away from her. But the reason that Lucy stayed away from the rest of her co-workers is that they were always hitting on her. Every single time, without fault, she knew it was expected, and it was stereotypical of them to do so. But there comes a point when it just becomes especially annoying, and it impedes her from doing her job.

It's like none of them have ever seen a Mexican girl with green eyes. And here was Dexter, not here to see the dinosaur, not here to see the work of art that she's working on. But to hit on her again. Dexter was a good-looking guy; tall, rugged, and down to earth. But Lucy preferred to keep her social life and work life separate. She would never date a co-worker. And for that reason, Lucy didn't bother to respond to his question. She went right back to working. "Do you know when the next dig is?" Lucy asks.

Dexter noticed her vibe change from the question, so he quickly changed the subject too. "Yeah," he says. "Should be in about a month, maybe a week after the unveiling, if I remember correctly."

"Where at?" Lucy asks.

"I think somewhere in Thailand," he says. "Can't remember where exactly. But there's rumors that it's a *Suchomimus*."

"Our dig site scout is an idiot," Lucy says. "You know his guess before this dig site was that it was going to be a ceratopsian of some kind? Where did he get his degree?"

"PLU in Washington State," Dexter responded, "and I think it's a project management degree."

Lucy gasped. "PLU," she mocked. "An entire university of the most *obnoxious assholes* you could find."

"I know, tell me about it," Dexter says. Dexter then crouched next to the skull on the table. He leaned in toward the animal's snout, as if he was face to face with the dinosaur. "Do you ever wonder what it would be like if these were still alive?" Dexter asks.

"Sometimes," Lucy responded.

"Imagine one of these just strolling around the streets of New York. Imagine driving over the Cascade Mountains and running into a stegosaur in the middle of the road. Wouldn't that be crazy?" Dexter says.

"There would be no *New York* if they were still alive," Lucy responded.

"What do you mean?" Dexter asks.

"I don't think humanity would be where we are now if dinosaurs were still alive," Lucy says. "We wouldn't be as technologically advanced as we are right now. We would have other things to worry about. We would stand no chance with these animals. No chance."

"Wow, Lucy," Dexter says. "At least try to be a little optimistic. I mean, we do just fine with all the animals that are alive right now. I mean, we stay away from them and we're doing just fine so far."

"Oh, it would not be the same if dinosaurs were still alive,"

Lucy says. "The biggest land animal in the world right now is the African elephant, and it's a herbivore. Every other dinosaur back then was at least three times bigger than an elephant. Animals like these, we would have no control over them. In fact, they would have more control over us, and humanity would not be the dominant species that we are now."

Dexter poked one of the sharp teeth with his finger. "Yeah, maybe there's some truth to what you're saying. I mean, imagine you live in the middle of nowhere and one of these things just comes across your lawn like a black bear. I mean, what would stop this animal from getting inside?"

Lucy didn't respond; she just kept working on the fossil in front of her. Dexter stood up and started to walk toward the door. "Well, it was nice seeing you, Lucy. I'll leave you to it," he says. "If you change your mind about the ceremony, let me know." Dexter stepped out of the room, leaving Lucy in silence again.

As she continued to work on the bones, her mind drifted again to the conversation with Dexter. She knew this for a fact. If all manner of Dinosauria were still alive, humanity would definitely be on the endangered species list. Which is why she chose this career. It's why she studied these dinosaurs. To study beasts from another time, to stand so close to the remains of the epitome of a *force of nature*.

Dexter was right. If one of these creatures walked across your lawn, there is nothing that could stop it from getting inside your home.

"Hello, can anybody hear me? We need help," Lucy says into the radio handset. "Hello. Can anybody hear me? Hello?" She then turned the dial to change the frequency again. "Hello. We need help. Can anybody hear me?" No response again. She had been switching frequencies and asking for help for the past ten minutes. She was hoping, praying that someone would answer and call for help for them.

The image of Kit begging for his life as he was torn apart was seared into her mind. The cruelty of the animal as it effortlessly tore his head clean off. The animal then tossed the head at the lodge almost as if it was *toying* with the humans. While the sight was incredibly disturbing, this level of violence was nothing new to Lucy. Living in Juarez, Mexico had given her an idea of what it means to be cruel.

Every day, without fault, someone would die a grueling death as they were tortured. Then they were torn to pieces and put on display for everyone to see. Everyone sees the consequences of trifling with the wrong people. Perhaps that was the animal's intention. It was a warning to stay away. But as Lucy heard the animal moving across the roof, examining every inch of the lodge, she quickly brushed away that theory. No, this animal was not done yet, and it was not a warning. It was just a display of what's yet to come for every single human inside the lodge.

Matt and Burns both rushed upstairs, following the sound of the animal's movement. They both had to make sure that there was no way inside the lodge, no way that it could force itself in. They rushed into one of the rooms and checked the windows and the skylight. There were windowpanes with thick metal caging welded on the outside. Surely there was no way to get through those. Burns spotted the animal's tail as it wagged across the skylight. It was moving in a different direction. Matt and Burns rushed to the next part of the lodge. They stood in the hallway for a second, listening to the animal move on the roof.

"My room has a balcony," Matt suddenly says. "That's where it's going right now."

Both men rushed to Matt's room. They stepped inside, and there was indeed a balcony on the far end. The balcony had a sliding glass door, but as soon as you opened the glass door, there was another sliding door with bars on it. It almost looked like a cell door at a prison.

"Is it locked?" Burns asks.

"I don't know. I haven't used the balcony," Matt says.

Both men rushed forward, but just before they reached the balcony doors, the animal hopped down and landed on the wooden balcony. The wooden balcony creaked at the animal's weight. Both men stopped in their tracks, shocked. The animal glared at them from outside. Even though the room was dark, they knew the animal could see them. The animal stood like a towering, dark shadow, an image torn from a nightmare. It then broke eye contact with both men and looked down at the cell door covering the glass door. It then extended its clawed arms and wrapped its clawed fingers around the bars. And it *tugged on it.* But the door wouldn't budge. It seemed to be locked tight; the animal couldn't get in. It then let go of the door, stepped back, and hopped up on the roof again.

"There's two more rooms to check," Burns says. "I'll go check one, you go check the other. Let's make sure it can't get in."

But Matt wouldn't move. He was stricken by the animal's behavior. "Matthew," Burns says to him.

Matt looked at him. "Did you see the animal's intelligence? The hand manipulation on the door?"

"Let's not worry about that right now," Burns says. "Let's go check the other rooms, *now.*"

Both men hurried into the hallway. Burns went one way, and Matt went the other. Burns stepped into his and Anika's room. No balcony but there were two windows and they both looked secured. As he was stepping out of the room, Burns caught Anika's scent coming from her side of the room. It briefly reminded him that she was still out there, if she was still alive. *Oh honey*, Burns thought to himself, *please be alive. I want to see you one more time.* He stepped into the hallway to see Matt already standing there.

"How's the other room?" Burns asks him.

"One window, secured with those welded bars."

"Okay," Burns says. "I don't think it can get in, at least not from the second floor."

"Let's go downstairs and check the back door, then the rest of the windows. I think our main priority is the front door. It seems to be the only opening that budges. If it tries to get in somewhere, it'll be the front door."

Both Burns and Matt went downstairs. The rest of the film crew was looking out the windows. Lucy was still sitting at the desk with the CB radio, trying to contact anybody. Matt and Burns walked through the kitchen and through the small hallways with the pantries, all the way to the back door. It was indeed a steel door as Burns had said. Burns gave the door a tug, and he got the impression that the door was extremely strong and stiff.

"Why the hell didn't Forrest put one of these doors up front instead of those double doors?" Burns asks, irritated.

"Guess we'll ask him when he gets here," Matt says. "Everything seems to be secure for now, like I said. Let's keep an eye on the front door."

Both men walked back to the living room. The first person they ran into was Lucy who was sitting at the desk. "Any luck, Lucy?" Burns asks her.

"No," she says. "I've been trying every single frequency that I can. I'm going to try the ranger station one more time. Someone's bound to hear us…"

Burns then looked around the living room, thinking of

possible solutions. "I reckon the only thing that's keeping us from reaching someone is this damn storm," Burns says, "so here's what we do: we prioritize the front door, but we also keep an eye on the rest of the openings. Even if they are barred and welded, it doesn't mean it can't force its way in. We don't know how strong this animal is. So we keep an eye on *everything*. If we stay on our toes about that, we can probably wait out the storm. Then maybe the radio will be able to reach someone."

"And if we still can't reach anybody after the storm?" Matt asks.

"Then we wait for Forrest," Burns says, "and we hope to God we can warn him in time before he steps out of his car."

"Do we even know when Forrest will get here?" Matt asks.

"No clue, we're fixin' to find out, I guess," Burns responded.

They heard hooting coming from outside the lodge. Burns and Matt looked at each other instantly. "Looks like the young ones are here," Matt says. Burns and Matt rushed to one of the windows and peeked outside. They couldn't see any movement, even with the floodlights, but they knew the cubs were there. The hooting was incessant for about two minutes, until the animal on the roof began crowing into the air. The cubs then rushed forward and revealed themselves from the tree line. They all darted forward to Kit's body. They started to tear into it, eating it as fast as they could chew.

Burns looked away from the sight, but Matt continued to watch the cubs rip into what was left of Kit's body. Matt saw one of the cubs stray away and hop toward Kit's head. It started to nibble into Kit's cheek, consuming bits of skin and flesh. It seemed to like it enough that it got greedy, as it started to roll the head away with its forearms into the tree line, to keep the meal for itself.

Matt heard some of the film crew sobbing, panicking. Mike,

the boom mic operator, was heaving, trying to keep himself from puking. "That Wiley fellow never stood a chance," Matt says. "Lived in the middle of nowhere, with no one to call for help."

"He had some ideas," Burns says.

"He tried to keep them away with fire. I wonder if it actually worked," Matt says.

"I think that's the kind of thing we leave for last resort," Burns says. "Burning down the house and an entire forest wouldn't do as much good right now."

The radio suddenly gave a deafening screech. The static grew loud and then died for everyone in the lodge to hear. Matt and Burns turned around to see Lucy covering her ears, handset swinging from the table. "What the hell, Lucy?" Matt says. "Don't break the damn radio."

"I didn't do anything to it. It just did that," Lucy responded. She picked up the handset quickly and clicked the button to speak into it but then hesitated.

Burns noticed it. "What? What's wrong?"

Lucy turned around to face Burns. She held the handset up to her face and she was clicking the mic button. It made no sound; there was no static, no radio traffic at all.

"What? What does that mean?" Matt asks.

"It has no signal. It's dead air," Burns says.

"How would you know that? We haven't had a signal. There's a storm," Matt says.

"There's no signal at all," Lucy says. "Even if the storm dies down, we can't reach anybody. I've worked with radios before, and this has no signal."

Burns walked over to her. He leaned in to look at the radio. On the screen for the frequency, in the top right corner, there was an indicator light switched on. It had a graphic of a satellite with an 'X' over it. "Do you know what that means right there?" Burns asks, pointing at the graphic.

Lucy adjusted her glasses and moved it to look at it. "Misalignment or no signal," she says.

"Misalignment?" Matt says. "Of the dish on top? How the hell did that happen? The storm?"

"Either it was a storm," Burns says, "or it was our friend on the roof."

"You're not about to tell me that it did it on purpose?" Matt asks.

"I don't think it did it on purpose, not consciously at least," Burns says. "I think it's poking and prodding at every inch of this entire lodge. It probably bumped into it or nudged it. It doesn't know what it is, but it is going to study it."

"Oh, for fuck's sake," Matt says. "If the radio dish is misaligned, what happens now? How do we fix it?"

"We'd have to realign it," Burns simply says.

"But we can't do that while it's up there," Matt says. "So now what? Can't even call for help if the storm clears."

"Now our only option is to stay in here, keep an eye on the entrances, wait for Valente to get here and, hope that that fucking thing doesn't find a way in."

"That really can't be our only option," Matt says. "There's not any way we can reach the dish without going outside? There was a skylight in one of the rooms."

"There's two skylights," Burns says. "But what's the point? The animal's on the roof. You really want to reach your hand out there through the bars?"

"How do we even know it's still on the roof? I don't hear it moving," Matt says.

Both men listened for a couple seconds, listening for any

creaking or movement on the roof, but they heard nothing. "Either way, I would say it's still worth a look," Matt says. "Don't you think maybe we can find a way to distract it? So someone can maybe reach up there? We need to widen our chances, Bill."

"Let's go take a look first, before we do anything else," Burns says. Both men turned around and walked up the stairs to the second floor.

Lucy stood up from the radio chair for the first time and walked over to the window. She hadn't looked out the window since Kit died. She saw a crowd of three-foot dinosaurs clawing and tearing into Kit's body in a frenzy. Their eyes glowing from the floodlights, their snouts and their claws covered in blood. She could hear the snarling through the window. They almost sounded like dogs playing a game of tug of war with a piece of rope. She hadn't had a chance to see these dinosaurs up close. She had only seen them in the video footage they showed her five months ago. But now, she had seen them kill a human being, and they were now feasting on it.

My God had this gone wrong so quickly.

She decided to study the dinosaurs, her face almost pressed up against the glass. She studied the tail, almost one and a half feet long as it met the thighs of the dinosaurs. The legs muscled and slim, same with the clawed forearms. The long snouts with the jagged teeth, and the pointed feathers from the top of their head running down their spine to the end of their tail.

Something then clicked in her mind. The claws on their hands. They didn't have just three claws, they had five. Except there were two smaller clawed fingers on either side of the three claws. *Wait a minute.* She recognized these species of dinosaurs. And just in that moment, it all made sense to what kind of dinosaurs they were. They were...

The glass in front of her suddenly flew toward her face,

but she didn't have any time to react other than to squint her eyes. She suddenly felt something grab her body and pull her forward into the bars. And her only instinct was to start screaming.

HUNTING GROUNDS

Anika held up the compass on her watch close to her face. She squinted her eyes and scrunched up her nose as she struggled to see the compass in the dark. Not only was it hard to catch a glimpse of the moonlight in the forest, but the rain sloshing on the forest canopy only made it harder. She was able to find a single ray of moonlight where she could put the compass.

She remembers that they had been heading more or less southwest when they first left the lodge. So by that logic, it would mean that she would head in the opposite direction to find the lodge, which was northeast. She didn't know how accurate that was, but what else could she do? She held up her wrist horizontally, and she slowly spun her body around until the dial on the compass was pointing northeast.

Now she knew the general direction she needed to go. The next order of business was if the male was going to let her walk in that direction and follow closely behind? Or was it still determined to push her in the direction it wanted her to go earlier? A theory appeared in her head: what if the male had been pushing her northeast the entire time? Of course, she would never know for sure as she never bothered to check the direction it was pushing her in.

If that were true, that would only mean that the male was guiding her home. Why would it do that? Why would the animal feel the need to push her back home back to safety? Maybe she was just overthinking it. How would an animal know the general direction? She could, however, test the theory right now. As she held the makeshift spear in her hand, she turned to face the male and looked at it directly in the eyes. She then lifted up her hand and pointed northeast to see if the animal could understand.

The animal didn't move; it just stood there blinking, staring right back at her. It made no noise, no movement or twitch of the muscle to indicate that it was understanding. So instead of waiting for a response, Anika started to walk northeast. She didn't stop to look behind her at any point. She wanted to see what the male would do. She walked about ten feet when she heard the dinosaur behind her start to follow.

She continued to walk, guiding herself with the compass on her wristband. The animal made no noise behind her; it made no effort to signal disapproval of their route. It didn't nudge at her; it didn't yank her or run in front of her and then ram her into another direction. It just followed Anika, and she continued her line of thought earlier. Even if the theory of the animal guiding her home seems to be dubious at best, what would give it some sense? Anika put all the facts she knew about these species onto her mental whiteboard.

She knew that these animals were amazingly powerful and rapid, but they were also highly sophisticated. These predators weren't like other predators. She remembers the stare-down among her, JJ, and Zeke. The alpha and beta were not impulsive; there was hesitation in the eyes; there was something more, something indescribable. The animals stared at their prey not like a regular predator would, calculating its next move, but they stared at the humans as if they were studying them.

Even when they reacted violently, it was not your typical predator-prey response. The animals attacked after JJ fired at them. It was only after the humans started wandering in their territory and antagonized them. After that, every move and killing blow seemed deliberate, with purpose rather than response or reaction. Perhaps Anika was right in her assumption at that very moment.

Had they submitted, had they chosen not to challenge these predators, they might have had a better chance of surviving. The outcome may have been different altogether. After the alpha and beta made the decision to murder the humans, the only thing that could explain the reaction from the male was disapproval of that decision. The male had not been fighting for prey, but it had stepped in to give its own opinion. But why was the male so against killing humans?

Anika had heard of instances where animals understood the need for humans. She had remembered hearing a story from one of her colleagues about a man in an African game preserve that drove a water truck. This man would drive a water truck out into the middle of the African bush, surrounded by all manner of wild animals, and would refill the watering hole. The animals had grown so accustomed to this routine that whenever they saw the water truck, they would follow the truck or even escort it. The man could walk around freely with lurking lions around, and they would not touch him.

The animals understood the need for the man with the water truck, and no predator would dare to touch him. Could that same logic be applied here? Could the male understand the need to keep humans alive for an unknown specific purpose? If that were the case, then this theory would have one simple explanation despite the unknown purpose. The male has either had a good interaction with humans, or a bad one. And these interactions would merit the response of not trifling with *human beings*.

Whatever the reason may be, she was here now, and the male seemed to be docile. At least toward her. This animal had put itself in harm's way multiple times in order to save her life. That had to mean something; that had to be a sign of some sort of emotional intelligence. Yet, there is always that worry in the back of her head. The worry that she was overthinking it, over-analyzing a set of coincidences and anomalies. The concern of a wild animal suddenly turning on her, as it had done many times in history, tapped her on the shoulder every time she considered the theory.

She suddenly heard a set of hooting. She crouched down quickly and looked around, holding the spear in her hands as tight as she could. The hooting was coming directly from her left. And it wasn't distant; it sounded close enough to her and the male. While crouching, she took a few steps forward to her right, so as to get away from the hooting.

She only made it a couple steps when the male grabbed her by the hoodie of her jacket with its teeth and gently yanked her left. Anika softly stumbled to the dirt floor. She looked up and saw the animal signalling her with its head to keep moving left. The male was urging her to go toward the hooting. Perhaps the male knows something that she doesn't. It would be an expert on the hunting practices of its own species.

She remembered her last encounter with the cubs. They didn't seem confident enough to attack her head-on. No that wasn't it. She had been a lone prey in the middle of the forest. They had the numbers, and they could have absolutely overwhelmed her. Anika had a brief flash in her mind of her running through the forest earlier. The cubs appeared every single time, attempting to herd her toward the beta.

Maybe that was it. That was the reason that they chose not to attack her. The cubs were attempting to herd her toward the beta for the kill. Is that what they were doing now with their hooting? Attempting to intimidate her and push her toward her death? Maybe that's what the male was trying to avoid by moving toward the hooting. Even if they ran into the cubs, the male would surely scare them away. Anika got into a crouching position and started to move toward the sounds of the cubs.

The male walked steadily beside her, its head hunched

down, claws on either side of its head. The male looked similar to a lion stalking its prey under the yellow African grass. Its head was huddled down, poised for the attack. Anika and the male slowly stepped through the forest, getting closer to the continuous hooting of the cubs. Anika knew she wasn't moving northeast anymore toward the lodge. But none of it would matter if she had walked straight into a trap laid by the beta or the alpha. She wouldn't stand a chance against either of them, even with the male at her side.

The male dinosaur at her side; the reality of the situation finally dawned on her. To anyone else, walking next to a dinosaur while being hunted might seem like someone's wet dream. Anika was terrified. Not only was she petrified of the alpha and the beta hiding in the woods somewhere, but she also had the concern that the male would just turn on her at any given moment. The male was a wild animal, a predator, and she needed to keep that fact in her mind without brushing it away.

Only then would she be as prepared as she needed to be.

The male then suddenly stopped in his tracks and yanked her by her hoodie again. This time, it was yanking her to the right, and Anika obliged. Now the hooting seemed like it was coming from behind her. *I thought the point of this was to avoid being herded?* The hooting behind her then stopped, and it started again directly in front of them. The cubs had changed direction; they had repositioned themselves and the male had sensed it. Could it see the cubs through the dense foliage and the dark? If that was true, it was all the more reason to pay attention to the animal's instincts.

Perhaps all this reasoning in her own head, trying to find a purpose or an idea or even a theory that would fit the situation, was moot. Maybe she needed to trust her instincts and the male's as well, in order to survive. The hooting then stopped completely, and the forest became very quiet. There's no noise, just the rain and the leaves twitching. The male very slowly took a couple steps forward in front of Anika. It gently raised its head into the air and sniffed. It did that for a second and then quickly turned its head to Anika.

Its eyes and expressions are of shock. Anika sensed immediately what had happened; the male's reaction gave her the answer.

Like a game of chess, their hunter was one step ahead of them. Their hunter had assumed that by appearing to herd them both in one direction, they would move in the opposite direction. And because of that, it had led them to exactly where it wanted them to go. It had led them right into its hunting grounds, perfect for an ambush. There was no evading anymore; no stalking, no hiding in the foliage.

The only way out was to fight.

SIGNIFICANT MOI

"Is it tall enough to see?" Burns asks. "Can you see the radio dish?"

Matt stood on top of a chair that was directly placed under the skylight. He was on his tiptoes, trying to peek out of the windowpanes above him. "I think I can see it," Matt says, "but it's nowhere near the skylight. We can't reach it from here."

"You think it's any closer to the other skylight?" Burns asks again.

"Maybe, it's worth a look," Matt says. He hopped down from the chair, and he grabbed it with one arm. Both he and Burns walked into the hallway and into the next room with the skylight. Matt did the same thing: he put the chair down under the skylight, stepped on top of it, and on his tiptoes again, he began to peek out of the windowpanes.

"Well, what's the verdict?" Burns asks.

"Yeah, I can see it," Matt says, "but again, it can't be reached from here. It's just too far away. It's not at arm's length. And honestly, even if we could reach it," he says as he looks down at Burns, "it looks way too fucking heavy to move with one hand."

"So we're back to fucking square one," Burns says.

"There's got to be another way out of here," Matt says. "There must be something we're not thinking of."

"I was just thinking to myself a moment ago. We could give a try to everyone who has a cell phone. You know, have them moving to different places of the lodge, see if we can reach anybody, see if we get any signal at all."

"That's a start," Matt says. "We should also ask the rest of the crew. Maybe they have different ideas or perspectives."

"We could, because I honestly can't think of anything else," Burns says. "We have no clue when Valente is actually going to make it here, or if anybody else is ever going to check up on us. We might be stuck here for a very long fucking time."

"Maybe there's a way we can distract the-" Matt was saying. But he was interrupted by a bone-chilling *shrieking* of a human being coming from downstairs. Matt quickly hopped down from the chair as Burns rushed out of the door and into the hallway. Both Matt and Burns ran down the stairs where the screaming got louder and louder.

They saw two things. The film crew's different reactions. Few of them held their hands up to their mouths in horror, while others were in shock like a deer in headlights; only a couple had rushed forward without any idea of how to help and were now just standing there, trying to frantically figure out what to do.

And the other thing that they saw was Lucy Benitez, her body up in the air, up against the bars of a broken window. Two sets of claws were on her back, holding her against the bars tightly, trying to pull her through. She screamed and shrieked in terror and in pain. Burns and Matt rushed forward, but Burns hesitated only a couple feet away. Burns joined the other two crew members who were just standing there, unsure of what to do or how to proceed.

Matt didn't hesitate. He rushed forward and put his fingers around the dinosaur's clawed fingers. He was trying to peel them off of Lucy's back. "Bill! Help me!" Matt screamed. Burns finally rushed forward. He went to the other set of the animal's claws, trying to pry them off Lucy's back. He struggled for a few seconds, blood started to trickle onto his arms and his fingers, but they weren't from the claws wrapped around Lucy's back.

Burns glanced up and saw that the animal's jaws were around Lucy's right arm. They were forcefully clenched around the flesh of her skin. The dinosaur was tearing her arm apart, its ragged teeth trying to pull Lucy through the bars. Matt was digging his fingers under the animal's claws, trying to pry the fingered claws one by one. But they were too strong. One of Matt's hands slipped, and he cut his palm on the sharp black claws of the animal.

"Marcus!" Matt screamed. "Grab the gun from the counter!"

Marcus quickly rushed over to the kitchen counter where Matt had set down Kit's revolver. He picked up the Taurus model 605, rushed over to Matt and tried to hand it to him. "Reach through, put it up against the dinosaur and pull the fucking trigger!" Matt yelled.

But Marcus didn't move. He could see more closely the blood rushing from Lucy's arm as she was still screaming. Marcus was watching the blood patter down onto Burns's and Matt 's clothes, soaking them red. The sight put Marcus into shock. He just stood there, not willing to risk his life to save another. Matt noticed it immediately, and with a quick swing of his arm, he snatched the revolver from Marcus's hands.

He swung the revolver around. He reached through the broken window and the bars, put the revolver up against the dinosaur's belly, and he pulled the trigger. But nothing happened; the hammer clicked on the revolver, and it fired nothing. Matt pulled the trigger a few more times and nothing happened. The hammer just kept clicking on the empty cylinders.

The revolver was empty; there were no more rounds in it.

Matt dropped the revolver onto the floor, and he frantically looked around the room for anything that could be used as a weapon. He saw a fire extinguisher inside a red panel on the kitchen wall. Matt quickly rushed over and opened the panel to grab the fire extinguisher. He pulled the pin on the handle, and he rushed forward to Lucy and Burns again.

Burns already had a knife in his hand, and he had stood up on the ledge of the windowsill. He had pulled his paracord fixed blade from the sheath on his belt and was stabbing the knife into the animal's snout and into its nose, attempting to get it to let go of its prey. Lucy was still staring into the animal's eyes, horrified. She was yelling and shrieking for help, in both English and Spanish, her throat sore from screaming.

Then she saw Burns's hand holding a knife come down into the animal's eyeball. The knife struck the bottom of the eyeball cavity, and the animal yelped. The animal miraculously let go of Lucy's arm, and she tumbled backward just as Matt was reaching them with the fire extinguisher. Matt dropped the fire extinguisher and caught Lucy in his arms. Burns stepped down from the windowsill and rushed over to Lucy. Matt was already setting her down on the floor, her eyes wide, but she had stopped screaming.

It was impossible to ignore the state of Lucy's arm, the skin and muscle tissue were almost shredded. Pieces of flesh were hanging from the bone. She was bleeding profusely, and they needed to control her bleeding.

"I'm going to grab my medical bag from my room. Stay away from the windows. Don't get anywhere near the windows," Burns frantically says. He rushed upstairs and headed into his room. He went to his backpack, unzipped it, and pulled out his trauma kit. He then exited his room and rushed back downstairs again.

As he was hurrying down the stairs, he could see that there was a significant pool of blood around Lucy's arm. She was losing too much blood; something needed to be done *now*. Burns hurried forward and kneeled down next to Lucy.

He opened the trauma bag and looked for a tourniquet. Once he found it, he wrapped it around Lucy's arm just below the shoulder, and he tightened it as many times as he could until it felt secure.

But she was still bleeding, so Burns grabbed another tourniquet. He put it just under the first one, and he did the same thing until it was firmly secured. The two tourniquets had minimized blood flow, but there was still a leak. "I need alcohol, anything with liquor for her wounds," Burns says. "I've slowed the bleeding and I bought her some time, but I need to clean the wound."

Matt rushed into the kitchen. He swung each cabinet open until he found a bottle of Captain Morgan rum. He darted over to Burns and handed him the bottle. Burns unscrewed the bottle open and poured a substantial amount of the liquor onto her wounds. But Lucy didn't move; she didn't make a sound. Burns expected her to wince in pain from the alcohol. Lucy was still wide-eyed, staring at the ceiling. Burns stared at her face for a couple of seconds until he saw her blink; she was still alive.

Burns put the bottle of liquor down, and he grabbed a couple rolls of bandages from his trauma kit. He examined the wound a lot more closely. The animal had wrapped its jaws around the lower part of her upper arm and elbow, and the top of her forearm. As he was applying the bandages to the wound, he did his best to put the flaps of torn tendons and muscle back together under the bandage. As he ran his fingers along her wound with the bandage, he could feel that not only her elbow, but her forearm was shattered. The animal had an unbelievable bite force, and it had broken her bones.

"No Lucy," Matt says, "don't close your eyes. Stay awake."

"She's lost a lot of blood," Burns says in a cold voice. "She's going to pass out either way. We just have to keep her stable and we have to minimize the bleeding."

"Her- Herre- Herrera-" Lucy says faintly.

"What is she trying to say?" Matt asks.

"Doesn't matter," Burns says.

Burns continued to apply several bandages. He then reached forward and felt for a pulse on Lucy's carotid artery. Her pulse was considerably high; her heart being tachycardic did not help her blood flow. Burns then checked her breathing next; it was slow and struggled.

Lucy Benitez was in a bad shape. She had lost a substantial amount of blood. And even with the two tourniquets on her arm, she was still leaking. Burns started taking another set of vitals, second nature from his time as a paramedic. Her breathing was slow, her heart was racing, and her face was already beginning to turn pale. He had bandaged up her arm, and he had done his very best to keep her stable. They suddenly started to hear barking and snarling coming from the cracked window. Matt peeked over and he saw a few cubs trying to squeeze through the bars to get inside.

Matt rushed over with the fire extinguisher again, pulling the pin on the handle. He was holding the nozzle in his hand, ready to spray the dinosaurs in hopes of getting them to back away. But Burns called out to him, an idea quickly formulating in his head. "Wait, wait," Burns says. He went over to the kitchen counter and picked up the empty can of bear spray. He walked over to the window where the cubs were trying to squeeze through. From a few feet away, he simply pointed the can of bear spray at them. The cubs' eyes grew wide. They quickly backed away from the window and scampered away.

"This should keep them away from the windows," Burns says. "Let's save the fire extinguisher just in case. We have no idea what will keep the adult away." The double door suddenly slammed into the couches, sliding them back. The alpha dinosaur was starting to slam its head into the doors again, attempting to break in. Burns and Matt rushed over and pushed the couches firmly up against the doors, trying to keep the animal from moving them away.

"We got to think of something quick," Burns says, his words straining under the weight he was pushing up against the couch. "We are not going to make it very far. Lucy doesn't have much time. She's going to bleed out."

"What options do we have left?" Matt says, his boots sliding on the hardwood floors from every push.

"We have two," Burns was talking very fast. "Realign the dish or go get the shotgun."

"Do you think the shotgun will work? The revolver sure as hell didn't."

Burns interrupted him. "We have no other options, no other choice. We can't wait for Valente. He won't get here in time. Starting to think even realigning the dish is doubtful, who knows when the storm will go away. And who knows how long it'll be before we reach someone. I think our best option is to get to the shotgun and pump this adult full of slugs."

"Bill, that can't be our only option," Matt was saying.

"Matt," Burns says grimly. "Lucy is going to bleed out, and we are all going to fucking die. Do you really think there is *anything* in this house that is going to *stop that thing*? Our only course of action is to fight back; *in any way we can*."

EROOM'S LAW

Valente was taking pictures with his phone, while Ward stood there looking at the scenery, still in awe. The complex was massive. It was miles of deforestation and habitat fragmentation. This patch of the island of Tasmania was once filled with green life. It had giant, ancient Huon pine trees, beautiful Pandani, and Australian blackwoods. Now it was full of pillars of black smoke, cut down trees, and bright white buildings made for elite tourists. Valente put the phone down in his hand, satisfied with the number of pictures he took of the exterior.

"Seen enough?" Ward says. "Can we go back and check on the lodge now?"

"No, this isn't nearly enough," Valente says. "I want pictures from the inside."

"Inside of what?" Ward says. "We have enough."

"It just looks like any construction site. It won't be enough," Valente says. "Come on, we have to go inside."

"*Go inside?*" Ward says, irritated. "What the hell else is there to see?"

"I want to see the medical building," Valente says.

"For fuck's sake, Forrest," Ward says. "Look around, *there's no one here*. Something's not right."

"Then grab your fucking gun," Valente says through his teeth.

Ward was going to retort again, but Valente was already

walking away toward the main road. Ward knew that there was no point in arguing with him, so he frustratingly walked around the 4Runner. He yanked open the passenger-side door, opened the glove box, and grabbed his holstered HK .45 USP. He clipped the holster onto his belt, then he grabbed the extra mag and put it in his pocket. Valente was walking very quickly. Ward caught up to him and yanked on his shoulder.

"I'm not leaving, if that's what you're going to say," Valente says.

"If we're going to be here, don't move in such a hurry," Ward snapped. "And keep an eye out."

"Keep an eye out for the dinosaurs?" Valente asks.

"Keep an eye out for anybody that doesn't want us here," Ward clarified.

Valente nodded, and they both began to walk slowly and carefully through the construction complex. They reached a fork in the road. There was a huge sign splitting the road in two. The top three lines on the board had arrows pointed right that said *Visitors Center*, *Hotel*, and *Coal Powerplant*. The bottom two had two arrows pointing left that said *Hunting Grounds* and *Medical*.

"Coal powerplant, that's what he went with?" Valente muttered.

"He'd need enough to power his whole city."

Valente sighed. He signalled Ward to go left, and they both went left. They kept walking until they saw the building. It looked more like an urgent care clinic than anything else; it was a lot smaller than the other buildings nearby.

And it also seemed to be the only building that was partially completed. Perhaps it was built first out of the entire complex. Valente took a step forward but then Ward cut him off. "Hold on there, kiddo," Ward says. He pulled his .45 pistol from the holster and held it in his hands up against his chest. Ward stepped forward first. He opened the door to the medical building and stepped inside, with Valente behind him.

He looked around, keeping the pistol level with his eyesight. Wherever his body turned, so did the pistol, looking around for any threat. The building was empty; there were no signs of life, no sounds to be heard. The reception desk had a ladder behind it, and there were cans of paint on the desk. A single landline phone still wrapped in plastic was sitting on the desk.

"I don't think this place is open for business just yet," Ward says.

"Let's go past the reception area. I want to see the rest of it," Valente says.

They walked past the reception area. There was a door-like opening with empty hinges on the left side. Evidently the doors have not been installed yet, so the entire clinic was wide open. They entered a long hallway with several rooms adjoining them. When they walked by the rooms, Ward cleared each one of them one by one, looking for a threat. All he could see was that they looked like patient rooms. The lights were on inside every room except the hallway. "Looks like there's power here, at least," Valente says.

"Most of this place seems fairly functional," Ward says. "Seeing the inside of this place makes me think. It looked like they were working on the hotel and visitor center, but then they stopped halfway to focus on this."

"I don't know," Valente says.

All they could hear was their own footsteps, slowly making their way down the hallway. They could hear the rain pattering on the roof, giving the building an eerie feel to it. Man-made buildings that were now derelict always had an eerie vibe to them when they were uninhabited. They reached the end of the hallway. There was another door opening but this one did have a door. There was a sign on the door reading

Warning: Biological Hazard, Authorized Personnel Beyond This Point.

Valente reached for the handle of the door, but again Ward stopped him. He signaled him with his hands to take a few steps back. Ward kept his pistol up with his right hand, and with his left hand, he reached forward to slowly open the door. As the door was opening, he scanned inside from left to right looking for a threat. When he cleared the room from outside the door, he quickly made his way inside and scanned the hidden corners of the room.

There was nothing except industrial grade refrigerators, a hazmat suit station, some desks, and a single computer sitting on top of one desk. The room was dimly lit, but the computer illuminated most of the room. The computer was locked, and it had a single screensaver with a graphic that read *Sky River Treatment Center.* As they walked through the room examining it, a stack of files sitting in front of the computer caught Valente's eye. He strolled over to the computer and started to skim through the stack of files.

"Lee, listen to this," Valente says, and he began to read out loud. *"I have never studied such a creature with such magnificent DNA. Who knew that such a vicious creature from the past carried the answer to most of our current health failures."*

"What's that?" Ward asks.

"A file labeled *Paleo-DNA: Project HI56203*, written by Dr. Sacksteder himself."

"That fucking prick."

Valente kept reading from the file. *"After further examinations, I've determined the animal's blood seems to have more purpose other than flowing through its veins. The blood cells are highly active, along with the white cells of the body. My hypothesis is that they're constantly looking for something to heal. Much like the animal's demeanor, the cells are incredibly aggressive toward anything foreign. Not only is it regulating its body and keeping its metabolism in check, but it'll heal any ailments, diseases, and wounds at a faster rate than any other mammal on the planet. So our question was: what would it do to any other ailments more prone to human beings?"*

Valente flipped the page. *"We tested with multiple concentrated doses of common diseases. There was no reaction; the blood cells did nothing. Which didn't make any sense as it seemed to do so when they were inside the animal itself. But not on the petri dish, with no reaction and no response whatsoever. However, I do recall that the animal's blood and saliva had a reaction with our very first reported victim. So there had to be a reason why there was no reaction in the petri dish. Then it occurred to me. The reason that it had killed the hunter is because he was prodding it. He was actively hunting the animal. Putting the animal in this situation would raise its heart rate and make its blood race as its metabolism prepared for a fight. We tested that theory. By putting the animal in stressful situations and environments, the DNA started to give the reaction we were looking for. Only under extreme duress does the animal's blood begin to have the needed reactions, thereby releasing epinephrine and cortisol."*

"It kills any bacteria, any parasite, any mutated blood cells you put in its way at a fast rate. Of course, it all depends on how fresh the DNA samples are. After a span of a couple hours, the animal's blood cells seem to lose their healing properties. By that logic, the subject must remain alive, in order for any human being to seek medical benefits from it. For future liable DNA samples, the subject would have to be close by for DNA extraction. I have forwarded all of my research and all of my findings to our project director, signed Dr. Sacksteder." Valente put the file back on the desk and stared at the wall for a couple seconds, taking in the information.

"You got what you needed," Ward says defiantly. "That is everything you came looking for. We can finally leave."

"Okay, okay," Valente says, his face still shocked by the

words.

"Are you going to take the file with you?" Ward asks.

"They might notice it's missing," Valente says sharply. "I don't want them to start cleaning the house because they think they might be exposed. I'm going to photograph it." Valente held his phone up a foot in the air, snapping pictures of each page as clearly as he could.

They suddenly heard a thud coming from the adjoining room. Ward held his pistol raised up to his chest. "We're not alone," Ward says. "We need to go now."

Valente glanced at the door from which the noise came. The door had a placard that read *Entry Forbidden Without PPE and Proper Authorization. Live Animal Beyond This Point.*

"Lee," Valente whispered.

"Don't you fucking dare," Ward says.

Valente stepped forward and yanked the door open before Ward could say anything else. As the door swung open, they both went into immediate shock at the sight beyond the door. There was a dinosaur, about eight feet long, massive, with muscled thighs and muscular forearms. It had a dark brown mane made up of small spotted feathers around its neck all the way up to its chin. The animal's leathery skin was dark red spotted with orange dots. The animal was hanging from the room's ceiling and walls by chains. Its snout had a muzzle wrapped around it, while its arms and legs were tied together by huge amounts of tape to keep them from extending. When the animal caught Valente and Ward in its peripheral, the animal whimpered.

"Holy fucking shit," Ward says. "This is bigger than I fucking thought. This thing is huge. How many of these were there again?"

"At least more than one."

"Doesn't seem very aggressive right now. But I can tell that it could easily change. We need to leave."

"Hold on, Lee."

Ward looked around the room. He saw cabinets and locked steel cases. Inside were both medical tools and non-lethal weaponry like cattle prods. Ward then looked at the animals in chains, its body covered in dark burn marks and bruises. "Guess they found a way to stress this animal out." Ward says.

"Like the file says, *stressful situations,*" Valente says. He took his phone and took as many pictures as he could of the animal in chains. Valente moved around the room, getting as many angles as he could. Then he put his phone back in his pocket, before he decided to walk away. The animal whimpered again and Valente looked into its eyes. He felt something in his chest, like a weight with an undeniable feeling; *immeasurable sorrow.*

"We have to take it with us," Valente says quickly.

"*Are you out of your fucking mind?*" Ward snapped.

"I can't in good conscience just leave it here to be tortured for who knows how long. How long do you think it'll take to get anyone to come out here and stop this?" Valente says.

"Boo-hoo for the fucking maneater."

"Lee."

"Do you know how many people this... *thing* has killed?" Ward retorted.

Valente walked close into Ward's face. "You told me to do something that for once didn't benefit me. Look at it in the eyes and tell me you don't feel a thing. If you don't, we can leave right now without it."

Ward sighed angrily. He glanced at the animal; it was looking right at him. Ward felt a weight in his chest, something he could not ignore. The grim feeling of hopelessness, a need to do something about the situation.

Ward began to smile nervously. He could not believe what he was about to say.

"The muzzle stays on," Ward says. "We drive it far away from here. We release it and that is it. No *ifs*, *ands*, or *buts* about it. I don't want to hear any other fucking thing."

"Okay," Valente says, "I can live with that." Valente moved around the animal slowly, starting to undo the buckles on the chains. The animal was warm, and its skin was rough. Valente noticed the feathers moved side to side as the animal's eyes followed him. He glanced over to Ward. He was just standing there, holding his pistol. "Are you going to help?" Valente asks him.

"Nope, I'm going to stand here with my gun," Ward says. "Unbuckle his body first, leave the head for last."

Valente moved around the room, freeing the animal's body little by little. Even after the animal's body was free, it didn't move. It just simply stared at Ward while its head and body was still hanging. "I'm about to release its head, are you ready?" Valente asks him.

Ward adjusted the grip on his pistol and held it steady. His muscles locked, ready to fire .45 caliber rounds into the animal should it decide to test them. Valente unclipped the last chain holding its head and torso. The animal's body tumbled to the ground, both men hearing its weight land on the tiles. Still, the animal didn't move; it didn't move its head or its limbs. It just simply stayed there. It was too weak; it was clear the animal was not going to be able to move on its own.

"Are you going to help me move it?" Valente asks.

Ward sighed, still frustrated at the fact that he had somehow agreed to do this. He signaled Valente to pick it up from the tail end of its body. While still keeping the pistol in his hand, Ward wrapped his arms around the animal's neck and chest. The men lifted the animal, and they instantly realized the reason for the animal's weakness. It was starving. An animal that at first glance would weigh at least 400 pounds, weighed less than 200. They could feel the animal's ribs and bones up against its leathery skin; there was little to no fat in its body.

"As soon as we clear this place, we let it go," Ward says.

"The muzzle," Valente recalled.

"I'll unclip it as soon as I know we're clear," Ward says.

They moved slowly through the medical building, making their way back to the front entrance. Ward could feel the animal's feathered mane and skin brushing up against his forearms, and it was surprisingly warm. They could feel its struggling shaky breath as it inhaled, its chest bulging from the rise. Just before coming up on the reception area from the hallway, the animal firmly placed its feet on the ground. It took two steps before it decided to dangle its feet again like before. Ward looked down and he could see the animal was beginning to move its forearms, its hands, and its claws.

"This thing is starting to regain some energy," Ward says.

"Then we better hurry," Valente says. They made their way through the reception area as quickly as they could. They stopped at the door, and Ward let go of the animal slightly. He pushed open the door with his hand, and they made their way outside.

"Shit, we forgot about the fucking perimeter fence," Ward says.

"We go to your truck at the end of the fence line," Valente says, "It's not far."

Ward didn't say anything. He simply grasped the animal tightly again. They continued to carry the animal to his Toyota 4Runner. Valente suddenly had to squint as they reached over a hill; there were headlights beaming toward them.

"Did you leave your headlights on, Lee?" Valente asks. Ward suddenly stopped, making Valente pause in his tracks abruptly. "What's going on, Lee?" Valente asks.

"Told you it was a fucking trap," Ward simply replied.

"What are you talking about?" Valente says. And as he says this, he stood on his tiptoes to glance over Ward's shoulder. He saw three shadows standing next to the beaming headlights. There was a second truck parked right behind Ward's Toyota 4Runner. Once his eyes adjusted to the light, he saw that it was his father, Rafe Valente, standing there. He was armed with his rifle and two mercenaries at his back armed to the teeth.

Rafe was just smiling. "Well, quite the conundrum we have here, don't you think?"

GERSON'S LAW

Anika Irving was being hunted by a predatorial dinosaur of apex stature. Realizing the weight of that statement in her head made Anika feel slightly hopeless. Not only has she seen how tenacious these animals were, but she had seen their cruelty toward their prey. But even though she was in a dire situation, for the first time in her life, she tried to stay optimistic. Because for whatever reason, she had a male dinosaur at her side, willing to fight with her. At the same time, she knew she could not rely on the male dinosaur to protect her completely. Not really.

If she turned tail and ran, leaving it behind while they were fighting, there was a chance that the cubs would finish her off shortly. The male had to survive in order for it to keep the cubs at bay. She had to fight back in her own way, which was easier said than done. She only had a couple weapons on her: her survival knife and a makeshift spear. She reminded herself that the adult dinosaurs had significantly more dangerous weapons on them, such as their sharp jagged teeth, their claws, and even their speed.

If she wanted to fight back and survive, she would have to keep her distance from these weapons. The spear was probably the best bet, but she didn't know how sturdy it was going to be against the animal. She looked around at her surroundings, anything in the environment that she could use against the hunter. It was completely dark now. She could barely see three feet in front of her as the moonlight peaked through the forest canopy. She could try to use the dark and maybe the dense foliage of ferns and scrubs to her advantage.

She didn't know how good the animal's visual acuity was, but using your environment was a start. She slowly kneeled down and took off her paracord bracelet. She started to take it apart, trying to undo the burnt ends with her fingernails and her teeth. Once she got a decent sized piece of paracord, she took her fixed blade out and she tied it to the handle in a firm knot. She then took the other end of the paracord and tied it around her right wrist. This would keep her from losing her only sturdy weapon. She then tucked the fixed blade into her jacket sleeve. She didn't need it right now; she had her spear.

Anika turned her head and glanced at the male dinosaur. It was meticulously moving its head from side to side, scanning every inch of the forest in front of it. It was looking for a hunter, whether it be the alpha or the beta, or *both*. Anika began to speculate what kind of predator these dinosaurs were. Would they stalk their prey until they were only a few feet away like a cursorial predator? While Anika was having these thoughts, she saw the male dinosaur lift up its head in the air and start to scan the trees around them. Why was it looking at the trees?

The male then charged without warning and rammed into Anika's back, sending her tumbling forward onto the ground. She lost the spear she had in her hands as her face hit the ferns and wet dirt. She could hear snarling and growling; scuffling noises were suddenly incessant behind her. Anika lifted her face off the ground and looked at the male. The male was rolling around on the ground, fighting with the beta.

The beta had managed to sneak up on them both, and the male had pushed her away from the killing blow. Anika got to her knees and frantically moved her hands around the dirt, searching for the spear. She finds it and holds it tight in her hands as she turns toward the fighting animals. She watches as the male and beta violently thrash around on the ground.

Biting, clawing, slashing, and kicking with growling anger.

Anika notices the beta seems to favor its arms, using them to pull the male's into its jaws for bites. Anika had to keep her distance if she wanted to survive. She had to stay out of the beta's reach. But she also wasn't going to just stand on the sidelines. Her only *ally* was risking its life to fight for her. Anika slowly walked around the fighting animals, looking for an opening to strike.

There was a moment in the fight when she saw the beta overpower the male momentarily. It held the male down and stood on top of its back. The beta was about to deliver a vicious blow to the male's neck with its jaws. Anika didn't hesitate; she charged forward, spear outstretched in front of her. The tip of the spear struck the beta in the side, barely breaking the leathery skin. The thick ribs of the beta snapped the spear with ridiculous ease.

Anika realized her mistake in thinking a makeshift spear would measure up to a seven-foot-tall dinosaur. The beta turned its attention to her and snapped its jaws at her. Its snout gave a loud *thunk* as its teeth closed just inches from Anika's nose. The male had rolled its body around from under the beta, and it pushed the beta off toward the dirt. The male then stood up and spun its body swiftly. Once more using its tail as a whip, it struck Anika's stomach and sent her toppling backward.

The male snarled at Anika right as the beta pounced on its back again. The male did not want her to join in the fight. It knew she stood no chance against the beta.

After the beta pounced on the male's back, it grabbed hold of the male's neck and head. The beta pulled back hard, and using the weight of its own body, it sent the male flying backward. The male tumbled hard and struck the trunk of a tree. Anika was on her feet when she saw the beta turn its head and glare at her. The beta darted toward her. Anika dove to the ground and scurried along the ferns and foliage, attempting to lose it in the dark.

The beta clawed and tore at the ferns and bushes, trying to find the small human. Anika kept crawling, low to the ground. She saw a tilted Huon pine tree with thick protruding roots. The opening in the roots was narrow but she didn't care. She crawled fast and tried to pull herself inside the roots. Her wounds ached as she scraped them by, squeezing into the base of the tree. She then felt a squeezing sensation in her right boot, and then her body started to move in the opposite direction.

Anika glanced over her shoulder. The beta had her boot in its mouth and was pulling her out. Anika pulled the fixed blade from her sleeve and swung it at the beta's face. It struck the beta in the bottom of its eyelid and slid in about halfway. The beta howled and let go of her boot. It retracted its head, and the paracord tied to the knife and Anika's wrist kept the blade from leaving her grasp. Anika then pulled the rest of her body in the tree roots. She could hear the beta bellowing in fury and pain at the fresh wound.

The beta then jumped forward and started to tear through the wood of the roots. It was plucking away giant chunks at a time with ridiculous ease. Little by little, the beta was destroying Anika's temporary shelter with its powerful jaws and arms. Anika needed to move. It would not be long before the animal made it to her. She looked around; there was nowhere to go. Where could she run to?

Her time for thinking was over. The beta was only inches away when she decided to crawl out of the roots from a different opening. Once she was out, she got to her feet and bolted toward another tree. She had no plan, but her first instinct was to climb. She climbed up the wet tree as fast as she could. She could hear the beta behind her running towards her. Her heart was pumping, her adrenaline making her muscles feel superhuman. She climbed the tree quickly, making it to a decent height in mere seconds. She then took a moment to look down to the base of the tree.

The beta was beginning to climb the tree.

It was doing it almost as quickly as she did, as if climbing was second nature to it. She started to climb higher and higher. The sound of the beta's furious snarling was getting closer. Anika suddenly felt that squeezing sensation on her boot again. And in an instant, she was yanked back and she was falling. She fell for almost fifteen feet to the ground below. She hit the ground with a thud, her back hitting the muddy forest floor. Anika was desperately gasping for air when she saw the beta hop down from the tree. She was attempting to get up when the animal pounced forward and landed on her body.

The beta had its talons on her chest and torso, holding Anika down. Anika could feel one of her ribs fracture at the weight of the predator. The beta lowered its head and gave a dominating growl to her face. Anika could see that beta's right eye was swollen shut from the knife wound. Drops of blood from its wounds dripped onto Anika's neck and face. Anika swung the knife in her hand again, but the beta caught her arm in its jaws. It was clenching hard, increasing the pressure little by little. It was going to snap her arm like a twig. Anika swung her other fist wildly, striking the beta in the snout and in the eye like one would with a shark.

The beta's talons in its feet were digging into her chest and stomach. She couldn't get free; she was at the beta's mercy now. Anika was yelling and cursing as she continued to punch the beta's face, hoping one of the punches would miraculously release her. Anika then felt the weight on her body disappear; the beta was pushed off her. She saw the male tackle the beta again.

The beta and male rolled away, once again caught in a wrestling match. Anika scrambled to her feet. She knew the male couldn't hold the beta at bay for long. Once Anika got to her feet, she saw the beta toss the male off its body using its mighty thighs. It sent the male flying toward Anika. Anika dodged the male's body by mere inches. She then saw the beta snarl at them both. It turned around and...

It climbed the nearest tree.

The beta, like before, climbed with ease, and disappeared into the tree canopy. Anika was in shock. She had lost sight of the beta instantaneously. She then realized a simple fact: these animals were *ambush predators*. The beta hadn't snuck up on them both earlier; it had laid a trap. It had been waiting on top of a tree, waiting for Anika to walk by. And the male had sensed it. It had pushed her away just in time.

Anika knew what it meant to be hunted by an ambush predator. She would never hear it, and she would never see it. It would somehow lure you into its killing grounds and pounce when you least expected it. Burns had taught Anika so much about survival. But the one thing Burns would always focus on was the near impossibility of winning against a ghost in the wind. Burns had indeed hunted down the jaguar that killed her mother, but with great risk to his life. And he had succeeded by mere luck.

Anika frantically looked around the forest canopy. She was searching for shadows or silhouettes lurking in the dark. Even then, it was hard to see. The rain kept splashing her eyes. As if the clouds over Tasmania were purposely trying to keep Anika blind.

Anika heard a loud splash behind her. She swung her head around and saw the beta standing behind her. In that moment, the beta swung its head around and snapped its jaws at Anika. Anika dove to her right, the beta's jaws nearly missing her face and neck. She crawled close to the floor, trying to conceal her body in the undergrowth. The beta roared in anger, twisting its gaze to Anika's last known location.

The beta had hidden in a tree, seen Anika, and pounced toward her. But as Anika hid her body behind a fallen log, she wondered why it hadn't landed on her. She took a quick peek over the log and saw the beta frantically looking around the ground and bushes. Why did the animal seem so confused? There was no way the animal had suddenly lost its…

The beta's right eye.

Anika could see it was still swollen shut from her knife wound. The beta was keeping its snout angled to the left. It couldn't see; its vision was impaired. The beta hadn't decided to land next to Anika instead of delivering a killing pounce. The animal had *missed* due to its damaged depth perception. Anika had assumed that she needed to keep a distance from the animal's best weapons, its claws and jaws.

But she was wrong. The animal's greatest weapon was its eyes—its demon eyes that spotted prey and sent it spiralling toward it like a heat-seeking missile. And she had wounded one, If only she could somehow wound the other. Then the beta would be blind, and Anika and male could kill it easily. Anika glanced at the survival knife dangling from the paracord on her wrist. That was the only weapon she had, the only hope she had left. She had to time her moment just right.

Shit, the beta spotted her. It bolted toward her. She had no choice but to turn tail and run. She ran to her left, hoping the animal's handicapped right side would assist her escape. The beta bellowed loudly behind her. The animal's feet splashed in the muddy ground. Anika felt the rush of air fly by her body, nearly missing her. Anika had found herself behind the animal. The beta had stopped in its tracks after it couldn't see her.

Anika saw her chance, and with all her might, she jumped on the beta's back. Anika wrapped her arms around the beta's neck, and acquiring a firm grip, she swung the fixed blade into the animal's left eye. The beta gave a deafening yelp as the blade split the cornea into two pieces. The beta began to buck Anika off its back desperately. It swung its body erratically and succeeded in sending Anika tumbling off into the dirt. Anika scrambled to her feet, and then she watched as the beta snapped its jaws blindly into the air. The beta was completely blind. It turned its body from side to side, confused and panicked as to why it couldn't see. Its roars changed to agitated whimpers, its predatorial instinct coming to a halt.

The beta had become *prey.*

Anika slowly moved around as the animal desperately tried to fight back its invisible attacker. The beta flailed its claws, quite literally grasping for anything at all. Anika then saw the beta tumble backward as the male tackled it to the ground. Even if the beta was blind, it was still sending bites and claws at the weight hovering over its body. The male clawed and bit, wounding the beta further as it held it down.

Anika looked around her feet. She saw a large rock by her ankles. Anika picked it up and rushed forward to the beta. She held up the rock and swung it down with all the strength she could muster. The rock struck the beta's snout, shattering the bone underneath its flesh, the skin giving way to a splash of blood. Anika raised the rock and swung it hard again, this time striking higher on the snout, the rock breaking the ridge over its right eye. This stunned the beta, making it temporarily stop fighting back. Anika picked up the rock and swung it down again, and again. Feeling the animal's blood fly up from its head and speckle her face and neck.

She kept striking with the rock until she saw the beta

stop moving. She took a step back and saw the beta's labored breathing. The once-terrifying predator was now taking its last breaths as it lay whimpering in the mud. The male then gave one final snarling bite with its jaws and severed the beta's carotid artery. The blood pooled from its neck, and in a matter of seconds, the beta finally died.

The male stepped off the beta's lifeless body and shook its head from the fight. It then looked at Anika and stared intently at her. The male's eyes for once changed their usual emotionless crocodilian look and gave Anika a different impression instead.

The male looked relieved.

THEY COME AT NIGHT

Lee Ward sat against the wall inside the old, abandoned, crumbling house. He peeked out of the window next to him, trying to spot any kind of life in the moonlight. The last bit of the Somalian sun had disappeared below the horizon more than twenty minutes ago, vanishing for the night. Now the cloudless night carried on and the full moon remained. The moonlight was the only source of light for the residents of Mogadishu. The cold night started to sweep in as Ward and the rest of his squad mates from his ranger battalion gazed out of the windows.

They all scanned the alleyways of the streets of Mogadishu, firmly grasping their Colt 723 ARs in their hands, ready for a fight. Ward let out a cold deep breath, the mist from his mouth catching his eye momentarily. It was getting colder, and the night had barely started. Ward leaned his head back from the window, tired of looking for threats and finding nothing. One of his hands let go of the rifle he was holding and unbuckled the helmet on his head. He slowly peeled the helmet off his head; the dried sweat and hair had made his helmet feel like glue.

He rested his helmet next to the wall where he was sitting, and he looked around the room. All of his squad mates had the same look on their faces. They were stuck. They had been cut off, caught up in an ambush they didn't see coming. Or maybe someone did see the ambush coming, they just chose not to warn them and sent them in anyways. Now all they could do was sit inside the room of this abandoned home and wait for dawn, or for orders. They could still hear the distant low cracking gunfire from another part of the city of Mogadishu.

"They're not calling for help," Rick Ryder says. "Why wouldn't they be calling for help? Sounds like the holy war out there."

"Maybe they can't reach them. That's why they haven't sent us out. I did a radio check not five minutes ago," Ward says. "Just 'loud and clear' was their response. They wanted us to stay put."

"That's bullshit," Ryder says. "Why would they want us to stay put?"

"My guess is they can see us right now," Ward responded. "It might be more of a risk to leave right now."

"Why would it be more of a risk?" Ryder asks.

"Do you do much reading?" Ward says to him.

Ryder just nodded and then shrugged, unsure of what Ward was asking.

"Von Clausewitz? Sun Tzu?" Ward asks him.

"I don't get you," Ryder says.

"Thinking about warfare, especially skirmishes like this," Ward says in a cold tone. "You fight infantry during the day, you know, regular soldiers. Not at night, not after dark. There's no soldiers at night. Only hunters."

"What the hell is that supposed to mean?" Ryder says.

"It means the whole city knows where we are," Ward says. "We're not exactly hiding right now. We're waiting for our turn in the fight."

Ryder didn't say another word. He simply looked away from Ward. Ryder looked out the window again, listening to the gunfire in the night. "Got movement," another one of his squad mates says. Ward grabbed his helmet and slipped it on.

He buckled it on his chin. He steadied the Colt rifle in his hand and sat up on his knees. He peeked out the window one more time and indeed saw shadows at the end of the street moving toward them.

"Soldiers during the day," Ward mumbled. "The hunters come at night."

The hunters come at night, Ward reminded himself of the phrase. He could feel the weight of that statement one more time in his chest. He had locked eyes with Rafe Valente and the two mercenaries at his back. The mercenaries held their ARs close to their chests, fingers over the triggers, staring at Ward and Valente. Rafe also wore military fatigues himself, which didn't make sense as Rafe was never military. Even his face didn't fit the outfit, neatly combed hair with large, framed glasses, like a schoolteacher or a suburban dad trying to look like a soldier. The only other thing that didn't fit the look was the Sabatti double-barrelled hunting rifle in his hands, an elephant gun chambered in .500 nitro express. Rafe continued to smile at his son, finding the situation amusing.

"Yes, indeed," Rafe says. "Quite the conundrum. What are you doing all the way out here on this island?"

Neither Valente nor Ward says a word in response.

"I'm talking to you," Rafe says. *"Lee Vincent Ward*. Son to Richard and Kayla Ward from Denver, Colorado. Former US Army Ranger, now lead engineer of Valtech Engineering, or is it *Industries* now?" He smiled even wider. "You got a brother somewhere in the Dakota's, right?"

"Passed away three years ago," Ward says, his voice sharp. "Brain cancer."

"The big *C*, huh? That's rough," Rafe says. "You really have no other family? Are you staying healthy like I asked you to?"

"Oh, you know..." Ward says.

"Yeah, it would be kind of hard to do around my son," Rafe says. "Speaking of which, what the hell are you doing now, Forrest?"

Valente smirked. He thought it was pretty obvious what they were doing as the dinosaur was wriggling in their arms.

"Did you forget how to talk?" Rafe pushed.

"I should be asking you," Valente says. "It was in your goddamn lab."

"Yes it was," Rafe responded. "Therefore it is my property. What are you doing holding it?"

"It's a living animal-" Valente began to say.

"Oh, don't start with that 'holier than thou' bullshit," Rafe says, cutting him off. "If you've seen my lab, and you've come this far, then you know exactly why I have it. In the world of pharmaceuticals and medicinal properties, this animal is the *motherload*. There is nothing in the world that will ever compare to the medicinal applications this animal has."

Valente's face tightened. "You would rather keep it here and torture it for its entire fucking life just so you can add more value to your stock shares?" Valente says angrily.

"This animal, believe it or not, is going to save lives," Rafe says. "*Save them*, a substantial change in comparison to what it was doing not three months ago."

"It doesn't matter how many lives it will save," Valente says. "This isn't right."

"Oh, such a non-consequentialist fucking attitude," Rafe got exasperated. "You know, for once in my life, I thought I was doing the right thing. And yes, I'll admit a raise in prices for my stocks does seem appealing. Do you have any idea how much my company has been struggling with a competitor like Horizon?"

"Well, when you put it that way," Ward responded in a

sarcastic manner.

"Jesus Christ," Rafe says, his voice exuding disbelief. "Look at the two of you. It's almost like you were made for each other. All right, let me put this in a way you can understand. You have two choices. One, you can put the animal down, get in your car, go home, and forget all of this bullshit. I promise I will leave you and your company alone for the rest of your life as long as you stay out of my way. Or option number two, we can let this little conundrum play out."

In the couple of seconds it took Valente to decide and respond for them both, *Ward saw it.* The tightening of their muscles, their shoulders perking up, their fingers entering the trigger guards. Despite the *options* Rafe had given them, it was clear they had made up their mind. There was no other way out of this. "I'm going to tell the whole world what you're doing here," Valente responded.

Either way, Ward thought, *that was the wrong answer anyways.* Just as Rafe and the mercenaries raised their rifles to fire upon them both, the dinosaur in their hands roared to life. It jumped up, and it started swinging its claws and legs wildly, startling the entire group of men. Ward and Valente had no choice but to let go of the animal. It hurried away from them with stunning speed. It went past the security booth and plunged into the forest. Valente was in shock. Ward reached out and yanked him by his jacket. Ward yanked him back behind the Toyota 4Runner as bullets began to pepper the SUV.

Ward kept his head down as the hail of bullets was roaring. After a couple of seconds, he peeked his head out and fired two rounds from his HK pistol. Ward saw that Rafe and the two mercenaries were hiding behind their own SUV, adjacent to the security booth.

"Forrest!" Ward yelled. "Get the fuck out of here!"

Valente gave him a blank stare. One moment, he was talking to his father, and the next, he was caught in the middle of a gunfight.

"Don't overthink it!" Ward yelled. "Just fucking go!"

Valente peeked out from around the 4Runner, looking for an escape route. While he was peeking out, he saw Rafe entering the foliage, pursuing the animal. Valente got to his feet, and he charged from behind the SUV, bullets flying by his body. Valente darted into the foliage too, after his father and the animal.

"*Not that way*! For fuck's sake!" Ward yelled. But Valente had already disappeared into the bushes. Ward stayed behind cover, keeping his pistol at the ready. The hail of bullets suddenly stopped. "Go after him! I'll stay here!" one of the mercenaries yelled. Just before the hail of bullets resumed from the automatic rifle, Ward saw one of the mercenaries charge into the forest too.

Now it was Valente against his father, a mercenary, and a predatorial dinosaur. Ward needed to act quickly. He took a moment to consider his situation. He knew that this mercenary was a former military. He didn't know how, he just knew. Every shot toward him was deliberate; no bullet was wasted. He was keeping him suppressed. Probably to make his way around to him and flank him at some point. Any move he made would have been calculated by his opponent. They had to have been briefed by Rafe on who Ward was, a former US Army Ranger.

So Ward decided to resort to the unorthodox. He laid on the wet asphalt floor and peeked under the truck. About ten or fifteen feet away, he saw the mercenary's boots sticking out from behind the SUV. Ward carefully pointed his pistol and he fired two shots, hitting the mercenary in the ankles. The mercenary staggered to the floor, grunting in pain. Ward scrambled to his feet as quickly as he could, and he ran from behind the truck, made his way around the security booth, and came behind the SUV until he found the mercenary on the floor.

The mercenary's eyes widened as soon as he saw Ward standing only a couple feet from him. Before the mercenary had a chance to react, Ward put two .45 ACP rounds in his face, killing him instantly.

Ward hesitated for a couple seconds after killing the mercenary. He realized this was the first time he had killed someone in over twenty years. It gave him the same feeling now as it did all the way back then. Ward shook the thought away and holstered his pistol. He crouched down close to the mercenary laying on the floor and grabbed the rifle. It was a SIG Sauer Spear MCX, chambered in 7.62×51mm NATO, and mounted on top was a Trijicon red-dot sight.

He carefully pulled the sling from around the mercenary's neck, blood and brain matter spilling from the exit wound on the back of his head. Pieces of brain and skull were scattered on the concrete. The .45 caliber rounds had turned his occipital bone into mush. Ward quickly examined the mercenary's plate carrier setup. The vest did indeed have one plate in front covering the chest. Under the chest plate were molle pouches with three 30-round AR magazines. Ward unclipped the side buckles on the mercenary's vest and took it off the dead man. He put the vest over his head and slid his head between the shoulders.

The plate carrier was at least one size bigger than him, so it wouldn't get in his way. He clipped the buckles on the sides, then picked up the rifle, and put the sling over his head. He then held up the rifle in his right hand, and with his left hand, he grabbed the fresh mag out of one of the pouches. Ward did a tactical reload to get a fresh magazine in the mag well. He then pulled the slide bolt back just enough to see if there was a round in the chamber. He finally let the bolt slide forward and rushed into the forest.

Valente had carelessly ran into the forest behind his father. He had no plan, not really. He could barely see him now that it was so dark, and the rain was making it harder. Valente knew that it was a terrible decision, but he wasn't just going to let his father kill the animal after he released it. He felt some sort of responsibility after freeing it back into the wild. Valente could still hear somebody running ahead of him in the bushes, even if he couldn't see him. He could still follow the sounds. Valente had to find a way to stop him. Rafe was a seasoned hunter, and there was no way of underestimating him. He would kill the dinosaur effortlessly and then boast about it.

Valente came to a sudden stop. He couldn't hear any more sounds, and he couldn't see anything. If his father had stopped moving, that only meant he was closing in on his prey to make a shot. Valente slowed down. He crept forward through the foliage, trying to find his father. He then spotted him, about twenty feet away. Rafe was crouched down behind a log, resting the tip of the double rifle on it, stabilizing it and aiming down the sights. Valente had to stop him, but he had no weapons. The best thing he could do was creep forward and alert the animal of an attacker. Valente continued to sneak forward as quietly as he could, trying to get as close as he could to his father to get the drop on him.

He was only about fifteen feet away when the ground next to Valente started to kick up and burst as he heard automatic gunfire from behind him. He glanced over his shoulder to see another mercenary, rifle at the ready, firing at him. Valente dove to his right behind a tree, and he hid behind it, taking cover. The rounds were pelting the wood of the tree as the mercenary fired at him relentlessly. He had to think of something quick because as of right now, he had no way out, and no weapons. The mercenary was going to kill him, and his father was going to kill the only dinosaur to still exist after millions of years.

Ward could hear automatic gunfire cracking in the distance ahead of him. Even though he was terrified that they were killing his best friend, at least the gunfire gave him a sense of direction. For the past minute and a half, he had been running wildly through the woods, hoping that he was heading in the right direction. He gripped the SIG Sauer rifle tightly in his hands. He needed to keep his training in mind. He needed to keep a level head, and he would not hold a single fiber of his being back from them. They were trying to kill him, but he was going to kill them first. As he got closer and closer to the gunfire, he raised his rifle to his eyes, ready to fire at any threat, ready to save Valente.

Then the gunfire suddenly stopped, but it didn't matter. About eighty yards away, Ward saw the situation that Valente found himself in. Valente was hidden behind a tree, taking cover, and the trunk of the tree was riddled with gunfire. The mercenary at the moment was switching his magazines out. And on the other end, he could see Rafe Valente moving around the forest, attempting to flank *his own son*.

That does it. Ward was going to kill them both.

Ward perched behind a tree, steadied his rifle, and fired a burst of 7.62×51mm NATO rounds. The bullets struck the mercenary in the back of his plate carrier, sending him tumbling forward. But they didn't kill him. Instead, the mercenary regained his balance and swung around with the rifle, trying to find his threat. At that moment, Ward fired another burst of rounds.

These ones were aimed a little higher than his chest. The bullets struck the mercenary's neck, chin, and forehead. It was an instant *lights out* as a bullet struck his head. It made the mercenary's body rag-doll to the floor, lifelessly. Ward then turned the rifle onto Rafe Valente. But it was too late. Rafe's Sabatti double-barrel elephant rifle burst loudly and sent a round flying toward Ward. The bullet struck the front of the magazine well of the assault rifle in Ward's hands.

The round spiraled through the rifle and then veered off into Ward's plate carrier. The single elephant rifle round had turned the SIG Sauer rifle into a grenade, sending bits of shrapnel and rifle parts into Ward's arms, chest, and neck. Ward tumbled backward onto the floor.

Valente had seen it all. Rafe had fired at Ward and struck him. Valente went into a fit of rage. He stood up from behind the tree and charged forward at his father, who only had mere seconds to react. Rafe attempted to swing the rifle toward his son, but Valente tackled him to the ground. Valente was using his left hand to push his father's face into the mud, and he was using his right hand to send punches into his father's sternum. Rafe growled in anger like an animal backed into a corner. Rafe couldn't get his son off of his body. Valente was amazingly strong. Rafe then pulled a knife from his belt and he swung it at his son's arms.

Valente felt the knife graze his forearms as he swung another punch. Rafe swung the knife again and he plunged it into Valente's thigh. Valente grunted in pain, and Rafe used the second of agony to heave his son off of his body. Rafe then quickly grabbed his rifle from the ground, held it up in his arms, and swung the butt of the rifle onto his son's face. He then rotated the rifle swiftly to point the barrel straight at Valente's face. Valente looked up, blood trickling from the blunt force trauma wound on his forehead.

"Stupid boy!" Rafe yelled. "I gave you a chance to walk away. But your fucking ego couldn't let it slide, could it?"

Rafe opened his mouth to say something else, but then he stopped. Something on the ground caught his eye. Something had fallen to the ground and rolled forward past his boot. Rafe kicked it softly with his boot to examine it.

It was a muzzle.

The muzzle was last seen around the dinosaur's jaws. Rafe slowly turned his body around, and the first thing he saw was a tail dangling from a tree. He followed the tail up to its owner, and he saw a dinosaur on the side of a tree, holding itself up with its arms and legs, sneering at him.

Rafe took a knee and swung the rifle around, but the animal had already jumped. It landed on him in a split second, and all Rafe could see was nothing but teeth and claws. Valente watched as the animal tore into his father, violently killing him. Once Rafe Valente went from screaming to groaning then to complete silence, the animal slowly raised its head up and stared at Valente. Valente didn't move; he didn't make a sound; he just looked right back at the animal. Valente expected the animal to kill him too, to take revenge on the species that had held him captive and tortured it.

But instead, the animal just looked away. It grabbed Rafe Valente's lifeless body and it started to drag it into the forest. Eventually, the animal disappeared from Valente's sight. Valente struggled to stand up, the knife still stuck in his thigh. He brushed the warm blood away from his eyebrows, and he started to limp toward Ward's body. When he reached him, he could see Ward's chest rise, and his exhale misted over his face. "Lee," Valente mumbled. "Are you alive?"

"Just get me to a damn hospital," Ward groaned.

Valente took the phone out of his pocket. He flipped on the flashlight and shone it on Ward's body. There were bits and pieces of metal embedded in Ward's forearms. His shirt was soaked in blood. He moved the flashlight over his face and he saw a single piece of shrapnel embedded in his cheek.

"Can you walk?" Valente asks him.

"I don't know," Ward says "You think you'd be able to carry me?"

"I have a knife in my thigh," Valente simply says.

Ward lifted his head just enough to take a glance at Valente's legs. He saw his right thigh definitely had a knife sticking out. "Fucking Christ," Ward says in a strange chuckle. "I bet you fucking wish we went to the lodge, huh?"

Valente ignored the comment. "I'm going to pull you from your vest and stand you up. You're going to have to use your legs. I'm going to try not to touch your arms." Ward groaned in agreement. Valente grabbed him by the vest, and he started to lift him up using his left leg for balance. He tugged him upward until Ward was able to stand himself up.

"Okay," Valente says once Ward is on his feet. "Back from where we came."

"Which is?" Ward mumbled.

"That way, I think," Valente says.

Ward once again groaned in agreement, and they both started to make their way through the woods back to the complex. As they were limping away, Valente could swear he could hear thumping noises emanating from deep in the forest.

After a couple minutes of limping through the foliage, Valente chuckled to himself.

"What's up?" Ward says.

"I see red and blue lights up ahead," Valente says with a smile. "Police."

"Thank fucking God," Ward groaned.

They kept walking until they reached the opening in the woods. There were two more SUVs and a police car parked at the front entrance of the complex. There were a couple police officers in uniform, and one single man in a vest standing in front of them, holding a flashlight and a pistol in his hand. Once the man in the vest spotted Ward and Valente walking out of the woods, he signaled to the other police officers to go help them.

The police officers moved forward and took hold of Ward by his vest and helped him walk toward their police cruiser. Valente simply limped as best as he could behind them. As Valente got closer, he noticed a single patch in front of the man's vest that read three letters: ICC. He didn't recognize the lettering, but he knew the man wasn't a police officer. He had to be some kind of federal agent. But what kind?

The man in the vest holstered his pistol. He was tall and slender, with dark gray hair slicked over his head. He walked over to Valente and grabbed him by the arm to help him walk. "You got a knife in your leg, sir," the man says to him. "Disagreement with your friend?"

"No," Valente says to him. "I had a disagreement with my father."

"Ah," the man says. "Parental disputes, aren't they the worst?" The man helped Valente lean up against the nearest SUV. He opened the trunk door, and he allowed Valente to sit in the back and rest his body. The man then looked over at the police officers holding Ward. They were carefully helping him sit down in front of their cruiser.

"It goes without saying, you should probably call for medical treatment for these boys," the man says to the police officers. One of the police officers rushed over to the front of his cruiser, swung open the driver door, grasped the handheld radio, and started to call for EMS to his location. "By the way," the man in the vest says. "Your father wouldn't happen to be Rafe Valente, would he?"

"He was," Valente answered. "Are you a federal agent?"

"Of some sort," the man in the vest says. "My name is Quinby Gunderson, of the International Criminal Court. We have been following your father's... *plunders*, for lack of a better word."

"Do you guys know what he's doing here?" Valente asks him.

"We have the most basic general idea," Quinby says to him. "We've only just become aware of him. We were actually following you."

"Following me?" Valente says. "What the hell for?"

"Because you decided to follow up on whatever is living in these woods. So were we. We have been for some time. We also heard you were going to bring an expedition out here. When were they coming out here by the way?"

"They're already here," Valente says to him. "They've been here for a few days now."

Quinby's eyes widened. "They're *already* here?"

"Well yeah-"

Quinby interrupted him. He pulled a satellite phone from his pocket and started to dial a few numbers. "Yeah, hey, Karen," Quinby says into the phone. "We have a problem. They've already been here for a few days apparently. Yes, the expedition. We need to go find them right now. No, I'm talking to Forrest Valente right now. He's in bad shape. He's going to need EMS. I would suggest taking everyone you can." Quinby slid the mic of the phone away from his face. "Do you know exactly where they are?" he says to Valente.

"I have the coordinates right here in my wallet."

Quinby shoved the phone forward into Valente's face. "*Tell her.*"

LODGE

Matthew Irving punched as hard as he could. He swung his fists wildly. He struck the animal's nose hard, its forehead, and its eyes, and he pulled on its ears. But it would not let go. The fierce jaguar would not let go of its prey. The growling jaguar kept its jaws clenched around Cassandra's throat. He couldn't hear Cassandra breathing anymore or screaming. All he could hear was the jaguar in front of him, snarling and rumbling, attempting to drag her away into the jungle. Matt finally swung his arms forward, and he put his thumbs in the jaguar's eyes.

The jaguar rapidly snarled, opened its jaws, and took a step back. The jaguar swung its claws wildly as it tried to regain its sight. Matt took a step backward too. While the jaguar was distracted, he grabbed Cassandra by her shirt and started to drag her away from the animal. The jaguar then shook the pain away from its face. It snarled at Matthew with its bloody fangs and then scurried away into the jungle. Matt looked down at his wife; he could see her chest rising and falling. She was still breathing, but blood was pouring out of the deep teeth marks on her throat.

Matt frantically took off his safari shirt. He rolled it up and put it around her throat, keeping pressure as much as he could. "Somebody help!" he yelled to the crew behind him. "Call an ambulance! Call somebody, please!" Matt looked down and saw his safari shirt was already drenched in blood. He looked over at his wife's face. She was looking right at him, life fading from her eyes. "Hold on, Cassie," he says to her. "Please, hold on, just hold on." She opened her mouth as if to say something, but the only thing that came out of her mouth were bubbles of blood. They trickled down her cheek and her face.

And as Matt was watching, Cassandra's eyes faded away into nothing.

"No, Cassie. No, please," Matt says, sobbing. "Don't do this. Just come back. It's okay baby please."

But he knew she was gone. There was nothing he could say or do to bring her back. Matt leaned back. He took his hands off her throat, and he held them up to his face. His hands were bright red, covered in his wife's blood. Matt saw shapes in his peripheral that broke his attention from his hands. He glanced to his left, and he saw little Anika standing there. Her mouth was open in shock, her cheeks, her ears, and her hair speckled in blood.

She didn't say a word to him, and neither did he.

Matthew Irving sat on the kitchen floor inside the lodge. He was resting his hands on his knees; his hands once again covered with someone's blood. The blood brought back images of his past, his mind tormenting him with dreadful memories. Every time he moved his head, he couldn't shake the image of his wife's eyes staring into his soul as she *expired*. He remembered his childhood, filled with violence and abuse that he would never dare to speak out loud again. He tried to remember the wonderful years of his life when everything felt like a dream. He tried to remember holding his daughter for the first time in his hands; she was so small.

But the dreadful memories always came back, as vivid as they could be. After his wife's death, his only real connection to this life was his daughter, Anika. Now Anika had gone missing in the woods of Tasmania. The expedition had gone awry; horrific deaths were involved. Matthew couldn't shake the thought away from his head. In comparison to the better years, his life actually had more death than good. Maybe this is what he deserved. Maybe this was God's way of telling him that he had chosen the wrong path, and He had been trying to correct him all along.

Or maybe this was life's cruel way of torturing those with good intentions. Matt looked around the room at the frightened faces of his film crew, whom he had doomed to their fate when he brought them here. Burns was on his knees over Lucy's injured arm, applying another set of bandages, struggling to keep her alive. His knees and his shins covered in blood as he was kneeling in the puddle of what was once running through Lucy's veins.

There was a series of thumping coming from the back door. Before that, it was coming from the far-left window of the living room. Before that, from the upstairs window. The devil was knocking, trying any which way it could to come inside and feast. The guilt inside Matthew's chest had never been heavier. It felt as if the weight on his chest was trying to drag him down through the floor and into the depths to where he belonged.

There was nothing he could do; he was going to die. Unfortunately, once more, he had brought along too many innocent souls with him.

"I need the keys to the truck," Burns says.

Matt looked over at him. He was still on his knees, but he was glancing over his shoulder at Matt. "The keys for the truck," Matt repeated.

"Yes," Burns says, "you have them in your pocket, right?"

"Are you going to try to drive us out of here?" Matt says, his voice no longer had the usual flair. It was cold and monotone.

"No, I'm going to go for the shotgun," Burns says.

"That thing will kill you before you even reach it," Matt says.

"Lucy is bleeding out," Burns says grimly. "She is going to die in the next couple of hours. Unless we do something right now. I'm going for the shotgun, and I'm going to kill that fucking thing. Then I'm going to get her to the nearest hospital."

"And if you die?" Matt says. "What happens to us? We just keep trying until we all die?"

"We have to try something," Burns says. "No matter the risks." Burns stood up, walked over to Matt, and held out his hand. "Give me the keys to the truck," Burns says. "I'm willing to take the risk. I just need you guys to make as much noise as you can. Do it on the opposite windows. Get its attention. Distract it."

"Did I ever tell you about where I came from?" Matt says, his voice sullen.

Burns was confused about the shift in tone from Matt, but he responded, "You told me you were from Texas."

"West Texas, a little town called Odessa," Matt says. "I grew up bad. My father was a drunk, violent. After all, his job required him to be. I hated my life. I hated the fact that I existed solely for the purpose of suffering. And as I got older, those feelings only increased. One night, the... home life... got so intense, that I hit my limit. I bolted out of the house, angry and resentful at not just my father, but God as well. I ran far, very far into the plains of west Texas. And as I ran, I pleaded to God to let me die, to take my life and end this suffering."

Burns didn't say a word. He never knew Matt came from a dark place. A dark place Burns was all too familiar with.

"I spotted a lion," Matt continued. "A cougar, feasting on a downed prey. It was by itself, tearing at a deer. It eventually looked up at me. It didn't waste any moment to decide my fate. It immediately strolled toward me. Its four legs moved up and down like pistons. I remember thinking to myself, *this is it, this is His almighty response.* I kneeled, I closed my eyes, and felt relieved that it would all end soon."

Matt sighed, his breath shaky as he continued. "But nothing happened. I could just... hear the lion breathing. My eyelids were closed, but I knew it wasn't moving. I finally gave up and peeked. It was just staring at me. It was only a few feet away, and my god, what a sight. Its fur around its jaws and neck covered in deer blood. I mean it looked like the incarnation of God's punishment. But it didn't move. It was just growling, watching me. I didn't know what to think, or what to do. All I could do was stare right back into its dark yellow eyes. Then it moved away and left me alone. Walked back to its downed prey. I was stunned, because I had noticed something in its eyes... something that set me on a different life path."

Matt looked up at Burns, his eyes glossy. "This life path I was put on created such... love. I didn't know it was possible. For the first time in my life, I felt like I belonged somewhere, among the rest of God's creatures. You have to understand the meaning of that. After so long, I belonged somewhere, where there wasn't pain. And I could finally prove to my father that there was love and passion to be found where he almost made me believe there was none. God, that evil bastard. You know, he laughed when I told him Cassie died?"

Matt grunted and cleared his throat. "All I ever did in my life was try to prove to him that he was wrong. I suppose we're all products of our fathers, aren't we? All I ever wanted was to share my love to the world. Was that so wrong?"

Burns kneeled down. He sighed and spoke softly. "It's not wrong, Matthew. But even the best intentions can bring tragic consequences if you're not careful. What matters is not just what message we're sending out, but how we send it in the first place. Do you honestly think you were doing it the right way? Teaching people correctly?"

"I tried, I really did."

Burns shakes his head in disbelief. Matt is still living in his own world. "Have you ever heard about Maisie Bennings?"

Matt shook his head.

"I know you didn't, why would you? I'm sure your lawyers kept it out of your view. She was a nine-year-old girl, who loved you and your show. She watched it every Saturday morning. She wanted to be you. She went out, into her backyard in north Tennessee, and came across a coyote. She walked up to it, just like you taught her. And the coyote attacked her. It only bit her a couple times. She was mostly fine... for a couple days. See, the coyote had *rabies*, and she got *infected*. She fought that infection for a week in the hospital. Then she died."

Matt's face has sunk, his eyes wide open.

"Her mom tried to sue you and your show. But your lawyers are too damn good. They plundered Maisie's family, left them with nothing. Just like Cassie's sister, Natalia, when she tried to sue for wrongful death."

Matt sighed, his breath shuddering. "I never knew..."

"I know."

Matt sighs again. "You know, what I saw that day, in the mountain lion's eyes?"

Burns is attentive.

"In its eyes was the answer I was looking for," Matt says, a tear running down his eyes. "I saw wild, violent eyes that were incapable of cruelty. This animal could have torn me apart, but it didn't, because it already had enough food. It didn't see a need to hurt me, to kill me. Killing for the sake of malice was a trait it did not possess. I thought, for once, I saw something that couldn't be cruel," Matt says. "Guess I was wrong about that too."

"We're in a different world now. We're living the consequence of our carelessness, whether we like it or not.

The punishment being: we are now left to survive like all the animals we study. What matters now is how we survive," Burns says.

"I know. Everything I have ever believed in is in shambles," Matt says. "All that matters to me now in this moment is to protect the only thing I've ever loved in this world. My daughter, Bill."

"It's best not to think about these things too much right now," Burns says. "It is what it is. We all made our own decisions. We all know exactly what we might get into. Just give me the keys."

Matt stood up as he was fishing in his pocket for keys. "It won't work," he says to Burns. "We start making noise trying to distract it, and it's going to know something is wrong. This thing is smart. There's another way to do this." He handed the keys to Burns. "We both go out there. I'll lead him away. I'll be the bait."

"No, we're not doing that," Burns says. "It will definitely kill you. I'm trying to prevent further loss of life."

"No, no," Matt says to him. "I'm not just bait. I'm going to run around the back and climb the ladder to the roof. I'm going to readjust the antenna as best I can. That way, if for whatever reason either one of us doesn't make it, at least the rest of us will have a chance."

"Are you sure you want to do this?" Burns asks solemnly.

"Yes, I do," Matt says. "It is the only way we can achieve some kind of success. I am done underestimating this animal. If we try to distract it from here, or even if I run out there and purposely holler at him to follow me, it's going to know. The only way this works is if we both have a mission, and whoever succeeds increases our chances of survival."

"Okay," Burns says. "No time to lose. We need to move now." Burns walked over to the film crew in the living room. "We're going to go out these double doors here. I want you all to be ready. As soon as we're out the door, I want you to barricade it again. I also need you all to keep a close eye. The moment we start coming back, you need to be ready to open this door."

"Someone should be at the back door too," Matt says. "Increase our chances."

"Let's do that too," Burns says in agreement. "One of you needs to go watch the back door. Y'all need to be watching, be Johnny-on-the-spot with the doors. We might not have a lot of time."

Marcus volunteered to go to the back door. He quickly strolled to the back to take his position.

"All right, you three," Burns says to three crew members. "Help me move these couches." They began to move the couches. As they were moving the barricade away from the front entrance, they could hear more thumping from the alpha dinosaur on the roof. "It's on the roof right now," Burns says. "You'll be running into it if you're going for the satellite dish."

"Don't underestimate it," Matt says. "It's going to make a rush at us. My guess is we'll have about five, maybe six seconds once we're out the door. No matter what happens, we don't stop. No matter what we hear, even if I'm screaming for fucking help, you keep going, otherwise the rest of us die."

Burns could tell that Matthew had no sense of showmanship in his voice anymore. He had never heard his friend be so serious in his life. Matthew Irving wasn't taking any more chances. He had finally become realistic. The couches were now away from the door, at a distance where they could easily be pushed back. Matt and Burns started to limber up. Then they both stood at the door, getting ready for the fight of their lives.

"You know, I never thanked you," Matt says.

"For what?"

"For raising my daughter when Cassie died. For taking her in when I failed as a father."

"She saved me too, you know. In her own way. She's a fighter. She's alive. I know she is."

"I know she's alive. She has the best from you and Addie, and she's as resilient as her mother," Matt says. He extends his hand to Burns, palm up for a handshake.

"Whatever happens next," Matt says. "*Godspeed brother.*"

Burns shook his hand, and for the first time in a long time, he felt a semblance of respect for his friend. He smiled solemnly, noticing a hint of melancholy behind Matt's eyes. He was expecting to die. They let the handshake go and opened the double doors.

And in different directions, they both ran into the night.

As soon as both men stepped outside the lodge, they were met by three cubs that scurried out of the bushes. As soon as the cubs laid eyes on both men, they started to snarl and crow into the air, calling for help. They then heard the loud, thunderous crowing response coming from the roof. Both men stopped in their tracks and looked up. They saw the enormous alpha dinosaur beginning to climb down the roof.

Both men turned tail and ran in separate directions toward their individual objectives. As soon as the alpha dinosaur hopped down onto the solid wet dirt below, it decided to go after Burns. Burns could hear the dinosaur behind him charging, its feet hitting the mud, making splashing sounds behind him. The animal was almost on him. The truck he needed to get to was almost ten feet away in the line of parked trucks.

So Burns dove to his left and frantically crawled under the second Ford F-350. He heard the dinosaur snarl as it lunged forward too, trying to grab Burns's legs as they disappeared under the chassis of the Ford F-350. Burns had gotten really lucky. The dinosaur's head was too bulky to fit under the truck's suspension, and its arms were just short enough that they could not reach him. The animal clawed fiercely under the truck, trying to catch Burns and pull him out.

Burn saw the axles and the chassis of the Ford F-350 start to wobble, as the dinosaur kept ramming its head into the side of the Ford truck. It was attempting to move it with brute force so that it could get to Burns. It growled and snarled in anger. The animal realized that the truck was too heavy for it to move. Burns then heard the alpha dinosaur crow to its cubs, calling them in. Burns took a glance at the dinosaur's feet as he was pulling himself across the mud. He saw the animal's taloned feet quickly run away in Matt's direction.

Burns wasn't in the clear just yet. He saw the cubs swiftly find him under the truck. They were a bit more slender, and they could get under the truck. They were clawing at the mud, trying to pull themselves under. Snarling and growling, snapping their jaws, they were trying to grab any part of his body. There were two at Burns's feet, and there was one that decided to crawl toward his face on the side of the truck.

Burns stopped for a moment. He pulled his fixed blade out, and he swung it at the cub crawling toward his face. The side of the blade hit the cub's snout. It yelped and pulled its head out in pain. Burns then felt something tugging on his boot. He looked down through the axle in the truck. He saw one of the cubs had crawled under just enough and had its teeth wrapped around his boot. Burns kicked off the dinosaur's snout with his other boot. The cub growled and continued trying to get under the truck. Burns took another quick glance around him. He couldn't see the alpha anywhere.

So Burns crawled out as fast as he could from under the truck. Once he was out, he made his way to the last truck in the convoy. He grabbed the keys out of his jacket pocket, unlocked the truck, swung open the passenger door, and jumped inside. Just as he swung the door closed, the cubs had jumped forward. They struck the closed passenger door and started to gnaw at the bars covering the windows. Burns clicked the button to lock the doors of the vehicle, then he looked around the back. He saw the rifle case containing the shotgun sitting in the pickup bed. He then looked out the windshield. He couldn't see Matt or the alpha dinosaur. All he could hear was growling in the distance.

Matt had made his way up the ladder with complete ease. When he reached the top and climbed onto the roof, he could see the satellite dish. He was moving carefully across the roof, trying not to slip on the wet shingles. After he got a closer look, he noticed the dish was simply pointed down toward the lodge instead of pointing up in the air. Matt put his hands on the edge of the dish, his fingers grasping the cold, wet steel, and started to tug, readjusting the dish. The loud, metallic screeching of the dish moving made him feel uneasy. The animals would know he was on the roof. Once the dish was sufficiently pointed up into the air past the tree line, he ran to the edge of the roof. He tried to look around and see where the alpha was, but he couldn't see it anywhere. It certainly wasn't at the truck, but he could see Burns inside trying to get to the pickup bed.

Where was the alpha dinosaur?

He then heard snarling, accompanied by loud thumping coming from the front door. Matt leaned his head over the roof, until he could see the alpha dinosaur. It was ramming its head into the double doors, trying to get inside the lodge. That's when Matt began to yell to get its attention.

The small sliding window separating the cabin from the pickup bed was too small for Burns to fit through. Burns was kicking the window, trying to shatter it, so that he could make his way through. He had already attempted to reach through with his arm, but the rifle case was too far away from his hand. He then suddenly heard yelling coming from the roof. He turned his body to see Matt yelling. He saw the alpha dinosaur ramming its head into the double doors. Every time the dinosaur rammed its head into the double doors, he could see them budge just a little more.

My God, it was going to get inside.

Burns turned his body around again and he kicked as hard as he could, harder and harder until the glass shattered. He then pushed the plastic edges out of the way and dragged his body through the opening. Once he was in the truck bed, he hunched over and pulled the rifle case toward him. He opened it and saw the nickel plated Benelli M4 semi-automatic shotgun held in place by gray pluckable foam. There were two boxes of shells right next to it. He grabbed the shotgun and held it in his hands. It was cold to the touch from the steel frame.

He then took the two boxes of shells and opened them both. There was a box of Federal double-ought buckshot and a box of Federal slugs. Burns knew how the shotgun worked. Whatever you loaded in the tube first was going to be shot last. He didn't know if the buckshot would work on the big dinosaur, but he for sure knew the slugs would. And he knew both the buckshot and the slugs would work on the cubs.

The only ones in his way at the moment were the cubs, trying to tear the door open. They were still clawing at the edge of the windows and the bars at the passenger side. Burns knew that the Benelli M4 shotgun could hold five shells in the tube. So he loaded three slugs first, and then two buckshot. He then pulled the bolt back and racked a shell into the chamber. Burns added one more buckshot into the tube. He stuffed the rest of the slugs in his right jacket pocket and the buckshot in his left pocket.

Burns pushed his body alongside with the shotgun back into the cabin of the truck. Burns put the key to the truck into the ignition, and he turned once so he could operate the inside buttons. He rolled the driver seat window down, making the snarling of the cubs louder as they were only inches away from him.

Burns simply put the barrel of the shotgun through the bars and pulled the trigger.

ANIKA

Anika Irving was tearing pieces of her jacket off with her Gerber fixed blade. She was tearing them into strands and then wrapping them around the defensive wounds on her forearms and hands. There were bites and tears in her skin along her arms, chest, shoulders, and back. All of them near misses from the beta's attack, all of them burning in pain at the moment. It was the first time in the entire night that she appreciated the cold rain splashing on her body.

She heard licking sounds coming from her right. When she looked over, she noticed the male dinosaur tending to its own wounds. Upon examining the animal's behavior, she noticed something extraordinary. Most of the animal's wounds, if not all, had stopped bleeding. And they weren't superficial wounds either. The male had taken the full force of the beta's attacks. There were deep cuts in the animal's skin and flesh, but they didn't appear to be bleeding anymore. Anika knew the probable explanation for this bodily function. It was not unheard of in the animal kingdom, especially in crocodiles. When wounded, crocodiles and alligators had the ability to redirect blood flow in parts of their body to refrain from bleeding out.

But as far as she knows, the only reason they could do that was because they were cold-blooded. This animal was warm-blooded. She had felt the warmth exuding from the animal's body countless times. Even when she swung down that heavy boulder onto the beta's head, she felt the warm blood speckle her hands and face. Maybe the redirecting of blood flow was no reason to compare them to crocodiles.

Perhaps it was just a normal bodily function for this animal, a trait undiscovered in this new species. This was all so fascinating and terrifying at the same time. By mere luck, she had survived the confrontation with the beta, but the encounter with the alpha might be a completely different story. Although they were both very cruel, she had noticed that the beta's behavior was more timid, and subservient to its alpha. While it seemed to be very skilled in hunting and tracking, the beta's attacks seemed rash and spontaneous.

The alpha was nothing but calm and collected when it was murdering JJ, staring back at her with those cold, indifferent eyes. Yes, indeed, their next encounter with the alpha might be the fatal one. It'll take a lot more than luck to kill it off. The male dinosaur suddenly stood up from the muddy ground and shook its body, shaking off the wet and the pain away from its body. Anika wiped the rain off her forehead; her skin was cold, and she could barely feel her fingers. She needed to find shelter, or she would not survive the night. She knew staying in one place would make it easier for her hunters to find her.

Anika could not shake the feeling in her gut whenever the male looked into her eyes. There was something more, something that separated it from the other animals she had studied before. She came back to the idea of emotional intelligence. Which was only ever present in mammalian brains, shared by animals like dogs, whales, and even humans. There was a possibility of rational thought. This dinosaur could not only problem-solve, but it had the capability of understanding situations. It had intentions. While mostly unclear, killing Anika was not one of them. This animal put itself through harm's way more than once to keep Anika safe.

Why the attachment? It couldn't be specific to Anika. It had to be toward her species in general. Was the male like this with every human?

Her thoughts were interrupted. She unexpectedly heard low cracking and echoing thumps in the distance. There were a couple of echoing thumps, then two more, and then a fifth. They were gunshots—consecutive, frantic gunshots. It had to be coming from the lodge or the search party if there was one. They had run into the alpha and her cubs. She was ready to run in that direction, but then she remembered the male dinosaur. The only ally that she seemed to have in this entire forest. She turned her head to look back at the male dinosaur. She wanted to say something, but she reminded herself that it could not understand English.

Maybe this animal was like any other species. Maybe with the sincere look in her eyes, it would understand. Anika waited for the male to lock eyes with her, and once it did, Anika nodded her head toward the gunfire. The male stared at her for a couple of seconds, and then it moved toward her. It lightly nudged her back, urging her to move in that direction. As she started to jog toward the gunfire through the forest, she could see the male dinosaur running alongside her.

PANDEMONIUM

The dinosaur cub began to gnaw at the strange piece of metal sticking out of the truck window. It wrapped its claws and snout around it, trying to tear it to shreds. Unbeknownst to the cub, the piece of metal was the barrel of a twelve-gauge shotgun. When Burns pulled the trigger, all nine pellets of buckshot turned the cub's head into mush, making it burst into a ball of red matter and mist. The loud bang of the twelve-gauge instantly frightened the other cubs trying to get inside the truck. They stepped backward and hissed, unsure if they should keep attacking the truck after the loud boom.

Burns slowly opened the driver's door and stepped out of the vehicle, holding his boom stick.

He raised the shotgun to his eyes, put the stock to his shoulder, and then put the sights right on top of a second cub. He pulled the trigger again, feeling the kick of the Benelli up against his shoulder. The buckshot pellets struck the cub in the face, neck, and shoulders. Its body flung backward, landing next to the last cub. The remaining cub charged forward, snarling in contempt. The second boom from the shotgun had caught the alpha's attention. It turned around just in time to see a third cub get blasted away by the Benelli. Then Burns turned the shotgun on to the alpha, who was already rushing toward him.

Burns pulled the trigger a fourth time, sending the first Federal slug round in the tube spiraling toward the alpha. It struck the alpha in the chest, but not before shredding parts of its right hand and forearm. The alpha immediately recognized that its prey had turned the tables. It turned right and darted toward the foliage. Burns fired another slug round toward the alpha but missed. Burns ran toward the front entrance of the lodge, trying to lead the sights onto the fleeing alpha. The alpha disappeared into the pitch-black forest surrounding the lodge.

Burns then rested the butt of the rifle on his shoulder. He was pulling another slug from his jacket pocket to load it into the tube. He was loading the slug when he saw the double doors of the front entrance begin to open. "No! Don't open them!" Burns yelled. "Close it! I'm not done!" But before Burns could say another word, he heard dashing footsteps from behind him. The alpha covered the distance around the lodge with alarming velocity. It was already behind Burns when he swung the shotgun around.

He was too late.

Burns felt jaws full of jagged teeth grab him by his thigh and send him flying forward into the air. His head struck the ground hard, sending him into a daze, his eyes seeing double. He quickly shook his head. He lifted his body just enough so he could glance back over his shoulder. The alpha was nowhere near his body.

The alpha was stepping inside the lodge.

Marcus heard screams coming from the front door. He ran from his post toward the living room and stopped in his tracks. The first thing he saw was the towering alpha dinosaur staring at everyone in the living room with dark eyes. No one moved. No one made a sound. The animal stood incredibly still; it almost looked like a wax figure. Until it opened its jaws and began to screech.

Matt had already made his way around the lodge to the ladder. He was about halfway down when he heard screams coming from the front door. This was shortly after the gunfire had stopped. Matt was praying that it hadn't gotten to Burns just yet. As he reached the bottom, he rushed over to the back door. He peered inside the window; there was no one inside. Marcus wasn't at his post, ready to open the door for him. He could hear loud thumping and movement coming from inside the lodge. The screaming was getting louder, and it was coming from multiple people. Matt turned tail and rushed around toward the front door.

Burns was struggling to stand up from the muddy floor. The animal had wounded his right thigh, but not deep enough to create a fatal injury. He stood up and looked around him on the ground, looking for the shotgun. Once he found it, he bent over slightly and picked it up with the tip of his fingers. He loaded another slug into the tube, then another, and he tried to load more but the tube was full. He could hear screams coming from inside the lodge; the front door was wide open. Burns limped as fast as he could toward the front entrance. He limped up the steps of the porch, across the floorboards, and to the front entrance.

What he saw inside, as he raised the shotgun to his eyes, was *gruesome*.

Burns saw the boom mic operator laying at the bottom of the staircase. His belly cut wide open, his entrails and intestines spilled out over the floor. The boom mic operator was feebly trying to pick up his slippery entrails and put them back in his stomach. He was coughing, watching a pool of red surround his body.

Burns could hear screams coming from the top floor. Burns limped forward and started to climb the staircase. He stepped over the boom mic operator's body. He reached out his hands when he saw Burns, pleading for help. Burns could not help him, not right now. He needed to put an end to the massacre. He limped up the staircase and heard more groans and screams accompanied by snarling coming from the hallway. As he reached the top of the staircase, he saw a single arm with a wristwatch still attached. He recognized the Casio watch he had last seen on Marcus, the editor.

Burns held the shotgun high, ready to fire, his finger anxious to find a target. The end of the hallway was dark. The screaming had stopped but he could hear groaning. He could hear something tearing, munching, chewing. Burns saw something get tossed toward him\. It rolled toward his feet. He saw bloodied, matted hair stuck to torn cheeks and lifeless eyes. It was the head of Megan, the producer. Burns looked up. He was about to pull the trigger into the dark hallway. That's when he saw the alpha dinosaur rushing from the end of the hallway.

Matthew Irving could see that the front door of the lodge was wide open. He couldn't hear any more screaming or any sounds coming from inside. Before he walked up to the porch, he looked to his left. He saw the mangled-up body of dinosaur cubs laying on the dirt. Their bodies were twitching, their faces and chest destroyed by buckshot. Matt finally walked up the steps of the porch and made his way through the front entrance. The first thing he saw was that there was blood everywhere. There was blood on the floor and on the walls. There was a body at the bottom of the staircase with his guts spilled out.

He saw Lucy Benitez still laying on the floor where they had left her. She no longer had just the injury on her arm. She also had deep gashes on her face and neck, and her head was twisted back over her shoulder. Matt put his hand up to his mouth, *was there anyone still alive?* He then heard two more shotgun blasts coming from the second floor. He looked up the staircase and saw Burns flying through the air from the top of the staircase.

Burns landed onto the hardwood floor with a loud *thunk*. The shotgun that was in his hands tumbled away toward the kitchen. Matt was about to run toward Burns when he heard the furious, angry roar coming from the top of the staircase. He saw the alpha dinosaur staring down at him, fresh wounds on its back and chest. Parts of the dinosaur's right hand were missing fingers and claws. Matt then heard Burns moan a simple phrase. *"Grab the shotgun."*

Matt rushed toward the kitchen, and he picked up the shotgun in his hands. When he turned around with the shotgun, the alpha dinosaur had already covered the distance between them with stunning momentum. It rammed into Matt's midsection, sending him flying backward, sending the shotgun flying in a different direction, again. Matt's head struck the lamp and his feet touched the kitchen counter as he flew through the kitchen. Matt was out of breath as he landed on the floor. He scrambled to his feet as quickly as he could. He saw a glimpse of the alpha dinosaur in his peripheral, clambering toward him through the kitchen. Matt ran toward the pantries, through the narrow hallways that looped around the living room, the dinosaur rumbling closely behind.

Burns was pretty sure that a couple of his ribs were broken. Even then, he still pushed his body to stand up from the floor. He could hear the alpha dinosaur roaring through the hallways of the lodge, chasing Matthew. Burns got to his feet. He limped as fast as he could toward the shotgun in the kitchen. He stepped over Lucy's dead body. He picked up the shotgun. He pulled the charging bolt back on the Benelli; there was one shell in the chamber. He checked the port under the shotgun.

He couldn't see any more shells in the tube. He searched for more slug rounds in his jacket pocket.

There were only three left. He pulled all three of them out of his jacket pocket. He pushed them slowly into the tube. Burns saw Matt run forward, out of one of the hallways into the living room, his face stricken with fear. And only a couple milliseconds later, the alpha dinosaur came crashing out of the hallway behind Matt. Burns held the shotgun steady, and he pulled the trigger once. The shotgun's slug went barreling through the air and struck the alpha dinosaur in the ribs. The alpha dinosaur bellowed in anger again. It turned its attention away from Matthew and ran toward Burns.

Burns squeezed the trigger again, but the shotgun wouldn't fire. He glanced at the charging bolt, only to notice that it wasn't pushed all the way forward. The shotgun was covered in mud. It was making the weapon jam. Burns wiped away the mud and struck the charging bolt with the palm of his hand. But the clearance of the malfunction on the weapon was too late. The alpha dinosaur had already sprung forward. It grabbed Burns by the arm with its jaws and swung its body around. The animal sent Burns flying in the air for the third time, the shotgun leaving his hands. Burns's body and his head struck the floor hard. His head felt woozy from the blow; he could feel his right arm was dislocated.

Burns was seeing double, even then, he could see the alpha dinosaur pounce toward him. The alpha dinosaur landed on his body, putting its full weight on Burns's torso. The animal plunged its head downward with its jaws open. Burns held up his left hand to defend himself, but it was no use. The animal tore through Burns's arm and into his chest, leaving deep wounds, sending blood flying everywhere.

When Matthew had made it into the living room, he had jumped through the front door. He had caught a glimpse of

Burns standing there, holding the shotgun. But he only heard one shot. When he turned around and looked through the front door again, he saw Burns flying through the air. The animal then pounced forward and started to tear into Burns. Matt had seen the shotgun slide toward his feet as he was standing at the front door. He picked up the shotgun, and he pointed it at the animal. He pulled the trigger, but the gun wouldn't fire.

Matt kept pulling the trigger as he saw the animal hurtling toward him, bellowing loudly.

LIFE AND DEATH

Anika was running through the woods as fast as she could. She could still hear some gunshots coming from the lodge. Through the foliage up ahead, she could see the bright floodlights shimmering from the porch. And then her boot touched something that didn't feel quite right on the floor. It didn't feel wet and grimy like a piece of wood, and it didn't feel like mud. It felt stiff and firm.

She stopped in her tracks. She looked down and saw an elephant rifle lying in the mud. She picked up the rifle and held it close to her face. She pulled the slide bolt back and noticed that there was a round in the chamber. Finally, she had a weapon and she stood a chance. The male dinosaur nudged her from behind, insisting her to keep moving. With the elephant rifle in her arms, she ran forward with a new sense of confidence. Both she and the male dinosaur then arrived at the clearing in front of the lodge. They both saw Matthew Irving suddenly fly backward from the doorway and roll across the mud.

Standing in the doorway to the front entrance was the alpha. It didn't take long for the alpha to catch them both in its sight. It snarled and began to roar loudly as it stepped out of the lodge. It had fresh wounds all across its body; the lodge had fought back. But it also had fresh blood dripping from its jaws. The alpha had dealt some damage too.

Anika knew a fight had occurred at the lodge. There were bodies of dinosaur cubs leading up to the front porch. There was a half-eaten corpse about ten feet in front of Anika.

The alpha had sent Matthew flying through the air and after landing on the dirt, Matthew wasn't moving. The simple fact that the alpha was stepping out of the front entrance to the lodge meant things had gone horribly wrong.

The alpha kept stepping forward with complete confidence and fury in its demeanor. Even if the alpha was severely wounded, it would not falter in its challenge to both her and the male. The fight was not over, but this time Anika stood more of a chance with the rifle in her hands. She didn't know how many rounds she had left in this rifle. There could very well be only one round in the chamber right now. She had to be steady with her shot; she had to keep it clean. She hadn't had much weapons training in the past. Burns had only shown her the basics of how to use firearms.

She knew that taking a shot from this distance with a rifle she's never tested would probably miss. Unfortunately, she had to let the alpha dinosaur get close enough for her to get a killing shot. She heard the male beside her snarl back at the alpha dinosaur. The alpha dinosaur didn't roar or snarl in response. It only kept taking its casual steps forward toward them. Even if the alpha dinosaur ever felt any shred of fear, the adrenaline running in its veins made it completely fearless. Anika pressed the stock up against her shoulder firmly. She kneeled, and she was ready for a shot. She lined up the barrel and the rifle scope.

Before she could pull the trigger, the male dinosaur rushed forward, springing into action. Both the alpha and the male dinosaur suddenly clashed together into a wrestling match. They were clawing and biting ferociously at each other as they rolled around on the floor. Anika slowly stood up. She meticulously fanned around the fighting dinosaurs, advancing closer and closer. She was waiting for the perfect moment, waiting for the fatal kill shot. And then it came, just as the alpha swung the male around and slammed it onto the floor, holding it down with its immense weight.

Anika took two calm steps forward. She was only five or six feet away. She had the rifle barrel pointed directly where she assumed the animal's heart would be. The barrel was aimed right above the breastplate. She pulled the trigger, and the elephant rifle thundered to life. The 270-grain round burst through the alpha dinosaur's breastplate. It pierced all the organs in its chest and then exited through the other side of its body. Blood sprayed from the exit wound. The animal snarled in pain and turned its attention to Anika.

Anika had already pulled the slide bolt back on the rifle, sending the empty casing flying. To her surprise, she saw another round waiting to be loaded into the chamber. She slid the bolt forward quickly, and she pulled the trigger again, just as the alpha dinosaur turned its body to attack her. The second bullet went straight through the front of the animal's chest. This time, the animal made no noise, no snarl, and no attempt to attack Anika. The alpha dinosaur grew wide-eyed. It took two tired steps forward, blood pouring from its wounds.

The alpha dinosaur then, in all its glory, tumbled to the ground, twitching. Life was fading from its mighty body. Anika slid the bolt back again. She saw a third round and chambered it swiftly. Without hesitation, she put the barrel of the rifle up against the alpha dinosaur's head and pulled the trigger. The top of the animal's head and brain cavity burst like a watermelon, sending feathers and flaps of leathery skin flying.

The alpha dinosaur was finally dead.

Anika lowered the elephant rifle, and she started to take a relieved deep breath. In the corner of her eye, she saw the male dinosaur start to stand up from the floor. It shook the daze away from its head and body. When it finally stood up on its own legs, it stared at the dead alpha dinosaur in front of it. It then looked at Anika and snorted. Anika suddenly heard scurrying coming from the bushes. She swung the rifle around and she saw four more cubs standing at the edge of the clearing. They were beginning to dart at her when the male dinosaur snarled fiercely, scaring them away. The cubs scampered back into the forest, no longer a threat.

She was safe. No other animals would disturb her now. The male dinosaur had won her complete trust.

She heard groaning coming from behind her and she turned around. Her father Matthew was starting to move where he was laying. She ran over to him. She didn't see any major injuries on his body. She touched his face, and it was cold from the rain. "Dad, can you hear me?" she says to him. "Are you all right?"

Matthew groaned. "Just give me a couple minutes here, sweetheart. I'll be right up. Fucker knocked the wind out of me."

Her father was fine. She stood up quickly and turned her attention to the lodge. She jogged over and went up the front porch steps. Before she even walked in the front entrance, she could smell the stale warm scent of blood emanating from inside. She then witnessed the aftermath of the massacre that had occurred inside the lodge. There was blood everywhere, body parts thrown about.

It was dead silent inside the lodge.

If there were any survivors, they would be keeping their noise to a minimum to stay hidden. "Hello!" she called out. "Bill! Are you here? Is anyone alive?"

There was no response; she heard nothing. No, wait, not nothing/ She could hear a faint wheezing coming from a corner in the living room. She saw a mangled body lying on the floor in the corner, a pool of blood beside it. She recognized the boots immediately; it was Burns. She rushed over to him, and she saw his body was deeply injured. There were long and deep slashes all across his body and neck. He was struggling to breath, coughing up blood.

"Bill, Bill," she was saying with tears in her eyes. "Hang in there, okay? We're going to get help."

Burns exhaled, and he gave a strange smile. "I'm okay, Addie," he says faintly. "It's okay, Addie. I'm okay, I'm right here."

"Bill, it's me, Anika. I'm here. I'm going to go get help, okay? Just stay with me."

"It's okay, Addie. Don't worry, I won't be gone long."

Burns was not in a good state of mind. The loss of blood had made him delirious. He thought he was talking to his late wife, Addie. She needed to get him medical help immediately. She needed to find a way...

She suddenly heard thunderous gunshots coming from outside. She heard the male dinosaur yelping in pain. She rushed out the front entrance and saw her father holding a shotgun in his hands, continuously pulling the trigger until the rifle was empty. Matthew had landed all three slugs into the male dinosaur's torso. "Wait! Stop!" Anika yelled. She darted forward and got in between her father and the dinosaur.

"Move out of the way, dammit!" Matthew yelled.

"No! Wait! Please!" Anika was crying. "Stop, just please stop. It helped me."

Matthew's expressions showed nothing but confusion at her last remark. Anika turned around and she saw the male dinosaur collapse onto the floor, coughing up blood. It had blood trickling from its gunshot wounds on its torso. She kneeled down beside the male, vision glossy from the tears. "I'm sorry," she was saying to it while sobbing uncontrollably. "I'm so sorry."

The male dinosaur was whimpering, its eyes looking up

directly at Anika, begging for aid. Anika didn't know what to do; there was nothing to do. The male dinosaur had been killed at the hands of her father. Even then, how could she blame him? Her father had not seen the lengths that this animal went to protect her. Her father had only witnessed cruelty at the hands of the alpha dinosaur.

The male dinosaur kept grumbling in agony. It kept its gaze fixed on Anika. Anika put her hands up against the animal's head, and she rubbed the animal's snout in a reassuring manner. She leaned in to whisper. "Thank you. Thank you for everything. I'm so sorry."

The male dinosaur then gave three more whimpered breaths, and the life faded from its eyes. Anika leaned her body back on her knees. She tried to shake the tears away from her eyes but she couldn't. She could not shake the experience that she had gone through with this animal.

Anika suddenly heard movement coming from the trees behind her. She stood up and grabbed the rifle. She swung it around and leveled it angrily. She was ready for the next fight; she was done with this whole expedition. That's when she saw a series of headlights coming through the foliage from the main road. Two black off-road SUVs came driving into the clearing and parked only a few feet away from her. Men in police uniforms stepped out of the SUVs. They looked around, shocked at the scene.

There was a woman that stepped out of one of the driver's seats. She had red hair in a ponytail. She was wearing a vest with three letters on a patch: ICC. She looked out to the front yard of the lodge, at both prehistoric animal and human remains lying about. The only words that came out of her mouth were, "Lord have mercy, *what the hell happened here?*"

EPILOGUE

All manner of experts and responders were dispatched to the expedition crime scene. Police, game wardens, park rangers, paramedics, as well as the magistrate court's crime scene investigators, tasked with processing the scene. The grisly sight of the remains of the expedition left all responders in shock. The warm and rancid smell of blood filled the air, and upon entering the immense lodge built by Valtech Industries, for the first time ever, paramedics had to take a moment to breathe. Police and game wardens had no clue where to start or what to make of it. For a brief moment, no one wanted to move forward. Some were terrified, some were confused, and some considered quitting on the spot to avoid it completely.

Luckily, federal agents were present to liaison. As incident commanders, they instructed all responders to either render aid or start their crime scene work. They were also instructed not to lift the blankets covering mysterious "animal" carcasses. The magistrate court's crime scene response team got to work immediately, and soon they realized the work would last for weeks. It was clear to the crime scene response team that some kind of fight-to-the-death had occurred inside the lodge of nightmares.

Dr. Hogan stepped out of the range rover as soon as it stopped. His boots touched wet pavement that had led up from a hidden path from the main road to a beautiful freshly built lodge that looked out of place in the middle of the Tasmanian bush. Hogan was instructed by a couple federal agents to stick to the bodies inside the lodge and to stay away from the mysterious 'carcasses' covered in sheets on the front lawn.

Hogan could smell it before he even stepped inside the lodge: the dry, pungent smell of blood. Lots of blood. Hogan was given a bright white forensic hazmat suit. After slipping it on, Hogan walked up the steps. It took them nearly an hour just to decide where to start first. Afterward, Hogan worked relentlessly with the other crime scene investigators to process the scene. After hour three, Hogan decided to step outside for a much-needed smoke break. As he lit his Camel cigarette, he noticed a young police officer standing a few feet away from him. Hogan, out of habit, offered him a cigarette.

The young officer politely declined. He only watched as Hogan began to smoke. He saw Hogan take a curious glance toward the bodies hidden under the white sheets near the porch. The young police officer says to him. "Don't get any ideas."

"Like you haven't taken a peek, mate," Hogan scoffed.

"I haven't."

"Neither have I," Hogan says. "But I know what's under there anyways."

"You couldn't possibly."

Hogan smiled at the young police officer. "Assuming I'd never guess what it is only proves you most definitely took a peek." Hogan took a long swig from his cigarette and smiled even wider.

"That under there," Hogan says, "is a *fucking dinosaur.*"

Paramedics examined several mutilated bodies of individuals inside the lodge. They estimated about five victims inside the lodge, each equally as mangled as the last. All with peculiar cuts and bloody injuries they had never seen before in Tasmania. Of the five victims, only one was still breathing. A male in his late 40s, with defensive wounds on his arms and chest. Paramedics quickly began to stabilize the individual. And eventually, they had to call for an airlift to the nearest hospital. The sole survivor was taken to Hobart General Hospital.

In the emergency room of Hobart General Hospital, there was a wing that no one other than police officers, authorized nurses, and doctors were allowed to enter. At the moment, Hobart General Hospital was surrounded by police presence. No one was allowed in or out without the proper vetting and permission. Emergency triage centers and surgery rooms were off-limits to the general public at the moment. All hospital staff had to wear proper PPE before they could enter the specific part of the emergency room. Past the police checkpoint inside the hospital, through the bright white hallways and past the nurse's station, sitting in the waiting room with bandages across his body was Forrest Valente.

He was one of the few whose wounds didn't require immediate emergency medical care or surgery. He was the first one to be attended here, and now, he was just calmly sitting while staring at the wall in front of him. He heard squeaking footsteps coming from the hallway. Valente turned his head and he saw Quinby Gunderson walking down the hallway toward him in the waiting room. Walking alongside him was Anika Irving, with brand new bandages on her arms, shoulder, and stitches on her face. Quinby asks Anika to sit down in one of the chairs. Anika didn't say a word in agreement; she simply sat down, her face completely blank.

"How are you feeling, Mr. Valente?" Quinby asks.

"I can barely feel my fingertips," Valente says. "Is that normal?"

"Oh yes," Quinby says, "that means they gave you the good stuff in the manner of pain medicine." Quinby's voice was monotone, and his accent sounded like it was from the East

Coast.

"What's going on with Lee?" Valente asks him.

"As far as I know, they took him out of surgery not ten minutes ago," Quinby says. "He's fine. But he's pumped full of morphine right now, so he might not know who you are or where he is."

"Were there any other survivors? From the expedition, I mean," Valente asks.

"Not many," Quinby says, "but it's best to leave those kinds of questions alone right now. We have to wait for my partner. She runs the show around here."

"You guys must have a lot of questions for us, I assume," Valente remarked.

"*A lot of questions* is an understatement, my boy," Quinby says. He finally sat down in one of the chairs. "Like I said, best to wait for the captain of the ship. She's the one who knows how to do all that stuff."

Valente nodded. He shifted in his chair, his wounded thigh making it uncomfortable to sit in any position. He glanced at Anika Irving. Before he spoke to her, he quickly examined the bandages on her body one more time. She wasn't wearing a jacket anymore; she only had a tank top, revealing the wounds on her shoulders. The thick wads of bandages wrapped around them, small specks of blood soaked through. The same with the bandages on her forearms; she was currently scratching them with dirty fingernails. Valente then notices her face; there were claw marks on her head that ran down to the temple. Dark black stitches kept her skin together, and they would surely leave a mark on her stern face.

Anika had been through it, that much he could tell.

"How are you feeling?" Valente asks her after working up the courage to do so.

"Stellar," she snapped.

"I'm sorry. It was probably a dumb question. I just-"

"I don't want to talk right now," she snapped again.

Valente didn't direct another word at her. He simply glanced at Quinby. Quinby's face said it all; his eyes were somber, and he slowly shook his head at Valente. It was best to let it go. Anika had clearly been through a lot. Valente decided to lean his head back and close his eyes for a few moments.

After a few silent minutes in the waiting room, there was a set of boots slowly making their way down the hallway. Matthew Irving, with only minor bruising on his face and neck, casually strolled into the waiting room. Matt was munching on a single Twix candy bar from a nearby vending machine. Matt strolled over. He stood between Quinby, Anika, and Valente. Valente was slumped in his seat, sleeping, while Anika stared blankly at the tiled floor. Matt walked in between them both, and he took a seat next to Anika.

"I just finished talking to the police outside. They're going to want to talk to us again, and they're going to have us stay a lot longer," Matt says.

"Federal agents are going to go over it all with us," Valente says without opening his eyes. He wasn't asleep, but he was trying.

Matt sighed and shook his head. "Sounds like we're going to be here a while, unfortunately," he says. Matt rubbed his face with his palms, his hands still shaky from the night of hell he lived through. Residual effects from the adrenaline pumping through his body for almost an entire night. "What about Lee and Bill?"

"Lee is in his room, hopped up on morphine. He's fine for now," Valente says.

"And Bill? I heard they were taking him to surgery for a second time?"

Anika finally looked up from her blank stare. She looked at her father directly, her eyes red and teary. Without saying a word, she kept her subdued gaze and slowly shook her head *no*.

Bill Burns was gone.

Matt leaned back in his chair, and he sighed with heavy sorrow. He felt helpless as he looked around the room. The man he had known for almost two decades was gone forever. The man Matt considered a distant brother, someone who had nothing but love and care to give to his family. The same man who had warned Matt about the consequences of his stupidity. *God*, he had done it again. He had dragged another innocent soul into his useless stardom *filled* with death.

His friend was gone.

For once, Matt felt like he couldn't say another word, his bottom lip quivering. His father was right; all those years ago his own father had told him he was nothing but a burden. He had nothing good to give to the world, nothing but death. And just before he broke down into tears for the second time in his entire life, he felt Anika touch his hand. She *squeezed* her father's hand, asking for comfort.

Matt squeezed back. "He's with Addie now. Where he wants to be…" he muttered in between tears. They held hands tightly, feeling an emotional connection between them neither had felt in years. Anika leaned her head on her father's shoulder, making Matt lean his head on hers. After nearly two decades, they were father and daughter again. They kept their embrace in the hospital waiting room for what felt like hours.

As both father and daughter shared their moment of sorrow over an old friend, one more person entered the waiting room. A stocky woman in her late 30s, with dirty ginger hair and interesting eyes. She scanned the entire room with a judgmental sneer until she chose her seat next to Valente, facing the grieving father and daughter. As she fished a phone from her pocket, she glanced at Quinby.

"Quinby, could you go check in on Mr. Ward? The nurses appeared to be wanting my attention, but I have more pressing matters," she says. Quinby nodded in agreement and stood from his chair. Before he walked away, he leaned in and whispered into the woman's ear. She nodded and thanked him for his report. Quinby then finally walked out of the waiting room.

"I saw you earlier," Matt says to the woman. "All the boys in blue seem to go to you before moving forward at all."

"Tends to happen when you're in charge," she replied rashly.

"Are you going to fill us in on what's going to happen next?" Matt asks with irritation in his tone.

"There's a lot more that needs to happen before I answer your question," the woman replied.

Matt was going to argue but Anika jumped in. "She wants to hear our story before she moves a finger. Typical cop stuff, to determine who's responsible for this bullshit." The woman smiled at Anika's blunt remark. Anika continued, "I apologize, I've been chased and mauled by dinosaurs for an entire fucking night. I'm Anika Irving, by the way. Could you at least tell me who you are?"

"Agent Karen Morrissey of the International Criminal Court," she says, her voice thick Scottish. "And I know exactly who you are, Dr. Irving. It's actually very surprising to find you here. I've actually been meaning to reach out to you for quite some time."

"Oh yeah? What's so special about me?"

"Because I read your paper on apex predators in arbitrary ecosystems this past year. Quite informative to the layman, a wee bit terrifying to people in my field at the moment."

"How so?" Anika pressed.

"Well, Dr., your research paper seems to suggest that nature has developed a dangerous toolbox of specific predators to dish out in dire circumstances," Morrisey says. "You know, I figure you must hear this a lot, but I firmly believe your theory could be perfected with more data than the one instance."

Anika squints her eyes. "Uh-huh, you didn't come all this way to talk about my paper, did you? Where did you say you're an agent of?"

"ICC, International Criminal Court. And to answer your previous question, yes, I am here to discuss your paper." Morrisey then shakes her head mid-sentence. "No, that's not the right term. Not 'discuss', more like apply it, in a sense."

"*Apply it?*"

"Yes, ma'am. See, out of the whole turmoil and critiques you received when you published your theory, I was one of the few who took it at face value and accepted that perhaps it's not devoid of merit."

Anika shakes her head. "I'm not understanding this at all. Why would the International Criminal what-have-you want to talk to me? Remind me, what is it that your agency does?"

"Investigate crimes against humanity. Mainly war crimes and mass genocide," Morrisey answered while pulling a small, tattered ledger from her jacket.

Anika jerks her head back slightly. "You can't tell me that is how you're investigating this situation? As a... genocide?"

"No, no," Morrisey simply says. "Not this one at least. Frankly, Dr. Irving, we're not sure what to call these occurrences anymore."

Anika remains silent, *occurrences, plural*?

"Now, no use in continuing this line of questioning. Like you mentioned, I'm going to need to hear your side of the story before we let you do anything else. I am afraid you are stuck here with us for the time being. So, if you could," Morrisey says as she then flipped to a blank page. "As crazy as the story or the details may seem, *start from the beginning please.*"

———————————